gone

but

still

here

gone
but
still
here

jennifer dance

gone
but
still
here

a novel

DUNDURN
PRESS

Publisher: Scott Fraser | Acquiring editor: Kathryn Lane | Editor: Robyn So
Cover designer: Laura Boyle
Cover image: beach: istock.com/Mike_Pellinni; trees: istock.com/CircleEyes; couple with dog: istock.com/tirc83; ibis: istock.com/danrichards_uk

Library and Archives Canada Cataloguing in Publication

Title: Gone but still here : a novel / Jennifer Dance.
Names: Dance, Jennifer, 1949- author.
Identifiers: Canadiana (print) 20210252359 | Canadiana (ebook) 20210252367 | ISBN 9781459748774 (softcover) | ISBN 9781459748781 (PDF) | ISBN 9781459748798 (EPUB)
Classification: LCC PS8607.A548 G66 2022 | DDC C813/.6—dc23

We acknowledge the support of the Canada Council for the Arts and the Ontario Arts Council for our publishing program. We also acknowledge the financial support of the Government of Ontario, through the Ontario Book Publishing Tax Credit and Ontario Creates, and the Government of Canada.

Dundurn Press
1382 Queen Street East
Toronto, Ontario, Canada M4L 1C9
dundurn.com, @dundurnpress 𝕏 f ⓘ

What an astonishing thing a book is. It's a flat object made from a tree with flexible parts on which are imprinted lots of funny dark squiggles. But one glance at it and you're inside the mind of another person, maybe somebody dead for thousands of years. Across the millennia, an author is speaking clearly and silently inside your head, directly to you. Writing is perhaps the greatest of human inventions, binding together people who never knew each other, citizens of distant epochs. Books break the shackles of time. A book is proof that humans are capable of working magic.

— Carl Sagan, "The Persistence of Memory,"
Cosmos: A Personal Voyage

prologue

My name is Mary, and I have Alzheimer's disease.

Lurching gut.

It makes me think of AA meetings I've seen in the movies: *My name is so-and-so, and I'm an alcoholic.* It's an acknowledgement, a way of facing your problem. Writing this is an acknowledgement, too. A way of confronting the truth.

I've been telling myself that I'm just having a few memory lapses — part of normal aging. But I'm slipping away. I can feel it.

Getting confused.

Losing logic and understanding.

Having to tell myself that red means stop, and green means go.

I've been trying to hide it. Hide *from* it. Ignore it. Make excuses. But one day I'll be gone, even though I will still be here. It's hard to accept. Hard to believe.

A living death. A dying life.

Will I know what's happening?

I hope not.

I type the awful words again, my fingers hammering away at the truth while my brain denies it:

My name is Mary, and I have Alzheimer's disease.

Sweating palms.

It sounds like someone else's reality, but at the same time there's a terrifying familiarity to it, like it's the truth, yet a lie at the same time — a strange contradiction that I can't figure out.

Racing heart.

A memory flits in: I'm carrying pink rosebuds and walking down the aisle of an English country church. Keith is waiting for me, his face lit with a broad smile, tears glistening in his eyes. But then the rosebuds I'm carrying are blood red and I am walking down a different aisle, toward a coffin covered in a blue altar cloth. I shut my mind to the memories — it's what I always do, taking myself to an empty space. It's safer there.

I catch my vacant gaze reflected in the sleeping computer screen. I must phone my children. Oh God, will I forget their names one day? Will I forget who they are? The odds say yes. I speak their names aloud, picturing each face and mentally attaching a label to their foreheads, names written in bold, uppercase letters. ALICIA! ZACH! KAYLA! I order myself to embed them in my memory and to never let them go. Reality tells me that willpower alone cannot stop dementia, but all the same, I try as hard as I can. Alicia! She works for an aid organization in Africa. Zach! He manages a hedge fund, whatever that is. And Kayla! She travels the world singing jazz in fancy hotels. Although maybe she doesn't do that anymore. I forget.

My lower lip trembles. I hold on to it with my teeth, my mother's words reverberating in my five-year-old head, "Nobody likes a crybaby."

Another voice comes to me. "It's okay, Sweetheart, I'm here."

The joyful lilt brings happiness to my heart. It feels so real, as if Keith is beside me, whispering in my ear, but he's gone. Long gone. I'm just hearing voices. It's a symptom of Alzheimer's.

Shit. I have Alzheimer's disease. An incurable degenerative disease of the brain. I can't grasp it, even though I speak the words. If I say them enough, maybe it will become easier. If I write them ...

My name is Mary, and ... I'm having a few memory lapses.

mary

I wonder how my life might have turned out if Keith had not sat at the desk next to mine on that first day of chemistry class. Easier? Perhaps. Duller? For sure. I had no idea of the saga that our meeting would ultimately create. But that day at university, I was smitten — with his broad, bright smile and his enormous dark eyes flanked with eyelashes so long that they grazed the lenses of his trendy Aviator shades. And I stayed smitten. Always.

Reading the words aloud, as a writer should, my voice quivers and tears sting my eyes. It takes me by surprise. I haven't cried for decades — not even when my mother died.

Although, when Paco passed away, I bawled my heart out in a dreadful expression of grief that was disproportionate to the life of a little black cat. Looking back, something was going on there: grief for Keith and my mother spewing out from some unfathomably deep place as I rocked the dying cat in my arms.

Crap. Writing a book about Keith is going to be harder than I thought. It was supposed to be easy. No convoluted plot or creative characters. Just me telling my story for our children, so they can learn about their father. It's not that I deliberately kept secrets about him. But it was painful to talk about. So I pushed it aside. Pushed *him* aside.

I stare at the backs of my hands, draped on the keyboard ... pale skin flecked with brown age spots and crisscrossed with blue-green veins. They belong to someone old, not to me. But the wedding band on my fourth finger is comfortingly familiar. The gold is worn thin. I twirl it, trying to figure it all out.

"You still wear my ring," a voice says, warm and lyrical, with the trace of laughter.

Until recently, I thought I'd forgotten the sound of Keith's voice. He died before the era of answering machines or cellphone recordings, and I wasn't able to recall his voice even when I wanted to. I'd forgotten *him*! It had been deliberate ... my way of surviving, because the grief was like quicksand, waiting to pull me under if I stepped too close. I had to keep my feet on solid ground for the sake of the children. I had to get out of bed and change diapers and feed them. I had to be the best mother I could be. They'd lost their daddy; they couldn't lose me, too.

But the kids are all grown up now. They never come to see me. Or phone me. Though they swear they do. How come my children turned out to be such big liars?

Keith speaks to me again. "Write about me. About us."

He sounds so close, so real that I can't stop myself from snuggling into the thought of him. But I know my mind is just playing tricks. Keith is gone. I want to bring him back, though, capture him in words on the page and give him immortality. But I don't want to go through the pain again.

I pull myself together, forging on in a well-practised technique taught to me at an early age by my stiff-upper-lip parents. I can still hear their words. "No point crying over spilled milk; there's always someone with a bigger problem than yours; and think of all the starving children in Africa."

Focusing on the screen, I read the first line again.

> I wonder how my life might have turned out if Keith
> had not sat at the desk next to mine ...

"Life can turn on a dime," I say aloud, feeling uncommonly wise yet morose. "One fork in the road — right or left — and everything changes. Meeting Keith all those years ago was the major fork in my life. My story should start there. But not today. My emotions are too fragile. I want to write about things that make me happy, not sad."

"Start with going to Trinidad then," Keith says. "*That* was the first of those life-changing forks in the road. *That's* where you should start your story."

In my mind, I lean against the ship's railing, yelling goodbye to my school friends on the wharf. It's 1966, a summer day. I'm seventeen years old, and the Beach Boys sing a Bahamian folk song in my head: "So h'ist up the *John B.* sails / see how the mainsail set / send for the captain a-shore / let us go home."

I start to type.

> Announcing our departure with deafening blasts of the horn, the S.S. *Golfito* eases away from the berth, and with tugboats alongside, manoeuvres into the busy English Channel. I wave at the well-wishers on the wharf, watching them get smaller — watching England grow smaller. Then, as my mother goes to unpack and organize our first-class cabin, I move to the bow, gazing to the exciting future ahead of me.
>
> For the first two days, however, there's not much to be excited about. The ocean is as grey as the sky and a fine drizzle mingles with salt spray, merging sky and sea seamlessly into one. But then, as we approach the Azores — an archipelago off the coast of Portugal — the Atlantic swell intensifies and the *Golfito* picks up its lurching pitch and roll.
>
> The *Golfito* is a Fyffes banana boat, a steamship that plies passengers and bananas between Southampton and the Caribbean islands.

A calypso pops into my head and I sing along. "Come, Mister Tally Man, tally me banana / Daylight come and me wan' go home."

The *Golfito* has a flat bottom, which enables her to come ashore to load bananas directly from the island beaches.

"Lift six-foot, seven-foot, eight-foot bunch! / Daylight come and me wan' go home."

On this outward journey to Port of Spain, there are no bananas in the hold to stabilize her, hence the sea-sickening roll. "It will be fine once we're past the Azores," the captain promises. I vomit over the railing and am ordered inside.

In the dining room, the round mahogany tables have their flaps up to stop food from sliding into our laps, but few passengers are attempting to eat. Bouncing off the walls like a drunkard, I stagger down the ship's narrow corridor back to the cabin, wondering how long it will take to get my sea legs. My mother, having thought of everything, doses me up with motion-sickness pills, and I escape into a world of sleep.

On the third morning, I wake to a blue sky and an equally blue ocean. My spirits soar. The soft, warm breeze tells me it's time to unpack the bikini and slather on the suntan oil.

Mummy is enjoying the holiday aspect of the voyage, sipping morning coffee while lounging in a deck chair, enjoying afternoon tea in the tearoom, and playing deck-shuffleboard at the stern. In her one-piece swimsuit with the built-in skirt, she's borderline embarrassing. Unlike the other passengers, she doesn't wear dark glasses or jewellery, slacks or chic dresses. Her hair isn't styled and she doesn't speak with a posh accent. But onboard ship, class seems of lesser importance than on land. Everyone mingles. Except for me. With no young people on board, I spend time alone at the bow of the ship, feeling the sun on my skin, the wind in my hair and the salt spray on my face.

It wasn't until I moved my own family from England to Canada, some fifteen years later, that I appreciated the challenges my mother faced — my father having flown to Trinidad weeks ahead of us, leaving her to single-handedly whittle down our family's possessions to fit into a few shipping crates in preparation for a five-year contract overseas.

When did I last see Mummy? I can't remember. It's been a while. I must drop by and see her. Right after I've finished writing this chapter.

I grab an orange sticky note and a black sharpie: *VISIT MUMMY*.

"Focus on writing, Mary!" I tell myself. "You don't get to stop until lunchtime."

I type the working title, *MARY'S STORY*, centring it at the top of the page. It's lame, but in my experience, the title is one of the last things to arrive. My third book, *Hawk*, was called *Blackbirds* when I was writing it. It was a good name for both the girl and the raven in the story. But I couldn't make the girl realistic. Odd, since I'm a girl — or I was. Sometimes I think I still am. It's a shock when I see myself in the mirror and I think, *Who's that?* Anyway, I changed the girl in the story to a boy, but then the title didn't work, so I turned the raven into a hawk, and voila, the new title was perfect.

An orange sticky note catches my attention: *VISIT MUMMY*. That's strange. My mother has been dead for years.

I read over what I've written, the soundtrack to the voyage taking me back half a century in the blink of an eye. "Come, Mister Tally Man, tally me banana / Daylight come and me wan' go home / Day! Me say da-a-ay-oh …"

I start to type.

For the first time in my life, I see the grandeur of a universe far beyond my expectations. In England, the sky often hovered, grey, over my head, and even when the clouds were high, the vista was restricted by buildings, chimneys, and trees. Now, I see the vast expanse of the Atlantic Ocean touching the sky on a distant curved horizon. I see the sun falling into the sea in a kaleidoscope of sunset colours and a night sky shimmering with billions more stars than I ever imagined possible. For the first time in my life, I can breathe! Yet I never realized that I couldn't! At the same time, I feel small and frail, in awe of a creative designer of this vast expanse of beauty.

Three times a day, I get our dog out of his crate and walk him around the ship's lower deck, his nostrils twitching at the salty smells in the air. As a puppy, Toby had been a roly-poly ball of creamy fluff, but as the weeks passed, his coat became long and silky and golden, nothing like his hard-working sheepdog mother, but confirming his paternity: a delinquent yellow lab from half a mile away. Toby inherited his mother's love of herding, but we didn't live on a sheep farm, so this was a problem. He would herd anything in sight, including children. There are no children on board, but when dolphins race alongside the ship like playful torpedoes, leaping out of the water in joyous jumps, Toby pokes his nose through the railings and whines, desperate to round them up.

On the morning of our tenth day, with shoals of flying fish skimming above the surface and grey pelicans flapping optimistically alongside, news breaks that land has been sighted. Everyone rushes port-side to see a thin, black ribbon on the horizon. Leaning on the railing, we watch the Northern Range slowly erupt from the sea until it becomes the lush, forested mountains that I'd seen in a library book. Navigating the Bocas Straits on the approach to Port of Spain, a flock of scarlet ibis fly with us, hugging the coastline — stark red against an emerald background.

Keith's ashes will be scattered in the deep waters of this passage, where the Caribbean Sea meets the Atlantic.

I feel sad. It's a familiar feeling, one that has lingered in the backwaters of my life for forty years. It's like a cockroach that comes out of the woodwork as soon as darkness falls — turn on the light and there it is. If I'm quick, I can stomp on it before it scares the crap out of me. Mentally, I do the deed.

sage

Jesse is my upright, my best human. We were pups together. I licked human food from his flat face and chubby fingers. It always tasted so much better than the food in my dish. He buried his nose in my fur and tugged on my tail, like my siblings did before I was scooped from my mother's side, leaving me cold and hungry and aching for the sound of her heartbeat. Jesse would snuggle up with me, his head against my side, his belly rising and falling in rhythm with mine. He was warm and soft, and the beat of his heart comforted me.

I was with him when he pulled himself up and stood on his two hind legs for the first time, turning into an upright before my eyes, wobbling and toddling and falling, then doing it all over again. But when I copied him, standing on my own hind legs and balancing my front ones against whomever and whatever was around, I got a knee rammed in my chest. A life on all fours was my destiny.

Jesse is much bigger now, lean and gangly like a wolfhound pup on the cusp of adulthood. He doesn't walk on all fours anymore, and he doesn't play much. That's okay, because I don't have the energy to play much, either, and I hurt in at least four places — maybe more, but I can only count to four because that's how many feet I have. I'm content to chew on the ball that Jesse occasionally rolls my way or to wait for the sound of his voice or the touch of his hand. These small gestures mean everything to me.

Since our puppy days, the pack has shrunk. Dad left a long time ago and never came back. Kyle and Krista went away, too. I don't miss them much. They never loved me the way Jesse and Mom do. They continuously challenged Mom, trying to take over as leaders of the pack. I'd bark, telling them to get in line, but they'd bark back, telling *me* to get in line, so I'd tuck my tail between my legs and slink off to my bed in Jesse's room.

Now, it's just Mom, Jesse, and me, and we each know our place in the pack. Mom is at the top, Jesse is in the middle, and I'm at the bottom. I don't mind being last in line. I don't want the responsibility of being the alpha. But all the same, I have an essential role to play in the hierarchy of the pack. It's my job to look out for Mom — our leader — because without her, we are all doomed. In the way of most gangly wolfhound pups, Jesse is no help at all, so it's all up to me.

"Mom!" Jesse shouts. "I need you to witness my signature on this."

My second-best human appears. I wag my tail, but she ignores my greeting, too busy studying the paper on the table. It's not the paper I'm allowed to hold in my mouth and carry from the edge of the street to the front door of our den, before depositing it gently in Mom's hands. This is another type of paper. I've learned to discern these subtle differences so as not to get into big trouble. I'm a smart dog.

"All done," Mom says. "Counsellor in Training! You're gonna have such a great summer. I'm so proud of you."

Jesse smiles. "Thanks! I have to mail it back. Crazy, eh? Who uses snail mail these days?"

Mom's pitch rises. "I don't have any stamps. Put it on the kitchen table with the shopping list. I'll go to the post office when I'm in town."

Mom isn't shining as usual, and she isn't singing like the Wild Ones in the wilderness. The weight that presses her down is invisible, but I know it's there. It's like the wind that blows through the trees — I can't see it, but it tickles my nose and ruffles the fur on my back. And sometimes I need to brace, with all four feet planted firmly on the ground, so as not to be swept away. I sense that Mom feels that way now. And I catch her feelings.

Jesse doesn't know how to catch feelings. He doesn't even see them! He's good at spotting a bird in the sky or a ball in the air, but he's inexplicably blind to things you see with more than your eyes — things you must know with your knower.

My nose and my knower both tell me that we're trapped in a difficult place and that Mom needs me. I nudge her hand, uncurling her fingers and making her stroke me. Soon her words pour over me like summer rain.

"Oh, *Sage*, I don't know what to do. A gig's come up overseas. If not for Jesse, I'd be on the next plane outta here. But I *can't* leave him for three months! I can't even leave him for a weekend. When the kids were little, I thought it would be easier when they got older. But teenagers ..."

She shakes her head and sighs. "I wonder if Ma would come here and stay in the house to keep an eye on him. She's retired. She doesn't have anything much to keep her in Montreal. I can ask."

She leans over and sinks both hands into the ruff of my neck. "*GoodGirlSage*. You are such a good listener!"

mary

I'm at my desk, staring at the page on the screen, ready to start a new chapter. My working day has always started at 9:00 a.m. and I'm a creature of habit, so I'm here, but the opening line has gone missing. A few minutes ago, it was in my head, clear as day. Now it flits just out of reach. I grab at it, thinking I have it, but before my fingers find the keys and lock it onto the page, it swirls away into the foggy cloud that hovers in my head. It's frustrating. I have to be at the library this afternoon. I need to catch the sentence and give it immortality. *Now*.

Damn it, I should have scribbled it down the minute it landed in my head. Instead, I made a cup of tea and now it's gone.

I close my eyes and try not to panic. Forgetting things occasionally is a common sign of aging. It doesn't mean I'm getting Alzheimer's.

I gaze around the room, seeing the accolades to a published author who bears my name. *She* is the one who insists I write my life story — my love story. But how can I do that? I can barely keep track of a movie plot, and technology has galloped away from me. Often, I can't remember what I just did. But despite all this, my memories of the past are stronger than ever, rising up, demanding a voice before it's too late.

Searching for inspiration, I scroll to the top of the document. A sentence jumps out at me.

> I wonder how my life might have turned out if Keith had not sat at the desk next to mine on that first day of chemistry class.

Suddenly, I'm in a different place. I see metal-framed chairs with curved plywood seats and attached desktops. I see windows without glass. It's familiar and comforting. I start to type.

I'm in the old pre-med lecture building at the University of the West Indies — UWI (pronounced "you-wee"). And it's the first day of classes.

I hear the unrelenting whomp-whomp-whomp of old ceiling fans. And the pinging of fat raindrops as they hit the corrugated metal roof.

With arms full of ring binders and textbooks with a fresh, new smell, I manoeuvre myself nervously into an empty seat directly under the slowly moving blades of a fan. It seems to me that in the tropics, everything moves slowly, even the fans, turning so lethargically that I can see the basket-weave pattern of the blades as they shift the sultry air, loosening fine tendrils of hair from my ponytail, wafting them across my damp face.

The desk is too small for all my supplies. My pen rolls onto the concrete floor. It's a maroon Parker fountain pen with an italic nib, the kind of pen you fill from a pot. I filled it the night before with blue-grey ink, making sure I was prepared for this important day. But now ink will have splattered into the cap and made a mess.

The most beautiful boy I have ever seen picks up the pen and hands it to me. He's lean and muscular, with brown skin and a smile that makes my knees go weak. He sits in the chair next to me, stacking his books on the desk. He doesn't need to introduce himself. His name is stylishly written in dark-blue ink on the covers: Keith W.D. Bowen.

This isn't the first time I've seen him. He drove past me at precisely 8:15 that morning as I walked the half mile from home to campus. The sun was already climbing high in the sky and was hot enough to make the walk unpleasant. On the short stretch of the Eastern Main Road, taxis passed me, men leaning out the windows, gesticulating. It wasn't aggressive, but there was a lewdness to it that made me uncomfortable. I was relieved to turn off the main road and cross the railway track onto campus. It was then that Keith drove by. Slowly. Turning his head to look.

I looked back:

A white Sunbeam Alpine with the top down.

Red leather upholstery.

Flashy.

The moment is frozen in time, like a snapshot: a warm smile lighting up his face; his arm resting comfortably on top of the wound-down window frame; his elegant fingers relaxed on the steering wheel. He wears a short-sleeved golf shirt, black and made from one of the new synthetic fabrics that don't crease the way cotton does.

My mother insisted that cotton was cooler for the tropics. Consequently, I'm wearing a sleeveless cotton shift that Hettie (the maid!) starched and ironed to perfection, but that now feels like a crumpled dishrag on my damp body.

Does he ask me if I want a ride? I think so, but perhaps that's just in my imagination. Anyway, I know better than to hop into a car with a strange boy, no matter how hot he is. He drives on toward the campus, and I follow on foot.

By the time I reach the pre-med building I'm already rosy from my walk in the sun. The Alpine is in the parking lot, its canvas top up in preparation for a tropical downpour, which, judging by the darkening sky, is on its way.

The phone rings.

"Hi Mary! It's Sally."

"Sally?"

"From the library."

"Of course! How are you, my dear?"

"I'm fine, but what about you? Are you okay? You didn't show up for your shift this afternoon."

I quickly bluff. "Oh, I'm so sorry, I should have phoned. I had a bit of a sniffle so decided to keep my germs to myself."

"Good idea. Can I bring you anything? Chicken soup?"

"That's kind of you, but I'm fine. I don't need anything."

"Okay then, I'll see you next week."

I've barely put down the phone before it rings again. It's Kayla! I haven't talked to her for the longest while, but she says we spoke two days ago.

No, we didn't.

"I have a huge favour to ask," she says. "I've got a job offer in Singapore. It's for three months. I really want to go."

"How exciting! Another country to cross off your list! How many will that make?"

"Thirty-eight," Kayla says.

"Is it with the military?"

"Military? Good heavens, no. It's singing jazz ... in a five-star hotel, six nights a week ... like I used to do in the old days. *Military?* Where did that come from?"

I laugh it off. "A slip of the tongue. I was just watching a show about women in the military. So you've been offered a jazz gig? That's great. You were so close to making a name for yourself, and you threw it all away when you fell for that man."

"David? Yeah, he swept me off my feet, for sure. But when I was back on the ground, everything was always about him: his job, his friends, his agenda. Then when Krista arrived, it was all about her. Then Kyle. Then Jesse. And I got lost in the mix. I couldn't be gigging all over the world with three kids in tow. And David was no help. These days, I prance around the stage, yelling out the lyrics of up-tempo pop songs, or I arrange the music for the church choir. It pays the bills and it keeps me singing, at least, but it's not me! I love jazz, Ma. I love the way it makes me feel when I sing it. It's like I *am* jazz. Part of me died when I gave it up … and the thing is, I thought it was too late. But now I have this opportunity. And if I take it, I'll come home with enough money to record an album … my own music! This is my last chance, Ma! I'm forty-five!"

"You can still be a jazz singer when you're old," I tell her, wanting to name some of the American greats I picture in my mind. Their names elude me. "And it's the one profession in the world where being Black is an advantage. If you want my advice, Kayla, I say, get out there and do it! Grab at your dreams! Reach for the stars!"

"Oh my gosh, Ma, thank you! You are always so encouraging, so full of good advice."

"You should have listened to my advice about David and kept your legs crossed!"

"What?"

Oh dear, I've upset her.

"You're right, Ma, but it's water under the bridge. We make mistakes and move on. The thing is, I want to take this job, but I can't leave Jesse alone. So, how would you feel about coming to stay at my place for three months? I just need someone to be in the house with Jesse and keep an eye on him."

"I'd love to," I squeal. "I adore little Jesse."

"He's not so little anymore! He's at a difficult age to be left alone. I worry about girls and parties."

"Girls? Parties? He's not even two!"

"Ma! Jesse is fourteen! What's with you? He's starting high school in September."

"Of course he is," I say, putting confidence into my voice, although fear strikes my heart. What is happening to me?

kayla

Kayla: Hey, Leesha, there's something wrong with Ma.

Alicia: Oh no. What?

Kayla: It's weird. I called her to ask if she'd look after Jesse if I go to Singapore. We were having a perfectly normal conversation … although now I think about it, it wasn't normal. She said a couple of things that were strange … out of character. But the biggie is she thinks Jesse is still a baby!

Alicia: That doesn't sound good. Gosh, I wish I weren't so far away. How about calling her neighbour and asking her to drop by and check things out?

Kayla: Chantelle? Good idea. I don't have the number.

Alicia: Zach has her contact info.

Kayla: Can you get it from him? I don't mind calling the neighbour, but I don't want to talk to Zach.

Alicia: Are you two ever gonna behave like adults? I'll ask him and get back to you.

mary

The noise of machinery wakes me. I get out of bed and walk to the kitchen. Headlights from the snowplow shine through the sliding door of my little balcony, right into my eyes. I'm on the second floor and have no door to the street, which normally makes me feel safe, but right now I'm lit up like a Christmas tree. Vulnerable. I should have put up blinds years ago. It doesn't seem worthwhile now.

The snowplow manoeuvres around the parked cars and moves on, the uncanny silence of freshly fallen snow once more engulfing the street. I make a cup of tea and watch the neighbourhood wake up. Lights come on in apartments on the other side of Rue de Cerise, and on the street, a few brave souls start engines and sweep off windshields. Then a man walks down the sidewalk, his snow-thrower at full throttle, hurling snow onto the parked cars. My little red car is usually easy to spot, but right now I don't see it. Is it buried under a foot of snow or did I park it under the building? I can't remember. I hope I don't have to go out today. What day is it?

I look at the calendar. A few squares have been crossed off in February. Does that mean it's early in the month, or have I been forgetting to cross the days off? I tap my iPhone to see the date, then cross off seven squares on the calendar, figuring that it's not my library day. Good — I don't have to brave the weather. I can spend the day writing, or I can stay in bed, or I can watch TV.

Grabbing the TV remote, I settle into the recliner. The remote isn't working. I look at it, perplexed. After a second or two, I realize I'm holding it upside down. It would be funny if not for the fact that my memory is failing. Brushing the fear away, like dandruff off my shoulders, I scroll through the guide, looking for *Judge Judy* or *Antiques Road Show*. I can't find either. Hundreds of channels and nothing to watch! I should be able to search for *Judge Judy* … if I could just find the right screen. When did it all get so complicated?

I peer at the remote, hoping to get a clue. The letters are too small. I need my reading glasses. Don't the marketing people know that we need bigger type as we get older? Frustrated, I turn to my laptop. Guess I'll spend the morning writing, after all.

Repositioning myself, I put my feet up, open the laptop and select the most recent document. My eyes see a jumble of meaningless words, but then a line jumps out at me. It's the Banana Boat Song. "Day! Me say da-a-ay-oh …"

The tune plays in my head and I'm back on the Golfito, disembarking into a new world.

The girl who steps off the gangplank in Port of Spain, Trinidad, is different from the one who walked up the gangplank in Southampton, England. Tanned skin. Fair hair, sticky with sea salt, streaked blond by the sun. A different person, inside and out.

After ten days of solitude and fresh air, the hot humidity of the busy harbour is oppressive. The smell of body odour vying with diesel fumes assaults my senses. And the frenzied whine of winches, cranes, and front-end loaders is at odds with the slow-moving dockworkers.

Toby, still on board in his crate, is doing an excellent impersonation of a pissed-off Rottweiler. The muscular dockworkers watch him, their voices filled with either alarm or respect. I can't tell which because I can barely hear their words above Toby's threatening growls or understand the strong island accent. But from their body language, I get the gist: no burglar in their right mind will be stealing from our house.

When the crate is finally lifted by crane, Toby flies through the air, announcing his intent to kill everything and everyone in a five-mile radius. When he sees me, he whines excitedly. Curiosity gets the better of the labourers and they gather around for a closer look, but when Dad opens the crate, they hastily retreat, climbing on ladders and machines, bales and bundles. Toby creeps out on his belly, his long, golden coat drenched with sweat, so delighted to see us that he promptly pees at our feet.

***

During the next six weeks, until the start of the university semester, life takes on a new rhythm, the slower rhythm of the islands. We enjoy the luxuries of being expats. Most afternoons, I swim in the outdoor pool reserved for university staff and students. I'm not yet registered as a student, but the boy who doubles as entrance official and lifeguard doesn't challenge me. In the cooler evenings, I join my parents at the tennis club, where the boys serve cocktails, along with tennis balls, to white members.

On Sundays, we pack Toby in the car and head across the island to Manzanilla Beach, where palm trees curve gracefully toward the ocean and waves roll relentlessly onto a sand beach that stretches for miles down the east coast. Other than an occasional fisherman unloading red snapper from a wooden pirogue and others mending their nets on the sand, the beach is deserted. Toby loves it. He herds the waves, snapping at the heels of the surf as it comes and goes.

Two crabs pop out of their holes and skitter sideways across the damp sand, going in different directions. Toby's instinct is to herd all scattering creatures into a group. But the crabs won't be rounded up. They stay firmly planted, pincers waving and eyes bugging out on

long stalks. Toby lunges and retreats, over and over, until
the crabs lose their nerve and fly across the sand in a mad
dash for safety. The game is on! Sometimes the crabs dive
down their holes before Toby can reach them, but sometimes he catches one and ... "Oh, no! Toby, it got you!"

He shakes his head, but it's futile — the pincers are
caught fast and Dad has to pry them off.

On the way home, in the back seat of the car, Toby
flops his hot body against me and sleeps. With my bare
legs sticking to the vinyl and my skin flushed from the
sun and sticky from the salt water, I doze off, too.

Regis jumps onto the arm of the recliner, trying to sit on the
keyboard. I love stroking him and hearing him purr, but I can't
work when he's here. I push him aside, encouraging him to nestle
into my legs instead, but he doesn't like being told what to do. He
jumps down and walks away with his tail in the air, settling in the
overflowing laundry basket. That surprises me because I just did the
laundry. These days, a minute goes by and it turns out to be a day.
Never mind. I'll do the laundry later, when I've finished writing.

So, what was I working on? The computer screen is dark, but
it quickly brings a document back up. It seems to be a story, but I
don't know what it's about. I read the last line on the screen. Ah, yes,
Trinidad! Images come to me. All I have to do is put them into words.

On our drives across the island to Manzanilla Beach, I
see bare-assed children bathing under hydrants in streets
that are shared with feral dogs. Bright-eyed boys play
cricket with coconut branches and tennis balls. On their
heads, women carry baskets overflowing with cassava and
eddoes. Men lean against shacks whose dilapidated walls
are covered with sun-bleached rum posters, whereas
others walk home from church, their wives and children in
Sunday-best.

We pass small plots of vegetables and big fields of sugar cane; tethered goats and Zebu cows. We get stuck behind a cart pulled by a donkey, mule, or ox. And all along the way, on the stoops of small homes teetering on wooden stilts, young and old sit together.

By stark contrast, our house in St. Augustine is like a centrefold in *Better Homes and Gardens*. It reminds me of Southern plantation homes that I've seen on TV — not as grand, but more upper class than anything in my former life.

I sit in a mahogany Morris chair on the wrap-around veranda, surrounded by a haven of tropical flowers — orange Bird of Paradise streaked with violet, bougainvillea in countless shades of purple and pink, and others I don't even know the names of. The polished cement floor is cool on my bare feet, and the decorative wrought-iron walls keep out intruders while letting in the jasmine-scented trade winds. Hettie brings freshly squeezed lime juice in a tall glass packed with ice and dripping with condensation.

Other than the veranda, the rest of the house is plastered white, with burglar-proofing bars on all the windows. The dining room alone is big enough to hold our entire English house and is linked to the back kitchen by a long corridor. Hettie, wearing a black dress, a frilly white apron, and a little hat starched as stiff as a crown, does the hike, pushing a trolley piled high with food. The lengthy corridor tricks my brain into thinking I'm still on the ship. I bounce into the walls, Hettie playfully accusing me of adding rum to my lime juice. I spent days on the *Golfito* getting my sea legs and now I have to get my land legs back.

I'm a budding biologist, and the biodiversity of Trinidad astounds me. I don't have to trek into the tropical rain forest of the Northern Range to discover it. It's within sight of my chair on the veranda or my bed at the end of the corridor. I see the huge broad leaves of banana plants competing for light with orange, lime, and mango trees. A prehistoric iguana basks on the stout limb of an avocado tree, so well camouflaged that my eye catches sight of him only when he stretches to chew a shiny, fresh leaf. A pair of iridescent hummingbirds dart and hover among the red hibiscus flowers, their wings nothing more than a blur. A metallic-blue butter-fly, the size of my hand, sails past in a slow, bouncy flight path, shimmering in the sunlight. And in the shade, a brown hen gathers her fluffy yellow chicks under her wing while a red rooster darts into the sunlight, chasing bugs and gobbling them down on the run, his iridescent feathers flashing purple and emerald. There's a wild, chaotic lushness that makes England seem tame and sterile in comparison. Exotic versus …

I've lost the word. Nothing. Waiting. Still waiting. Terror fills the void. Is it Alzheimer's? I should book a doctor's appointment. I'm too scared.

Blood pounds through my ears, and over the roar I hear Alicia's voice: "Take a big breath in … and let it go."

I breathe deeply and feel calmer.

Turning back to the screen, I read the words aloud, reflecting that it's way too descriptive. Readers want action. Too bad! They can suck it up. If I have Alzheimer's, I won't be able to write like this much longer. Words, especially adjectives, have always come easily, but now they are hiding from me. Exotic versus …

Bland! There it is! Exotic versus bland. I don't have Alzheimer's.

As the afternoon sun gives way to the violet and tobacco hues of dusk, colossal moths emerge, fluttering and flapping against the lights. A semi-transparent gecko who lives behind a painting in the living room tentatively peeks out, scampering across the ceiling on pink adhesive feet, his long tongue snatching up wayward mosquitoes, who have voracious appetites for fresh English blood. In darkened rooms, cockroaches as big as your thumb disappear into cracks in the woodwork the instant you flip the switch. But I'm …

Diverting? Divulging? Distracting?
It begins with a *d*, I'm sure, but I can't find it.
My teeth clench, my gut tightens.
Maybe I'll play Sudoku on my laptop. That always calms me.

The doorbell startles me. I ignore it. I don't feel like being social — it's too much like hard work. But the bell keeps ringing insistently. I set aside my laptop and struggle out of the recliner.

It's my neighbour, chattering so fast I can barely keep track.

"Mary! *Est-ce que ça va?* I was worried about you. Were you sleeping?"

"*Oui, je dormais,*" I say, rubbing my eyes pretending I've just woken up. "*Va bien, merci.*"

"I'm sorry to disturb you. I haven't seen you for a few days. Do you need anything? I have to go to the grocery store, so it's no trouble. *Viens avec moi!* We can stop for coffee, have a nice chat and catch up. The roads are plowed and the sun is shining."

Her words are overwhelming.

I tell her I'm fine. I don't need anything. And I've just started to work on a new book — a memoir about me and my husband — so, thanks, but I'll take a rain check on the coffee.

And I don't call her by name because I've forgotten it, even though I've known her for years.

kayla

Kayla: Do you know that Ma is
writing a new book?

Alicia: No! That's great.

Kayla: I found out about it
from the neighbour!

Alicia: Chantelle?

Kayla: Yeah. BTW, she says Ma is okay.

Alicia: Good!

Kayla: She doesn't want any help.

Alicia: She *never* wants help! What's the book
about?

Kayla: About her and our dad!

Alicia: Wow! That's awesome. Perhaps we are
finally gonna learn something about Keith! I
wonder what brought that on.

Kayla: Don't know. But I'm getting more
concerned about her memory.

Alicia: Didn't Chantelle say she was fine?

Kayla: She did. But remember that bowl you made for her when you were in high school?

Alicia: Yes! The purple one with the yellow splotches that were supposed to be daffodils. Ma said it was the nicest bowl ever!

Kayla: Remember how upset she was when Zach broke it?

Alicia: He knocked it off the counter playing ball in the house! It smashed on the tiles. There was a lot of yelling! Total uproar. One of those childhood memories you never forget.

Kayla: Yeah, well, that's the thing. She's forgotten! She thinks she LOST it. Said she's searched high and low.

Alicia: Did you tell her Zach broke it?

Kayla: Yeah, but I don't think it registered because two minutes later, she said the same thing ... that she lost it and searched high and low. Same story told the same way.

Alicia: That doesn't sound like her. What did you say?

Kayla: Nothing! I changed the subject. But I just called her doctor. It's so difficult to get any information out of them — the whole doctor-patient confidentiality — but he said that he'd ask her to come in for a checkup.

Alicia: Can you get up to Montreal
any time soon?

> Kayla: Not this week or next. I have a
> wedding on Saturday, then a big corporate
> gig in Toronto. We just got a new keyboard
> player so we need to rehearse. And Easter is
> just two months away, so I have a ton of work
> to do at the church. I can't get away right now.

Alicia: That's a shame, but glad to hear
you've got work. What did you decide about
Singapore?

> Kayla: I'm not going. Ma can barely take care
> of herself, let alone Jesse.

Alicia: Sorry about that. I gotta run. I'm doing
a nutrition clinic with a group of pregnant
moms in a village outside Kigali.

> Kayla: Wish I had some of that Rwandan
> sunshine right now. It's brutal here.

Alicia: Hang in there! Spring should be just
around the corner! I'll watch out for anything
odd when I speak to Mom.

mary

"I'll book an MRI," the doctor says, "just in case there's a tumour or something vascular causing reduced blood flow to the brain. And we'll do a carotid Doppler. It could be stenosis. Or an infarct."

I look at him quizzically.

"A stroke," he explains. "Or a transient ischemic attack. Either could affect memory. Are you eating well? You look as if you might be losing weight. Hop on the scale. Careful, watch your step there. Yes, you're down seven pounds since your last checkup. That's a lot for a tiny person like you. Malnutrition can cause memory loss, so that could be your problem right there. Tell me what you ate yesterday."

I shrug.

"Tell me what you ate this morning? Did you have breakfast?"

I don't know the answer, so I make one up. "Egg and bacon."

"Excellent! Let's do a cognitive test right now. It will give us a baseline for the future, so we'll know if your memory is getting worse, staying the same, or maybe getting better."

He sounds cheery, but I feel anxious. I hate tests — I freeze and can't think straight.

He smiles at me reassuringly. "Don't worry, Mary. It's not like an exam at school. No passing or failing grades. Can you tell me your name?"

"You know that! I'm Mary Bowen."

"And what is your date of birth?"

"May 26, 1949."

"What year are we in now?"

I hesitate and take a stab. "2000?"

"And where are we right now?"

"At your office."

"Excellent. Now can you tell me what these animals are?"

I name the three animals drawn on the page.

It's baby stuff. I'm acing it. He shows me a diagram with numbers and letters, then hands me a pencil.

"Can you join them up in a single line? I'll show you what I mean: A-1, B-2, C-3, et cetera."

I make a start, then freeze. "What do you want me to do?"

He repeats the instructions, and I complete the task perfectly. Feeling good!

"Mary, I'm going to tell you five words now. I want you to memorize them: *banana, rose, basket, forest, motorbike.* In a few minutes, I'll ask you to recite them back to me, so remember them, okay?"

He repeats the words as I try to picture them in my mind ... placing the banana and the rose in the basket. Before I can finish, he moves onto another problem, asking me to copy a drawing of two overlapping cubes. I have to concentrate but I do well ... I think.

Next, he asks me to repeat a sentence back to him, but I don't like the sentence structure, so I correct it as I repeat it.

"Now, Mary," he asks, "can you tell me the five words I gave you at the beginning of the test?"

"What words?"

"The ones I asked you to memorize. I told you I was going to ask you about them later."

"You didn't give me any words!" I say, angry that he is jeopardizing my chance of passing the test.

"I'll give you a clue to the first word — it's a fruit." He's trying to convince me that he really did give me five words, but I know he didn't. Maybe it's a trick question.

"Apple," I say tentatively.

"No worries, Mary. Can you count backward from one hundred by sevens?"

"One hundred, ninety-nine, ninety-eight ..."

"By sevens, Mary. Like this: one hundred, ninety-three ... now you try."

"Are you mad?"

"Okay, let's see if we can draw a clock, an old-fashioned one with ticking hands."

I don't like the patronizing way he says *we*. It's me doing the test, not him. Regardless, I feel sure that I can draw a clock. I start with a circle. It's pretty good, but the numbers don't fit inside it. They mysteriously land outside the circle.

"Can I start over?" I ask. "I can do better than that."

"No, Mary, this is good! Now I want you to draw the hands on the clock. Set them at twenty to four."

I think hard and do it. I know that one hand should be longer than the other, and I can't figure that out. The test is stupid! And dated! Who uses clocks with hands these days?

"Okay, Mary," he says, getting up from his seat. "I'll see you again when I have the results of the scans. In the meantime, do puzzles. They're good for the brain."

"I already do puzzles," I say. "Sudoku. And crosswords."

"Excellent! Keep that up. You need to challenge your brain. And try to eat well. Everything that is good for the heart is good for the brain, too. Same goes for physical exercise. It gets the blood flowing ... gives your brain some oxygen so you can think clearer. Use it or lose it, they say."

I stopped listening to him after Sudoku.

"Mary," he says, looking me in the eye. "Listen to me, this is important. Have you told your family that you are having problems remembering things?"

"No, I don't want to worry them."

"This would be a good time to share what's going on. I think you need some support, especially because you live alone. I'll make you an appointment with the gerontologist, and I'll do the paper-work to get you a social worker. We'll get you some services, okay?"

In my mind's eye, I see old folk parked in reclining wheelchairs, staring at the ceiling of their care home, mouths flopped open, drooling. I cannot — will not — join them. "I'll tell my children," I say. "They'll help me. I don't need social services."

"Okay," the doctor says, "but I want you to bring one of your children to your next appointment."

I nod.

He ushers me to the door. "Oh, just one more thing … you aren't still driving, are you?" The way he frames the question suggests he doesn't think I should be.

I panic. He's gonna take away my licence!

"No," I say. "I don't drive anymore."

I leave the doctor's office, climb into my little red car, and drive home.

The concierge greets me in the foyer, telling me that my mail-box is filled to overflowing. I stuff it all into my purse and head to the elevator. Only after I hit the button for the second floor do I remember that the doctor said I should use the stairs. Next time.

In my apartment, I toss the mail onto the kitchen counter. It's mostly junk. There's a bill for the TV. It's red. Overdue. Final noti-fication. Service discontinued.

I turn the television on. Nothing. How can they do that without warning? I used to write cheques and mail them, but everything is different now. Kayla showed me how to pay my bills on the com-puter. She says it's easy, but I get confused. And she's never here to help me. She doesn't visit these days. None of the children visit me.

I phone Zach about the television. He says he'll fix it. He says not to worry. However, I am worried. I'll play Sudoku on my lap-top. That always calms me.

sage

It's too early in the morning for Mom to be bustling around like this. Something must be happening. I follow her anxiously, not wanting to be left behind. She throws a big, soft bag over her shoulder. The leather smells delicious enough to chew, but I know better than to try. In the past, I've been on the receiving end of Mom's wrath for chewing her leather shoes, which, with their delicious scent of both cows and human feet, are almost impossible to resist.

She wakes Jesse. "I'm heading to Montreal now. I'll be home in four days, but I'm just a phone call away, and Mrs. McClutchy is going to look in on you."

"Got it," he mumbles.

"There's plenty of food in the house, and don't forget to let *Sage* out. Her bladder's not as strong as it used to be. And no parties!"

"Okay Mom," he says, rolling over to face the wall and burying his head under the covers.

I follow Mom to the door. "Look after the house," she says, stroking me gently, "and look after Jesse." Then she opens the door, blocking me with her body. "*Sage! Stay.*"

I rest my chin on the window ledge by the door and watch *Minivan* disappear from sight. Then I go back to Jesse's room and flop on the floor to wait. But boredom soon sets in. Jesse stays hidden under the covers, so I settle down on my own bed, waiting for him to stir. Eventually, he does and is soon rummaging around in *TheFridge*. I sit at his feet, drooling, wishing he would hurry because my belly is right in line with its cold breath. There's not much hair there and I'm getting chilled.

He tips crunchy things into both our dishes. After I wolf mine down, he shoos me into the backyard, startling the chickadees, who take to the air with a whooshing of wings. I sniff out the perfect spot to relieve myself, and watch the birds return, taking turns to flutter onto the feeder that hangs from a branch in the big tree.

The day passes: I come and go into the backyard. *KingDoberman*, from next door, comes and goes, too. I can't see him, but I know he's there, snuffling up against the fence. I snuffle back. Sparrows, juncos, and nuthatches fly in and out on a constant quest for food. Jesse looks for more food, too. Then more. Then more again. He shares with me, which makes me happy, but as the shadows lengthen, I miss Mom.

With just a sliver of sunlight left in the sky, Jesse takes me *Walkies*. He gives me time to stop and sniff and learn which of my friends have recently passed by. The delicious fishy aroma left by *MitzyTheSharpei* tells me that she is having a good day. Same goes for *KingDoberman*, the scent of red meat he ate yesterday remaining on the grass even though his human carried the poop away. *PeteyThePitbull*, from across the street, has a severe case of the runs. *TerrorTheTerrier* isn't doing well, either — he vomited up grass, along with a mouthful of over-ripe *Chicken*. It's too far gone to eat but well worth rolling in. I'm about to lean my shoulder into it when Jesse jerks the leash and drags me away. He stops to let me poop only after I've already assumed the position, and he doesn't collect it in a baggie, the way Mom does. Instead, after looking around with a furtive glance, he tugs me down the street toward home.

I wait at the door for Mom to return, but she doesn't. Instead, some of Jesse's friends arrive. They play loud music, which hurts my ears, so after I've helped them eat the pizza and pretzels and cleaned up all the spills from the floor, I go to my bed and bury my head under my tail.

I miss Mom. My nose leads me to where her scent is strongest — her room. My legs have no choice but to follow my nose, even though I am not allowed here. I snuggle into her pillow and breathe her aroma. It makes me think she's still here.

kayla

Kayla: At the gerontologist now … waiting.

Zach: Patch me in if you need help.

Alicia: Good luck.

Kayla: Shall we do a conference call later to discuss?

Zach: Sure. Anytime is good for me.

Kayla: As soon as Ma is asleep — around 9? Is that good for you, Leesh?

Alicia: That will be 4:00 a.m. here. I can do earlier if you want. I'll be up anyways … worrying.

Kayla: I'd rather wait until Ma is asleep, so she can't eavesdrop. Especially if it's bad news.

Zach: Text if it's *good* news, then! So we don't worry.

Kayla: Going in now.

———————————

The gerontologist is reading Ma's file, silently assessing the scans, blood work, and cognitive tests. I wish he'd skip to the diagnosis, because I've been waiting for this moment for three months, ever since I first noticed Ma's confusion and memory loss, ever since I first got the feeling that she might have Alzheimer's.

I watch his face for a hint as to where this consultation is going but he's impassive.

Finally, he takes off his reading glasses, thoughtfully lays them aside, and gives my mother a sad glance before making eye contact with me. *Shit!* It's bad news.

"The good news is ..."

My heart plummets in anticipation of the bad news, which he's saving for last.

"... there is no evidence of stenosis, strokes, or tumours. In fact, your mother's cerebrovascular system is in good shape."

"That's wonderful," Ma says, her face lighting up, but I anticipate what's coming next.

Strangely, I feel gratitude. I'm glad I made the six-hour drive to be with my mother for this weighty, life-changing moment. I'm glad she's not alone.

"But there *is* cognitive impairment," the doctor says.

Ma is quiet, her expression flat. I don't know if she is taking it in, or not.

"Is it Alzheimer's?" I whisper to the doctor.

"Hard to tell for sure, but I don't see any other reason for the memory loss. We'll know more as time goes by. I'll see her again in three months and do another cognitive test then, to see how fast or how slow things are moving."

I don't want to alarm Ma, so even though I want answers, I can't ask the right questions. The doctor seems to read my thoughts, answering the question that is at the forefront of my mind.

"Everyone is different. And every person's journey is different. For some people, it's five years; for others, it's twenty-five."

On the drive back to Ma's condo, we are both quiet. "I told you I was fine," she says. "Just a few memory problems." I don't respond.

After Ma goes to bed, I get Alicia and Zach on a conference call, not an easy task as we are all in different time zones. Alicia, in Rwanda, is seven hours ahead, and Zach, in Vancouver, three hours behind.

"Did he say it was Alzheimer's for sure?" Alicia asks.

"Not for sure," I say. "You need an autopsy for that ... to see plaques and tangles down the microscope. But he's ruled out other things, and he prescribed Alzheimer's medication. So I think it's most probably Alzheimer's."

"Meds! That's good!"

"The doctor didn't sound too optimistic about them. There are a few we can try, but some people get side effects, and the meds aren't a cure ... they won't stop it. At best, they might slow it down. And when I was leaving ..." I pause to regain my stoicism. "... the doctor gave me a pamphlet from the Alzheimer Society of Canada ... said I should connect with the local chapter."

"Crap! How did Ma take the news?"

"Fine! She says, it's 'just a few memory problems.' But I don't know how much she took in."

"Should we force the information down her throat and try to get her to accept it?" Zach asks.

"Why would we do that?" I reply. "Ignorance is bliss."

"If it were me, I'd want to know. I could make plans ... do the things I always wanted to do ... before it's too late."

"I think we should go along with Ma," Alicia says. "If she thinks it's just a few memory problems, she still has hope. Let's not take that away from her. But we don't need to make that decision right now. I think today's priority is assessing her capabilities so we know what help she needs, if any. I mean is it safe for her to be living alone?"

Suddenly, they both expect me to be the authority on our mother's abilities.

"Can she still cook or go grocery shopping?"

"Can she handle money, pay the bills, use a bank machine?"

"Can she read, write, take a shower?"

"Is it safe to leave her alone? What if she leaves a pan on the stove? What if she wanders off and gets lost?"

"Should we get her a MedicAlert bracelet or a GPS tracker? Should we register her with the police?"

"This is all so overwhelming," I say.

Alicia, a problem-solver by nature, takes the helm, deciding that for now we will divide and conquer, each of us taking a topic to research. She volunteers to investigate in-home help and the Alzheimer Society. Zach does what he's best at: annoying me.

"Kayla, you'll have to bear the brunt of this," he says. "You're the closest to her."

I'm pretty sure he means geographically, not emotionally, but both are equally true. The relationship I have with Ma is a strange one. As pathetic as it sounds, my mother is my best friend. I tell her everything, even though she tells me nothing — at least nothing about her emotions, and nothing about her past except that the aggro between Zach and me started as soon as I was born. I know that my brother was caught between a rock and a hard place: His daddy died when he was less than two years old, his mother became an emotional wreck in the process, and I arrived four months later, making him a middle child with baggage far heavier than most.

"Zach!" I protest. "It's six hours to Montreal! I know you don't think being a singer is a real job, but it is! Right now, I have lots of bookings. Plus, it's Easter next week. You do know I *work* at the church, right? I've got all this special music to arrange and the choir to lead."

"I don't expect you to drop everything. Why are you always so touchy? How about going back the weekend after next? The reality is that none of us are in a good position to take care of Ma right now, so we should be looking for some sort of … facility."

"That's heartless," I shriek. "Plus, it's expensive. And quite honestly, it's Ma's worst nightmare. You know how independent she is.

Anyway, she looked after *us* all these years. Isn't it our turn to look after *her* now?"

"What option do we have?" Zach asks. "I can't take her, at least not full time."

"Can't or won't," I mutter.

"Do you want her to move in with you and Jesse and the dog? Or should we rotate her around the world? A month with Leesh in Rwanda, a month with me on the West Coast and a month with you back east?"

"Don't be ridiculous!"

"Come on guys, be nice," Alicia says. "We have to work together on this. We have to share the responsibility."

I take a deep breath and try to express what I've been thinking. "I hate the idea of putting her in a home. And we can't leave her in Montreal alone, at least not for much longer. That's just plain wrong. Now that Kyle is living in residence, and Krista's old bedroom is empty, I was wondering if Ma could come live with me."

"That solves the problem then," Zach says, as if it's a *fait accompli*.

"I didn't say yes for sure," I say, feeling manipulated, "but I do want to think about it."

Picturing myself cleaning out Krista's remaining junk and making a nice room for my mother, I feel pretty sure I've made the decision: I won't put her into a nursing home, at least not yet, and if that means taking her into my own home, then so be it. But Zach has made me uneasy. It's the way I usually feel after conversations with him.

Alicia, ever the peacemaker, changes the subject, suggesting an interim phone schedule so that Ma will have contact with one of us each day. We bicker over times, days, and availability.

Zach, the financial guru, says he'll work with a lawyer to draw up the power of attorney for Ma's finances. "We can implement it as soon as she's no longer *compos mentis*."

"What?"

"Of sound mind," he explains.

"You mean like insane? Surely we're a long way from that."

"I'd say we're nearly there, Kayla," he says with an unusual amount of sympathy in his voice. "You said she handed you her wallet in McDonald's because she couldn't figure out how to pay for the coffee."

"That's true. She was frustrated, even angry over it, but that doesn't mean she's lost her mind."

"I hope you're right, but it's best to be prepared. If we do it now, while she still knows what she's signing, it's just a simple trip to the lawyer's office. If not, then it's a whole other problem."

"You mean she has to *agree* to us taking control of her money?"

"Yes, but it might be a big relief for her. If we leave it until she's totally lost it, we have to get her certified, and that's a lot more complicated. I can take a trip to Montreal, talk to her about it, get her on board, and go to the lawyer's office all at the same time. We'll get the power of attorney for health, too … end-of-life decisions, et cetera."

"You mean like turning off life support?" Alicia says.

"More than that. If her heart stops, for example, do we want them to attempt resuscitation? If she gets pneumonia, do we want heroic treatments to keep her alive, or just keep her comfortable?"

"Oh my God!" I blurt out. "This is awful. There's no way we should keep her alive once her brain is gone."

"But it's not about what *we* want," Zach says. "We need to know what *she* wants. And that means discussing it with her soon, while she still has the mental faculty."

I'm horrified. "I can't do that!"

"Don't worry, Kayla, I'll handle it. I'll make it a priority. I'll fly out there in the next few weeks and get it all done. And I'll commit to going … say, once a month, until we get something better arranged for her."

On the other end of the line, Alicia is crying.

Zach's voice cracks, too. That's a first. "I know it sounds awful," he says, "but it will make things easier for us as we move forward."

Alicia speaks through her sniffles. "It's best you do the power of attorney stuff, Zach. She'll take it from you whereas she'll fight with me and Kayla. She holds you on a pedestal."

"Only because I remind her of Keith," Zach says.

"What?" Alicia and I both screech. "I never knew that!"

"I didn't know, either, at least not until I was sixteen, when I got my black belt. Ma said that I looked so much like Keith, it took her breath away. I'm just lighter skinned, that's all. When Ma told me, it was like she turned on a tap for a few seconds — emotion poured out, then she turned the tap back off and went back to her old self. Apparently, Keith did karate, too, but he didn't take it up until he was an adult. I've often wondered why he felt the need to learn self-defence ..."

Zach pauses for less than a second, then moves right along. "I already put her TV on pre-authorized debit ..."

It's a light bulb moment for me: Zach hides his emotions, too! Our mother taught us both to soldier on.

"... The cable was shut off not long ago," he continues, "because she didn't pay the bill. I did the same for the gas, the hydro, and the phone. And talking about money ... you know how easily old people get scammed, and how common it is? If someone calls saying there's an unauthorized payment on her credit card ... if they ask her to confirm her card number, she'll give it to them without blinking! We have to take away her cards! Kayla, lift them from her wallet ... now, while she's asleep."

"You mean I'm supposed to steal my mother's cards and leave her here alone for two weeks without any money?"

"If you bring her groceries every couple of weeks, what else is there to spend money on? Leave her a hundred bucks cash for emergencies. Two hundred, tops."

"Go find her wallet and do it now," Alicia suggests, "while we're still on the phone for moral support."

I do as I'm told, feeling like total shit. How can this be happening?

"How's she supposed to put gas in the car?" I ask.

"She shouldn't be driving! That's the next thing to deal with. We'll have to sell the car. If she doesn't agree, then we'll wait until we have the power of attorney. I'll think about that. But we've made a good start. Well done, Kayla. You've done a great job."

We say goodnight. I feel closer to Zach than I ever have.

sage

In the morning, I whine at Jesse, telling him I need to pee. We pick our way over sleeping bodies and he shoos me out into the backyard. By the time he lets me back in, the humans are awake, upright and using lots of words that I don't understand. Words, I reflect, are a human superpower, almost as excellent as hands. As hard as I try to coax words from my mouth, all I can achieve is a limited variety of garbled sounds accompanied by a puddle of drool.

Eventually the strangers go away, but Jesse climbs back into bed, not wanting to spend time with me.

I wait faithfully by the front door, *FloppyBunny* at the ready, looking out the window, but our hope that Mom will soon return fades fast.

As the day goes by, *PinkPiggy* joins our vigil. And then *Mouse*. They are damp and bedraggled, but like me and *FloppyBunny*, ready to greet Mom the instant she returns. However, we despair that she will ever come home. She never leaves the den for this long. If she doesn't come back soon, I don't hold out much hope for Jesse and me. I love Jesse, but I don't think he's ready to lead our pack just yet. Although I have to admit that the menu has been quite varied, including the red meat burgers we both love so much but Mom never gives me.

The thought of food drives me to the kitchen. I follow my nose. It's what I do, what I've always done since the beginning of me, when I was blind and deaf and learned about the world through aroma.

Right now, the scent of a pretzel distracts me. It's under *TheFridge*, just out of reach. I lie down and watch it. It's good to know it's there, in case the rations get really limited.

kayla

I divide yesterday's lasagna into individual portions for the freezer so Ma can pop them in the oven, but then I worry that she might leave it on.

"Do you use the oven much these days, Ma?"

"I made a lovely roast dinner yesterday."

"No, you didn't! I made lasagna for us last night."

I go into the bathroom and call Zach, whispering my concerns. We agree to turn off the breaker for the stovetop and the oven. Ma has an electric kettle, toaster, and microwave. She can use those.

I tell her there's a problem with the oven and leave a note on it to remind her. *OVEN IS BROKEN. USE MICROWAVE.*

"Don't worry," she tells me.

"I do worry, Ma. Stouffville is such a long way from Montreal. I wish we lived closer so I could see you all the time and help you out more. What would you think about living with Jesse and me?"

"I don't need your help, Kayla. I know you mean well, but I don't need you mollycoddling me. I have a life here! I run the book club, and what about my job at the library?"

"You retired, Ma."

"Did I? Oh, yes, but I go in and help out. I'm a ..."

"Volunteer?" I suggest.

"Yes! They need me."

Her negative reaction is upsetting. I hear her say that living with me would be merely one step up from living on the street. But when

I look at her critically, I see a woman who is already living on the street: mismatched socks and hair that hangs, limp and grey, on her shoulders, looking like it hasn't been washed for weeks. Ma's hair used to be blond and long and silky, and when I was a child, I wanted hair like hers.

"How about a girls' beauty day," I say, enthusiastically. "I'll take you to the hair salon at the mall."

"Sure," she says, "you could use some styling yourself. What's with the Afro? Don't you straighten it anymore?"

"No, Ma, that went out of style years ago. It's all natural now, but most hairdressers don't know how to deal with hair like mine. I have a lady at home — Jasmine. She's mixed race, too. I'll stick with her, thanks. Now, go get changed, and put on matching socks, 'cause we might even go for a mani-pedi! Are your feet clean?"

Ma says nothing. The faraway expression in her eyes makes me realize she didn't hear a thing I said.

"Take off your socks, Ma."

Dust flies into the air along with the socks — my mother's dead skin sparkling in the sunlight.

"Eek! When did you last shower?"

"This morning."

"No, you did not. I was here. I would have heard you. Go have a quick shower now, before we go to the mall."

She doesn't move. I put more enthusiasm into my voice. "We can eat lunch at the mall … the Thai food you like!"

She seems keen on that idea and heads off to the shower. Two minutes later she reappears in the same clothes and the same mismatched socks.

Abandoning the mani-pedi idea, I offer up her goose-down coat and she plunges her arms in. The coat hides her odd attire, plus it will keep her warm. Montreal is always so much colder than Stouffville, and spring takes so long to arrive.

"Why don't you drive?" I suggest, thinking it will be a good opportunity for me to evaluate her driving skills.

She takes the car keys off the hook and passes them to me. "You drive, dear."

"I've done enough driving," I say. "Six hours here and it will be six hours back."

"Six hours? The mall is ten minutes away!"

"I mean six hours from Stouffville."

She frowns, then recovers with a quick, "Oh, yes, of course."

Her driving isn't bad … no wrong turns, no emergency stops. But I sit anxiously in the front passenger seat, feeling like I did when Kyle and Krista were learning to drive, anticipating the moment when my right foot will slam to the floor, hitting the non-existent brake. She stops at a green light.

"Are you waiting for any particular shade of green?" I say. It's a phrase that the family has used for as long as I can remember.

She laughs, and I see the younger version of Ma, the one who was my rock. I want to hold on to her and beg her not to leave me. Tears well in my eyes, but I don't let them fall. I blink and sniff, telling myself there's still plenty of time to do things with Ma. Five to twenty-five years, the doctor said.

The haircut goes well, and we eat Thai at the food court, Ma tucking in as if she hasn't eaten in a week. I wonder if she's getting enough nutrition. She looks a little gaunt, but swears she's eating well and is still perfectly capable of cooking and grocery shopping, though I haven't seen her make anything other than tea since I arrived. I should not have taken over in the kitchen.

People in the mall stare at us. They've done it my whole life. When I was little, strangers would smile, pat my hair, and ask if I was adopted. Then, when I hit my twenties, they assumed I was the maid. Now that Ma is old, they think I'm her caregiver. Hardly anyone realizes we are mother and daughter. Ma is as white as they come, and I'm Black. Technically I'm part Black. The DNA in my saliva sample has proven that almost half my ancestors came from Togo, in Africa, undoubtedly captured and taken to the West Indies in chains. I'm part white, of course, but

I'm never seen that way even when my birth mother is standing right next to me.

We pop into the grocery store to pick up a few more packs of microwavable entrees and soups, then head out to the parking lot. We both stare around blankly.

Ma turns to me and asks, "Where did you park, Kayla?"

I want to say, "For goodness' sakes, Ma, *you* drove! *You* were supposed to remember where you parked," but I button my lip and mentally retrace the parking process ... when we got out of the car, I was busy making sure she didn't wander into traffic. Parking lots are such dangerous places ... cars pulling in and reversing out. I had to grab onto her like she was a pre-schooler.

With a general location in mind, I take her hand and head off.

I test her by asking, "What colour is your car?"

"Red," she says confidently. "There it is! I see it!"

Phew.

Next day, I admire the neatly stacked cans and jars in the pantry: tuna, salmon, baked beans, chili, pasta sauce, and cat food — the tins with the pull rings — along with packages of microwavable side dishes. The fridge is stocked with her favourite cheeses, eggs, and salad items, along with the all-important milk for her tea. The freezer section has individual frozen entrees that can be microwaved. And a bowl of fruit sits on the counter. She should be good until I come again in two weeks.

I label the cupboards, wash her bedsheets, do a quick vacuum, and get ready to head home, telling her not to come outside to wave me off because it's raining and it will make a mess of her lovely hair. I settle her in the recliner in front of the TV and kiss her on the forehead. As I turn to sneak away, I pause to take a picture in my mind — she's smiling at *Judge Judy*. Then I hold up my iPhone and take a quick shot, in case *my* memory goes, too. Finally, I lean over her shoulder and take a few selfies of us together. It makes me sad, but I get the feeling that when I look back later, the pictures will make me happy.

I shut the door quietly and walk down the corridor to the elevator with conflicting emotions.

Hope that she'll be safe.

Fear that she won't be.

Guilt that I'm leaving her alone.

Relief that I'm returning to my own life.

mary

It's time to face reality, I tell myself, settling at my desk and opening the laptop.

> My name is Mary, and I have Alzheimer's disease. It makes me think of AA meetings I've seen in the movies: *My name is so-and-so and I'm an alcoholic.* It's an acknowledgement, a way of facing your problem. Writing this is an acknowledgement, too. A way of confronting the truth.

But is it the truth? Maybe the doctor is wrong.

The sticky notes on the wall by my desk are curling up at the edges. I flatten them with clear tape, reading as I go. *CHALLENGE YOUR BRAIN.* The doctor told me that. He suggested learning a new language. At my age? I don't think so. But I could speak French more often. I used to be fluent but these days I'm lazy. I let people speak English.

I grab a pink sticky note and a purple sharpie. I like purple. *SPEAK FRENCH.* Huh, there's already a green note saying that!

PLAY WORD GAMES, an orange note says. I like word games. I love how you change one letter, and you make a whole new word. Like *true* and *tree*. I have a word game on my phone, the one where you search for words hidden among jumbled letters. I'll do that now. Opening the phone ... scrolling ... what am I looking for again? I forget. Never mind. I'll get back to writing.

I stare into space, hoping that an idea for my memoir will drop into my head. Suddenly, Keith's voice breaks the silence. He sounds so real that my heart fills with love. "Write about meeting me."

I start writing with a smile on my face, feeling warm inside and safe.

I met Keith when I was ...

Panic surges through me. I can't remember how old I was when we met! Was I seventeen? Or sixteen? How can I have forgotten that?

Pounding heart.

It was such an important year in my life.

I'll figure it out. I was born in 1949, and we went to Trinidad in 1966. Damn it! I don't know *how* to figure it out.

My stomach flips.

"You never were good with mental arithmetic!" Keith says.

I hear the smile in his voice.

"You're right," I say. "I need paper and pencil. Hey! I didn't fail the doctor's memory test because I have Alzheimer's — I failed it 'cause I'm no good at mental math. Never was. Words are my thing, not subtracting backward by sevens. Who can do that?"

"I can," Keith says. "One hundred, ninety-three, eighty-six, seventy-nine, seventy-two, sixty-five, fifty-eight, fifty-one, forty-four, thirty-seven, thirty, twenty-three, sixteen, nine, two."

I see him! Not just in my imagination, but in flesh and blood, a broad grin spreading across his face.

"Show off," I say.

He fades from my eyes.

"Don't go," I say.

"I'm still with you, my love. Always. Now, write some more about Trinidad. About that first day of class. Do you remember the rain?"

Suddenly, I'm back in the old pre-med building.

A tropical cloudburst — torrents beating so hard on the
tin roof that it drowns out the voice of the professor; the
kind of rain that hits the tarmac and bounces back four
feet before falling again, wind ripping through the class-
room, paper tugging at the moorings of ring-binders.
Five minutes and it's over.

At the end of class, Keith casually offers to drive me to
our next lecture in the new part of campus. I accept his
offer, using sandals and splash-back as an excuse. As we
drive, I'm too intoxicated with the breathtaking prox-
imity of Keith behind the wheel to take in the stunning
vista that would be the back drop of my life for the next
four years: the royal palms standing guard on either side
of the main avenue, and the original university building
set in colonial splendour on an island of verdant lawn.

Steam rises from the tarmac, sparkling in the sun,
and the scent of damp earth and flowers mingle with
the scent of Keith. It makes me giddy! Everything is so
fresh, I feel as if I'm in the Garden of Eden — the first
day of a new world … the first day of my life!

Keith tells me he is just turning nineteen and has already worked a year in the oil fields in the south of the
island, winning a scholarship to continue his education
with a degree in engineering. Thanks to UWI's pre-med
course for all students in science-based degrees, Keith
and I find ourselves in many of the same classes. Pre-
med was also what saved me from being left behind in
an English boarding school when my parents relocated
to Trinidad.

Even though my father was of the opinion that travelling the world was the best education anyone could
have, he didn't want my academics to suffer. The logical

solution was to leave me behind so I could finish A-levels and go to an English university. But then Dad discovered that UWI offered pre-med — a crash course at A-level — and that instead of being the subpar university he assumed it would be, UWI was affiliated with the University of London and was the seat of the world-renowned Imperial College of Tropical Agriculture.

Ever since my mother had brought Africa's starving children to my attention, I'd had this vague, idealistic notion that I could help feed them. At Southampton's Grammar School for Girls, there had been no avenue for this. I'm not sure it was ever a serious career choice, but I'd discovered that it brought approving nods when used in response to the perpetual question: What do you want to do when you grow up?

My desire to go to Trinidad with my parents had nothing to do with academics or job opportunity. It came solely from the centrefold in a library book, showing a golden beach fringed with palm trees; drinks served in green coconuts; lush, forested mountains swooping down from a sapphire sky; and white surf breaking from a cobalt ocean.

It was all so vibrant — nothing like the dreary palette of my childhood, with its pebble beaches and the cold grey water of the English Channel.

The phone rings. It's the doctor's office. I missed an appointment. Now I have to pay a twenty-five-dollar cancellation fee. That's outrageous. Where do they expect me to find money like that?

I think the cab driver forgot to come for me. It would never have happened if the Ministry hadn't taken away my licence. There are far worse drivers on the roads than me! It's a moot point, anyway, because someone stole my car.

I check the time: 4:30! How did that happen?

I haven't told anyone yet about my memory lapses. I feel ashamed. I don't know why, but I do. I've been hiding it as best I can, but I don't think I can hide it much longer. I don't want to worry the children unnecessarily. And I don't want to be a burden to them. They're busy with their own lives. Kayla has a family of her own now: two young children, plus a new baby. Jesse! He's such a cutie — big dark eyes, brown curly hair. His smile lights up my life. He reminds me of my own baby — Zach. He'll be home from school soon. I must make supper.

I rummage through the fridge, finding a half tub of coleslaw, a sad tomato, and a carton of eggs. I beat two and put them in a pan on the cooktop, but the stove doesn't work. Damn it! I need a repairman.

I put the eggs in the microwave. I'll have them with Swiss cheese, my favourite. I lay a slice on the plate. But it reminds me of a slice of brain I saw on the computer when I googled Alzheimer's: full of holes created when tiny feeding tubes collapse like crumpled drinking straws; when the brain starves to death cell by cell and shrivels away to nothing. Is this my future?

After seeing the cheese this way, I don't fancy eating it, and the microwaved eggs are rubbery and stinky. I slather them with ranch dressing. It doesn't help much. I offer them to Regis, and with a heavy heart, I go to bed, hiding under the comforter with the purple irises and the yellow daffodils.

sage

Mom is making a big mess in Krista's old room. Bags and boxes everywhere.

I creep in. I never felt welcome here. Krista was the only upright in the pack with a sense of smell, but she didn't like my aroma, and I didn't like hers.

"*Sage*, you stink," she'd say, clamping her long, delicate fingers over her nose.

Sometimes, I would cover my nose with my paws, trying to keep her perfumed stench from stinging my sensitive nostrils, but it didn't work. So I learned to stay out of Krista's room, preferring instead to inhale the sweet, sweet smell of Jesse's feet.

Krista went away a while ago, but the dust bunnies who sleep peacefully along the walls still retain her odour. I snort, sending them swirling into the air.

Something about the bags and boxes takes me back to when Dad left the pack, to when the rest of us moved to a new den, and then to another, and another. An uneasy feeling flits through my belly. Are we moving to a new den? I don't think I can survive getting stuffed into my puppy-sized crate again, and then into the belly of a great smelly beast who roars and races until my ears pop ... until everything swirls around me ... until I throw up. I can't even re-eat it because I feel so bad, abandoned by my pack, sharing the cramped space with a pile of vomit, and desperate to pee ... holding on and holding on, hoping that someone will hear my plaintive whimpers. When I'm finally reunited with my pack, I'm so overjoyed that I can't control myself ... at first, a few drops: no big deal; it happens occasionally when I get overexcited. But then a deluge splashes over the hard tarmac. Jesse jumps out of the way, acting disgusted, making me feel thoroughly ashamed, although I don't know why, because when he was short, he peed on the floor all the time.

Jesse pokes his head into Krista's room. "What are you doing, Mom?"

"Cleaning out your sister's stuff. Can you take these bags out to the garbage, please? I want a nice place for your gran when she comes to stay."

"She never comes to stay! You always go there."

Mom is using her cheerful voice, trying to hide her irritation. "She's coming here for a change. She needs more help these days, and I can't keep going to Montreal every time she loses the can opener."

"But I hardly know her!" Jesse complains.

Mom stops piling things into boxes and perches on the end of the bed. "When we lived in Montreal, she'd drop by nearly every day. She loved you so much. You loved her, too! You'd gurgle at the sight of her. If the weather was nice she'd take you to the park in your stroller. *Sage*, too. She'd sing you songs and read you stories. Sometimes I wonder if your dad dragged us out to Calgary to get me away from her! After the divorce, I wanted to move us back to Montreal, but then I got the music director job at the church here. It pays the bills and Stouffville is close enough to Toronto, so I can still do some gigging, yet it's far enough away to have that small-town feel."

"But why isn't Krista dealing with all this? It's her mess."

"She's already taken everything she wants. The rest is garbage."

"It's not fair, Mom," Jesse says, dragging a bag to the door. "Krista should be doing this, not me."

I follow him, but he slams the door in my face, saying, "*Stay!*"

I squish my damp nose against the window, watching him pile bags on the grass at the edge of the street, where the neighbourhood dogs pee. With a heavy sigh, I accept my fate: we're moving to a new den, a place where I will have to figure out the hierarchy of the new dogs — who is dominant and who is submissive (that would be me). A place where new cats will swat, lunge, jab, and hiss, commanding respect with a glare of the eye, and proclaiming their menacing superiority by the liquid rise and fall of their shoulders ... just like their bigger cousins who stroll across the grassland on *TeeVee*. Even the small, fluffy cats that look as harmless as *FloppyBunny* are not to be trusted. Never, *ever*, turn your back on a cat.

A fresh wave of panic hits me. Is Jesse leaving me now? Like Dad did? Like Kyle and Krista? If Jesse leaves me, I'll die. I can endure moving to a new den so long as Jesse comes with me, because home is wherever he is. Sure, I have to keep Mom calm and focused so she can be a good alpha, and I have to prevent intruders from entering our den, especially the one called *YooPeeEss*, but my number-one role in life has always been to look after Jesse. And believe me, he needs a lot of looking after. He's never been quick to learn. I still have to push my snout under his hand over and over before he strokes me. I still have to carry *TennisBall* in my mouth for ages before he rolls it for me. And I've given up following him around the den, telling him I'm hungry. I go to Mom instead.

I slink off to my bed and curl into a worried ball, tucking my muzzle as far under my tail as it can go, until I'm invisible. Eventually, I hear Jesse approach. I pop my head out and wag my tail, then, with a big sigh, I tell him I'm worried he's going to leave me and to please, please stay. As usual, he doesn't get it. He's so slow.

He has problems of his own. His shoulders slump and his head hangs low. I nudge under his hand with my muzzle, trying to make him feel better. That's my job.

mary

A new day. And I'm trying to be thankful. Alicia says gratitude will lift my mood.

I'm grateful for the sun, which shines through the sliding door of my little balcony. But it highlights a film of dirt, telling me I need to find the glass cleaner. I have no idea where it is.

I'm thankful for Regis. But he's licking the dirty dishes piled in the sink. As soon as he sees me, he jumps down, meowing in the voice that says he's hungry. I only just fed him, but his dish is already bare, dried pieces caked to the sides. I open the cupboard labelled *CAT FOOD*, take out a can, and look around for the can opener.

Regis winds himself around my ankles, caterwauling. I look in the drawer labelled *CUTLERY*. No can opener. I look in the sink. It's a mess. I rummage through the cupboard labelled *CANNED FOOD*. Baked beans? Regis doesn't like beans. Glass cleaner? Nope. Tuna? That will do. The cat can have half and I'll have the rest for my lunch. But where's the can opener?

Anger bursts out of me. "Damn it, Regis, stop your wailing. I can't think straight."

He doesn't stop. In fact, he amps up the noise, jumping on the counter and getting right in my face. I screech at him and he scampers away, watching me from a safe distance. Feeling bad about scaring him, I mush a slice of bread in milk and make a peace offering. He seems to like it. I have some, too, mashed in a bowl with a spoonful of sugar — the dessert of my childhood. I should visit Mummy. I will, after I've done some work. It's past 9:00 and I should have started already. I'm editing a manuscript for a client. There's a deadline to meet.

Where's the laptop? It's on the kitchen counter, charging.

I pull up a chair and enter the password: *Keith1*.

Tea, in my favourite mug — a necessity for the writing process — is already on the counter. It's cold. I'll reheat it. Huh, there's already a cup in the microwave. It's cold, too. Oh, dear. I'm forgetting things. I should tell Kayla. Oh God, I hope I never forget her name. I hope I never forget who she is. "Kayla, Kayla, Kayla." If I say it enough times, surely I'll remember it forever. I'll write it on an orange sticky note: *KAYLA*. I wish she'd come to visit me. She said she would. But when? I didn't write that down. And what do I tell her, anyway? I'm not accustomed to asking for help. I've always been independent.

Self-pity creeps in. I throttle it. "Good God, Mary. Get a hold of yourself ... Tea! That will help."

I move around the kitchen, looking for the things I need. I take the last clean mug from the cupboard labelled *MUGS* and find teabags in the canister labelled *TEA*, but I can't remember the order for doing things. Maybe I should make a note. I grab a pen and a square of fluorescent pink and start writing.

1. *Fill kettle with water.*
2. *Hit switch.*
3. *Get teabag from blue ...*

I need a bigger sticky note. Where are they? I look in the fridge. There's the can opener! Who put that there? Crazy! But at least I can open a can of cat food now.

Shit! The stupid opener doesn't work. Nothing works these days. I'll write it on the shopping list. Where's the list? I'll start a new one. Where are the sticky notes? There's one on my laptop. It says, *BOOK — "MARY'S STORY" SAVED IN MY DOCS.*

I open up the document. It needs a better title, something strong, persuasive, and memorable. If I know what the story is about, maybe I can suggest a better one.

I love editing. I've always been good at spelling, punctuation, and grammar, but there's more to editing than that. It can transform a mundane piece of writing into a riveting one, a confusing ramble into an enlightening thesis. And an out-of-place comma can change the whole meaning of a sentence. Over the years, I've seen so many comical examples of this, but right now, I can't think of a single one.

The story sounds familiar. Memories of university days. It was the best of times, it was the worst of times. That sounds familiar. Of course — it's Dickens! *A Tale of Two Cities.* Oh my goodness, am I editing Charles Dickens?

Seconds go by, or minutes, or maybe even hours before I realize my stupidity. I laugh at myself, but I'm appalled that I could have such a crazy, irrational thought. I start to feel the dreaded swirl of emotion pulling me, like water down a drain; confusing, nauseating. I push it away, focusing on the words on the screen. The manuscript may not be Dickens, but it needs editing, for sure.

Keith's voice sounds again in my head. "Mary! Move on with *writing* the story. You don't have time to edit."

I don't? Why not? Oh, shit! I have Alzheimer's.

My chest tightens. Why am I wasting my time editing someone else's book?

"It's *your* story," Keith says. "*Ours.*"

"That's crazy! I can't write a book! I have dementia. I'll never get it finished."

Keith is insistent. "Write now, Mary, before it's too late."

I catch his sense of urgency and type as fast as my fingers will go.

Keith and I had chemistry, for sure, right from the first moment. Our physical chemistry translated nicely to the chemistry lab, where it didn't take us long to pair up as lab partners. His brainpower floored me. I'd always been told I was smart, but Keith was smarter. Especially at physics and math. I was better at biology and at creative things like writing. I never procrastinated. He did. He had a T-shirt with a cartoon character's head squeezed in a vice. Sweat was flying, and the caption read: *I do better under pressure*. He did.

We are in the chemistry lab — together — spinning test tubes in a hand-operated centrifuge. He asks if I want to go water-skiing on Wednesday.

Hell, yes.

Other than an early morning class, Wednesdays are free, and although I have never tried water-skiing, it looks cool.

That first Wednesday isn't really a date because other people are with us. I discover that I'm a natural at water-skiing and that Keith always has access to a boat, his older brother, Brian, being the island's top designer, builder, and distributor of performance powerboats.

Every Wednesday after that, Keith and I get together, sometimes with others, but increasingly alone. Often, with the top down on the Sunbeam Alpine, we drive north to Maracas Bay, the road clinging perilously to the side of the mountain, twisting and turning, rising and falling, then sweeping down to the crescent-shaped bay … every bit as magnificent as the centrefold in that library book.

But our favourite Wednesday activity is to go "down d' islands" to the sheltered cove of Scotland Bay, nestled into the mountainside and accessible only by boat. Turning the motor off, we wait for peace to settle, for the mirror image of lush tropical forest to reappear and for the vervet monkeys to come back out of hiding.

Dappled light filters through leaves, bouncing off salt water, layer upon layer of verdant shimmering green. Magical.

We lower ourselves over the edge of the boat and swim slowly, without splashing, so as not to disturb the reflection. Water droplets catch in Keith's Afro, glistening like diamonds gathered in a net. Peaceful. Floating. Perfect. Senses alive.

It's there, on a Wednesday, when we first kiss. Salt water on our faces. Sunlight dancing on our heads. Endless shades of rippling green.

On the weekends, Scotland Bay is a busy place, people water-skiing and "liming" with music and rum, but on those Wednesday afternoons, it's just the vervet monkeys and us. It's our sanctuary, protected from the ocean swells and the tribulations of life.

Sometimes, in the distance, we see an ocean liner pass through the deep-water passage, and I imagine travellers leaning on the railing, as I had once, staring toward the steep, forested slopes of the Northern Range.

This is where Keith's ashes were scattered ... in our Wednesday afternoon ocean. The location was my choice. He'd been a prisoner in his body for three appalling months, conscious yet unable to talk or move or eat or communicate. I wanted him to be free, where the Caribbean Sea mingles with the vast Atlantic Ocean. Drifting. No longer confined. Surrounded by diamonds sparkling in the sun.

I never told my parents about those Wednesday afternoons. I knew they wouldn't approve. Most days after class, Keith drives me home in the Sunbeam Alpine, dropping me off out of sight from the house, on the corner of the Eastern Main Road and McCarthy Street. Then one day, about six months in, I ask Keith to come to the house and meet my mother.

If she is shocked or appalled, she doesn't let on. But later, when Dad comes home, the shit hits the fan.

"I should never have brought you here," he says, his face flushed red. "I should have listened to Jack Wicks. 'Leave her in England!' he said. 'If she comes out here, she'll hook up with a darkie.' But honestly, Mary, I never thought you'd do it! I thought you had more sense!"

I can't believe what I'm hearing.

He's on a rant. "You have no idea what's happening around the world. The U.S. is on the brink of a race war, and if Enoch Powell has anything to do with it, England won't be far behind."

I don't know who Enoch Powell is, but I don't admit that.

"I've seen a lot more of the world than you have. There are places you won't be able to go, countries you won't be able to live in. Do you know that mixed marriage is illegal in the southern states? Even the burial grounds are segregated! And look at apartheid in South Africa!"

"What about Martin Luther King?" I argue.

"Peace! Love! Non-violence! He's getting nowhere. Race riots are happening all over the States. People are being killed on the streets of Detroit — buildings set on fire, right now! They'll kill Martin Luther King, too, you mark my words. Look, I've worked in the States. I've seen how Negroes are treated. And the places they live — ghettos! Marry him and he'll drag you down."

I haven't been thinking of either getting married or moving to the States, but the only argument I can come up with is that Keith is studying engineering, and has a scholarship, so there are bound to be opportunities for him when he graduates.

"Even with a degree," Dad yells, "he won't get the same opportunities, believe me, Mary … it's a racist world! Accept that. And move on. Now! Before you get hurt."

"If it's a racist world, why not do something to make it better?"

My father sinks his head into his hands. "You are so young! So naive. Do you really want to sacrifice your future, maybe even your life, for a cause that isn't your own? And think about the next generation! If you have his children, they'll be pickaninnies. Misfits! Not accepted by anyone."

He calms down for a moment and I think he's done. But he picks back up, with sadness in his voice.

"Look, Mary, you're my daughter and I'm concerned for your safety and happiness. I know that if you continue seeing this boy, you're heading for a life filled with difficulties that you cannot even begin to imagine."

I'm a million miles from thinking about marriage and children. But I hate being told what I can or cannot do, especially by a man who doesn't wear jeans.

"Times are changing," I tell him, paraphrasing Bob Dylan, a skinny white kid who is shaking up the world with his music, telling politicians and parents alike that they'd better start swimming before they sink like stones.

But my father doesn't listen. He forbids me to see Keith. And if I defy his jean-less authority, I'll be shipped straight to boarding school in England.

My mother says that I'm too young to know what true love is — she calls it puppy love. She wants me to be happy, but she's caught in the middle, trapped between her uncompromising husband and my naive resolve. And she promised to obey my father.

Since there's no way I'm giving Keith up and no way I'm being shipped back to boarding school, deception is required.

mary

A noise wakes me. I pull back the bedroom curtain and stare down at a boy on a mower. Isn't there a law about making noise so early in the morning? The clock radio says 7:02. I guess 7:00 must be their start time.

In no time, the grass outside my apartment is buzzed, and the boy moves on to wake up the rest of the neighbourhood. Stillness returns. Shafts of sunlight slice through the nearby trees. Dust sparkles. A hymn drops into my head, "Morning Has Broken." I'm in my blue Girl Guide uniform, standing in a field, my plimsolls wet from the dew. Mist hangs in the air, blackbirds sing ... and the smell of sausages drifts from the cook tent. It was all so long ago: before I left England, before I learned about loss and grief, hate and love.

The stillness is shattered once more by the roar of a weed whacker. The young man who wields it looks familiar, although I can't quite place him. Dark curls poke out from his baseball cap and a grassy-green haze coats his baggy pants. It's Harry! He's here! Smelling of garlic and shaking a dented pail of grain. The chickens come running, some of them flying down from their perches in the trees. I squint and the chickens vanish, replaced by pigeons. What the heck? I'm seeing things! But it's good fodder for my story.

Reciting the name Harry over and over, so I don't lose it and the associated imagery, I go back to bed and open my laptop.

> Harry lives in the servants' quarters of the house in Trinidad, on top of the garages — four of them. He

takes care of everything in the yard and orchard, including Dad's car, which he washes every morning. Harry never has a worry in the world. Or if he does, he doesn't let it show. His black hair coils out from under a stained baseball cap, and long, grey pants flap limply around his skinny legs. Lithe. Barefoot. He could be anything from twenty to fifty. But despite his age, he's called "boy"… the yard boy.

Harry is mixed, Black and Indian. And he is Hindu. I figured that out by the colourful prayer flags that wave on bamboo poles outside his door, although for quite a while, I thought Harry just had a flair for decorating.

Hettie sashays past the bedrooms toward the back entrance, her curves squashed into a stretchy black tube dress, a big wicker bag over the crook of her elbow, and a broad-brimmed straw hat on her head. Monday to Saturday, Hettie cooks, cleans, and does the laundry by hand with a washboard, in an outside tub plumbed into the back wall of the house. Cold water only. She starches the cottons and linens, then drapes them over the bushes to bleach in the tropical sun until they are crisp. Next day, she irons everything, including underwear. At the end of the day, and with the food cooked, she puts on a fresh white apron and a little white hat and serves us dinner.

I liked Hettie from the first time I saw her. She calls me Miss Mary, and no matter how busy she is, she always has time to stop and chat with me.

When my parents rented the house on McCarthy Street, it came with Hettie and Harry. My mother had never had "help" and didn't want any. However, Hettie and Harry needed the work, and my mother was sensitive to the needs of the less fortunate, so they stayed on.

I must have napped. That's the problem with working in bed. My laptop has gone to sleep, too. I wake it up and, through bleary eyes, see words on the screen — pages of them. I look them over, unsure what it is … probably something that I'm editing for a client. *Mary's Story!* What a lame title. Perhaps a better one will come to me later, once I know what the story is really about. Where's the outline? There isn't one. Where's the cover blurb? I can't find that, either. This author is an amateur!

Gradually, it comes to me that I am the author who has forgotten to provide an outline and the blurb. I go back to the beginning of the document, reading slowly and trying to remember what I'm working on. Shit, the story is about me. Apparently, I have Alzheimer's. Is this fiction? My gut says no, this is for real. My heart sinks. How can I write a clear storyline when plaques and tangles are choking my brain.

Keith speaks. "Don't doubt yourself, Mary. You're really good at writing. You can do this!"

"You always had faith in me, Keith," I say aloud. "More than I ever had in myself. But it's different now. My brain is dying."

"You can still do it! Do it for us. For Alicia, Zach, Kayla. They have no memories of me. Just write whatever comes into your head. You can fix the title later."

His voice is so real. But he's not here — at least I don't think he is. My mind is just playing tricks. All the same, his words encourage me.

"Okay, I'll write, but I'm feeling hungry."

"Get something to eat," the voice says.

"Good idea! I'll walk down to the place on Rue de Cerise, and get poutine."

Keith sounds alarmed. "No! I mean get something from the kitchen … from the fridge."

"I want poutine!" I say, heading out the door.

sage

Jesse pushes my nose away from his leg. "*Sage!* You're getting hair all over my new pants."

My uprights use the word *Sage* to get my attention. They say it quietly and gently when they love me, and deeply and gruffly when I'm a *BadDog*. In between, there is room for misinterpretation, but I usually get the gist. Today, by the expression on Jesse's flat face and the way he waves the rolling brush in his long arms, I know it's playtime. Overjoyed, I grab the brush in my teeth. Wrong gist.

Jesse points his finger. "*Bed! RightNow.*"

Bed is a word that always takes the fizz out of my feet, the tone, volume, and body language telling me just how bad I have been and how quickly I should obey the command.

The finger means Jesse is in no mood for disobedience. I plod down the hall toward my bed in his room. Depressed. Banished. Exiled. And unsure why, because I didn't eat the garbage.

I see Mom putting on her shoes, a sure sign she's going out. "We're running late, Jesse," she complains. "This is an important milestone: grade eight graduation."

Jesse pushes past me and grabs his shoes. They're both going out! Nooooo! I don't want to be left behind, but no one has released me from the *Bed* command. Mom is by the front door, looking out the window, her back toward me. Like all humans, her eyes are on the front of her face, so she shouldn't be able to see behind unless she turns her whole body or swivels her head like an owl. However, I suspect she has other eyes on the back of her head, hidden under

her hair, like *GeorgeTheSheepdog*, because, although her ears don't
hear as well as mine and her nose hardly works at all, she's remark-
ably good at catching me entering the forbidden parts of the den or
drinking from the big water bowl in the small room. If she filled my
bowl in the kitchen more often, I wouldn't have to drink from hers.

"*Sage! Stay!*" Jesse says as they both rush out the door, closing
it in my face.

I flop onto the mat and wait. Alone. Lonely.

Time passes. My tummy begins to growl, and the sky outside
grows dark. It's dark inside, too. My uprights are usually home
by this time, filling the den with their light and with the moving
pictures that appear on *TeeVee*.

I follow my nose around the kitchen, sniffing the darkness for
something to help me survive. Anything! My snout leads me to a
small crust of toast under the table. It's not enough, but it heartens
me all the same.

The hunger, however, intensifies. I groan, fearing that if Mom
and Jesse don't return soon, I might die. Resting my chin on my
paws, I lie in front of the closed pantry door, breathing in the multi-
tude of aromas that sneak out the bottom, including that of my
kibble. I give the door a nudge. I don't know why, because I've done
the same thing countless times before and it never, ever opens.

Eventually, I hear *Minivan*, then Mom's footsteps. Like bacon
in a pan, I start to sizzle — joy fizzing and farting out of me. I
snatch *FloppyBunny* by a hind leg and race to the door. By the time
it opens, I'm ready, my paws treading the ground enthusiastically.

Mom enters, filling the den with light in her special way. My
greeting is a lame excuse for the leaps and bounds I used to perform
when I was young, but I make up for it with my voice — a welcom-
ing whine, muffled by *FloppyBunny's* damp leg.

"Aw, *Sage*," Mom says, taking my gift, "you brought me
FloppyBunny! Thank you, *Sweetiepie, You'reSuchaGoodGirl*."

She offers him right back to me, the way she's supposed to. It
took many attempts to teach Mom this trick, so I wag my tail in

appreciation, grasping *FloppyBunny* gently around his soft belly, then lying on the floor to chew his ear.

She pours herself a drink and holds the glass in the air. *"Sage!* Let's toast our boy! To Jesse — Athlete of the Year!"

She takes a few sips of her drink, then fills my dish with kibble, adds a dollop of meat from a can and puts it on the floor. *"LeaveIt!"*

She always makes me wait! It's her way of telling me she's the boss. I stare at *dindins* intently to make sure it doesn't get away. Salivating.

"Okay! YouCanHaveIt!"

I pounce and wolf it down.

Once the dish is licked sparkling clean, Mom lets me into the backyard so I can sniff our whole territory, right up to the fence, making sure all is well with the entire world. When I come back inside, she is talking on the phone. I hear the sharp inhale of her breath and I smell the surge of fear.

"Oh no! Where is she now? ... I can be there tomorrow. I'm in Stouffville ... north of Toronto ... yes, I agree she can't be left alone, but you don't want to keep her in jail, surely? She's seventy-five and has Alzheimer's! Give me a few minutes. I'm calling my brother.

"Zach, we've got a problem. Ma is at the police station. Someone found her wandering down the street, not far from the condo. She was lost, talking about wanting poutine. She's okay, but the police won't send her home alone. They'll take her to a hospital unless we can find someone to spend the night with her. I don't know what to do."

Mom runs out of words, but I hear another voice speaking far, far away.

Mom talks some more. "No, Zach, I can't go to Montreal this minute! I've had two glasses of wine. And it's too far for me to drive at night. I'll head out at the crack of dawn."

The far away voice speaks for a while then Mom speaks again: "You mean Sally LeBlanc? From the library? Good idea! She offered to help any time ... you'll sort it out then? Thanks!"

Mom puts the phone down and races around the den, throwing things into her leather bag, and saying *OhGod* over and over. I know it means she needs help so I follow her, telling her that I'm willing to share her burden and that if she talks to me, she'll feel better. But she ignores me.

Finally, she sits. I nudge my snout into her clenched fist, loosening her fingers until she rests her hand on my head. It's heavy.

When Jesse gets home, I explode in pure joy, the way I always do, wriggling and whining until I almost wet myself. I'm even more excited than usual because I smell meat on Jesse's breath — the red meat he calls *burgers*. When he bends over to scratch me, the aroma compels me to lick the corner of his lips. He yells, pushing me away and swiping a hand across his mouth.

It's been a lifetime since my mother taught me how to beg for food this way — learned, she said, from the Wild Ones — but despite my many attempts to teach Jesse the same lesson, he still doesn't respond correctly. He never pukes up food for me … well, almost never. He's always been a slow learner.

Mom is excited to see Jesse, too. "Let me see the trophy," she squeals. "Oh, Jesse, I'm so proud of you!"

Soon, she sighs and her tone changes. "Remember how I told you that your gran has Alzheimer's and that she was gonna come here to stay with us?"

"Yeah."

"It's happening sooner than I thought."

"How much sooner?"

"I'm driving up to get her tomorrow."

"What! Why?"

"I just got a call from the police."

"She's in *jail*?"

"Not exactly. They found her wandering in the street. She was lost and disoriented. Fortunately, she was wearing the MedicAlert bracelet, and Uncle Zach had registered her with the police, too.

So they were able to get all her contact information. I'm going to Montreal first thing in the morning to bring her here."

Jesse's voice is strident and alarming. "You mean just for a short while, right ... then she'll go to an old folks' home?"

"I don't know — maybe. But for now, she'll move in here with us."

"For how long?"

"I don't know exactly. It will depend on lots of things. Listen, Jess, she needs our help. She can't take care of herself anymore. She can't shop or cook. I don't even know if she's eating."

"I thought someone was taking care of her."

"That didn't work too good. The first person quit, and Gran fired the second one."

"Why are you driving? Why not put her on a plane? That would be way quicker."

"Jesse, don't you get it? She has dementia. Airports are busy places — confusing even for me. She couldn't cope with security or checking her bag or getting to the right gate. Who knows where she'd end up."

"I was only eight when I went out to Calgary to see Dad," Jesse mumbles. "They drive you around in golf carts."

I sense that Mom has words piling up in her mouth, but instead of letting them burst furiously into the air, she swallows them and walks away.

Jesse sighs and stomps to his room. I follow. He helps me onto his bed and throws an arm over me. I work my magic and he cheers up. "Hey! I'm going to camp soon ... for the whole summer. I just have to survive the next two weeks. Then it's *hasta la vista*, baby!"

mary

The police ask me questions. I don't know why. I didn't do anything wrong. But they have a file on me, so I guess I must have.

"You're registered with us," a young man says. He's dressed like a policeman, but he looks like a teenager. Maybe he's an imposter. "We have your contact information and medical history and medications. We even have your photo. Look!"

The photo is of a much older woman. She looks like my grandmother. Good heavens! Is Granny a criminal?

"That's not me," I complain, raising my voice in alarm. "False arrest!"

"We aren't arresting you, Mary! *Vous êtes perdue.* Lost! We will help you go home … *chez vous.* But you have to stay here … right here … until someone comes for you. Do you understand?"

"Oui! Je comprends."

But I want to go home. And I want poutine. So I walk toward the door.

Another officer spots me. "Quit trying to escape, you hear? Or we'll have to take you to the hospital." He brings me back to his desk and points to a chair, talking to me as if I am Toby. *"Asseyez-vous. Reste ici.* Sit! Stay right here!"

They bring me poutine! What a nice surprise. And a cup of tea!

The lady from the library comes to spring me. "Hello, Mary! Let's get you out of here."

"Allons-y. Vite," I say, giggling. "Are we going to the *bibliothèque*?"

"Yes! But first we're going home, okay?"

She offers me her hand. As I take it, her name jumps into my mind. Sally! Together we walk across the parking lot.

"I can't remember where I parked my car," I say.

"That's okay," Sally says. "Here's mine."

As soon as we enter the condo, Regis rubs against my legs, cater-wauling as usual. He sounds hungry.

The library lady says she'll feed him and make us a cup of tea, but when she adds milk, the whole thing curdles. She pours it down the drain, invisible underneath all the dirty dishes.

"I'm sorry for the mess," I say. "My brain isn't working these days. I have Alzheimer's. I haven't told Kayla yet. I don't want to worry her. I haven't told anyone."

She touches my hand. "That's a lot to deal with all on your own."

Her words bring tears to my eyes.

"I see you have notes stuck all over the place. That's a good way to remember things. *FEED REGIS. TAKE SALMON OIL. PLAY SUDOKU. TAKE PILLS. PLAY WORD GAME.*"

"After a while, I stop seeing them," I tell her. "Even if I do all those things, they won't cure me. At best, they may give me a little more time."

As I say the words, I know they are true. I have Alzheimer's disease and my brain is dying. Then the truth fades. Sure, my thoughts, mem-ories, and abilities *are* changing. Not a lot, but I'm hardly the best one to judge, as I can't remember if I've forgotten something, and I forget the things that I've forgotten. How can I keep track of how much more forgetful I am today when I've already forgotten yesterday?

"It's a conundrum," I tell the library lady, who is washing dishes. "I can't have Alzheimer's if I can come up with a word like *conun-drum*. I should write it down before I forget it."

I open the laptop while repeating the word: "Conundrum, con-undrum, conundrum."

"Conundrum," the library lady says. "What a funny word it is!" She laughs and I join her. "Conundrum, conundrum, conundrum." She looks at the screen. "Are you writing another book?"

"Yes. It's a memoir of sorts … a few things that I hid away because they were too hard to talk about."

In my mind, I see an old-time coal miner swinging a pickaxe, chipping away at the wall that protects my heart. It's starting to crumble. I *need* the wall! I'm firing the coal miner and hiring a bricklayer.

The library lady interrupts my thoughts, showing me a note: *SPEAK FRENCH.*

"*Oui, c'est bon pour le cerveau*," I tell her.

"Good for the brain, eh? I didn't know that!"

"*Je suis fatiguée*," I tell her. "*Je veux aller au lit.*"

"*Moi aussi, Mary. Je suis trop fatiguée pour conduire.* Is it okay if I stay over?"

"*Oui! C'est bon!*" I point to the couch. "You shouldn't drive if you're tired."

kayla

"Sorry to wake you, Zach. But I really need your help."

"What's happened?'

"I'm on my way to Ma's, but there's been a big accident on the 401."

"Are you okay?"

"Yeah. It's five kilometres ahead, according to the radio. A transport truck jackknifed and blocked the westbound lanes. I'm going to be hours late getting to Ma's."

"It's not the end of the world."

"Yes, it is! Sally can only stay with Ma until one and I have movers arriving at two. I was supposed to be there way ahead of that! What's Ma gonna think if people start taking her furniture away?"

"Yeah, I see the problem. I'll phone the neighbour. Maybe she can help. I'll call you right back."

"Chantelle isn't picking up. But I can phone Ma and talk her through it with the movers?"

"I can't see that working well."

"Me, neither. I'll keep trying Chantelle. What time did you say Sally has to leave?"

"One o'clock, latest. She has to go to work."

"That reminds me: What did you decide about your job?"

"Obviously I didn't go to Singapore! I'm gonna continue with twenty hours a week at the church, but I can do a lot of it from home. I think I can cope with that as well as look after Ma. As for other gigs, I'll see how it goes. I'll cut back if I need to."

"Thanks for stepping up, Kayla. I'll call the neighbour again. In the meantime, listen to an audiobook or music. Enjoy some alone time! You aren't gonna have much of that soon."

mary

It's morning and the lady from the library is sleeping on my couch! I don't want to wake her, so I go back to bed.

Beams of sunlight shine through the window, spreading warmth from my chest right down to my toes. I'm lying on the beach. Keith is sitting beside me, cross-legged, sand between his toes, his fingers strumming *my* song on the cuatro: "You Are My Sunshine."

I'm happy, knowing that I'm the sunshine in Keith's life, and he's the sunshine in mine.

I sing along with him as I have so many times before, but suddenly the sun disappears behind a dark cloud. Heaviness settles on me. Keith is gone, just like the sunshine in the song."

A female voice calls out. "Mary?"

Someone is in my apartment! A thief! Stealing my things! I cautiously creep to the kitchen.

"Coffee is ready," the female voice says, sounding warm and friendly.

"Who are you? What are you doing here?"

"I'm Sally! From the library, remember?"

"Of course," I say, trying not to let confusion show in my voice.

"I was going to make you breakfast, but your stovetop isn't working, so let's go out to eat. Would you like that?"

We go down to street level and eat crepes piled with strawberries and crème fraîche. Then she takes me back home, but she doesn't come in. She says she has to go to work at the library. I want to go with her ... after all, I'm the head librarian, and I don't think I should trust this woman to do my job. She says that I have the day off because Kayla is coming to visit me. It's the first I'm hearing of it.

After she leaves, the apartment feels empty and quiet.

Something rings in my ears. It's the phone. It's Zach! He says that Kayla is on her way to my place, that she's going to take me to her house, that she'll take care of me.

It's a lot of information to process. I don't want to burden Kayla. After all, she's got a job and a young family to take care of.

More ringing in my ears. This time it's the doorbell.

I say goodbye to Zach, but he keeps telling me not to hang up because he wants to talk more.

I hang up and open the door.

"*Bonjour, Madame*," the man says. "Mary Bowen, *oui?*"

"*Oui, c'est moi.* What do you want?"

He shows me some papers, but the print is small. When I turn away to get my reading glasses, he comes in. The phone is ringing, but I dare not turn my back on the man again. He's walking into my bedroom now. I need to get out, I need to run, but the phone is ringing and ringing and ringing. Another man blocks the doorway. The phone is still ringing. It won't stop.

I pounce on it.

"Hi, Ma — it's Kayla!"

"Kayla! Thank goodness! Two men are here! They just barged in."

"It's okay, Ma. They're from the moving company. I sent them to bring a few of your things to my house — the big things that won't fit in my van. Your chest of drawers, your recliner, your desk ..."

"What? Why didn't you ask me first? I'm happy to give you anything you want, whatever you need, but you should have spoken to me first."

"I did! I mean, I'm sorry, Ma. You're right, I should have asked you first. I'll stay on the phone until the men leave, okay?"

"They're taking my recliner!"

"I know. Don't worry! They're bringing it to my house. It'll be there when you arrive."

"Arrive?"

"Yes! I'm driving up to you right now, Ma. I'll be at your place *real* soon."

"That will be nice, dear."

"I'm going to bring you back to my house, Ma, just like we agreed … so you can live with me and Jesse. I'm going to help take care of you."

"I don't need any help! I can manage."

"I know you can manage, Ma. You are very capable, but all of us — Alicia, Zach, and I — we all think that you need a little extra help, and Montreal is so far away: too far for me to pop in every day. It'll be easier if you come to live in my house."

"Kayla! The men are taking my chest of drawers."

"I know, Ma, they're taking it to my house."

"You can have it. You can have anything you want. But I wish you'd asked first. I don't like this."

"I'm sorry, Ma."

"Why are you crying, Kayla? I'm the one getting burglarized."

A third man arrives. "D'you need a hand with the desk? It's a big one."

I scream at the top of my lungs, aiming the phone at their chests. "Stay away from me! I'll shoot. Leave me alone!"

The men back away, their hands raised. "Okay! Okay! *C'est bon, Madame. C'est bon.* We're going!"

"*Vite!*" I shout, as they drag the desk out the door.

"*Merde! Elle est folle! Totalement.*"

"*Vous êtes stupides, mes amis! C'est un téléphone, pas une arme à feu!*"

They think I don't know French. I slam the door and fumble with the safety chain, but my fingers are trembling. The chain won't go where it's supposed to. I slide down the door and curl up into a ball.

mary

Leaning against the door, I hear footstep approach. Heavy ones. Threatening ones. Then loud knocking, and a male voice.

"Police! *Ouvre la porte! Maintenant!*"

I freeze and hold my breath, pretending I'm not here.

I hear a man and a woman argue, then a gentle knocking and a soft female voice. "It's the police, *Madame*. We are just checking on you. Your son said you were having a problem. Are you okay?"

I don't reply.

"Mary, please let me in. I need to see that you are safe. If you like, I could make us a cup of tea."

"Do you have cookies?" I ask.

"I'll send my friend to get some. They'll be here in two minutes."

I open the door. It's a girl wearing a police uniform. She looks about twelve.

"How old are you?" I blurt out.

"*Vingt-neuf.* Twenty-nine. *Et vous?*"

"*Je ne sais pas. Vingt-neuf, aussi, je pense.*"

"We are the same age!" the girl says excitedly. "Twins!"

She walks past me and goes to the kitchen. "First things first, let's put the kettle on. And we'll put the phone back on the hook. And now I want you to tell me what happened. Why did you get so frightened?"

"Men! Racists! Rapists! I don't want to talk about it."

"Okay, let's just sit for a while and drink our tea."

A man wearing a police uniform barges in. He reaches toward me and I shrink away, but it's just a packet of cookies in his hand. The girl opens them and soon we are munching chocolate digestives together. "Your daughter will be here soon. She is on her way. Her name is Kayla, right?"

"My furniture is gone," I say, getting up and walking around the apartment. "Look, my recliner is gone! And my desk ... it should be right here. Someone stole it all."

"Nobody stole it, Mary," the police girl says. "Your daughter is keeping it safe for you."

In the bedroom, I see Regis sleeping on my bed. "Thank goodness they left my bed. And my comforter. And my laptop. I guess Kayla must need the other things. Maybe she's fallen on hard times. I'm happy to help her whenever I can. I am her mother, after all. But I do like my desk. Without it, I feel ... I feel ..."

Suddenly, Kayla comes through the door, hugging me so tight I think she's going to break my ribs. Then she speaks fast to the police girl, too fast for me to follow, but I sense her fear. Kayla isn't white, and that's always a strike against you.

"I'm so sorry I wasn't here," she tells the police girl. "I was stuck on the 401. Gridlocked for three hours! But Sally LeBlanc was with Ma all night, from the moment she left the police station last night, and all morning, too, right up until one o'clock. You can check my story. Sally LeBlanc. She works at the library."

The police girl smiles. "It's okay! You aren't under arrest. We just wanted to know that Mary is safe. Sounds like you did your best."

Kayla exhales, and I feel her relief. I'm relieved, too. Kayla isn't going to be arrested.

The police girl leaves, and Kayla suggests we lie down on my bed, so she can stretch her back after the long drive. In no time, she nods off.

I get out of bed, carefully so as not to disturb Kayla, and look around for my laptop. My desk is gone! I don't know where it went. How can I have lost something as big as a desk? I look in the closet and then in each of the kitchen cabinets. No desk. I decide to work from my recliner. It's gone, too! I must have been burgled!

I phone the police. The officer says they'll send someone around, but I hear talking in the background. "Danielle was just there. She's still writing up the report. We picked her up yesterday, too, on Rue de Cerise ... she was lost. And she's the one who reported her car stolen, a month back, but the family sold it, remember?" They laugh.

I feel sorry for the woman whose car was stolen. She's probably Black — the police only help white people. There was no justice for Keith. No effort to find the gang who attacked him. Skinheads, witnesses said, but no one wanted to get involved. The horror of that day rushes at me. Keith screaming at me to run ... my legs unable to carry me away from him. Steel-toed boots thudding into his skull ... his chest.

Broken ribs.

Ruptured spleen.

Fractured skull.

Bruises.

For no reason other than the colour of his skin ... and that he was with me?

kayla

Hi Siblings,

I have a few spare minutes so thought I'd bring you both up to speed. Things have gone better today, thank goodness.

I'm still at the condo, but the van is packed, and I'm heading over to the library in half an hour to pick up Ma. Sally took her there first thing, so I could get everything cleared out of the apartment without freaking her out. And I don't want to upset her by bringing her back to an empty condo, hence the rendezvous at the library. With luck, I'll be on the road by three and home before dark. Gotta remember the cat!

Sally has been a godsend. Her husband, too. He took the big items down to the Dumpster … the bed, the couch, and all the junk. And he took boxes of stuff to the charity shop. I've just finished packing up her clothes and a few personal items. And that's it! It's all in the van, except the cat. A cleaner is coming after we are out.

I've been reflecting on how blind we all were. I'd been calling Ma every few days, yet I didn't see this coming, at least not this fast. I thought we had more time. I didn't notice anything out of the ordinary until the end of January, when I wanted to go to Singapore. She must have known, though, don't you think? She tried to hide it from us. Even after the gerontologist appointment, two months ago when we knew it was probably Alzheimer's, I didn't think she was bad enough to require around-the-clock supervision. I thought she was in the early stages and we had lots of time. Then, all of a sudden, she's getting lost in her own neighbourhood! I feel bad ... like we were negligent.

And yesterday, despite all my phone calls, she still wasn't expecting me. That was shocking. And she still thinks she works full time at the library, even though she only volunteers once a week! And according to Sally, she missed the last few sessions. She just didn't show up.

She can't use a can opener, but she also doesn't realize that you don't *need* a can opener. The cans all have pull-tabs! I watched her try to open a can of food for Regis this morning. She couldn't open it, either with or without a can opener. No wonder Regis is thin. There are still ten unopened cans in the pantry! Poor cat! This intervention is just in the nick of time for him as well as for Ma.

Getting the movers to pick up those few big items ahead of time was a BIG mistake. From what the police officer said, it triggered a memory of when men attacked her, maybe even molested her! God, I can't begin to imagine.

I'm so glad you sold the car, Zach — one less thing for me to deal with today. But she's confused over it. Yesterday, she told me several times that it had been stolen. She was upset that the police weren't doing anything about it ... and that it was because Keith was Black! I didn't follow her logic. I told her the car was in the parking garage under the building, right where she left it. I'm becoming quite the liar! Hopefully, she'll soon forget about it.

Okay! Time to go. Wish me luck.

Gotta remember the cat!

Kayla

sage

Jesse has shut me in the laundry room. Intruders clomp past on heavy feet, grunting and puffing. I raise the alarm, throwing myself at the door with booming barks, but Jesse yells at me: "*Sage! ShutUp.*"

When he finally lets me out, Krista's empty room is full again.

He joins me in sniffing around, then leaps into a big chair that suddenly springs to life with a groan, laying him flat on his back. I scoot to safety, yipping at Jesse to get away from the manic beast, but he laughs, encouraging the creature to repeat the action until it bucks back and forth vigorously.

"Yee-haw!" he shouts. "Ride 'em, cowboy!"

YeeHaw bucks Jesse off, instantly becoming a big, soft chair again, with no life of its own. But I don't buy it. I've seen how quickly things can change. *YeeHaw* is deceptive and dangerous and not to be trusted. He frightens the crap out of me.

"*Sage!* You're such a *chicken*," Jesse says.

Chicken lives in a can and gets spooned onto my dry kibble. Optimistically, I wait for it to appear. It doesn't. I flop down, dejected.

Suddenly, Mom is home! I greet her with more than my normal exuberance, my nose delighting in the familiar scent of home and family and love. But another aroma lingers on her skin: anxiety. I pick it up and make it my own.

Jesse smells of frustration and impatience. Growling like an irritable dog, he skulks to our room and slams the door behind him.

I barely have time to finish greeting Mom before an old one is reaching out to stroke me. "Toby! There's my boy. Where have you been? I've missed you so much."

"This is *Sage*," Mom explains. "And she's a girl ... a purebred golden retriever. Toby was your dog when you were a girl."

"Yes, of course!" the old one says. "Silly me, I get things muddled sometimes."

The scent on the old one's breath is familiar. It's often found clinging to both old dogs and old humans, and it reminds me of rotting logs on the forest floor. But another smell seeps through the newcomer's skin, too, telling me her vital force is weak. My nostrils crinkle, remembering the bitter pills Mom sometimes hides in my favourite treats, the ones I spit out before I gulp down the treat. And then Mom will say, *What-are-we-going-to-do-with-you-Sage?*

I haven't figured out what that means yet.

I twitch my nose, pushing aside the tangled odours of pills and rotting logs, sniffing deeper still, waiting for my nose to tell me the rest of the story. An image of an upright from long ago comes to my knower, along with the taste of the treats she would give me when Mom wasn't looking.

"Look what I've got, *Sage!*" Mom says, speaking with the high-pitched voice that tells me something exciting is happening.

The aroma of cat is already stinging my eyes. No. *No*. NO!

It's not that I hate cats, but cats generally hate me, looking down their short, stubby noses, telling me I'm a pathetic excuse of a creature. Eternally optimistic, I wonder if maybe this cat will be different.

Keeping *PinkPiggy* in my mouth — it's always good to come bearing gifts — I approach cautiously, stretching my muzzle to sniff the ball of fluff in Mom's arms.

Whack! A paw snaps out and bats my face.

"Regis!" Mom says in her boss-dog voice. "Be nice."

I retreat, dropping *PinkPiggy* and licking the speck of blood from my snout. Glaring at Mom from a safe distance, I beg her to take Cat back outside where he belongs. Instead, she puts him on the ground and strokes him. He arches his back and rubs against her legs. She smiles as if this is a sign of his affection. I know better. He's leaving his scent on her — marking her as part of *his* territory.

I watch and wait, still prepared to be friends if Cat shows any friendliness, but he hisses right in my face. I can't help but cringe. He seems satisfied. With tail held high, he presents me with his rear end and strolls away. Typical cat!

"Good boy, Toby," the old one says, stroking me lovingly. Memories rise like fog in the early morning ... memories of a more vital version of this old one, energetic and spirited, laughing and smiling, calling me *MyBeautifulSage* and letting me chase squirrels while a much shorter version of Jesse plays with other short ones. My knower tells me that long ago, this old one was part of our pack. She was called Gran, but when we moved to a new den, she wasn't put into a crate and loaded into the belly of the beast like I was. She was left behind.

Reassured about who she is, I greet her warmly, with a vigorously wagging tail and a squirm of delight, but Gran ignores me, her face crumpling, like *MitzyTheSharpei* from down the block.

"Where am I?" she says.

"At home. This is where you live now."

Gran doesn't appear to understand Mom's words any more than I do. "Where am I?" she repeats.

"At home!" Mom says loudly, leading Gran into Krista's old room. "This is where you live now. Look! Your furniture is here already. Jesse will bring your suitcases in from the van, and I'll help you unpack. We'll put your favourite comforter on the bed, and there's plenty of room in the closet for your —"

Gran interrupts, panicked. "Kayla! Where am I?"

Every pack needs a bold leader, and right now, Mom's pungent scent of alarm says she's not up to the task. I go on alert, looking for signs of danger. Nothing seems amiss, but feeling leaderless, I slink toward my safe place — my bed in Jesse's room. The door is closed, so I flop on the floor outside, my nose pressed against the crack at the bottom, breathing in the reassuring scent of Jesse and whimpering softly until he lets me in.

Cat is on my bed! *My* bed! I glare at him, but he glares back, his enormous bright eyes forcing me to look away. I woof at Jesse until he abruptly picks up Cat and plonks him outside the door. Cat turns to look at him with disdain, then with his asshole proudly on full display, he saunters away.

I nudge Jesse's leg, thanking him for putting Cat in his place and telling him he should take a run at the alpha position. A scent of uncertainty oozes from Mom, a sign that her reign is coming to an end. Maybe the era of burgers and pizza is upon us! Jesse, after all, has passed the first test, proving that he can keep us alive without Mom's help. I tell him that he has my support and will do everything I can to ensure a seamless transition of power, but he ignores me, wrapped up in his own heavy cloak of anger.

I try to leap onto his bed, but my hind legs refuse to lift me from the ground. I wait, building up strength, then with a mighty heave from the front end, I clamber up, curling into the crook of his knees and breathing his scent. It calms me. Him, too. But it doesn't last long.

"Jesse!" Mom calls. "*Come* and say hi to your grandmother."

Jesse's body tenses, but he doesn't move.

Mom calls again. And again.

He charges out the door and I follow.

"Do I know you?" Gran asks.

Jesse looks stunned, like he does when he first wakes up.

Mom speaks in the high-pitched, squeaky voice she usually reserves for short ones. "Ma, this is your grandson Jesse, remember? It's been a few years since you've seen him, and he's growing like a weed! Gosh, some nights, I swear he grows an inch in his sleep, so it's not surprising you don't recognize him. He just graduated from grade eight and is starting high school in —"

Gran cuts her off. "Where am I?"

"This is where you live now," Mom says, cheerily.

Silence.

Gran looks back at Jesse. "You look familiar. Have I met you before?"

He frowns. "Er ... yes, I'm Jesse, your grandson."

More silence.

"Where am I?" Gran says.

Mom speaks slower and louder, her brow furrowed. "Ma, you're at my house. You're going to live here now — with Jesse and me."

"Where's Jesse?" Gran says.

"He's right here."

"No, the other Jesse — the baby."

Silence.

"I want to go home," Gran whines.

Mom's scent tells me she's on the brink of panic. Her fear flutters through my own body. She continues talking in the high-pitched voice. "This is your home now, Ma. We're gonna have such fun together, wait and see. You don't have to worry about a thing, because I'm going to look after you. Okay?"

Cat reappears from his jaunt around the den, his plaintive meow filling the silence.

Mom picks him up, attempting to laugh. "Yes, Regis, I'm going to look after you, too. You need fattening up. I think Ma has been forgetting to feed you."

More silence in which Jesse stares at his feet and fidgets. Then, like a spooked bunny, he dashes back to our room. I follow, sniffing at my bed on the floor. Cat has left his odour there. I nudge Jesse, and he helps me onto his bed, but Cat has been there, too. I snuggle up to Jesse, selectively inhaling his reassuring scent, trying to ignore the jumbled odours of Cat, bitter pills, rotting wood, anger, and uncertainty. Maybe tomorrow will smell better.

sage

Today the odour is worse. It wreaks of stress.

"We have to talk about this," Mom says, pacing around the house after Jesse. "I know I handled it all wrong. I should have given you more of a heads-up, but it all happened so fast in the end. I told you that I wanted Gran to come here eventually."

"Yeah, but I thought it was way down the line."

"I had hoped for more time, too."

"Why can't you put her in an old folks' home?"

"She's my mother! I need to look after her. And anyway, I'm the one who makes decisions for this family, not you. But there was really no choice. I have to do this."

"She doesn't even know who I am," Jesse whines, plonking himself down on a kitchen chair.

"She knew who you were once. And she loved you to bits. She still loves you. I don't think the love ever goes away. It's just that a chunk of time has been erased from her brain. Imagine an eraser rubbing out part of a picture. Unfortunately, with Alzheimer's, there's no stopping that eraser. All the things she learned and experienced as an adult will be erased and eventually she'll be as helpless as a baby."

"You mean she won't be able to speak, or feed herself?"

"Correct. She'll even have to wear diapers."

Jesse looks horrified.

"I know you've hardly seen Gran. When you used to go out to Calgary to stay with your dad, that's when I went to Montreal to see her. But she always asked about you, every single time we spoke. She never forgot you."

"It's not even about her," Jesse says, sounding a little more reasonable. "I don't hate her. It's just that for years this house was really crowded. I never had my own room. I always had to share with Kyle. Finally, I have the room to myself. Finally, I can stretch out on the family room couch and have total control of the TV remote. It's taken me an entire lifetime to reach this point. And now everything is ruined!"

"Try to understand, Jess, I can't keep going to Montreal every week. It's too far, it's too hard on me, and anyway Gran needs more help than a weekly visit can give. She needs someone with her nearly all the time. And people aren't lining up to look after her! But that's water under the bridge. She's here and you have to make the best of it."

"But why not put her in an old folks' home? Isn't that what they're for?"

"Jesse, I'm going to ask that you try very, very hard to put yourself in her shoes. I know it's almost impossible to imagine, but one day you will get old. If you don't get old, it will mean you're dead. That's a fact of life. Imagine how you would feel if your family — the people you love and who you thought loved you — looked you in the eye and said, 'We don't want you here. You're too old, too much trouble. You take up too much space.' Ma looked after me my whole life … like I look after you. And now it's time for me to give back some of that love. I need to do this."

Mom's eyes are starting to leak salt water. Before I can get in there for a lick, she mops her face with a tissue and blows her nose. I watch the damp tissue as she tosses it in the bin. As soon as no one is looking, I retrieve it, chew, and swallow.

mary

Everything is unfamiliar. The ornaments and paintings, the bathroom and kitchen, even the views from the windows ... all new and troubling.

I walk up and down a hallway, seeing Hettie in a clean white apron and a starched white hat, pushing a trolley with our dinner. I amble in and out of rooms, but they don't have high ceilings or fans that move the air. Finally, I find a room that feels more like home. The comforter on the bed has purple irises and yellow daffodils, and the recliner creaks and groans with reassuring familiarity. I run my hands over the battered thesaurus on the desk, finger the well-thumbed dictionary, and leaf through a few books — all old friends from another time and place.

Framed certificates on the wall tell me that I'm a woman of excellence and the recipient of an Ontario Achievement Award. It's hard to believe. And three books, displayed in stands on the chest of drawers, tell me that I accomplished something, though I can't quite remember what. I see a photo of a woman, her long blond hair in a ponytail, talking to schoolchildren. She's familiar. I know what she is telling the students: *What a gift to be able to express your ideas as symbols on a page, so that someone on the other side of the world sees what you are seeing, feels what you are feeling, laughs out loud or even cries.* I sense the woman's passion for writing, but also for life. Am I that woman? Was I that woman? I don't know.

The cat rubs against my legs. I'm glad he's here. I've forgotten his name. My chest tightens, and my heart races. How can I have forgotten his name? He's been my companion for years.

Kayla tells me that this is my home, but she's lying. Home is a small apartment where the neighbours speak French. Or maybe home is a cottage in the English countryside, or an apartment at the top of a Victorian house in London, or even the tranquil green water of a sheltered bay in the Caribbean. All these places merge in my head, swirling in confusion ... getting muddied, like the ocean between Venezuela and Trinidad. In a flash, I am flying over the islands, stunned by the clarity of the Caribbean Sea, with its countless shades of blue and green ... until it meets the Atlantic current that sweeps past the Orinoco delta, carrying soil and silt from the Venezuelan Highlands, making the sea look like marble cake batter.

Toby nudges me, clearly telling me he wants a scratch. I sink my fingers into his long, golden coat and the swirling stops.

Out of the corner of my eye, I notice the laptop on my desk. I recall that I have a manuscript to edit. Someone is paying me good money, so I'd better get the job done. I feel a sense of urgency — there must be a deadline. There always is.

I read a few pages. "Huh, look at this, Toby. I'm writing a story. It's not bad. But where's the story going? I have no idea."

I tell myself to type, regardless. It's an exercise I learned as a younger writer: even when you think you have nothing to say, it's important to put words on paper, inviting the story to flow whenever it so desires. I lay my fingers on the keys and wait to see what comes.

I breathe.

Kayla appears, looking over my shoulder. "Ma, I know you hate people reading your work too early on, but please can I read it?"

I shrug.

"I'm going to start at the beginning, okay?"

She reads aloud, "Prologue. My name is Mary, and I have Alzheimer's disease."

"My name is Mary, too," I tell her.

Kayla reads on. "I've been trying to hide it. Hide from it …"

She turns to face me with tears slipping down her cheeks. "Me, too," she whispers.

I'm shocked. "Oh my goodness, Kayla, do you have Alzheimer's?"

"No! No! Not me," she says. "It's just that for the longest while, I told myself that it was just normal aging. Most people forget things as they get older, right?"

I suspect she's talking about me, but I can't be sure. It's confusing. She reads on in silence. Then, "Wow! This is good."

"What's it about?" I ask.

"It's about you and Keith! Oh my gosh, Ma, please write some more."

"I don't know what to write."

sage

I'm learning to understand Gran's words. *ComeToby* means the same as *ComeSage*. When I go to her, I get a scratch as a reward. And *GoodBoyToby* means the same as *GoodGirlSage*. Both these words make me feel warm and fuzzy inside. But there are times when I don't know what she means. She's acting that way right now.

"Who took my money? I left a whole dollar right here, and it's gone. Who took it?"

She thinks I ate the bathroom garbage! Or licked her dirty underwear! I don't remember doing either of those things.

I slink away to Jesse's bed, to suck in his comforting smell from the covers. But another smell assaults my nose. Cat! His rank odour is settling into the very bones of our den. I wish he would take his smells and go away. But he doesn't. The birds have gone, though. Some ended up in Cat's belly, leaving just feathers and claws as a remembrance. I still hear a few birds in *KingDoberman*'s trees, sounding alarm calls whenever Cat is on the prowl. But they don't sing their lively ditties in our yard anymore.

Mom is still unhappy, even though she pretends to be happy. Gran is still confused, even though she pretends to be okay. And Jesse is still bad tempered, although he doesn't pretend to be anything else. I try to improve his mood by telling him how much I love him, but he doesn't listen. He doesn't speak much *Dog*.

Compared to *Human*, *Dog* is elementary. It has very few sounds — in fact, it's more of a sign language. That's the problem: humans rarely notice signs. They lean too heavily on words. My entire life, I have tried to make my sounds come out as words they can understand:

I bark at various speeds and volumes to say, *Danger! Intruder!*

I woof to say, *Here I am — don't forget about me.*

I yip to say, *Quick — give me dindins before I die of starvation.*

I yip higher to say, *I need to go out for a pee.*

I grunt to say, *I'm so happy — I just don't know what to do with myself.*

I whimper to say, *I'm hurt — inside or out.*

I groan to say, *I think I'm dying.*

And on very rare occasions, I growl to say, *Back off — this is my territory, these are my humans.*

Then there's the whine. I use it to say lots of things, such as *There's a squirrel — let me at it,* or *Please touch me, stroke me, play with me, talk to me ... anything!*

And, finally, the sigh that says, *Why aren't you listening to any of the above?*

Often, to clarify, I add actions such as the wag in my tail, the squirm of my spine, or the drool landing on my toes; maybe the bounce in my step, the upward nudge of my nose, or the sideways tilt of my head; even the alternating lift of my eyebrows or a downcast gaze. Simple, right?

Mom sometimes understands what I'm saying, but Jesse, not so much. It works both ways. I don't understand most of the things that he says, either, but at least I pay attention, waiting for familiar words to jump out at me and using all my senses to discern his meaning. Jesse doesn't try as hard as I do. Sometimes, I don't think he tries at all.

When he was shorter, he would talk to me all the time, going on for so long that I'd often fall asleep, no matter how hard I tried to stay awake. These days, he talks to me only when he's sad or angry. Right now, he's angry. I can tell by the energy of his words — fast and choppy.

"Gran doesn't stay in her own room and watch television like Mom promised. She's always on the couch, watching mine, always getting in my way. How can someone so small take up so much space? She doesn't even know that she's my grandmother. I have to call her Mary because calling her Gran gets her confused. I can think of plenty of other names I'd like to call her. I shouldn't even be here! I should be at camp, but Mom screwed up everything. How could she have forgotten to mail my contract?"

Growling like an angry dog, he leaps off the bed and charges from the room. I struggle to keep up with him, but he storms out of the house, slamming the door in my face. I flop onto the mat ... waiting.

mary

There's a crispness to the early morning air that borders on chill. I suck it in, knowing it won't last long. The tropical sun will soon be brutally hot. Its orange glow is already piercing my closed eyelids.

I love to sit on the veranda at this time of day, the leather cushions of the Morris chair cool against my legs and the rich mahogany frame smooth on my arms. Nearby, I can hear traffic building on the Eastern Main Road, humming with life ... the start of a busy new day. But here, for now, everything is peaceful.

The polished concrete is making my bare feet cold. I attempt to tuck them under myself for warmth. I open my eyes and see loose flesh falling away from sharp shin bones. I'm alarmed. What happened to my legs? I wonder if I'm dreaming. But no, I can hear Hettie in the kitchen, and I can smell pancakes and bacon.

Toby whines from behind the screen door, his snout pressed against the mesh. He wants to join me, but he's not allowed to run free. He chases Harry's chickens, rounds them up like sheep. Harry says the stress makes them stop laying eggs.

Hettie calls from inside the house. "Breakfast is ready."

I heave myself from the chair. It's white plastic, not red mahogany. That's strange. I gaze around. I'm on a small front porch, overlooking a quiet street. Parked cars. Bungalows. A scraggly red geranium struggling to grow in a clay pot. A rotting net dangling from a bent basketball hoop. Nothing makes sense to me. It's not just my surroundings. I barely recognize myself. It seems like I'm in a different body — the wrong one.

In a split second of complete lucidity, I grasp the truth. This is dementia. This is Alzheimer's disease. What are the chances of me getting better? Exactly zero. There's no cure for Alzheimer's. It's progressive and eventually terminal. It can drag on for years, though, until everyone around you just wishes you'd stop procrastinating and get on with dying.

Pneumonia is called Alzheimer's best friend. Heart attack and stroke come in a close second and third. The unfortunate folk who defy these maladies lie around year after year, Alzheimer's destroying brain cell after brain cell ... until life is nothing more than a beating heart and heaving lungs. These basic functions are controlled by the deepest part of the brain, disturbingly known as the reptilian brain. This is what scares me the most. Not so much for me — I assume I'll be out of it by then. But I can't imagine my children sitting around for years as I continue breathing. In and out. In and out.

Oh, God! Please let pneumonia be my best friend.

Kayla takes my hand, leading me back inside the house. She has become the mother, and I am the child.

sage

The whole pack descends on the kitchen at the same time, even Cat, who jumps on the counter. Mom yells and waves her arms, but he glares at her with dagger eyes, defying her leadership until she picks him up and drops him from such a height that his paws hit the floor with a thud. He flattens his ears, locks his death-gaze on me, and hisses — as if it's *my* fault!

The moment Mom turns away, he springs effortlessly back onto the counter, acting once more as if he's top dog. To be fair, the job *does* seem to be up for grabs. Mom isn't the strong leader she used to be. She even lets Gran be boss. Mom doesn't cower or roll over on her back like a submissive dog, yet she gives off that same vibe. It makes my gut churn because every pack needs a strong leader.

"I see you got yourself dressed today!" she says, bearing down on Gran. "Your head is through the armhole. Let me fix it."

"No," Gran shrieks, her arms flailing. "I can do it myself."

Mom backs off. "Okay! But here — put your slippers on, before you get cold feet. No! You're putting them on the wrong feet. That can't be comfortable. Let me help."

"I'm not a child," Gran protests.

Jesse joins in. "Leave her alone, Mom. What difference does it make if she looks like a homeless person?"

"You're right," Mom says, turning her attention back to Gran and speaking once more in the voice for short ones. "After breakfast, Ma, I want you to write some more of your story. Won't that be fun!"

"Good luck with that!" Jesse says, grabbing *Basketball* and bouncing it up and down the hall.

"Not in the house," Mom shouts.

I follow him out the front door and flop onto the grass, watching him hurl *Basketball* toward the bent ring over the garage door. When he jabs it playfully toward me, I close my eyes. Once, I tried to wrestle a ball like this into my mouth. All its breath whooshed out and it wouldn't move after that. When Jesse discovered that *Basketball* was dead, he shoved it in my face and yelled at me until I peed myself.

Even in the darkness behind my closed eyes, the orange ball taunts me with its haunting voice: *bounce-bounce-bounce-whoosh* — like a beating heart. *Bounce-bounce-bounce-whoosh.* A reminder of the life I took.

"It's two months before school starts," Jesse says, dropping onto the grass beside me. "Sixty days! That's, uh … one thousand, four hundred … and forty hours! I plan to sleep through almost half of that, which leaves, uh … seven hundred and twenty waking hours. Urrrgh. I don't think I'll make it."

For a while he stares at the sky, then, with a sigh, he starts talking again, his words heavy and sluggish. "Two weeks ago, I was worried about starting high school. I wanted summer to last forever. Now I can't wait for it to be over. Summer sucks! There's no one here to hang out with."

He holds *Basketball* a little too close to my face for comfort. I look away, embarrassed, but Jesse, unaware of my shame, keeps talking. "Mom says that the move's been hard on Gran — that messing up her routine has made her even more confused than usual, that we need to give her time to settle in. But she still doesn't know who I am and she's been here two weeks already."

I'm panting. It's hot in the sun and *Basketball* is stressing me out.

"*Sage, Let'sGo,*" Jesse says. "Looks like you need a drink."

Gran greets me as soon as we amble through the door. She reaches out to stroke the thick hair at the back of my neck. "Toby! How are you, boy? *You'reSuchAGoodDog.*"

Jesse rolls his eyeballs, showing me the whites. It's another of his gestures that I don't understand.

"Did you have a good game?" Gran asks.

"It wasn't a game," Jesse says, kicking off his shoes and using his toes to guide *Basketball* into the corner. "I was just shooting hoops on the driveway."

Gran nods.

I'm slurping the water from my bowl when, from the edge of my vision, I notice *Basketball* creeping out of the corner and rolling toward me, silently sneaking up on me. I sidestep, giving him a wide berth.

"Did you have a good game?" Gran asks again.

"Agree with her," Mom whispers.

"Yes! I had a great game," he says, smiling. "Kawhi Leonard passed me the ball, and I drained a three-pointer!"

"Leonard sounds like a nice boy!"

Jesse's laughter escapes as a snort.

"Do I know you?" Gran asks.

Jesse groans and goes to his room.

kayla

"Hi, Leesha, did I wake you?"

"Not really. I'm still in bed, under my mosquito net, but the sun is up and the roosters are crowing."

"I had an awful day and I just need to dump on you. I'm hiding out in the garage, so Ma and Jesse can't hear me."

"What did Ma do this time?"

"It's Jesse who's the problem."

"I thought he was away on a training program for camp counsellors?"

"That's the problem. I messed up. He signed the contract a couple of months ago and we had to mail it back. Who uses mail anymore? I didn't even have a stamp, so I said I'd swing by the post office. But I forgot. I've had a lot on my mind. Anyway, it must have got buried under a pile of junk mail and got thrown out with the recycling. Last week, Jesse called to confirm his check-in time and they said he hadn't returned the contract so they'd offered the spot to someone else! Now he's mad at me because he's stuck here all summer. I get it. I really do, but he's not letting it go. I'm not sure he ever will."

"I have no idea how to deal with your son, but at least Ma is on the list for the Alzheimer Day Centre, now. That will give you a break from her."

"Yeah, but it's a long wait! Could be six months, depending on who graduates to a nursing home, or who dies. I don't know if I can survive six months! I was so naive, thinking I could look after Ma

as well as hold down my job at the church. It's only twenty hours
a week and I can do a lot of it from home, but add a wedding or a
baptism to the mix, and I'm up half the night, planning. The boss
is already breathing down my neck about missed deadlines."

"Which boss? The pastor? Or God?"

"Pastor Jeff! Last week there were two funerals."

"The ultimate deadline! Oops, sorry."

"Seriously, Leesh, I can't lose this job! It's our bread and butter.
I'm worrying about Christmas already, all the extra services, the
kids' pageant and special music to plan."

"Whoa, Kayla! It's only July! Anyway, as soon as Ma's condo
sells, there'll be some money, Zach says enough to pay for ten years
of nursing home care, so we can dip into it a little sooner and take
the financial burden off of you ... hire a personal support worker to
come in while you're working, or pay *you* if you want, so that you
can say goodbye to the job."

"You mean pay me to look after my own mother? That doesn't
seem right."

"But it's not right for you to look after her for free, especially if
you get fired or have to quit your job! I'll talk to Zach. But right
now, how can I help you, Kayla? Tell me what you need."

"That's the problem. I don't know what I need. I'm too stressed
and too tired to think straight. But talking like this helps. Can we
have regular chats so I can dump on you?"

"For sure! And I'm thinking I'll ask Zach to take Jesse under
his wing. My gut says the boy needs a male role model. David isn't
much help, is he?"

"That's an understatement. He said he was coming to Jesse's
graduation. He never even showed up!"

"What a dick! Poor Jesse — he must have been devastated."

"Yeah, but you know this family ... he won't talk about it! I
agree that he needs a role model ... but *Zach*?"

"He's not as bad as you think, Kayla. In fact, he's a great guy.
He wants to help. He doesn't have a son. It might be a great match."

"What can he do from Vancouver?"

"Zoom, FaceTime, messaging. Look at you and me … chatting as if I was down the street, yet I'm in Central Africa. Leave it with me."

"Thanks."

"Are you still going to yoga?"

"You're kidding me!"

"You've gotta take care of yourself, Kayla. It's like being on a plane. If the cabin pressure drops, they tell you to put on your own oxygen mask first before helping your children, because you're no help to anyone if you're unconscious or dead."

"Yeah, well, who's gonna stay with Ma while I go off to yoga?"

"Aren't there some babysitters in the area?"

"Looking after an old woman with dementia isn't exactly cool."

"What about Jesse?"

"When hell freezes over!"

"I bet Zach could get him to gran-sit!"

"Don't hold your breath."

sage

Mom pushes everything on the kitchen table to one end. "Jesse!" she calls. "Come and see what I have."

"Colouring? I'm not four!"

"I'm trying to find things for Gran to do ... something to keep her occupied. Life must be so boring for her, sitting around doing nothing. Can you help her get started?"

Jesse sniffs one of the little sticks. "Takes me back to when I was a kid," he says.

I sniff, too, remembering the smell and the taste. Fruity. Waxy.

Jesse guides Gran to the table, and they both sit down. Jesse flicks through the pages of a book. "Choose a picture, Mary. Which one do you like? How about this? A little girl chasing a butterfly! Or there's a boy building a sandcastle at the beach!"

I flop at their feet in the little patch of sunlight that streams through the window, listening to Jesse's unusually cheery words.

"The boy on the beach! Good choice. Let's decide which colours to use ... the sand should be yellow for sure, and the sea blue. The boy's skin ... we've got pink, brown, or black. What do you think? Brown? And what about his hair —"

Mom cuts him off. "Too much talk, Jesse. One step at a time, remember. Give her time to respond before moving on. The rule is six seconds."

For a while, it's peaceful. I'm almost asleep when Jesse's cheery voice rouses me. "Red seagulls! That's interesting, Mary. Very creative! I love it."

Gran stabs at the book with the little stick, snapping it in two. I gobble up the piece that rolls onto the floor. It's not as tasty as I remember, but it's better than nothing. I'm still licking the flavour from the floor when Gran pushes the chair away and starts wandering around in a hunt for something she never finds.

Snatching up *FloppyBunny*, I follow her. Eventually, she takes my offering and sits on the couch. I rest my head in her lap, nibbling one of *FloppyBunny*'s ears, sharing the weight of Gran's heartache, sharing the smell of butter that clings to her skirt. Surely, she won't mind if I lick that up while we sit here together.

mary

Kayla sets up my laptop on the desk in the room she says is mine. A sticky note on the screen directs me to a document. *MARY'S STORY.* Huh! My name is Mary, too.

The cursor blinks hypnotically and my fingers rest on the keyboard, waiting for something, but I don't know what. Kayla tells me to write about my university days. Wanting to keep her happy, I try.

I'm one of a handful of white students in a class of several hundred taking a mandatory course on West Indian History.

When I was in the Lower Sixth at the Southampton Grammar School for Girls, I learned from Miss Easton that colonialism was a good thing, helping those in underdeveloped countries, enabling them to become developing countries and eventually developed countries. If they were really good, they could gain their independence. This was a messy business and fraught with problems, which was to be expected since they no longer wanted our help. But once everyone was back in their right minds, these new nations could become part of the Commonwealth, even getting an invitation from the Queen for a state visit to Buckingham Palace. All's well that ends well.

Now, at UWI, I'm learning about colonialism from the *colonized* rather than the colonizer — taught by a

Black professor with a Ph.D., far better qualified than
Miss Easton both academically and in life experience.
I want to slide off my chair and hide under the seat
to escape the hundreds of dark eyes boring into me.
Logically, I know I'm not responsible for events that
happened generations before I was born. These students, and this professor: they know that, don't they?

Going right back to the 1700s, my ancestors were
shopkeepers and farmworkers, not a sea captain or a
slave-owner among them. But even if my forebears were
not personally involved in the slave trade, they con-
doned it, and they dressed up colonialism to be grand
when it was nothing more than thievery.

I bow my head and bury my face behind my long hair,
trying to hide my shame.

In England, I'd been white in a sea of white. My blond
hair meant nothing. My skin and blue eyes gained me
no special privilege that I was aware of. In a school filled
with daughters of businessmen and the gifted working
class, I was invisible. But in Trinidad, I stand out. I'm
the visible minority among a population descended pre-
dominantly from African slaves and Indian indentured
labourers. I feel the blazing heat of the other students'
eyes on me. Eyes that convict me.

White privilege.

Travelling first class.

Pulling strings with the chancellor to get me into pre-
med, a course that was already full. Yes, we can make
room.

I stand condemned.

I'm conflicted, too. Part of me enjoys the luxury of
having someone make my bed and clean the bathroom.
There's nothing wrong with paying someone a fair wage
to do a job for you, but how condescending to call a
grown man "boy" and a grown woman "girl," and how

disturbing in the context of slavery and everything those labels represent.

Part of me wants to climb onto my desktop and shout that I'm sorry for the past, that I'm taking a stand for equality and justice. But the bigger part of me wants to hide behind my hair, because taking a stand is scary and daunting, and anyway, I'm just a single person. What can I do?

Suddenly, I feel drained. A familiar, warm voice surrounds me from the inside out. "It's okay Mary, take a break. Sleep. You can pick this up in the morning."

"Will my brain still be with me in the morning?" I ask. "Or will the plaques and tangles take over in the night, like brambles choking a flower garden? If I go to sleep ... will I be here when I wake up?"

"You'll be here, my love, and I'll be here, too."

Reassured, I let myself drift away.

sage

Cat leaps from the kitchen counter to the top of the wall cabinet in a single bound. One has to admire his agility, if nothing else. He stalks along the top, settling down behind a swimming bird that looks like the ones we see at *ThePond*. This one, however, has no life in it, which explains why it allows Cat to get so close.

I really don't like having Cat in our den. Jesse doesn't, either. He often clenches his teeth and growls under his breath. I know better than to talk like this, but Jesse is middle dog. He can get away with it … sometimes. All the same, I watch closely, brows raised, my eyes darting between Mom and Jesse, waiting for her to do the top-dog thing and swiftly put him in his place, but she doesn't. She talks to him quietly and gently, the same way she generally talks to Gran. It's worrisome because I sense that Mom is hiding something, but I can't figure out what or why. Exhausted, I flop onto the floor, letting human words wash over me — words that I hear often these days but are still meaningless to me.

"What day is it?"

"Tuesday."

"Where am I?"

"At home."

"What day is it?"

"Tuesday."

"Where am I?"

"At home."

———

I'm almost asleep when Gran changes her rhythm. "What's the thing with the wheels called? And why isn't it there on the street where I left it?"

I open my eyes to see her looking out the window, beating her fists into her head.

"*You'veGottaBeKidding!*" Jesse says.

This word is confusing for me. It can mean something good is happening or something bad. Right now, pungent whiffs of rage burst from Jesse's skin.

"You don't have a car anymore," he says.

Gran talks fast, her words running into each other. "Of-course-I-have-a-car-and-it-should-be-parked-right-there. Someone-stole-it. Did-you-steal-it? These-days-people-steal-things-from-me-all-the-time. Why-are-they-doing-that?"

"Nobody stole it," Mom says calmly. "I took it to the mechanic for an oil change, that's all."

Gran's face crumples into a deep frown. "But we just changed the oil! You're throwing away good money! How much is it costing?"

"Fifty bucks."

"What-the-fuck-were-you-thinking? That's-a-fortune, a-fuckin'-fortune! *Fifty-fuckin'-bucks?*"

Jesse's laughter brings a fizz to my feet. But Mom points her finger at him. "It's not funny, Jesse. *Out!*"

We leave together, Jesse repeating Gran's words. But not for long. Mom stomps after us, her voice stern.

"Listen to me, Jesse. I might have to take bad language from Gran — she's lost her filter — but I'm not taking it from you. You *don't* get to copy her!"

"Okay," Jesse says, exploding into a fresh fit of laughter.

Unexpectedly, Mom joins in, and suddenly, they are both doubled over in full belly laughs.

"Stop!" Mom begs, crossing her legs. "Stop, before I wet my pants!"

Jesse laughs harder, until salt water leaks from his eyes.

I didn't see that coming.

When the laughter dies away, the pack gathers once more in the kitchen. All is well — time for me to take a short nap before *dindins*. Just as I'm drifting away, Cat pounces, startling the crap out of me. I forgot he was hiding up there, behind that lifeless bird! He doesn't whack me or scratch me, but the cackle in his voice as he races away sounds a lot like *Gotcha*.

sage

"Chirrup, chirrup."

My head pops up, and with ears pricked and nose twitching, I use all my senses to pinpoint the crunchy creature. It's in the corner. No, it's under Jesse's shoe. Suddenly it leaps, jumping around in all directions, then it stays so still that even the long, wavy-feely things on its head don't twitch. It looks dead, but it's only pretending, like I do when Jesse says *Bang! You'reDead.* I tap it with my paw, and it leaps into the air again.

I give chase.

It stops.

I tap.

It leaps.

Usually, we play together this way until its legs fall off. After that, it doesn't want to play anymore.

But today, I forget the Number One Rule of playing Cricket: I catch the little critter in my mouth. It hangs from my lip by the hairy hooks on its legs.

I whimper, asking for help.

"Oh no, Toby, it got you," Gran says, but she does nothing to help me.

Jess comes over, but he just laughs. "I gotta get a photo! This is so Insta-worthy!"

"Help him," Gran begs. "Get the crab off him."

"It's just a cricket, Mary! She'll rub her face along the ground in a minute … its legs will fall off and it will be game over." He laughs again. "Look, there she goes."

I rub my face along the ground, pieces of the creature falling away until I'm free. I crunch up the remains.

mary

I read over the last chapter, waiting for ideas to flow. Kayla brings me a glass of water with an ice cube, its tip breaking the surface. An analogy falls into my mind. Wanting to outpace my forgetfulness, I type as quickly as I can, my brain and fingers falling into sync.

> The hulking mass of racism, like an iceberg, is hidden under the surface of our everyday lives. Keith works with white people who are warm and welcoming, but when he is alone, white women clutch their purses a little tighter, or cross the street to avoid him. And when I am out alone, or at work, I hear hurtful and ignorant things that most people would never say to my face, at least not if they know my husband is coloured.
>
> Even among well-educated people, fear and hatred lurk in conversations about rising crime rates, the declining economy, and fewer available jobs. Immigrants are blamed for these things — not white immigrants, but people of colour. Fake science is used to prop up arguments that whites have evolved further than our common African ancestors. And this promotes an agenda that keeps people of visible African descent as second-class citizens … pariahs taking advantage of the social services in Britain. I want to deny it from the rooftops or justify it as payback for all the assets Britain stole from "her" empire and its people. But I bite my tongue, scared of confrontation.

Music, however, is changing the world. Melting the icebergs! The addictive beat of American groups like Diana Ross and the Supremes, Martha and the Vandellas, and the Four Tops, all with their synchronized dance moves and stylish matching clothes, are climbing the charts in the U.K. And at Woodstock, Jimi Hendrix stuns the world with his guitar rendition of the U.S. national anthem. Music is a door, and the younger generation is opening up to the other side: integration, acceptance, equality.

But Enoch Powell, a Conservative Member of Parliament in Britain, is stirring the pot with his anti-immigration talk, his prophecy of blood in the streets and his proposal for repatriation of immigrants. His words make racial hatred acceptable and mainstream, giving credibility and power to white supremacy and to the growing number of disenfranchised young white men who are taking their racial hatred to the streets.

My heart leaps to my throat and I know it's time to change the subject. The Drifters sing in my head and my mood changes in an instant. Keith takes my hand and we walk barefoot on the boardwalk. But there's something wrong with the memory. Is it fantasy or reality? Is it daydream or delusion? I can't tell. But I want to hold Keith's hand forever, so I step off the boardwalk onto the sand and head to the water's edge. When the first wave wets our feet, a terrifying familiarity washes over me. I suddenly know where this dream is going.

I snap open my eyes and rush to the kitchen, trying to outrun the fear. Toby follows me, offering me his bunny. "Thank you, Toby! You are such a good boy."

sage

For most of my life, whenever Jesse has left the den, I've lain down on the mat by the door and waited for him to return. These days, I have Gran to look after, which gives me a purpose and makes life more bearable, but I still wait for the sound of his feet on the porch outside the door. Sometimes he makes a big fuss of me and other times he ignores me. I never know what to expect, but I'm always hopeful.

Today, he almost flattens me as he barrels in, charging to *TheFridge* and talking to the food inside.

"I need a ride to Markville Mall to get new *Basketball* shoes. My old ones are … ur … they're just old, and they're tight! I'll need new ones for tryouts when school starts. Can we go after supper?"

Mom sighs. "We can go tomorrow — all three of us."

"*Seriously?* Take Gran to the mall?"

"We can't leave her alone!" Mom says, her voice alarmingly shrill.

"Not even for a couple of hours?"

Mom sighs deeply. It's a sound she makes a lot these days. "I wish you'd be more understanding, Jesse. And close *TheFridge*, for goodness' sake."

"Understanding? I understand everything. It's Gran who doesn't understand things."

"Keep your voice down," Mom whispers. "I don't want her to hear."

"We can take her with us," Jesse whispers back, "and lock her in the car in the parking lot — just for half an hour. She'd never figure out the kiddie locks. Even you can't do that, Mom. The weather's perfect — not too hot, not too cold, and we could leave her with a bottle of water."

"She's not a dog, Jesse!"

Jesse almost bursts with explosive words, but taking a breath, he walks away.

Grabbing *Mouse* by the tail, I follow him, but he doesn't notice me. I offer *Mouse* to Gran instead, but she doesn't notice me, either. She keeps on searching, getting too close to *YeeHaw*, who creaks and lays her horizontal. "Someone stole my keys," she whimpers from *YeeHaw*'s clutches.

"I'll help you find your keys in a minute," Mom tells her.

"This is crazy," Jesse whispers. "She doesn't have keys! She doesn't even have a car!"

Mom drops her head into her hands. "I know that, but it's easier than arguing with her. Distract and divert, the experts say. And when all else fails, lie."

"Mom! You always told us not to lie … under any circumstances."

"It's called therapeutic lying — therapeutic for *me*. Listen to me, Jesse! I can't take it anymore. Please, please, please, give me some alone time. Take Gran for a walk."

Jesse's mouth flops open wide enough to catch flies. "Where do you expect me to go?"

"*ThePark*. Any place! Take *Sage*, too. Just get outta here, both of you, before … before … before I leave home! See how you manage then."

Jesse raises his arms in the air and backs away from her. "Hey, Mom, none of this was my idea, remember." He picks up my leash. "C'mon, Mary. Let's take *Sage* to *ThePark*."

YeeHaw bucks Gran off. "I need my wig," she moans, rummaging through drawers, throwing things into the air as if she wants me to play catch. "I can't go without my wig."

Her odour tells me that she's definitely not in a playful mood, but I can't stop myself. I lunge across the room, catching soft objects in my mouth: my favourites — underwear!

"*LeaveIt!*" Jesse shouts, laughing.

I look at him, asking for clarification because laughter and *LeaveIt* are two sounds that don't usually go together.

"*Sage! DropIt.*" No laughter.

Reluctantly, I allow the damp items to fall from my mouth.

Gran twists her knobby fingers into her hair. "All of this! It attracts too much attention. Someone will tell my daddy."

Mom makes an entrance. She's calm now, speaking slowly in a soothing tone. "You don't have to worry, Ma. Your daddy died years ago, remember?"

"He died? Daddy died?"

"Yes, you know that!"

For a moment, Gran freezes. Then she starts grabbing clothes from the open drawers.

"What are you doing?"

"Packing."

"Where are you going?"

"Home to Mummy, of course. She'll need me."

"Your mummy's dead, too."

Gran staggers backward, collapsing into *YeeHaw*, who comes to life with a loud groan, laying her flat out.

"Both of them dead?" she says, her feet flailing. "When?"

"Years ago," Mom replies.

"Why didn't you tell me? Why did you hide this from me?"

Mom and Jesse both seem stunned. They don't know what to do. Yet again, it's all up to me. Gingerly, I creep closer until my head rests on Gran's lap. *YeeHaw* is unpredictable and dangerous. I'm a *very* brave dog.

Gran stops flailing and strokes me. Gradually, her heart slows and steadies.

Mom and Jesse leave, but I stay with Gran until the aroma of cheese drifting from the kitchen is too much to ignore. Cheese is the solution to all of life's problems. The mere thought of it gives me courage. Tentatively, I move my head from Gran's lap. *YeeHaw* doesn't stir, so I make a dash for the kitchen and ask both Jesse and Mom for cheese. Deep in conversation, they ignore me.

"She won't remember what happened," Mom says. "Every time she hears her parents are dead, it'll be like she's hearing it for the first time. She'll grieve, all over again, every single time."

"No problem. We won't mention her parents again. If Gran brings them up, we'll pretend they're still alive, maybe out of the room ... at the store, whatever."

Mom gasps. "I've been pushing her to write her life story before she loses her memories, but what was I thinking? I don't want her to relive all the grief she's tried to stifle, especially about Keith."

Jesse shrugs. "I don't get how she can remember things that she forgot years ago — I mean, how is that possible? She can't even remember things that happened two minutes ago! It makes no sense!"

"Recent memories are always the first to go. Something blocks them from getting to the storage area or stops them from being processed into long-term memories. On the other hand, things that happened years ago, when the brain was healthy, were stored correctly, so they're still there."

"Reminds me of our old computer," Jesse says. "Kyle told me to get as much as I could onto an external hard drive before it crashed and we lost it all."

"That's what I've been trying to do," Mom exclaims, "get Gran to write down her memories before they're lost forever!"

Jesse chuckles. "I think it's too late. Her RAM's already fried!"

mary

Through the kitchen window, I see a young man playing basketball. My heart leaps in my chest. It's Keith! I look again. It's not Keith. His skin is too light. Perhaps it's the boy who does the yardwork ... Harry? Whatever his name, he doesn't do much yardwork. He spends most of his time fooling around. Kayla should nag him more, like she nags me to work on my story. Right now, she's scrolling through it, stopping on a page she likes.

"Ma, you were writing about that little apartment you lived in."

"What little apartment?"

"Your first home together, the bed-sitting room at the top of the Victorian house in South London, when you and Keith were newlyweds. I'll read what you wrote ... 'it was only one room, with a bed, a couch, a hotplate, and a sink.' Tell me some of your *good* memories about that place."

"There was a Bob Marley billboard on the lamppost outside."

"Excellent! Write it down. Let's see if we can think of five good things. You type and I'll do the numbers."

1. A Bob Marley billboard on the lamppost outside.
2. Lots of West Indians. Jamaicans, mostly.
3. Reggae, calypso, and pop music in the air.
4. A communal bathroom down the hall. It was always dirty. Several people shared it, and no one wanted to clean.
5. Putting coins in the gas meter for hot water — shillings. Running out of shillings. If you misjudged it, the water ran cold.

"That doesn't sound very nice," Kayla says. "Why did you stay there?"

I start to tell her, but she insists I write it down. I've had enough of her telling me what to do, and anyway, typing is too much effort, so I refuse.

She drags the laptop across the counter toward her. "You talk, and I'll type."

"We tried to rent a nicer place in a better neighbourhood," I tell her, "but every place we went, they had an excuse. They'd take one look at us and say the place was rented, even though we'd just called them from the phone box down the street. Or they said, 'We don't rent to Coloureds,' or 'You'll bring down property prices,' or 'I'm not personally racist, but the other tenants won't like it.'

"Keith carried the brunt of it. He didn't want to fulfill my dad's prophecy: that he wouldn't be able to look after me in the manner I deserved. I didn't care where we lived, as long as we were together."

"So what did you do?"

"Do?"

"How did you find a place to live?"

"Seren … seren … Serengeti," I tell her.

"Serengeti? Do you mean 'serendipity'?"

Kayla laughs and I feel humiliated, but not for long. Suddenly I'm with Keith, walking down Clapham High Street. I feel his hand in mine, and sense him shorten his stride to match my pace. My heart swells with love. I want to stay with him forever, the frayed hems of his bell-bottom jeans touching the pavement, his toes poking out of leather sandals, but Kayla is hustling me along, wanting me to tell some story called "serendipity."

A spry old Black woman bumped into us on Clapham High Street, telling Keith she knew him and was related to his family in Trinidad. She owned a big terraced house close by and rented out rooms. One was available on the top floor. We jumped at the chance to rent it, sight unseen. Her name was Phyllis and she lived on the main floor and we'd go down once a week to drop off the rent. She always invited us in, made us a rum and Coke, and we'd chat for a while. She said she didn't like to drink alone, so we were doing her a favour. I think she was lonely. She talked about her son, but we never saw him. Then one day we went down to give her the rent and she wasn't there. Her son was. She'd died in the night. The building went up for sale. And we had to start the hunt all over again.

Kayla lays her hand on my arm and tells me she is sorry. Tears prick the corners of my eyes — I don't know why. It's not like I knew Phyllis very well.

"What happened after that?" Kayla asks.

"After what?"

"After Phyllis died. How did you find another place to live?"

We signed up with a rental agency, but it was the same old story: *No Coloureds … it's rented … I'm not prejudiced but …* So we decided that I would join another agency by myself. I'll never forget the first place I went to. A man with a South African accent answered the door. He was really pleased to see me. Said, 'I told the agency no Blacks, but that's all they've been sending.' I was furious. At him, at the world, and at myself for not coming up with the right words to shame him. I still regret that. It left me realizing that my dad was right: there *were* places Keith and I couldn't live. I really hadn't believed him until then. Keith's take-away was that we needed to buy a place of our own so we weren't at the mercy of racist landlords. Maybe we were a tad paranoid, but we worried that white people wouldn't even sell to us. So we'd look at the outsides of houses

together, then I would contact the agent and schedule
the inside tour *alone*. When we were finally ready to
make an offer, Keith showed up to sign the papers. He
never even saw the inside of the house we bought until
we moved in.

The neighbours must have been shocked when they
saw us, but there was no outright racism. Not like in
London.

A memory explodes in my head like a bomb going off ...
A gang ...
Shaved heads ...
Checkered shirts ...
Blue jeans cuffed above the ankle ...
Steel-toed boots.

Rushing to escape, I push my chair back so hard that it falls
over. Toby is startled. Kayla is alarmed. She wants to know what
happened and why the chair is tipped over.

I don't know.

Maybe Toby knocked it over. I think something frightened
him. But he's licking my hand now, reassuringly. All is well.

sage

Mom and Jesse are shouting at each other. Mom is shouting the loudest, which isn't like her at all. It frightens me. I whine at them to stop, but they take no notice of me, so I retreat with my tail between my legs and nuzzle Gran. Her hands tremble like leaves on a tree, her fear so strong I can taste it.

Eventually, Jesse stomps off to his room and slams the door. Mom does the same.

Gran is on the move, too, but she doesn't seem to know where to go or what she's looking for. I follow her until she finds her bed. She lies down with her knees to her chest and pulls the covers over her head. I wait until her breathing is shallow, then I head off to check on Mom. *Mouse*'s tail is caught at the bottom of the slammed door, so I nose the door open and peek in.

Mom is on her bed, twitching — a sure sign that she's still agitated. She needs me, but there's a problem; I'm not allowed in her room, and since I'm a *GoodGirlSage* who understands the rules, I don't enter. Instead, I lie on my belly where wood meets carpet, my snout touching the no-go line. My paws, however, refuse to obey the rules of the line. Irresistibly tempted by the presence of a distressed Mom across the room, they wriggle and squirm and claw at the ground, dragging me across the line at the speed of a snail. Bad paws! But I'm a little closer to Mom now and poised to go the whole way.

Surprisingly, she doesn't yell when I tippy-toe across the carpet and cautiously sidle up to her. She rests her arm across my back.

"Oh, *Sage*, I totally lost it. I got so angry. I hate that Ma saw me like that. It wasn't her fault."

She sinks her fingers into the thick fur on my shoulders and massages me as she talks. I understand only that she's troubled.

"I feel like I'm in the middle of a tug-of-war," she continues, "one hand holding on to Ma, trying to stop her from slipping away, and the other holding on to Jesse. On both counts, I'm failing. Looking after Ma is harder than I thought. She's always interrupting me, always asking the same questions, always following me around the house like a shadow. I'm not as patient as I thought I was. But Jesse makes me angry, and then I'm mad at myself for getting angry. I want to quit! But I can't run away from my mother or my son."

She jerks up in bed, breathing fast, like she can't get enough air. Reassuringly, I touch my muzzle to her hand, but her stress zaps my wet nose.

"Oh God, I'm having a heart attack," she says. "No, it's just a panic attack … just a panic attack … just a panic attack … just a panic attack."

I nuzzle and nudge her, even though I really don't like the tingly, zappy feelings that fly from her fingertips. Gradually, her breathing settles and I sense that the anxiety is leaving her, but I'm wrong. She leaps off the bed and stomps to the kitchen, where she opens a bottle that gives off a fermented smell. She pours herself a drink and downs it rapidly. I need a drink, too. My bowl is empty, but Mom is in no mood to fill it, so I sneak off to the little room to help myself from the big bowl. Cat is already there, tapping his forepaw against the roll of paper that hangs from the wall. Without warning, he launches himself at it, scrabbling with his claws and sending clouds of soft, shredded paper to the floor, like feathers from inside a pillow.

Mom sees me with the eyes on the back of her head. "*Sage!* Are you drinking from the toilet again?"

I lower my head in shame, even though I didn't do a thing. Mom advances, her face contorted in fury.

"Regis!" she shrieks.

Cat careens past me, a tortured yowl coming from his throat, claws grappling helplessly on the tiled floor as he makes the turn, skidding like the cars Jesse sometimes watches on *TeeVee*. Cat is way too fast for Mom. She lags behind, fist raised in a display of anger that I haven't seen since Jesse cut up her bedsheets.

Cat does a lap around the house at full tilt, then, before Mom catches up, he bounds to the top of the kitchen cabinets, his feet barely touching the counter on the way. He hides behind the dead bird. She will never find him. She can't sniff him out, the way I do. Her nose is good for nothing — other than blowing, snorting, snotting, and breathing. Right now, she's trying to do all four at the same time and has become a gasping, mucousy, salty mess. Before I can clean her up, she picks up a handful of the soft paper billowing on the floor and hides her face in it.

"Oh *Sage*," she says, blowing and mopping. "I kicked the cat. I didn't hurt him, but all the same … what an awful person I've become."

I lick her arm, telling her that I love her and am delighted that she put Cat in his place. If we're lucky, he'll stay out of our way for a while. But I mustn't forget he's behind the swimming bird because he's well positioned for another ambush.

kayla

"Hi, Leesha. I had a bad day."

"Oh, no, I thought you were doing better. The last time we spoke you seemed quite positive."

"Yeah, well, it's up and down like a frickin' roller coaster."

"What happened?"

"I really needed to get out of the house today. Sometimes I feel like I'm in a prison. So I figured we'd pop into Newmarket to get Ma some adult bibs, and some socks ... ones she can slip on and off more easily. I'm getting a backache from leaning over to help her. I must have been nuts, but I seriously thought we could have lunch out! Nothing fancy, just the food court. Before we lined up to order, I asked her if she needed to use the washroom. She said, no, so we get our food and find a table. After two mouthfuls, guess what. She has to go to the washroom. She can't wait ... I mean she *can't* wait! So I ask the guy at the next table to keep an eye on our food, and off we go."

"Do you think she has a bladder infection?" Alicia asks. "I'm googling ... it's a common cause of incontinence. Or it could be irritable bladder. Both are common with Alzheimer's patients, especially if they wear diapers. That's good to know for the future. It says here that meds might help. Sorry ... I interrupted your story. Did you get to the bathroom in time?"

"Just. The family one was in use, so we used a regular one, and the stall was extra small. I didn't think there was room for both of us, so I stood outside and talked her through it. 'Don't lock the door, Ma. I'm right here. Nobody will come in.' I should have put my toe in, 'cause guess what?"

"She locked the door?"

"Yup. And then she couldn't unlock it! I freaked. I couldn't leave her to go and get help."

"Shit! What did you do?"

"I crawled underneath! It was one of the most disgusting things I've ever done. Face down on that floor, my hair in goodness knows what. I still feel contaminated even though I came home and jumped in the shower."

"Oh my God … good thing you didn't get stuck."

"I almost did!"

I suddenly see the funny side and start to giggle. Alicia joins in. We have a long history of laughing together. Soon we are both hooting and snorting and egging each other on. It feels good.

"Did you still eat lunch after all that?" Alicia asks when the laughter fades away.

"I was planning to. Thank God there was soap and paper towel in the washroom, and even sanitizer. But when we got back to the food court, the guy at the next table was gone. And so was our food! I would have complained but there was a line-up at the counter. I wanted to scream."

"That's not like you."

"No, it's not. I don't know what's happening to me, Leesh. My emotions are right at the surface. And sometimes they get away from me."

"Sounds like you need to talk to someone."

"What do you think I'm doing? Chatting with you is better than seeing a shrink."

"That's good to hear. I feel so far away. I feel like I'm no help at all, and that I'm leaving it all to you."

"Believe me … *this* is helpful. I need someone to dump on, someone to laugh with, someone who understands me. I think I'm a bit like that pressure cooker Ma had in the old days. Remember when it literally blew its top?"

"Yeah …! *Kapow* … beef stew all over the kitchen ceiling."

"Exactly! You help me let off steam, so I don't explode."

"I'm glad. Did you get the socks?"

"What?"

"The socks for Ma, and the bib?"

"Yes! I got them before we went to the food court. But that was a disaster, too! When we left the store, we set off the alarm. Turns out Ma had stuffed her pockets with some mighty fine hair accessories. It was more than embarrassing — frightening, actually. You know what it's like being in a store while Black!"

"Yeah, everyone expects us to steal things. Did security come?"

"Oh, yes! They were there in a flash. I kept my distance!"

Alicia starts to laugh again. "You left Ma to deal with it?"

"Yup! I figured I'd make things worse for her. It worked! Security figured it out pretty quickly and let her go. The store manager even gave her one of the hair ornaments!"

Alicia's laughter is infectious, but this time I'm crying as well as laughing. I figure it's all good. It's giving me some much-needed release, so I don't blow up inappropriately at Ma.

"Oh, by the way," Alicia says, "do you know that Zach and Jesse are talking?"

"No way! Jesse didn't tell me that."

"Of course not. You're his mother — the last one to know anything important. But from what Zach says, they've really hit it off."

"That's amazing, Leesh! Thanks for doing that."

"One more thing … I found out that long-term care homes keep a few beds open for what they call 'respite care.' I thought maybe Ma could go in for a week, when you feel you can't cope anymore … you could have a break. I'll text you the phone number."

"That sounds fantastic. Although I'm not sure if I could persuade her to go. Long-term care is her worst nightmare. But I'll call them and check it out."

kayla

"Good morning. I want to book a week of respite for my mother."

"Certainly! I can help you with that. Did you have a date in mind?"

"ASAP. Like tomorrow! I'm at my wits' end."

"Oh dear, I'm sorry to hear that, but we are booked solid for the next six months."

"Six *months*! You've gotta be kidding me? I'm having a breakdown now, not six months down the road."

"We have a bed in Sudbury in two months … if you don't mind the drive."

"Sudbury! That's five hours away. Twenty hours' driving to get a week's break! That's insane!"

"Yeah, it's a long way. I can start the application right now if you like. Do you have a case file number?"

"I don't think so."

"I'll have to set that up before we can proceed. We'll have to do an in-home appraisal, of course. Let's see … I have an opening in three weeks. Are you available on September seventeenth at ten thirty?"

"Yeah, I don't have anything else on my calendar," I say facetiously.

"And have you started the process for getting your mother on the wait-list for long-term care?"

"No!"

"Ah … that will slow things down a bit. We need to —"

"Oh, for God's sake," I yell. "This is crazy. I just need a break. And I need it now."

"I'm sorry. The good news is .·. you are eligible for a personal support worker, to come three times a week to bathe your mother. The visits are thirty to sixty minutes. Would that help you?"

"Not really. Ma can still bathe herself. She doesn't like the process, so I let it go for about a week. But I don't need someone to actually do it."

"She's not physically disabled, is she? I could get you more hours if she was disabled, or if she lived alone. But she lives with you, right?"

"You mean we are being penalized because I brought my mother to live with me? And I'm now juggling her, my son, and my job?"

"I wish I could do more, but there's never enough money to run the programs people need. If you don't mind my saying, it sounds like you need a companion rather than a PSW — someone to come in for half a day, maybe twice a week, so you can have a break and know she's safe and taken care of."

"Exactly!"

"I'll send you the names of agencies that handle that."

"Perfect. Thank you."

"It's not covered, but if you can afford it, it might help you out. Another option is the Alzheimer Day Centre. And it's reasonably priced because it's sponsored by donations."

"Ma's been on the list for months already."

"I'm sorry. So shall I arrange for the PSW to come three times a week to bathe her? We try to get the same person coming each time but unfortunately, because of scheduling, that doesn't always happen."

"Instead of three times a week, can I get the three hours in one chunk, so the PSW could bathe Ma and then interact with her, play some games, or socialize ... and give me a break?"

"I'm sorry, it doesn't work that way."

Anger rises up inside me and bursts out of my mouth. "Oh, fuck it! Ma would never agree to go to your stupid home, anyway! Fuck-fuck-fuck-fuck-fuck-fuck-fuck!" I burst into tears and slam the phone down.

Jesse comes running. "What the heck Mom? What's going on?"

"These people are supposed to help us! We pay them with our tax dollars, yet they make you jump through so many hoops. Typical bureaucracy!"

"Calm down, Mom! Your blood pressure must be through the roof. You're gonna give yourself a stroke."

I take a deep breath and blow it out, my heart not really in it. But three more breaths and I feel sanity return. "It wasn't that poor woman's fault. I shouldn't have taken it out on her. It was totally out of character for me. I'd better call her back to apologize."

"Just relax for a second, Mom. I'll put the kettle on and make you a nice cup of tea. And here's Sage to work her magic."

"Ha! She just wants a cookie! But thanks, Jesse. And thanks, Sage. You brought me Pink-Piggy. Aw, sweetiepie, you're such a good girl."

"Gran's really upset," Jesse says as Ma walks tentatively toward us. "She thinks you're mad at her."

I hug my mother, saying that it wasn't her fault.

"I'm a nuisance," she sobs, "I know that."

"That's not true, Ma. I'm so sorry for making you feel that way." She's small and fragile in my arms. And sad. I vow to do better.

"Jesse is making tea," I say, with a smile on my face and love in my heart. "Would you like a cup?"

Jesse sits with us at the kitchen table, which is quite remarkable.

"Do you know Labour Day weekend is coming up?" he says. "It's the first day of high school next Tuesday."

"Oh gosh, Jesse, I completely forgot. Was I supposed to help you register or buy you supplies? What about clothes? And you never got those basketball shoes."

"I went to the school and registered already. I have my time-table. D'you wanna see it?"

"Please."

"I still need to pick up the basics from the dollar store … paper, pens, binders. And I need a scientific calculator. I could get one here in town, but I figure I'll get the bus to Toronto. Uncle Zach says he'll give me two hundred and fifty dollars toward jeans and a pair of Nikes."

"That's nice of him! How are you feeling about starting high school? It's been a long summer for you."

"Yeah, back in June, I couldn't wait for September, even though high school scared the crap out of me. I just wanted out of here. When I'd leave the house, even just to shoot hoops on the driveway, I felt lighter. And when I came back inside, I'd feel heavy again. But it's not so bad anymore. I still have my ups and downs, though ... still get irritated, still feel like I've gotta get outta here."

"I feel the same way," I say. "It's been a hard adjustment for both of us."

"Uncle Zach said that, too. He helped me see things through *your* eyes. Once school starts, I won't be here much. I'll be trying out for the team — so with practices and games, I'll be busy. But you'll still be here, with no break. He thinks you should get back to your yoga class ... once a week at least. I told him you do yoga in your bedroom sometimes, but he says it's better to go to a class. You need to get out of the house, just like I do. You need to see other people."

"I'd love to do that, but getting someone to stay here with you-know-who is the issue."

"That's the thing, Mom. I'll do it. At least I'll try."

"*What?* Seriously! That would be wonderful. Hang on a moment ... did your uncle bribe you?"

Jesse grins. "Sorta."

"Works for me."

sage

Over the years, I've learned that when the nights turn cool, the routine changes. Jesse goes out a lot, leaving the den after a hurried breakfast and not returning until *dindins* time, or even later. I don't know where he goes. I hear words like School, Practice, Game, Tournament, as if I should understand — but I don't. When he returns, the remnants of his day cling to him, but I can't piece the mystery together, no matter how hard I sniff.

But now Mom is trying to go out. This is different. I get under her feet, saying I want to go with her. So does Gran.

"Please co-operate," Mom says, prying Gran's fingers from her side. "I need to go, or I'll miss the start of the class. I won't be long, and Jesse is here with you."

Mom's special mat is rolled up under her arm — the mat she lies on sometimes, waving her arms and legs in the air and taking deep, slow breaths. At first, when she got down on her mat like this, I thought she wanted to wrestle with me, like Jesse did when we were young, so I bounded over the no-go line and romped with her. Wrong! She showed me her pointing finger and yelled, "*Sage*, get off the mat!" I didn't understand the word, but I understood the finger and backed away. But then Mom must have seen my disappointment because she executed a perfect *Let'sPlay* pose, with her head and hands on the mat and her butt up in the air!

I thought, she was finally learning *Dog*! So I put my forepaws on the mat and pushed my hips as high as they would go, my tail waving and everything in my vibrating body saying, *Yes, yes, yes ... Let's play.*

"Get off the mat," she yelled.

Confused, I waited for clarification, holding my pose. Mom moved into a sitting position, breathing deeply and facing me eye to eye, then, with arms above her head and her magnificent fingers splayed like the wings of a bird, she gracefully leaned to the side. This was a clear invitation for me to sniff her stinky armpit. I obliged, but she snapped her arm back to her side, pointed her finger again and yelled, "*Out.*" So many mixed messages! It seems my humans are incapable of perfecting the art of clear communication.

Since that day, I have learned the rules of the mat. I try to respect them, I really do, but sometimes I just can't help myself. Mom on the floor is irresistible.

Right now, she's still trying to leave the den, but Jesse tempts me and Gran away from the door with *Cookies.* I swallow mine whole, then lick up every one of Gran's spilled crumbs, and by that time, Mom is gone.

Soon Gran is pacing the floor, confusion lining her face and the whiff of fear seeping from her. I feel her panic. I chew on *FloppyBunny*'s ear to calm myself, and then I offer him to Gran so she can do the same. She ignores me, talking instead to Jesse. He replies with one long word, which he says over and over: *She's-gone-to-yoga-she'll-be-back-soon.*

I can tell he's losing patience. It's like the day he tried to teach me to jump through a hoop. *ThroughTheHoop*, he said, getting louder and louder as if deafness was my problem, but my hips were sore and I didn't want to do it.

Right now, Jesse is getting loud with Gran. "*She's-gone-to-yoga-she'll-be-back-soon.*"

Pain flashes into Gran's eyes. "Why are you angry with me? What have I done wrong?"

"Nothing," he says, taking a deep breath. "I'm sorry I shouted. I'm just having a bad day. It's not your fault."

"I want Hettie," Gran wails. "Where's Hettie?"

Jesse frowns. "Who's Hettie?"

"Hettie! You know … she looks after me."

Jesse sounds shocked. "You mean Mom?"

"Where's Hettie?" she asks again, staying close to Jesse's side like I do when I'm worried.

Jesse breaks free and charges to the little room, the one where my spare water bowl lives. Even though there's barely room to turn around, both Gran and I try to follow him. We're too slow. Jesse closes the door in our faces.

I press my nose against the bottom of the door, breathing Jesse's scent and listening to his muffled voice. "Damn it! I don't have my phone with me."

Gran turns away and paces in and out of all the rooms, and up and down the hall. She needs me, so I follow her. Eventually, she sinks onto the couch. I want to rest my head on her lap to let her know I'm here, taking care of her, but I'm leery of a surprise attack from Cat. He's balanced on the window ledge, just one leap away, a hind leg stretched toward the ceiling, his raspy tongue licking his butt. Not that I judge him. I do the same — lick my butt, I mean, not stretch my leg like that. But when my humans need me, I know better than to indulge myself with butt-licking. Cat, on the other hand, is self-centred. Whenever Gran pats her lap, giving him a clear invitation to jump up for a cuddle, he turns his head away, his body language saying, *I will not respond to your bidding. I shall be your lap-cat only when I desire it.* Then, when he finally decides to sit on her lap, he's quick to remind her of the terms of the arrangement, smacking her hand with a paw if she overdoes the stroking.

I watch Cat now, absorbed in self-grooming, his body contorted into a pretzel shape. I don't know how he can do that without falling off the ledge. Despite his personality flaws, he does have skills.

Confident that he will be occupied with excessive licking and grooming for a while, I push my snout under Gran's fidgeting fingers until I get her attention and she rubs behind my ears. Sadness flows through her hands to me. It's mixed with fear, confusion, and loneliness — dark and heavy. I don't know why Gran feels this way, because no one is choking her with a leash or shouting *BadDog* at her. No one is shutting her in the laundry room, alone. No one has forgotten to feed her.

"Sometimes, I think you are the only one who understands me," she whispers. "*GoodBoyToby. You'reSuchaSweetBoy.*"

I can't help but wag my tail. *She loves me! She loves me! She loves me!*

Jesse reappears, stroking me like he's glad I'm here. I wag my tail some more. *He loves me! He loves me! He loves me!*

Gran struggles to her feet, hopping on the spot, making ouchy noises. Jesse holds her shoulders and steers her to the little room with the big water bowl. When she reappears, I squirm and wriggle, glad to be reunited. She's happy, too.

"Hello *Toby*! Where have you been, my *SweetBoy*? I missed you so much."

Jesse chuckles. "Look at the two of you. It's like you've been separated for months. It's been two minutes tops."

He escorts us back to the couch. I lie at Gran's feet and in no time, she nods off to sleep. I do the same.

Cat pounces. I forgot he was there!

kayla

The iPad rings at exactly the scheduled time. My smiling sister is on the screen. This is Day One of a new idea: Alicia and Zach will FaceTime Ma on alternate days at a prearranged time for thirty minutes. On this opening session, Alicia has planned a singalong to get Ma breathing more deeply, using some of the songs Ma taught us as children. She says I can join in if I want, or go off and do something else for half an hour.

I stand the iPad on the kitchen counter, planning to escape as soon as they are settled.

"Hi, Ma," Alicia says. "It's me ... Alicia!"

Ma turns to me, confused.

"It's Alicia," I tell her. "You can talk to her just like you're on the phone, but you can see her at the same time."

Ma leans in close to the screen and shouts: "Alicia?"

Alicia waves enthusiastically, smiling from ear to ear.

Ma smiles and waves back, and it warms my heart. I no longer want to shut myself in my room for half an hour; I want to stay here with my mother and my sister.

Alicia speaks clearly and slowly. "I was thinking back to when Kayla and Zach and I were small children. You sang songs with us all the time. It was such fun. I remember 'Head, Shoulders, Knees, and Toes.' Let's stand up and do the actions together."

Ma is captivated. She watches Alicia on the screen and copies the actions, singing along, laughing.

"Eyes and ears and mouth and nose ..."

I join in and even Jesse appears. We repeat the song in French. *"Têtes, épaules, genoux, oreilles, genoux, oreilles …"* Then we progress to "Five Little Monkeys Jumping on the Bed." It's the best fun I've had in months.

Even after the call ends, the happiness lingers, the tunes running through my head as I lay in bed. I go to sleep smiling at the memory, not only of my beautiful sister and mother on the FaceTime call, but of us all, forty years earlier, bouncing on the bed, singing "Five Little Monkeys Jumping on the Bed."

Kayla: That was brilliant yesterday, Leesh. I enjoyed it!

Alicia: It was fun, wasn't it! I've got several more songs lined up … and some chair yoga.

Zach: And I was thinking about reading her a bedtime story … P'raps *The Velveteen Rabbit.* She used to read it to us when we were kids, remember?

Alicia: I love that one!

Kayla: How about reading the books she read to my kids when they were young? I still have a copy of *Love You Forever.* I remember Ma reading it to Jesse when he was about two! It might jog her memory, too.

Alicia: How about even older books … like *Winnie the Pooh?* Or *The Wind in the Willows?* Books that Ma's mother might have read to her as a child.

Zach: Good idea, but we don't need a new
story each night. She won't remember that we
just read it to her!

> Kayla: Yeah, repetition is good for little kids. I
> expect it's good for Ma, too.

Alicia: I agree. We find her favourites and use
them over and over.

Zach: I have another idea! A family concert
on Zoom. Kayla can be the lead singer and
Leesha and I can do the backups!

> Kayla: That's a great idea. Ma loves Motown!
> We can start with that.

Zach: Maybe get her dancing!

Alicia: We can all dance!

sage

My job is quite demanding these days. One or other of my humans is always in need of emotional support. As soon as I get one settled, I have to start work on another. Right now, it's Jesse.

"Shoot," he mumbles, "where did I put my phone? Am I getting Alzheimer's, too? Is it contagious?"

I don't know what he's looking for, but I follow him around, finding *PinkPiggy* along the way. Eventually, he picks up *iPhone* and we go back to bed.

"Hey, Siri. Is Alzheimer's catching?" he says.

"Okay, I found this on the web. Check it out."

He's quiet for a while, then, "Hey, Siri. Is Alzheimer's hereditary?"

"Okay, I found this on the web. Check it out."

Panic spurts from him with its many different layers. I can taste it — bitter and foul. I can see it — dark and ominous. And I can feel it with a surge of my own heart.

"Mom," he yells weakly, his skin suddenly damp and clammy. She doesn't hear him.

I jump off the bed and race to Mom's side, yipping at her. She's smart. She knows what I mean. She follows me back to Jesse's room.

"Everything's blurry," he says. "I'm seeing stars."

"Get your head down," Mom commands in her alpha voice. "And tell me what's going on."

Jesse holds up *iPhone*.

Mom squints at it. "That's for young-onset Alzheimer's disease! Gran has ordinary Alzheimer's."

"What's the difference?"

"Young-onset means the symptoms start early in life ... maybe around forty. Gran's didn't start until she was past seventy. The article is right about young-onset — there *is* a strong genetic link. But for ordinary Alzheimer's, the link is weaker."

"I thought ..."

"I know," Mom says. "I was worried about it, too." She holds Jesse's chin in her hands. "Look at me Jess. Listen! Young-onset Alzheimer's is rare. Gran doesn't have that, so your chance of getting Alzheimer's isn't much higher than the average person. Plus, there are things you can do to reduce that risk. You already exercise a lot, and you keep your brain active. Things like learning music and other languages ... that helps protect you."

"So *Basketball* and French school and playing the guitar help me not get Alzheimer's?"

She nods. "And the other thing is diet. We can work on that if you want."

Jesse lets his breath go in a big whoosh. "Would you want to know, Mom? Say you could get tested to find out if you were going to get it — would you want to know?"

She replies quickly. "Absolutely not! To know that one day I'll go to the store and get lost on the way home, or that I'll wake up one morning and not know how to make myself breakfast, or ..." Her voice quivers. "Or that one day I'll look at you and see a stranger?"

"But if you knew it was going to happen," Jesse says, the words catching in his throat, "you could make a bucket list and do it all."

"Or I might get frantic every time I forget a name or a word."

"I get worried when I forget anything," Jesse confides, "especially my phone!"

Mom smiles, despite her quivering chin and moist eyes. "It's normal to lose your phone now and again. It's *not* normal if you forget what your phone is *for* when you have it in your hand."

Jesse inhales sharply. "Just the other day, I pointed the home phone at the TV and expected it to change the channel!"

Mom laughs. "Everyone does that occasionally. You were probably just distracted. Don't live your life as if you have a death
sentence hanging over you. Worst-case scenario, let's say that you
are destined to get it: it would be decades from now. They will have
a cure by then, for sure!"

"I hope so," he says.

The doorbell rings. I rush to do my guard-dog routine. It's the
boy called *TakeOut* so my barks turn to delighted grunts, but all I
get is dry kibble. I follow the empty containers to the garbage bin,
watching Jesse close the lid tight, staying for as long as I'm allowed,
nudging it with my snout. My efforts are in vain — another cruel
reminder that I don't have hands.

"Hey, *Sage*," he says, when we go back inside. "*Come* and watch
this."

I trot alongside him to the couch. Dogs are on *TeeVee*. A whole
pack of them without leashes or collars or uprights. The mother
suckles the pups in a den underground while the others carry food
to her in their bellies. One of them throws back his head and howls.
Another answers with a different timbre to its voice. Then another,
until together, they sing one joyous song of freedom, love, and family.

Quivers race up and down my spine. These are the Wild Ones
my mother told me about ... the ones I see in my dreams. I'm so
mesmerized by them that I barely notice Jesse leave my side.

Mom approaches, chasing the Wild Ones into the cover of
darkness. She seems mad with Jesse. "What have I told you about
leaving the television on when no one is watching?"

"*Sage* was watching!"

"*You'veGottaBeKidding*," Mom says, her tone suggesting that
she's rolling her eyes. I can't see her, though, because I'm sniffing
around trying to get inside the black box with the Wild Ones.

"I'm serious," Jesse says. "*Sage* loves animal shows, especially
National Geographic. Turn it back on and see what I mean."

The Wild Ones reappear, running together through deep snow.
My forepaws dance on the spot.

"How about that," Mom says.

Totally absorbed, I allow the voices of my uprights to fade into the background. Eventually, when the Wild Ones run away into the darkness, I go outside to do my nightly check for intruders. The *TakeOut* containers are chewed to pieces, and fresh raccoon poop is piled by the open bins. I alert Mom to it. She grumbles, cleaning up and re-securing the lid. Raccoons are crafty creatures. They can get into a bin almost as quick as a human. They have hands!

sage

It's bacon for *dindins*! Bacon for *dindins*!

Bacon is the best, the best, the best.

"*Out!*" Mom yells. "This is spitting."

I retreat one step. Then two more. But it's not good enough for her. She doesn't understand how hard it is for me to back away from bacon. With a silent glare, she points her finger. I high-step my front paws and slide my back ones, reversing to where the kitchen meets the hall. Because when Mom gives me the finger along with the *Out* word, I must always go to the closest boundary, where one part of the den meets another. Sometimes these boundaries have doors, sometimes not. Sometimes there's a change of floor texture. Sometimes not. It could be confusing to a dog without a knower, especially this particular boundary where the kitchen meets the hall. It has nothing to identify it. No door. Same slick tiles, except for one that has a crooked crack running through it, marking the perfect spot to see almost every place in the den — the kitchen, the front door, the door to the little room with the big water bowl, and even part of the TeeVee room. Plus, if I turn my head as far as it will go, I can see the doorways to Jesse's room, Gran's room, and, way in the distance, Mom's room.

I flop down onto the tile with the crooked crack and wait until my humans sit down to eat. Then I sneak back into the kitchen.

Before Gran joined our pack, I would sit next to Jesse during feeding time. Occasionally, he'd drop a crumb or even sneak me something under the table, but if not, I still had the satisfaction of leaning against his leg. These days, in hopes of something more substantial to tide me over, I sit close to Gran because she spills more than Jesse. I'm poised, ready to gulp anything down before Mom says *LeaveIt* or *BadForDogs* — words that mean I must stay hungry.

The next opportunity for me to get a smidgen of sustenance is dishwasher-loading time. For some inexplicable reason, Mom doesn't appreciate my help. "*Sage! GetOuttaThere*," she yells, giving me the pointy finger.

Gran tries to help with the cleanup, too, but not by licking dishes — her tongue is way too short to do a good job. She uses her hands, snagging the plates with her knobbly fingers and magical thumbs, dropping them into the dishwasher, lickety-split.

My stumpy, fingerless paws are perfect for digging a hole in the backyard or uprooting one of Mom's freshly planted flowers. They're great for running and excellent for scratching an irritating itch, but they have severe limitations. Despite a lifetime of trying, they still can't turn a door handle. If I had hands, no door would imprison me! I'd be able to follow Jesse wherever he went, never forced to stay home alone. I'd be able to open the cupboard where my treats live, or pry the lid off my kibble in the pantry. I'd even be able to get meat out of *TheFridge*. I'd never be hungry ever again. Life would be perfect.

Mom's voice breaks into my fantasy. She's watching Gran put dishes into the dishwasher. Generally, Mom doesn't appreciate Gran's help any more than she does mine, but today it's different. She uses her high and happy tone. "Good job, Ma! You're such a good helper."

I wag my tail because it sounds like *GoodGirlSage! You're-SuchaGoodGirl*. Gran beams from ear to ear, then ambles away on her never-ending hunt for the bone she stashed away. Usually, I'd follow her on the hunt, but I stay in the kitchen, drooling onto my paws and looking at Mom with pitiful eyes because she hasn't fed me yet. She's busy rearranging everything in the dishwasher, but the plates are spotless by this time because when she wasn't looking, I'd licked them all squeaky clean.

"Gimme *dindins*," I yip.

She understands! Picking up my dish, she pours in the kibble. Then I hear the familiar scraping sound and I can barely contain my excitement — bacon grease in my *dindins*!

Sit — Stay — LeaveIt.

A fresh strand of drool hits my toes.

"YouCanHaveIt."

I wolf it down, licking every trace from the dish. I lick my nose to get the last smudges from there, too. Finally, I do a quick butt-lick, just to make sure no bacon taste has escaped. Not yet, but I'll check again later.

kayla

"Hi, Leesha, are you awake?"

"I am now! What's up?"

"Nothing much. I had quite a good day, for a change. I think I might be getting my head around this caregiving thing. I just wanted to hear your voice and let you know I emailed you a video of Ma. She's putting on her fleecy jacket all by herself. She's so independent and really doesn't want my help, but if there's a wrong way to do it, she will: inside out, back to front, upside down ... you name it. She can't even tell when it's wrong!"

"Hang on ... let me watch it while we're talking."

"You can do that?"

"I think so ... here we go ... oh dear, she's putting her feet in the armholes! She thinks her jacket is a pair of pants! She's pulling it up. Oh no, Ma, that's not gonna work. Your legs are bigger than your arms ... they won't fit."

"Keep watching. She's gonna make them fit!"

"Gosh, Kayla, she really has her mind set on pulling those sleeves up to her waist."

"Yeah, I thought she'd give up and realize something was wrong, but no!"

"Oh my goodness. She can't even walk! It's like her legs are in a straitjacket!"

"That's when I stopped videoing. I was concerned she'd topple over."

"Wow, Kayla, that was amazing. Sad but funny, too, and it gives me an insight into what you're dealing with."

"Oh, that's just a snippet! The whole process took fifteen minutes but I edited it down to two, because big videos won't send. Then it took me another ten minutes to extricate her … I thought I was gonna have to cut her out!"

Alicia laughs robustly, and I join her. It feels good.

"Honestly, if I hadn't been trying to video Ma surreptitiously, I'd have jumped in at the get-go and told her she was doing it wrong. I've got to stop doing that! Or I would have taken over and done it for her. I've got to stop doing that, too. It was a good lesson for me."

"It must be hard," Alicia says.

"Uh oh, she's calling me. She doesn't know where I am. Gotta go."

"You hang in there, sis."

mary

Kayla is irritated. I don't know what I did to upset her. She tries to be nice, but I can tell she's angry inside. She insists I write some more of my story. I tell her there is no story inside of me. I'm empty.

"Just write about how you feel today," she says, leaning over and typing. "I'll start you off … Today I feel …"

Today, I feel …

I take over.

Empty.
Stupid.
Helpless.

Usually Kayla makes me feel safe, but sometimes she gets impatient. I think it's because I don't understand what she tells me. When she asks me to fetch something, I panic because I know I'll forget what she asked, or I'll do it wrong and she'll get cross with me. I don't like it when she gets cross with me. She talks to me as if I'm deaf, or stupid. I feel scared, useless.

Kyla looks over my shoulder. "I'm so sorry. So sorry."

I don't know why she's sorry, but I enjoy her hug. It's warm and loving. And familiar.

"Let's sit on the couch and watch TV," she says. "I'll find us a new episode of *Judge Judy*."

She snuggles against me, her arm around my shoulder. I feel warm and cozy inside. Protected.

Suddenly, the screen is filled with angry white men, carrying flaming torches, shouting racist words.

My heart pounds against my ribs.

The men come at us out of nowhere. Six of them, maybe more. Shaved heads, steel-toed boots, faces twisted in hatred.

Two of them push me back and forth between them, like a rag doll.

Spit flying with their laughter.

Crooked front teeth.

Jabbing me in the chest.

"Wanna find out what it's like with a real man?"

Keith is fighting to help me. But they push him to the ground. They kick him ... over and over ... until he is still.

I scream. "Oh God. No!"

"It's just the news, Ma. I've turned it off!"

When I come to my senses, Kayla is holding me in her arms. "It's okay. You're safe. I'm here."

We are both crying.

kayla

Kayla: Ma just had a meltdown.

Alicia: What happened?

Kayla: Did you see those white supremacists
on the news? I think it triggered a flashback.
She was terrified! Literally trembling. And
sobbing her heart out. I've never seen
her like that.

Alicia: I'll phone you.

Kayla: No, she's right here. She'll hear me.

Alicia: Go to the garage.

Kayla: I don't want to leave her.
I made tea and she's drinking it.
I gave her a cookie.

Alicia: Does that help?

Kayla: Big time.

Alicia: So you think it's a flashback to when
Keith was killed? Ask her some questions.
Get her to tell you what happened.

Kayla: I can't ask her to describe something that terrified the shit out of her, especially now she's calming down. I can't put her through all that fear again.

Alicia: Good point. What can I do?

Kayla: Nothing! You're too far away!

Alicia: How about if I visit her on FaceTime? Maybe seeing me will distract her.

Kayla: Okay.

Alicia: I'm calling now.

mary

A pretty woman with long curly hair is here, waving and blowing me kisses. Her broad, bright smile is so familiar, yet I can't quite place it. No matter … I know I love her, and I know she loves me. She says she's Alicia on TimeFace. I tell her my daughter's name is Alicia, too.

I ask her if she wants tea, and I offer her a cookie from the packet — oatmeal chocolate chip. In her smile, I see my Alicia, and in her chuckle, I hear both my little girls. It makes me laugh, too. The woman doesn't take a cookie — she says she just ate. She wants to sit with me for a while and chat.

"I hear you're writing another book!" she says excitedly. "I can't wait to read it."

"How about we read it together," Kayla says. "Right now, over FaceTime. I can read your last chapter. It's about when you and Keith were at university.

> "We started hanging out with a group of mixed-race students: combinations of Syrian, Black, white, Indian, and Chinese. A rainbow of ethnicity and religion. One of the light-skinned boys pretended to be my boyfriend … to throw Dad off the scent. His name was Ian, or was it Howard? Maybe it was Ian Howard. And his real girlfriend was …"

"Anna-Mae," I chime in, the name coming to me in a flash, alongside a picture of a pretty girl with long, black hair. "It's been a while since we all got together." I grab the phone off the coffee table. "I'll phone them and arrange something."

"That's the TV remote," Kayla says. "And anyway, everyone is at work right now. I'll help you call this evening, after you've finished work, too."

The yard boy looks over my shoulder and talks to the TimeFace woman. "Hey there, Auntie Leesh, I thought I heard another voice."

"Hi, Jesse," she says. "How was school today?"

"Did I do a school visit today?" I ask the TimeFace woman. "I love talking to students! Afterward, they all line up so I can sign their books. It's always thrilling to see brand new copies of my books in the store, but the best books in the world are the grimy ones in the classrooms … dog-eared and ragged. It means they've been read by lots of kids."

"That must be very satisfying," the TimeFace woman says. "And now you are writing another book. It's about Keith and your friends, Ian and Anna-Mae. Kayla is reading us a chapter."

> "Ian's father is a diplomat. If truth be told, he's a bit full of himself, but he's a good friend. He phones the house and asks to speak to me, then he comes by to take me out. My parents think he's my boyfriend. They like him. Who wouldn't? He has a big personality, and he's well spoken. He has an expensive car and, best of all, he looks white, even though he's Syrian.
>
> "When we drive away, they wave at us from the veranda. Then as soon as we get around the corner, I stuff my hair into a curly black wig."

"What?" the TimeFace woman shrieks. "You wore a wig?"

I nod and run my fingers through my hair. "All this long blond hair attracts too much attention. I don't want anyone to recognize me and report back to Dad that I was with Keith. Dad has forbidden me to see him."

The TimeFace girl throws her head back and laughs. "You raised us three kids to never tell a lie! Now look at you! I'm proud of you, Ma ... Mary!"

"I'm not proud of me," I say. "It's deceitful. But Dad won't listen to reason. He won't give Keith a chance. He's stubborn and authoritative — and wrong. I'm equally stubborn and defiant — and right!"

"Shall I read some more?" Kayla asks.

"Yes, please!" the TimeFace woman says, her bubbly enthusiasm infectious.

"This part is about the first home that you and Keith bought in England.

> "It was listed as a cozy artisans' cottage, the artisans being brick-workers from eighteen-something, and 'cozy' meaning it was not much bigger than a doll's house, each room ten feet square. But it gave us peace of mind, knowing that a landlord wasn't going to throw us out on the street. The cottage was in a row of 'two-up, two-downs.' Its door opened straight from the street into the front room — no porch, no entrance lobby, no coat closet. I made a stuffed dachshund to block the draft that whistled under the door, and I stripped off the dated wallpaper — cream with golden ferns — and painted the walls white to give the illusion of more space.
>
> "The kitchen was a 'new' addition tacked onto the back around 1920, and despite its minuscule five feet by seven, it doubled as a bathroom, with a Victorian hipbath hidden under a removable kitchen counter."

As Kayla reads, I see Keith flattening himself against the gas stove in the kitchen so I can squeeze past. I feel him, smell him. Then he is gone.

"The toilet was *outside*, in a lean-to shelter. It had the original mahogany seat and a long pull chain from the overhead water tank. Spiders lived there. We would light a paraffin heater to stop the pipes from freezing. In the bedroom, condensation ran down the windowpanes, freezing into fern-like patterns that made a crystal wine glass look clumsy. On winter mornings, we leaped out from under the duvet and bolted down the steep staircase to the kitchen, warming up around the gas stove, making toast at the same time. For me, it wasn't that different from my early childhood, but for Keith, it must have been awful. He never complained, though."

"We were young and in love," I say, smiling.

"You were blessed to have had that," the curly-haired TimeFace woman says, wistfully. "Some people never find love."

"Love hurts when it ends," I tell her.

In the silence, Kayla sighs, then she puts on her bright and cheery voice. "Let's read some more."

"When the cottage walls closed in on us, we would take the footbridge across the race of the old watermill, climb over the style into the cow pasture, and hike up the steep slope of Box Hill."

"It sounds exactly like a place where Keith and I lived," I say.

Kayla hugs me. "I think it *is* that exact place! The story is about you and Keith. Listen.

"At the top of the hill, we would lie in the grass on the chalky hillside, our hearts pounding from the exertion. From there, we could spot our little house on the outskirts of Dorking. It looked like a toy village beneath us, complete with trains trundling along the tracks, whistles blowing."

As I listen to Kayla read the words on my laptop, a feeling of déjà-vu zaps me like an electric shock. I feel it right down to my toes.

"I'm sitting on a faded velvet seat in a non-smoking compartment of the British Rail train. As it pulls out of Dorking station, I watch Keith on the platform, waving. It's our morning routine; we walk to the station together, and after I board the train bound for London's Waterloo and my job at St. Thomas' Hospital, he goes down the steps and crosses under the track to platform three, to catch the Victoria train.

"This day, from the rear-facing seat, my eyes never leave him. The train gathers speed, he waves a final time, then turns to walk toward the steps. In that instant, knowledge hits me like a bolt of lightning: Keith is going to die. I crane my neck to keep him in my vision until the last possible moment. Then he is gone.

"Stunned, I stare out the window, my belly filled with dread and the edge of my vision filled with stars. For the first time in my life, I am truly afraid. Death is no longer something on the distant horizon, for the old or infirm. Death is real. It is coming for Keith, and the certainty of that knowledge steals my breath away. This isn't the plan! With decades of smiles etched into our wrinkled faces and hair turning silver, we'll grow old together. Then, and only then, will death come close.

"I tell myself that my imagination is working overtime. Keith is twenty-five, strong and healthy. All the same, sweat breaks out on the palms of my hands and pricks my skin like needles.

"More commuters board the train, men in business suits grasping the overhead rail, each in his own world, with paperbacks and newspapers and briefcases, all of them oblivious to my distress.

"I am surrounded by people, yet totally alone.

"In desperation, I pray to a God I have no real faith in. *Please, God, No! I can't live without him. Please don't take him away.*

"The green hills of the Surrey countryside fly by, replaced by suburban backyards: swings and slides and fish ponds. Through windows, I see kitchens and living rooms, faces and families. And then the gloom of the city. Everything seems normal. Yet my feelings of impending doom linger.

"I contemplate the possibilities. Will his train crash? Will he be hit by a car on the street? Or killed in a random act of violence?

"As the day goes by, I muddle through my work, telling myself that from a scientific perspective, a premonition happens when a confused brain tries to sort out an information overload. It is *not* a glimpse into the future. But keeping all my options open, I continue pleading with God, justifying Keith's life, explaining how much good the two of us could do in the world, showing bigots that mixed marriage is nothing to be afraid of. But all the while, my selfish heart is screaming that I don't want to be left alone. *Please, God, no.*

"My spirits don't lift until I walk through the door that evening and see Keith in the kitchen. I hug him tighter than usual, discreetly wiping tears of relief from my eyes. And I don't tell him anything about my premonition."

"That's as far as you got," Kayla says, her eyes damp with tears. The TimeFace lady is crying, too. I don't get why they are both being such crybabies.

sage

After *dindins*, Mom sits next to Gran on the couch, watching the moving pictures on *TeeVee*.

I stretch out on the floor, my chest against Mom's feet and my chin on Gran's, keeping one eye on the moving pictures — just in case a dog shows up to eat his *dindins* or to race around with his friends.

TeeVee speaks. "When people in power condone hate groups, even encourage them, it gives them permission to come out of the woodwork and integrate themselves into mainstream society. You can see it happening right now. We need to take a stand."

"Jesse," Mom says. "You need to watch this."

"What is it?" he asks, looking up from *iPhone*.

"A debate on racism."

"I'm too young to do anything about it, so what's the point?"

Mom's voice goes higher. "Young people can make a huge difference! Look at the Black Lives Matter movement. And look at the Civil Rights era. It was the young people who protested and were willing to fight for our basic rights! They changed life for all of us!"

Gran's scent changes but Mom doesn't notice — she's nose blind.

Suddenly, Gran yanks her fuzzy slippers out from under me, sending my head to the floor with a clunk. Standing on her two spindly legs, she wags her finger in Jesse's face.

"Look, young man, you've got to stand up for equality. Black people are as good as white people! You should know that. You might try to pass for white, keeping your curly hair cut short, but there's Negro blood in you for sure. Do you know that in the southern states, even a few drops means you can't be buried in the same cemetery as a white person? Do you know that mixed marriage is illegal? All over the world, white folks will lynch you, shoot you, and accuse you of things you never did ... to get you locked away. You need to take a stand, you hear me? *You* need to make the world a better place."

Gran's alpha act works. Jesse responds like a whipped puppy and stares at *TeeVee.* The pictures aren't moving fast enough to hold my interest, and there are no animals, so I close my eyes and rest ... until a dog barks. I reply with a friendly woof, but he ignores me — he's too busy chowing down on *dindins.* Before I get close enough to catch the scent, both the dog and his *dindins* disappear into darkness.

Mom tries to shoo Cat and me into the cold night air. Cat sits on the mat in front of the open door, blocking my way, his tail waving, which in cat-talk means he's not happy. Then he turns and hisses at Mom, obviously telling her he'd rather stay inside and use his litter box because it's cold enough outside to freeze off his non-existent balls. Mom doesn't get it. She gives his rear end a firm tap with her toe and he flies out the door, leaping onto the fence in a single bound, then stalking along the top.

Down below, I follow him through the gloom at a more leisurely pace, sniffing out the perfect spot to relieve myself while feeling a twinge of envy for Cat's athletic abilities. Happily engrossed, mid-poop, I watch him jump down, defecate in the snow, then quickly bury it with two scrapes of his front paws. This is always a mystery for me. He's proud and haughty in so many ways, yet when it comes to poop, he's compelled to hide it. I never make any attempt to hide mine. I leave it there for Mom to gather and keep in her special bag. She grumbles when she does this, but secretly, I think she enjoys it. Why else would she keep it for herself?

All pooped out, I investigate Cat's steamy turd.

"*LeaveIt!*" Mom orders sternly — proof she wants it for herself! I do as I'm told. I don't much like the taste of fresh cat poop, anyway. I prefer it when it's frozen or air-dried with the crunchy coating from the litter box.

"Hurry up, both of you," Mom says, shivering in the doorway.

Cat dives between her legs and races for the comfort of Gran's bed. I dawdle in behind him, ambling along to Jesse's room, but the door is closed. Mom goes to her room, too, shutting the door behind her. I'm alone! Not the good type of alone, when I can enjoy a quiet lick of my intimate parts without Jesse acting disgusted and telling me to stop licking my hoo-hoo. I mean, *lonely*-alone. Lonely-alone is *not* a good feeling. It's a hollow, relentless ache inside, one to be avoided at all costs.

Gran's door is open a crack. I nudge it with my muzzle and creep in on silent pads. *YeeHaw* is sleeping. That's good. But Cat is making circles on Gran's bed. That's bad. I wait, a safe distance away, while he treads the bedding, checking for snakes or poisonous spiders, his retractable claws opening and closing in a clever way that mine can't.

I wait until he curls up by Gran's feet, then I settle down on the mat at the side of the bed and close my eyes. Gran is sleeping fitfully, faint moans coming from her throat as if she's having a bad dream, but the Wild Ones are calling me and I lope away to join them.

A high-pitched scream startles me. I jerk back to the mat at the side of Gran's bed, Cat whooshing over my head like a startled jackrabbit. My instinct is to follow him as he rockets down the hall, but Gran needs me — she's terrified. I move closer, to let her know I've got her back. Too close. She whacks me on the nose. I reverse, colliding with Jesse and Mom.

With eyes open wide, Gran looks right at Jesse. "*OhGod*, I thought you were dead!"

"It's okay," Mom says. "You're safe, now. And Jesse is safe. You were dreaming, that's all."

"I was not dreaming," Gran says, grabbing Jesse's head and groping through his hair like she's searching for fleas. "It was real! You were bleeding from your ear ... right here."

Jesse pushes her hands away and backs out of range.

"I saw you on the ground, Keith! You were out cold. And they were still kicking you with their steel-toed boots. You were hurt, really hurt!"

Mom's hand is covering her gaping mouth. She doesn't seem to know what to do, so I nuzzle Gran's hand until she grabs on to the thick fur around my neck. I wait, motionless as her breathing slows and her grip on my neck loosens. The tension leaves her. Soon, her eyes droop in sleep.

Mom strokes me tenderly. "You are something else, *Sage*! *Let'sGoToBed*."

I take a step, then hesitate and turn back to Gran, easing myself down beside her bed. She might need me. Closing my eyes, I wait for the Wild Ones to appear, or even the squirrels, but they don't come. I hear Mom and Jesse go to the kitchen. A midnight snack! Irresistible.

"Hey, *Sage*, you couldn't sleep, either?" Mom says, offering me a piece of cold pizza crust. "That was upsetting, wasn't it?"

"How could she possibly think I was Keith?" Jesse says. "He'd be ancient by now — like seventy-five."

"For starters, she was disoriented and confused — she'd just woken up from a terrifying nightmare. But when people die young, they don't grow old in our minds — they stay the same age forever, so even if Gran didn't have Alzheimer's, she'd probably still remember Keith as a young man, not a senior citizen. And you look a lot like he did when he was sixteen, so it makes sense. I have a photo hidden away in my bedroom. Wanna see it?"

"Sure, but why's it hidden?"

"Mom didn't let us have photos of him around the house ... guess she wanted to forget and move on. I kept one tucked away out of sight. As far as I know, it's the only one of him."

I follow them down the hall to Mom's room, stopping with my front feet obediently placed on the no-go line.

Mom reaches up high and hands Jesse something.

His mouth drops open. "Wow! He was a real person! I never thought of him that way. It makes me feel like we're connected. I can actually see myself in him! That's so strange. If I Photoshopped it to lighten the colour ..."

"Yeah, he was darker than you, but other than that, you are two peas in a pod. Same face shape. Same body shape — lean and muscular. And the smile!"

"The other day Gran said I should smile more often because I have a beautiful smile and it reminded her of Keith. But she also said he was much nicer than me. That's the first thing anyone ever told me about him. It's kinda cool. What do you know about him, Mom?"

"Nothing. He died before I was born."

"But didn't Gran tell you anything? Didn't you ask?"

"I grew up knowing not to ask. It was like he didn't exist. She wouldn't talk about him, or about what happened, or how he died, none of it."

"Why not?"

"Sometimes, when terrible things happen, we block it out."

Jesse inhales sharply. "You think he was killed? Like in her nightmare?"

Mom shrugs. "I always assumed it was a hate crime. I have no proof ... it's just something I feel in my gut. Interracial marriage was taboo in those days. But whatever happened, Ma blocked it out of her life. And mine."

"You mean she pretended it never happened?"

"I think it's nature's way of enabling us to survive something traumatic. The only thing I know for sure is that I grew up without a father."

I hear Jesse's words crack in his throat. "I grew up without a father, too."

Mom reaches out and touches his arm. "I'm sorry, Jess."

I can tell Mom wants to snuggle into him as she does with me sometimes, but he turns away from her.

She hands him another picture. "This is Ma. Isn't she gorgeous? I think it's when she was a teenager in Trinidad."

"No way!" Jesse shrieks. "Getting old sucks!"

kayla

Crap! Where's the invite for the Zoom call? I'm late! Zach sent me the link in an email so I just need to search my inbox ... here we go ... join meeting. Damn! Why is the internet so slow tonight?

"Jesse! Are you watching Netflix? Can you stop for a few minutes?"

Finally, Alicia and Zach pop up on the screen. They are both smiling. I know that my news will soon wipe the smiles off their faces.

"I'm taking Ma off the Alzheimer's meds."

"Why?" asks Zach.

"The first one upset her stomach. She was so worried about not making it to the bathroom in time that she'd sit on the toilet for hours, then rush back within a few minutes of leaving, forgetting that she'd just been! Now the second one is giving her really bad nightmares."

"Oh no, that must be awful," Alicia says. "But are you sure it's the medication, and not advancing dementia? Hallucinations are par for the course, right? They might play out in her sleep, too."

"The doctor says medication can worsen flashbacks and cause bad dreams."

The screen freezes. Crap! I don't have time for this!

"So, are we out of options?" Alicia asks when the service resumes.

"I think so."

"Let's try CBD oil," Zach says.

"*Weed?*" Alicia exclaims. "I know you live on the West Coast and all, but weed? For our mother?"

"Pure CBD oil doesn't make you high," Zach replies. "It's THC that does that. I've been reading up on it. CBD can calm agitation in Alzheimer's and Parkinson's patients. Maybe it will help Ma sleep."

"Yeah, she'll be stoned!" I say.

Alicia giggles. "And chowing down on pizza."

Zach ignores her. "I'll order some and have it delivered to you."

Alicia is fast to respond. "Pizza or weed? You can't have one without the other!"

"I'm serious," Zach says. "If it doesn't work for Ma, you can try it yourself, Kayla. In fact, maybe I should just order a bottle for you, too."

"None for me, thanks. I need to keep my mind clear to deal with all this."

mary

I'm getting dressed. The woman sighs, tuts, laughs, and even cries a little. Her emotions are all over the place. I know that I know her. Her name is on the tip of my tongue, but it won't come to me. It's frustrating. Finally, she approves of what I'm wearing and insists that it's time to start work on the computer. I tell her I want to watch *Judge Judy* on TV, but she says I must do my work first. Sometimes she is so bossy.

She makes me sit at the kitchen table in front of my open laptop, but she can't make me write. She can't make the words come. Through the window I see a young man working in the yard. He gets off the mower and aims a ball at the hoop on the garage wall. The woman calls him Jesse. The only Jesse I know is a baby. I don't know this Jesse. She says he's my grandson. He's not. If I had a grandson, I'd know about it for sure. The young man looks strangely like Keith, but lighter skinned. Plus, he's impatient, so he's not like Keith at all. But when he smiles, he lights up my heart. The harder I try to make sense of it, the more my brain freezes.

I twirl the ring on my finger, waiting for thoughts to come — thoughts I can convert to symbols on the screen.

Waiting.

Waiting.

The ring is loose, yet it won't slide over my knuckle.

"Write about our wedding," Keith says.

I see him waiting for me at the altar — strikingly handsome in a dark suit, a white carnation in his buttonhole.

I feel the hope of that day, the dream of a future together. But then I'm walking toward a rough-sawn box, covered with a royal-blue altar cloth, topped by four blood-red rosebuds.

I type aggressively, trampling the emotion with every stomp on the keyboard.

> Keith didn't get down on bended knee and ask me to marry him. We both had a hippie mentality about the traditions of our parents' generation. But when we talked about it, we discovered that it was something we both really wanted to do. I would have been happy popping into the closest registry office, but Keith wanted to be married in church, under the eyes of God. He wanted us to have God's blessing.
>
> I bought yards of oyster satin from a street market in London's Petticoat Lane, borrowed a sewing machine, and made a wedding dress.
>
> I walked up the aisle alone — nobody gave me away.
>
> Mummy and Daddy didn't come.
>
> They had already given me away years earlier.
>
> Mummy and Daddy didn't come — that's all I remember.

"I remember," Keith says. "You were beautiful! You still are."

Our conversation is cut short by the woman.

"Tell me why you and Keith left Trinidad," she asks. "Why did you go to live in rainy old England and then snowy Canada? A tropical island sounds much more appealing."

The woman's questions get tangled in my brain. I look at her blankly.

"Why did you and Keith go to live in England?" she asks.

I tell her that Keith was offered a job there, right out of university. He was so bright! A shining star.

Keith smiles in recognition of my praise. I smile back, feeling the warmth of his love.

"What kind of job?" the woman asks.

I don't know what she's talking about. I hate it when this happens. It makes me feel so stupid.

"Keith's job … in England," she says. "What was it?"

I tell her that Keith was a systems analyst. I never understood what that was — something to do with computers. They were transitioning from massive beasts that filled an entire room to much smaller machines the size of a fridge, which were programmed by holes punched in cards. I didn't understand that, either, but Keith did and he said they were poised to change the world.

The woman prompts me with another question. "What about you? Did you get a job in England, too?"

"Yes, in the Virology Research Department at St. Thomas' — a big teaching hospital in London."

"That's quite a leap from agriculture."

I shrug. "I had a solid background in science. Then I moved to an antiviral research project at a large pharmaceutical company. My team did the early research work on interferon, a possible cure for virus infections."

"Wow, Ma, you were a research scientist! I never knew! There's so much I don't know. When did you get married?"

"Soon after getting to England. Keith's parents came up from Trinidad for the wedding, but mine didn't."

"Oh my gosh, why not? Were they still living in Trinidad?"

"Yes, but that was no excuse. They flew all over the world. They could have come, but they didn't. My father told me not to marry Keith, and I did. So that was that."

Tears start to prick my eyes. I fight them by slamming the laptop shut, but it won't slam with the satisfying noise of a door, so I get up and find a real door to slam. Then another, and another.

The woman tries to calm me, showing me a book with numbers and squares. It looks familiar, but I don't understand what I'm supposed to do. It's senseless to me. I feel bad for not understanding, so I scribble the pencil across the page as hard as I can. The woman turns and walks away from me.

I want to call her back and say I'm sorry that I upset her, but I can't remember her name. "Stop," I shout.

She turns and looks at me, an inquiring expression on her face. She's beautiful, although she looks tired. She reminds me of someone I once knew, but I don't know who.

"Yes?" she asks. "What do you want?"

"I don't know."

She comes back and hugs me.

That's what I wanted.

sage

As darkness creeps into the den, Gran gets restless, heading to the front door and rattling the handle. "It's time to go home." she wails. "Home before dark, that's the rule. Mummy will worry if I'm not home before dark."

Jesse and Mom try to calm her, but she's determined to escape. Over and over they lead her back to the kitchen. And over and over Gran says the same long word: Mummy-will-worry-if-I'm-not-home-before-dark.

"Your mummy can't worry," Jesse snorts. "She's dead."

Gran's face crumples. "Dead? Mummy's dead?"

Mom glares at him.

"Sorry," he whispers. "I forgot!"

"Your mummy's not dead," Mom says. "I saw her this morning, and she said, 'You take care of Mary tonight! You give her supper.'"

Gran's face lights up. "What are we having? Coconut cake? I love coconut cake."

"I don't know how to make coconut cake. I've never made it in my life!"

"That's not so, Hettie! You made it for me all the time. It was my favourite, remember?"

Mom makes a face as if she's screaming, although no sound comes out. Then she takes a breath. "You've got things muddled! How could I have made coconut cake for you when you were little — I'm thirty years younger than you!"

Snapping a banana off the bunch, she hands it to Gran, who launches into song. "A beautiful bunch of ripe banana / Daylight come and me wanna go home."

Instead of joining in, which would have put everyone back in a good mood, Mom stomps off to her bedroom, my hope for *din-dins* disappearing with her. Weak from lack of sustenance, I dither. Should I follow Mom, sidling up close to her so she can hear my groaning belly and hopefully save my life, or stay in the kitchen where the food lives.

Jesse gets my attention with a loud, "No!"

I don't know what I did wrong … phew! It's Gran in trouble, not me.

"Mary! Don't eat the peel!"

He tries to take the banana away from Gran, who's still singing, "Six-foot, seven-foot, eight-foot bunch! Daylight come and me wanna go home," but she won't let the banana go. The skin splits, and the goop oozes into her hand.

"Now you've made a big mess," he complains. "Give me the banana, Mary, and you can have a *Cookie*."

My ears prick up and I watch, hawk-eyed. Gran opens her hand and lets the banana fall to the floor. I'm not that fond of banana, but as I'm dying of starvation, I'm not picky. I swoop down, inhaling it, licking the floor clean, working my way toward Gran's sticky fingers, which are now also covered with *Cookie* crumbs. Jesse beats me to it, wiping her hands with a warm cloth.

In no time, Gran starts wailing again. "I want to go home. Home before dark — that's the rule. *Mummy-will-worry-if-I'm-not-home-before-dark.*"

Jesse sighs. "Your mummy says you're to stay here tonight."

"Are we having coconut cake?"

"Yes, we are!" Jesse says. "Right after eggs and bacon."

His laughter tickles my ears. Laughter is my favourite sound.

Then bacon aroma fills my nostrils. Sizzling bacon is my favourite sound, too.

After what feels like forever, I hear kibble landing in my dish and the sound of plates being scraped. I can barely contain my excitement — bacon in my *dindins*! Bacon in my *dindins*!

Jesse puts my dish on the floor, saying, "*Sit — Stay — LeaveIt.*" I keep my eyes riveted on the food, making sure it doesn't escape.

"*Okay! YouCanHaveIt!*"

My life is spared.

Later, he helps me into his bed, inviting me to snuggle against his legs. He seems to be in a better mood than usual, stroking me rhythmically and talking like he used to when he was shorter. "There's this girl. Her name's Ashley. She comes out to *Basketball* practices. I think she might like one of the players. It would be nice if it was me, but I doubt it. Sometimes I think she smiles right at me ... although she's a long way off, so I'm never sure. I smile back anyway."

I close my eyes and wander off to chase squirrels.

mary

The woman is trying to confuse me. She says her name is Kayla. Liar. It's Hettie! She shows me a story on my laptop. She reads parts of it. She says I wrote it. She tells me to write more, but I have nothing to write about.

"Please, Mary, just try."

"No!"

"How about if you write a cover blurb," the woman suggests. "I'll get you a cup of tea when you've done that."

"Done what?"

"Written a cover blurb. You used to do that all the time for books you were editing."

"But to write a blurb, I need to know what the story is about."

"It's about you and Keith — your life together."

"*You* write the blurb," I tell her. "*You* know the story."

"Me?" she says. "I don't know what happened because I wasn't alive for any of it, and you never told me! But I'll help you get started."

She types on my laptop, reading aloud as she goes.

COVER BLURB — Drafts

1. The tragic love story of a young interracial couple navigating their way through the racially charged sixties and seventies.

2. Love in the face of hate: the journey of a
   young Black man and a young white woman
   in the turbulent times of the Civil Rights era.

"Oooo, I like that one a lot! Okay, Mary. Your turn now."
I try to co-operate.

1. Keith W.D. Bowen — the love of my life.
   Gone. The End.

I feel a touch on my face as light as a butterfly's wing — the blue
morpho from Trinidad, as big as my outstretched hand. I wonder
if it's Keith stroking my cheek. I doubt it, but all the same, I melt
into his touch, soaking up his tenderness like parched earth soaks
up a gentle rain.

"Let's go to our happy place," he says, "to the cottage on
Holmwood Common. Do you remember the first time we saw it?
The muddy potholes in the lane? The stream where trees arched
overhead and hid the sky?"

The line between the past and the present blurs until they are
one. I type.

> The lane is damp and gloomy, but then at the top of the
> hill, there's a sunny clearing, with oaks and birches and
> bracken, and footpaths radiating out through hundreds
> of acres of National Trust Land. A solitary red-brick cot-
> tage sits in the clearing. Never in a million years did we
> think we'd be able to buy such a perfect place. A little
> part of heaven.
>
> As with our first home, this cottage lacks modern
> amenities, but with nature on our doorstep, we consid-
> er ourselves the luckiest people alive. We put on rub-
> ber boots and tramp the footpaths, our feet feeling the

springy turf of summer, the hard frost of winter and the soft mud of all seasons.

I take the seasons for granted, but Keith has lived his life in a land where there are no changes in the length of the day or the temperature. He sees the English seasons with fresh eyes, paralleling them with the seasons of life: the birth and freshness of spring, the growth of summer, the maturity of autumn, and the death of winter. We are in early summer. Winter is a long way off.

Alicia and Zach are both born when we live in that house. I see Keith dancing in the living room with newborn Alicia in his arms, singing along with Stevie Wonder: "Isn't She Lovely?" His movements are fluid and there is so much love in his eyes, so much joy in his heart. In the back garden, I see Zach riding on his daddy's shoulders, squealing with delight. And Alicia picking daisies from the lawn, the sun transforming her curls into a halo of gold.

I remember our last night in the cottage, sleeping on the floor, on a mattress that was going to be trashed the next morning, Alicia and Zach sandwiched between us. All four of us entwined. I wish I could have stopped time. I loved our life there, and I worried that we'd never be that happy again. But Keith was thinking of the future, of a safer place where our children would have the chance to reach their full potential. He didn't want them living in fear. He didn't want them to be held back by skin colour. He was so excited about Canada, so optimistic, that I couldn't bring myself to tell him I was scared. I trusted him, though. I always trusted him. I felt safe with him. He was my rock. My compass. I knew he'd never let me down.

But then he died. And I never was that happy ever again ...

I want to cry, but the tears don't come.

I want to go home, back to Holmwood. To the sunlit clearing in the English woodland. To Keith and the children. To who I was then. But I can't find my car keys. Maybe I can walk. I feel young inside, but walking is an effort.

My shoulders slump.

My skin sags like it's too big for me.

Did someone switch bodies on me?

If I could find my way back home, everything would be all right.

If I could just find my keys.

Hettie brings tea and cookies. What a nice surprise.

sage

Mom has gone to yoga, so I'm looking after Gran. She's moving restlessly around the den, in and out of rooms in her endless hunt for something. I follow her, letting her know she's not alone.

Jesse is at his desk in the bedroom, playing with *Mac*. He's as obsessed with *Mac* as I am with *FloppyBunny* and *Mouse*, but *Mac* confuses me. He's a shape-shifter, with lots of different voices. Sometimes he's a dog, but when I touch my nose to his in a friendly greeting, energy cracks like lightning, giving me a painful buzz.

Mac's loud ring startles us all, especially Gran. "What's that?" she says with alarm.

"It's Ashley!" Jesse says, his scent bursting with excitement.

"Ring-ring," says *Mac*.

"What's that?" says Gran.

"Crap! I look a mess!" says Jesse. "She's never Skyped me before! She's never even spoken to me before!"

"Ring-ring."

"What's that?"

Jesse swipes both hands over his head in a quick grooming motion, pastes on a smile, and taps the screen. "Hi Ashley!"

Mac speaks in the voice of a female upright. "Hi Jesse! I saw you were online, so I thought I'd just say hi."

Gran has picked up the home phone and is yelling down the receiver, "Hello! Hello! Hello!"

"Hang up!" Jesse says.

"Excuse me?" the female voice says.

"No, not you, Ashley. One sec, please."

Leaving *Mac* on the desk, Jesse snatches the phone from Gran and hangs it up, muttering, "For crying out loud!" Then, returning to *Mac*, he puts the smile back on his face. "Sorry about that."

"It's okay," she says. "Looks like I caught you at a bad time. I'll talk to you later."

"No, wait," he says, with both urgency and pleading in his voice.

Gran is now peering into the face of *Mac*. "Who's that?" she asks.

"Hi there," the female voice says.

Jesse laughs out loud. "Ashley, meet Gran. Gran, meet Ashley. Yeah ... this isn't such a good time for me. I'm babysitting my gran."

"Aww," the female drawls. "That's so sweet. I like it. I'll see you at practice then ... tomorrow. Bye."

Jesse strokes me and whispers into the fur of my neck. "Huh! I may have been wrong about wanting to hide Gran from everyone. Girls like boys with puppies. Seems they like boys with grannies, too!"

mary

I'm hungry but the woman tells me I already had oatmeal and rasp-
berries. I had no such thing! She also tells me that she's my Kayla.
She must think I'm stupid. She's *way* too old to be Kayla. She looks
familiar, though: brown-skinned, middle aged, curvy. But I can't
remember her name. Hettie, maybe?

She says she'll make me toast, but I want fish and chips —
wrapped in newspaper, with salt and vinegar. I close my eyes and
remember sitting on a park bench, eating fish and chips with
Keith … right from the newspaper. We are a million miles away
from eating shark-and-bake on the beach at Maracas, with the surf
crashing in. Or biting into chicken roti from the shop in San Juan.
Or slurping oysters from the shell at a food stall on the Savannah in
Port of Spain, while drinking coconut water from the shiny green
husk after the vendor deftly slices off the top with a single stroke
of his machete.

"The fish and chip shop isn't even open," the woman says. "It's
nine in the morning! Time to start work. Come, sit down here at
the kitchen table. Let's open up your laptop, and you can do some
writing while I get on with a few jobs?"

"I don't have anything to write about."

"I don't have fish and chips, either," she mumbles.

"Pardon me?"

"I was just saying I'll send Jesse up to the fish and chip shop
later, but in the meantime, write! You're logged in and ready to go."

I push the laptop away, saying I'm too tired to write.

"Okay. You talk and I'll type," she says, sitting next to me. "Let's talk about how you and Keith came to Canada. You said it was because Keith was looking for a safe place to live, but how did it happen?"

"We flew on a plane."

The woman chuckles. "I mean, did Keith have a job lined up in Ontario, or what?"

"Yes."

Keith had a big job: national support manager for a large computer company. It was a big deal for a Black man. I was so proud of him. He could have gone so far.

We bought a big house in Toronto. I must have gotten pregnant almost as soon as we moved in, so I wasn't at my best. I was so tired. And Keith had a lot of responsibility and was working long hours. One day, he came home from the office, shaken. He'd strayed out of his lane on the 401 and almost hit another car. He wondered if he had gone to sleep at the wheel. I told him he was still getting used to driving on the right side of the road, and the North American highways were much more intense than the narrow, winding streets of both England and Trinidad. All that was true. But a few days later, I saw him bounce into the bathroom door frame. I thought it was funny and asked if he'd been drinking. But when he scratched my new Honda — all the way down the side — walking past it with a screwdriver, I was furious with him for being so careless. It was my first-ever new car — still fresh from the showroom. Later, though, after Keith died, I treasured that scratch. I'd let my fingers graze over it and remember him.

"I don't want to talk about it anymore," I tell the woman.

"Okay," she says, poking things into my ears. "Let's listen to music on the MP3 player. It's a gift from the Alzheimer Society. They loaded it up with all your favourite songs."

"Wow!" I shout. "This is amazing. It's Otis Redding!"

I sing along … walking hand in hand with Keith. Ahead of us, on the dock at the end of the bay, two chairs beckon. Behind us, our footprints mark the damp sand. The sun is going down, the tide rolling away. Something bothers me, something I should have done. Something important.

Emotion surges up my throat like bile. "If I'd paid attention, you might still be alive," I whisper. "We might be sitting on that dock, watching the sunset."

"It wouldn't have changed a thing, my love," Keith tells me. "Nobody survives this. If you want to blame someone, blame me … I knew something was wrong and I hid it from you for as long as I could. For too long. Because by the time we had a diagnosis, I couldn't speak. I couldn't kiss you or squeeze your hand. I lost everything so quickly. I was never able to tell you goodbye. I never thanked you for being my wife, the love of my life, the mother of my children. That was the hardest part of all. And I knew you weren't ready to let me go. So I stayed as long as I could …"

The song in my ears changes. One of my favourites: Martha and the Vandellas, "Dancing in the Street."

"Fish and chips!" the woman calls out. "It's in the paper, just the way you like it."

"I'm not hungry."

"Oh for goodness' sake," she says, stomping away.

mary

The woman who looks after me says it's October 28th, almost Halloween. The date makes my stomach lurch, transporting me to a place and time I never wanted to revisit. Keith tells me that I need to write about it. I tell him it's too painful and that, anyway, writing is hard work these days. "Just try, Mary," he says. "I'll be here helping you."

> Kneeling at the altar rail in the chapel at the Toronto General, I'm doing what billions of people have done at times like this … negotiating with God, promising I'll do anything if He will just spare my beloved. I'm both impatient and reluctant to return to Keith's bedside. I hate leaving him alone; I want to be with him at the end. Yet I'm scared, too — scared of the future and of what death looks like.
>
> Getting a firm grasp on my emotions, I make the familiar elevator ride to the fourth floor. The door slides open and immediately, I hear Keith's loud and laboured breathing. He's had difficulty breathing for a month or more, but this is different. I race to his room and see the agony written on his face as he fights for every breath. It's unbearable.
>
> I rail at God. "Why aren't you doing something? Keith is your man! Why are you kicking him in the teeth when he's already down? What kind of betrayal is that. Oh, God, please make it stop."

A voice speaks inside me. "He's holding on for you, Mary!"

I know in my soul that it's true.

I tell my beautiful husband not to hold on any longer. I tell him to let go. That I'll be okay. The kids will be okay.

Slower breaths.

His eyes are open, looking into mine. Softening. The anguish has gone.

Death is at hand. I know it. He knows it, too. All I can do is shower his forehead with kisses and say three little words over and over. "I love you, I love you, I love you."

His eyes say it back to me.

And then there is silence.

And with it, peace.

***

As Keith deteriorated over the months, I took Alicia and Zach to the hospital once a week. I didn't want them growing up thinking that their daddy had walked away from them because he didn't love them enough. After his death, I bring them to the hospital one last time to say goodbye and to see with their own eyes that there is a difference between life and death.

The nurses have removed the tubes and straightened his limbs and closed his eyes. He looks as if he is sleeping peacefully. Alicia climbs up on the bed, the same way she always does, talking to him and showing him her latest drawing. I tell her that Keith can no longer see. Alicia says that his eyes are shut and she tries to pry them open. Then she taps his arm, trying to wake him. I say that he can no longer feel anything, either. She smacks him hard — really hard. I tell her that her daddy's spirit has left his body and gone to live with God … that he was too sick and in too much pain to stay with us … that he didn't want to leave us. I tell her that his spirit, the part of him we know and love, will never die.

Zach just wants to check out everything in the room. His fingers snag the sheet that covers his daddy's feet. We all see the cream-coloured card tied with string to his big toe — a number written in black ink.

"Wot dat?" he asks.

Alicia answers. "It's so God knows who he is when he gets to heaven."

A few hours later, when we leave the hospital, peace covers me like a warm blanket on a cold night. Is it denial? I don't think so. I think it's the peace that people talk about — the peace of God, which passes all understanding. Finally, after three months of anguish, my body, heart, and soul are at peace. As I close the door, a wealth of symbolism touches my heart. I'm walking into a new life — strangely, one filled with hope, one in which I am both mother and father to our children. I vow to do the best job I can.

Six months later, out of the blue, at suppertime, Zach says the words he was too young to say that last day at the hospital: "Daddy's not coming home for supper. He's dead."

kayla

After Ma is in bed, I read the latest chapter of her story, bawling my eyes out. As soon as I can see straight, I copy and paste it into an email for both Alicia and Zach.

Within half an hour, Alicia FaceTimes me. She's emotional but excited, too. "When I was reading, I remembered! I actually remembered the last time I saw my daddy. I was wearing a red-check dress with lace on the hem, and white sandals. I didn't take them off when I climbed onto his bed, even though I knew I should have. The sheets were crisp and white and had dark-blue writing on the top corner where they were folded back on his shoulder. I knew that it was very bad to write on sheets, and I wondered if someone would get in trouble. With hindsight, I know it was the name of the hospital."

Alicia laughs but her face looks as if she's ready to cry. "I thought he was sleeping. I talked to him, but he didn't wake up. I showed him my drawing — he always liked to see my pictures, but he didn't open his eyes." Alicia's voice quakes and she struggles to continue. "He wouldn't wake up! He wouldn't wake up!"

My sister's face crumples. I want to rush to her and wrap her in my arms. But there are twelve thousand kilometres between us. She sobs. I sob, too. Two little girls who have lost their daddy.

mary

The woman brings me a cup of tea. I sip it, watching maple leaves drift past the kitchen window. They flutter against a backdrop of a bright blue sky, taking me back to the crematorium chapel … to the day of Keith's funeral.

Despite death hovering close by, the weather on October 30th has the audacity to be perfect. Bright blue sky without a cloud in sight.

Red and gold leaves trembling in the gentle breeze.

Rustling.

Fluttering.

But ever since that day, autumn leaves have been synonymous with death.

Darkness.

Depression.

Approaching winter.

They say winter is a time for plants to recharge and prepare to burst forth again with the glorious freshness of spring, but I see only winter's hardship, the animals that must struggle for food and shelter. Life is cruel and harsh. And then we die.

The feeling of peace I had felt the day Keith died is gone. Hope is gone, too, and from what I can tell, so is God. I am alone, with no one to help me.

In the gloom of my mind, Keith speaks to me. "Death is not the end, my love. Like the flowers, we come back!"

"You were always so full of crap!" I tell him.

He laughs.

"But the day *after* the funeral was even worse," I say.

Keith seems surprised. "How come?"

"You don't know?"

"I was busy for a few days around that time. Tell me what happened."

> On October 31st, I had to pick up your cremains from the funeral home. Your parents were flying back to Trinidad the next day, and I wanted them to take your ashes to scatter in our Wednesday afternoon ocean ... where vervet monkeys play ... where grey pelicans hunt flying fish ... where diamonds sparkled in your hair ... where we fell in love ...

So much was taken from me. From us.

"Write it down for the children," Keith says.

> I drive to the funeral home in my little green Honda with the scratch down the side.
>
> I am intending to just pop in and collect the ashes, a small task after everything I have been through: the final one ... and then it will be over.
>
> I leave Zach and Alicia in their kiddy-seats in the car and go inside.
>
> The funeral director hands me a rectangular parcel wrapped in brown paper. There's a shipping label for Customs.
>
> I'm not prepared.
>
> I hadn't anticipated a brown paper parcel ready for international mail.

It's the size of a shoebox, and when I take it in my hands, it is heavy.

This is all that remains of you.

I'm about to vomit or faint or both. I sit down, my head between my knees, your box of ashes traded for a sick bag like the ones on airplanes. I'm reeling with the horror of a finite end.

That's when I hear the wailing: a gut-wrenching sound coming from a part of me so deep I didn't know it existed, a sound that ushers in a season of total hopelessness.

Suddenly I remember that Alicia and Zach are still in the car. Alone. I pull myself together and with your ashes in hand, I rush outside.

The children are excited about the parcel. Alicia, the only one with a vocabulary, is spokesperson. "What's in the box?"

"I don't know. It's not for us." It's the first time I've lied to them.

"Who's it for?"

"Your grandparents. We're just dropping it off to them."

"Can we open it to peek inside?"

"No, we can't."

I put the box on the front passenger seat, wrap the seat belt around it, and head to Pickering, driving on the same road we had test-driven the Honda just a few months earlier. You had always been the driver, but this car was going to be mine, so I drove it that day. You were in the passenger seat, and Alicia and Zach were in kiddy-seats in the back. Now, here we are, together again in the little green car, in the same seats, on the same road. But how different things are.

I hand your ashes to your parents, almost on the run, determined not to let emotion rear its ugly head again, getting the hell out of there as fast as possible, as if speed is going to solve my problems. I don't wait to witness their shock or grief. I can't even deal with my own grief, let alone theirs. With hindsight, I regret this. I have lost a husband, the love of my life and the father of my children. They have lost a son. Their grief is no less than mine. We should have grieved together.

With a sense that my mission is accomplished, I hurtle home to trick-or-treat with the children, moving at a frantic pace that becomes the story of my life, doing everything I can to outrun the horrendous emotions of that day.

Weary from the effort of typing, I sit back and close my eyes, but my mind won't go still, so I keep writing.

During the months that Keith was in the hospital, our subdivision transformed from a muddy construction site to a finished neighbourhood with sod and sidewalks and trees. Now, on October 31st, the streets are humming with excitement: groups of fathers stroll down the middle of the quiet square; mothers on the sidewalk keep a watchful eye on children who run from door to door.

Alicia is wearing a bear costume and Zach is a bunny with floppy ears. They both carry plastic pails shaped like pumpkins. I can see them in my mind's eye, looking so adorable, so innocent. But I can't remember who gave us the costumes or the plastic pumpkins. It must have been one of the new neighbours — such a wonderful gesture.

Several people ask me about Keith. They never met him. They know our tragic tale only through the neighbourhood grapevine.

He died, I tell them, matter of factly. Trick-or-treat, the children sing, eyes wide, candy pouring into their pails.

sage

It's dark in the den. I don't care about that. I see quite well in the dark, plus I can sense things with my whiskers. I'm more concerned that Mom isn't in the kitchen, the way she always is at this time of day. Instead, she and Gran are sitting in the gloomy family room, like they're hiding. My tummy rumbles. I need *dindins*!

Jesse gets my leash and says *Walkies*. I jump up, the hunger pangs vanishing at the anticipation of patrolling my territory with Jesse. I surge out the door to the street. Lots of short ones are there, going to all the doors of all the dens. They want to talk to me and pat me. I love short ones, but most of these are way too excited for my liking. They can't stand still for even a heartbeat. All the same, when they scamper off, I want to follow them. Jesse won't let me.

"They're high on candy," he says. "Can you imagine all these kids ringing our doorbell and saying 'trick-or-treat'? Gran would be terrified! Good call that Mom decided to light candles and hide out at the back of the house."

Suddenly, his scent changes and his knees start to tremble. I follow his gaze to a group of uprights. I'm sure he wants to race over to them and have a good, hard sniff, but something holds him back. Maybe it's his legs — they aren't working! He's shifting his weight from one foot to the other, as if he might fall over.

One of the uprights bursts away from the group and runs toward us. "Hey, Jesse," she says. "You've got a dog! What's his name?"

"Sage! He's a she. A golden retriever."

"You're so lucky. I love dogs, but we can't have one. My dad's allergic. Can I share yours?"

"Sure! I'm gonna take her for a walk tomorrow. You can come, if you like."

"That would be cool," she says, darting away. "See you tomorrow."

Jesse stares after her. "Wow," he says, reaching down to scratch my back. "That was easy! Ashley likes you! You're the best, *Sage*!"

When we get home, there's still no *dindins*. Everyone else is eating but when I beg for some, they say, "Chocolate-can-kill-dogs," as if I am supposed to understand what that means.

I follow Jesse to bed and soon drift away to play with the Wild Ones.

"Stop watching me," Gran howls, waking me from sleep.

I ease myself off Jesse's bed and follow her voice to the little room with the big water bowl.

Jesse stumbles in after me. "What's going on?"

"Stop watching me," Gran sobs.

"What the heck is your problem?" he says. "If you don't want us watching you, just shut the bathroom door."

Mom staggers in, rubbing her eyes, but quickly comes to her senses and assumes the top-dog role.

"Quick, Jesse, get some push-pins or something!"

"What? Why?"

"To fasten this towel over the mirror. Get the pins — we'll talk later. And Sage ... get *Out*! There's not enough room in here for all of us."

In no time, Gran stops wailing.

"Why did I let you eat chocolate last night?" Mom says.

"I love chocolate," Gran says. "It's my favourite."

"Mine too, Mary, but it's got too much caffeine and too much sugar. Let's get you back to bed."

Jesse strokes me slowly and firmly and talks as we snuggle down together. "I can't imagine what it's like to have your brain waste away so you don't even recognize your own reflection. When Gran first came to live here, she got on my nerves big time, but these days … when I see the look on her face, or the expression in her eyes, it makes me feel sad. I'm gonna be nicer to her from now on. I really am."

For a while he's quiet, but then he turns over again, yanks the covers from under me and thumps the pillow as if he wants to kill it. "Crap! Ashley makes me so nervous. I can't act cool around her, no matter how hard I try. I fall over my words, and my feet!"

He throws his arm over my shoulder, and eventually I feel him slipping away.

sage

When Jesse wakes, he's even more anxious. "What a weird dream," he says, rubbing his eyes. "I've never even met Ashley's dad, but I know it was him. He just looked at me and said in this Southern red-neck voice, 'Where d'you get those curls, boy?'"

He leaps out of bed, knocking me under the chin, calling for Mom in a panicked voice. "Can you give me a haircut?"

Mom clutches her chest. "I thought there was an emergency."

"There *is* an emergency! I need a haircut."

Mom reaches out to stroke Jesse's head, like she often strokes mine. "Aw, no! Your curls are lovely. After you have a shower, just crunch them and they'll go into little ringlets, like when you were little."

Jesse pulls away from her. "Stop it! Give me a trim, just a quick one."

"What time are you meeting Ashley?"

"Eleven."

"There's no time. I haven't made Gran's breakfast yet, and she's not even dressed. Go with the curls; they're cute."

I can tell that Jesse wants to stomp his feet and shriek, like he did when he was short, when he wanted a *Cookie* and Mom said no. But he doesn't. He flops onto his bed, rolling his eyeballs up and away until the whites look enormous. Then he charges into the room where the rain falls. I try to follow him, but he yells, "*Out!*" and closes the door, leaving me with nothing to do than pull his dirty shorts from the basket and lick them.

When he reappears, all his good smells are gone, replaced with soapy ones that make my eyes burn. He puts on clothes ... then takes them off and puts on others. Sensing that he's going out, I prick my ears and try to make eye contact, clearly telling him that I want to go, too. But he won't look at me. Instead, he thrusts his chin forward and talks to the shadowy upright on the wall. "Hi, Ashley, it's good to see you."

He changes position and smiles. "Hey, Ash, what's up?"

Then he opens his mouth and grins widely. "You're looking fine, girl."

The grin vanishes from his face. "I don't know what I'm doing, *Sage*. You're gonna have to help me out, big time."

I nuzzle his hand, but he pushes me away. "I don't want to smell like dog."

When he puts on shoes, I know for sure that he's leaving the den, so I stare at my leash, willing him to take me with him. My message gets through!

"*Sage! Let'sGo.* We're gonna meet Ashley."

We're at the front door when Mom reaches out and touches his arm.

"Jess, you've got to be careful, especially with Ashley. Promise me. Don't provoke anyone."

"Okay," Jesse says. "But where's this coming from?"

"There's a lot in the news these days about hate groups ... Proud Boys, white supremacists, the alt-right, neo-Nazis, the KKK. Different names, same xenophobia."

"Mom, this is Canada!"

"Hate crimes are on the rise here, too! It's a fact. And those are just the ones reported to the police — most go unreported. Do you know that Proud Boys was started by a Canadian? And look at the treatment of Indigenous people ... and Chinese people! It goes back centuries. We are not immune in Canada! Just be aware, that's all. And remember your phone is a great tool."

Jesse laughs. "You mean I should hit them with it?"

"No!"

"Don't worry, Mom. I know what you mean. I gotta go. Ashley's gonna be waiting for us."

Trotting at Jesse's side, I feel the cold breeze in my fur and inhale the occasional scent of wood smoke from a chimney. We reach the place where I'm supposed to sit on the edge of the sidewalk. As always, I park my butt on the cold ground and wait for Jesse to pause, look both ways and say, *Okay!YouCanCross*. But Jesse keeps right on walking. I hustle to catch up.

At the next crossroads, I turn my head toward *ThePark*, but Jesse pulls the leash in a different direction, taking me outside my territory. My nose picks up new aromas. I want to stop and sniff them more thoroughly, but Jesse's in a big hurry, his scent and energy level telling me he's excited but anxious at the same time.

Suddenly, his scent thickens into an aromatic soup. I follow his gaze toward the upright we met on the night of the excited short ones. She rushes toward us, patting my head enthusiastically and making friendly noises.

I respond by moving in for an introductory sniff between her legs, where all uprights keep their special aromas, but Jesse pulls me away, reminding me that uprights don't like to be greeted this way. I've never understood why they have their best-smelling parts at nose level if they don't want me to sniff there, but I never give up trying.

We walk ... and stop ... and walk ... and stop. Both Jesse and the other upright ignore me, so I sniff around to my heart's content — not at the two-legged one, though. Jesse yanks my leash as soon as I try that.

We stop in sniffing range of a fire hydrant. It has so many different aromas that my senses go into overload. Since we seem to be paused here for a while, I begin to unravel the layers of scent peed onto this small space. As always, I search for the smell of my mother. Even after a lifetime of separation, I have no doubt that I would recognize her scent of milk and damp meadow hay, with an occasional stab of sharp thistle.

A fresh, intimidating fragrance high up on the hydrant belongs to a stranger. It makes the hair on my back bristle. I snort, blowing the comforting smells of friends to my nostrils, along with new, scary ones. I sort them out, savouring each one: *KingDoberman* tried to mask the stranger's scent with his own; *MitzyTheSharpei* had fish again for last night's dinner. There's no trace of her waste — her uprights must have collected it for themselves — but the wrinkly dog wiped her butt along the ground, leaving a robust fishy scent in her wake.

The smell of yet another dog gets my attention: young and healthy with copulation on her mind. I'm at a complete loss to understand this frantic urge. I don't like it when other dogs try to jump me, or hump my head, although doggy etiquette dictates that I return the favour.

Alas, my mother's scent is not to be found, so I squat, covering the copulating smell with a few dribbles of my own. Then I follow my nose to the next urine-soaked message, sprinkling that, too.

"What's she doing?" the female upright says, a disdainful frown on her face. "Does she have a bladder infection or something?"

Jesse laughs. "She's checking her pee-mail — leaving a post on Facebook and reading everyone else's posts."

The girl's eyes light up. "She's like me! Can't walk more than five steps without checking my messages!"

Unexpectedly, Jesse turns toward me. "*Sage! GimmeFive.*"

I slap his waiting hand with my paw. The girl grins and pats me on the top of my head. I don't much like having my head patted. It shakes up my knower and makes my eyes wobble. I prefer to be stroked or rubbed or scratched. Jesse knows this, but others often don't. I tolerate it because I'm *GoodGirlSage.*

She stops patting me and holds her hand out, saying, "Will you give me five, too?" I don't know what she means, but her hand is inviting, so I push my head under it, hoping for a scratch behind the ears. They both laugh. Joy bubbles up inside me.

"*Bang! You'reDead,*" Jesse says.

I know what he means, but it's going to take me a while to respond because I'm sore, and the ground is hard and cold. He gives me the command again — louder and firmer, as if I'm deaf. Reluctantly, I ease myself down and roll onto my side. I'm supposed to lie still, but I can't resist stretching my neck toward the fishy scent left by *MitzyTheSharpei*. This behaviour isn't generally allowed, but today, Jesse doesn't seem to care what I do. He even forgets to say *Up* when they start walking again, leaving me to scramble to all fours so quickly that it hurts. He's focused entirely on the upright and the words that fly from her mouth.

Eventually, the girl goes away. Jesse rubs the special spot between my front legs, the place I can't reach with either my claws or my teeth. "You were a big help today, *Sage*," he says. "Ashley loved you! *GoooodGiiiiirl.*"

It's the best sound he can make.

sage

I'm alone in the den. No Mom. No Jesse. No Gran. I stretch out on the mat by the front door and wait, keeping one eye on the dog called *Mirror*. She's a beautiful dog with a long, flowing coat, but despite appearing kind and friendly, she has a cold, hard nose that is decidedly unfriendly. I often sit in front of her anyway, just watching what she's doing.

When we first met, I bowed down and wagged my tail in a *Let'sPlay* greeting. *Mirror* did the same, saying that she, too, wanted to play, so I bounded forward to introduce myself. Unexpectedly, my back legs crashed into my front ones. Jesse laughed and said the word that always makes me feel embarrassed but happy at the same time — *You'reSuchaSillySage*.

Since then, I've learned that the best approach with *Mirror* is to play hard to get. I watch her from a distance, giving her clear signals that I'm waiting for her to make the first move.

When Jesse finally comes through the door, I greet him with even more enthusiasm than usual, telling him I'm overjoyed he came home, because *Mirror* isn't much fun. Jesse is excited to see me, too, but instead of taking *FloppyBunny* from my mouth, he falls to his knees, thrusts both arms into the air, and shouts, "Yes! We have the house to ourselves!"

I get in on the action, hopping around him, *FloppyBunny's* long legs and ears gambolling on either side of my mouth. Finally, Jesse gets it! He takes *FloppyBunny* from my mouth and tosses him across the room. I scamper off to retrieve him, and we repeat the game.

Soon, Mom staggers into the kitchen with bulging bags, a sure sign that she's been hunting and has returned to the pack with food for us all.

"That was a disaster," she moans. "I'm never taking Gran grocery shopping again!"

"Pardon me?" Gran says.

"Nothing. I was just telling Jesse how much fun we had at the grocery store."

"Grocery store? I can't remember when I last went grocery shopping."

Mom sighs. "Where do you think all this food came from?"

Deep tracks etch Gran's face as she wanders away, searching. I don't know why she'd hunt for her old bone when fresh food is right here.

"I just needed a few things," Mom mumbles, unpacking food and putting it in places I can't reach. "I thought I could quickly pop out with Gran. What was I thinking? She puts something in the cart, I take it out, she puts it back in. Half this stuff we don't even need!"

"Where are the chips?" Jesse asks, searching through the bags.

"I didn't buy chips. We've got to start eating healthier. I watched a webinar on nutrition and dementia. Gran needs better food for her brain ... fewer carbs, more healthy fat, less junk. Same goes for you and me."

"Did you at least get something good for supper?"

Mom sighs. "I was planning to pick up one of those nice lasagnas with the fresh pasta and the organic sauce, but while I was in line at the deli counter, Gran wandered off. I left the cart and went chasing around the store like a madwoman! When I saw her, she was already past the checkout and going out the main exit. I grabbed her just as she was crossing the road to the parking lot. She was following a young woman, calling her 'Mummy.' I had a panic attack, right there and then, hyperventilating and —"

Jesse interrupts. "What happened to the groceries?"

"Nothing! Once I grabbed her, we went back inside and got the cart. I'd left my purse in it! Luckily, no one stole it. I was really spaced out — like I was disconnected from the real world. I forgot all about picking up the lasagna."

"I'm hungry," Jesse whines.

Anger bursts out of Mom in a cloud of pungent breath. She storms off, calling over her shoulder, "Make your own damn supper for a change. Feed Gran, too. I've got a wicked headache, and I can't see straight. I'm going to bed."

Jesse stares into *TheFridge*. I sit bolt upright alongside him, ears pricked, eyes focused, clearly telling him I could use a snack, but nothing edible comes my way. By the time he slams the door, cold, foggy breath has settled around my feet and chilled my belly. I curl up to warm myself, Jesse's words floating over my head.

"I feel like having peanut butter on toast. D'you want some, Mary?"

"Yes, please."

"I'll make the toast. You get the peanut butter."

She looks around … and around … and around.

"It's in the pantry."

Gran opens *TheFridge*, staring into it in the way Jesse does.

Jesse closes the door and speaks slowly. "Listen to me, Mary. The peanut butter is in the pantry." He points his finger. "Look! That way! Follow my finger."

She stares at his finger, moving in closer to examine it.

"No, Mary, follow my finger." He moves his whole arm as if throwing a ball. I get up and head toward the pantry in anticipation of catching said ball in my mouth, but there's no ball. He tricked me. Gran is still staring at Jesse's finger. Following a pointing finger is a skill that takes time to learn. It requires a healthy knower. Gran can't do it.

Jesse holds her shoulders and turns her toward the pantry. "There you go! Now look on your left. Left! The other left! Good.

Now look on the shelf by your shoulder. Your shoulder, Mary. That's your knee. Higher."

He bursts into song. "Head, *shoulders*, knees, and toes! That's it! Well done!"

The jar in Gran's hand is not my favourite, but I'll eat it all the same because starvation is an ever-present threat.

Pop! Toast flies into the air, getting everyone's attention.

Jesse wolfs his down. Gran eats slower and shares with me.

The peanut butter gets stuck to the roof of my mouth.

mary

Keith is telling me to write about Kayla's birth. I can't. My brain is tired. I tell him to do it.

"Me?" he says, laughing. "I can't write!"

"Of course not," I say, sadness darkening my mood. "You weren't there."

"That's not what I mean. I *was* there, but you couldn't see me. I'd write about it if I could, but I can't. You have to do it."

Kayla was born four months after Keith died. She was darker skinned and darker haired than both Alicia and Zach, more like her father. But something wasn't right. She clenched her fists and jerked her arms, like a boxer firing quick jabs. Her legs, too, kicked out. And she howled. It was not the cry of a healthy newborn. It was much more distressed. They took her from me and nobody would tell me what was going on. My worst fear was that she, like Keith, would die.

I remember lying on a blue pad, in a hospital bed with rails on the side. The plastic under the pillowcase rattled and crackled every time I moved. The IV line in the back of my hand hurt. Machinery pulsed and beeped and flashed. This was what Keith had endured for three months. The night Kayla was born, I lived it all over again. I couldn't make it stop. I just wanted to get out of the hospital and take our baby home and be with Alicia and Zach. I discharged myself. I couldn't stay there with all those memories.

A week or two later, the doctor said Kayla had fetal stress disorder.

It made perfect sense. She'd floated in my stress hormones for nine months. My heartbeat had orchestrated her prenatal life. Of course she would have shared my anguish.

The doctors said she'd probably get over it eventually, and that I should keep her peaceful and quiet. Like that was possible with Alicia and Zach! Especially Zach. Even if he quietly peered into the crib, Kayla woke with a start and a high-pitched wail, jerking her arms and legs. It was like she was lashing out, protecting herself from everyone and everything around her. It was awful.

The doctor said I might have PTSD, but I didn't have time for PTSD. I had to be father and mother. I had to get up and feed our three children and change diapers. I had to do the best I could. I was just having a few nightmares, that was all. One in particular:

I'm on the beach with Keith, but he's on a gurney, paralyzed. The tide is coming in. The wheels are stuck in the wet sand. I can't move it to safety. I try and try but the water is rising. I can't turn the tide. I can't save him …

I burst into tears and walk away from my desk, pacing up and down the hallway as fast as my legs will carry me. Toby follows me, carrying his stuffed rabbit and nudging me. I bury my face in his ruff. I forget what I am upset about.

kayla

As soon as Ma is sleeping, I get Alicia and Zach on a conference call, keen to tell them the latest news.

"The Alzheimer Day Centre called today. Ma can start the program next week. Two days a week, from nine to four! I can't believe it! I'll be able to pick up groceries, read a book, or have a bath! I'm so excited."

"And you'll be able to have a phone call without hiding in the garage," Alicia says.

"That is really good news!" Zach says.

"There's other news, too. Maybe you both know this already, but I didn't! I was born with fetal stress disorder!"

"No way!" they both say.

"Ma just wrote about it in her book. I'll email the chapter to you."

"It makes sense," Zach says. "Keith died when Ma was pregnant with you. She must have been under incredible stress. You would have absorbed all that."

"You're right. But I never put two and two together. It's given me a whole new outlook … envisioning myself in the womb, absorbing Ma's grief and sharing her nightmares. Unimaginable, really. And as a newborn with fetal stress disorder, I needed peace and quiet and comfort. I needed to be swaddled and assured I was safe. And instead of that, I got a single parent who was grieving and a pair of siblings who were probably swinging from the light fixtures. Apparently, you scared the crap out of me, Zach."

"I'm so sorry," he says. "I didn't know!"

"You weren't even two!" I tell him. "Jesse and Kyle were terrors at two — climbing the walls. There's no way they could have been quiet and peaceful."

"Do you think you grew out of it?" Alicia asks.

"It's not at the level of a soldier returning from a tour of duty in Afghanistan, but I think it's still part of me. My earliest memories include panic attacks — shaking and sweating and wanting to run away but my legs not being able to move. To this day, I'll sometimes break out in a cold sweat — tunnel vision, chest pain, the whole nine yards. The last time it happened was when I lost Ma in the grocery store. I thought it was a panic attack. But maybe it was stress disorder? I guess I could talk to the doctor about it. Oh! I almost said I don't have time to go to the doctor, but that's not true anymore! I'll have Mondays and Wednesdays!"

"I'm glad," Zach says. "You deserve a break. By the way, how's it going with the CBD oil?"

"It's helping — more than I expected, actually! She's still having a few nightmares, but not every day, like before. The psychiatrist wanted to put her on anti-anxiety meds —"

Zach interrupts. "What! You took her to a psychiatrist and you didn't tell me?"

"Yeah, the one at the memory clinic."

"You mean the place where they do the clinical trials?"

"Yes."

"Good God, Kayla, why didn't you tell me that? A trial? We should all have discussed it!"

"Calm down, Zach! She's not doing a trial. We went there to see if she was eligible for one, but she wasn't. Anyway, it was Ma's idea, not mine! *She* wanted to go. We talked to the psychiatrist about her nightmares. He suggested a cocktail of anti-anxiety meds and sleeping pills, but I decided to try the CBD first. Happy?"

"I'm sorry," Zach says. "I'm glad it's helping … for now at least. There's so little I can do to make life easier for her, or for you.

Down the line, antipsychotics might be helpful, but if we hold off as long as possible, that's a good thing."

"Let's talk about this another time. I gotta go. Ma's sleeping, and I've got some church work to catch up on."

"Right, okay. We'll talk later. Bye, guys."

sage

Mom has washed Gran and brushed her and put her into clean clothes. This is often a sign that my humans are leaving the den, so I get underfoot to make sure they can't leave me behind.

"*Sage!*" Mom says. "I'm just dropping Gran off at the Day Centre. We aren't going *Walkies*. You have to *Stay* here and guard the house."

The words *Walkies* and *Stay* don't usually go together, so I'm confused.

"I don't want to go," Gran wails, refusing to put on her shoes.

"But you'll have so much fun," Mom says in the encouraging voice. "You'll play games and sing songs! Let me help you with your coat. Here we go. One arm in …"

Gran fights Mom off. "I don't want to go."

Mom switches to the begging voice. "Please, Mary. Please don't make this difficult for me!"

Gran resists, her bottom lip puckering. "I'm not going."

Mom finally finds her alpha voice. "I know you don't *want* to go, Mary, but you *need* to go — for *my* sake. I've got high blood pressure and frickin' atrial tachycardia. The doctor says I'm under too much stress. So suck it up. You're going! Are you listening to a word I'm saying?"

Everything about Gran's posture and expression says she's not going anywhere. If she had claws on her feet, she'd be digging them in right now.

"Goodbye then," Mom says, stepping outside.

Gran rushes after her, anxious not to be left behind. So do I. Mom blocks me. "*Stay!*"

I do as I'm told. Gran leaves with Mom. Jesse has gone, too. I'm alone. I lie on the mat by the door and wait.

Before long, Mom returns — without Gran. She's upset. She goes to her room and collapses on the bed, turning away from me, facing the wall. My knower says she needs me, so I shamelessly cross the no-go line and stride to the far side of the bed, to find her face. It's squished and strained. I nudge her with my nose, trying to focus her mind on stroking me, but it's like she's in some other place. I nudge. Nothing. I nudge again. Eventually, she strokes me lethargically. But then the talking starts and I settle in to listen, searching for familiar words.

"I thought the day program was going to give me a break. I'd been looking forward to having some alone time. But she clung to me like a toddler being left at preschool. I think she was scared I was leaving her there for good. She looked so helpless, so vulnerable ... it broke my heart. But it makes me angry, too, because she isn't considering *my* needs and *my* feelings. I know it's not her fault. It's the disease. I understand that with my *head*, but sometimes my feelings don't line up."

Her hand stops stroking, and she starts to close up again.

I nudge, more vigorously this time.

"*You'reSuchaSweetiepie*," she says, leaning over to kiss the top of my head. "You're such a good listener — better than a therapy session. Sometimes, I swear you know what I'm thinking."

I wag my tail.

"What shall we do with the rest of the day?" she says, her voice sounding happier. "We have a couple of hours to ourselves. We could do laundry, or *Vacuum*, or cook a nice supper, or we could stay right here and have a nap ... Let's do that! *Come* on up here."

I don't believe what I'm hearing. I must have got it wrong. Never, ever, has Mom invited me onto her bed. I was there during turkey season, but that was Jesse's idea, not Mom's.

I look at her, stunned, awaiting clarification.

She pats the bed. *"Come."*

Her bed is lower than Jesse's, so I make it up in a single bound. She throws her arm over me, and I snuggle into her warmth. This is the best day of my life!

sage

Vacuum is prowling around the den, hunting for food scraps. Pickings are slim. I know, because I already did a thorough clean, leaving nothing but desiccated flies and dust bunnies. *Vacuum* is on a leash, but he still gives Mom a hard time, fighting her about where they should go. Mom is damp and she's losing control. I'm frustrated because *Vacuum* is sucking up the familiar smells, but I'm scared, too, because *Vacuum* is after my toes, and although I try to be brave, I find myself high-stepping away from him … backward. It's humiliating.

Jesse yells over *Vacuum*'s roar. "I don't see why we have to do all this. It's only Uncle Zach coming. What difference does it make if the house is a mess?"

"It matters to me," Mom yells back. "I don't want him to think I'm a slob."

"He's coming to see Gran, not inspect your housecleaning! Anyway, what's up with the two of you?"

"Nothing! We were never close, even as children. It's like you and Krista. But it's getting better now."

Vacuum catches *Mouse* by the tail … roars, coughs, then falls silent. Mom wrestles *Mouse* from *Vacuum*'s teeth and tosses him my way, but he smells different — and his tail is gone!

When *Vacuum* starts up again, he races toward me. I jump out of the way because I like my tail exactly where it is. I retreat to the kitchen, where Jesse is slopping scented water around, rubbing away the sticky spills that I should have already licked. Suddenly,

I splay out on my belly. I scramble to get up, but the floor beneath my feet is soapy, and I may as well be on a sheet of ice.

Instead of helping me, Jesse yells and gives me the finger. "*Out.*"

I get control of my wayward feet and slink away, looking for a safe place. *Vacuum* is still dragging Mom around. Gran is on the couch with a towel wrapped around her head. She gives off the scent of *Bath*. I have a sinking feeling that it might be my turn next.

Mom shoves *Vacuum* back into his crate, hangs his leash on a peg, and shuts the door. Good riddance. But before long, she reappears, holding the little white sticks that she likes to poke down my ears. I tuck my tail and slink off to hide under Jesse's bed.

Gran doesn't move fast enough — her whimpers are a sure sign that she's getting her ears poked. Soon, her whimpers change to a yowl!

"For heaven's sake!" Mom shouts. "I'm just combing your hair."

"You're pulling it out!"

"Forget Gran's hair!" Jesse says in his alpha voice. "Just stick it in a ponytail."

Mom's face collapses. "I want Ma to look nice. Not like I'm neglecting her."

"Neglecting her? Send her to Vancouver! See how long that lasts!"

"Why are you both so cross with me?" Gran sobs. "What did I do wrong?"

Jesse's voice changes in an instant. "You didn't do anything wrong," he says gently. "We aren't cross with you."

Though he repeats these words several times, Gran won't calm down. From my hiding place under the bed, I watch her feet shuffling up and down the hall in her never-ending hunt for a bone.

"What's she lost now?" Mom asks.

"Her mind," Jesse replies.

"Jesse! Don't say that! Don't ..."

Unexpectedly, she snorts like a pig, and in no time, both of them are laughing so hard that I come out from under the bed and jump up and down with them.

Mom ruffles my coat. "Oh, *Sage*, dear sweet *Sage*, we don't laugh enough these days, do we?"

mary

The woman who looks after me says that Zach is coming soon. I think he's at school. I'll go outside to wait for him. He must be six by now. Or maybe nine. I get six and nine muddled up.

The woman steers me away from the door, telling me I'm half naked and need to get dressed first. She chooses a top that I don't like and insists I put it on.

I pull it back off and start rummaging through the closet.

"Mary! I just folded all those clothes, and you're messing them up. That top looked lovely. Very elegant. It goes perfectly with your black slacks."

"I don't like it. I want to wear *this*."

I push my arms into the sleeves of a purple cardigan, but it feels wrong. The woman tells me it's upside down and back to front. She fixes it.

"What are you looking for now?" she asks.

"The circular skirt with the strawberries on the bottom. Mummy gave it to me for my birthday, just last week!"

The woman groans. "Maybe it's in the wash."

"But it's brand new! I've only worn it once. It doesn't need washing!"

Suddenly, I remember the woman's name — Hettie! In my mind's eye, I see her at the outside sink, humming a tune and rhythmically rubbing clothes against the wooden scrubbing board, hanging them over the bushes in the hot sun so they dry stiff.

"Don't starch my skirt," I tell her. "I don't want it crisp."

"I won't," she says, holding up black slacks, telling me which leg goes into which hole.

I totter on one leg, and she steadies me, ordering me to sit down before I fall. I sit but I really wish she'd stop telling me what to do.

She kneels to help get my feet into the holes of the slacks. If I had my skirt, we wouldn't be having this trouble.

I tell her I want my new sneakers, too. She says she'll look for them right after she's ironed my skirt. She seems to find this amusing.

She pulls up my slacks. I yank them down, stumbling as they get caught around my ankles. She's not pleased.

"Oh, for goodness' sakes, Mary! What are you doing? I got you dressed already."

"I want to wear the circular skirt that Mummy gave me for my birthday."

"Listen to me, Mary. It's in the wash."

"But it's brand new! You didn't need to wash it."

She cuts me off, impatient and short tempered. "You spilled something down the front, so I put it to soak."

"Mummy just bought it for my birthday," I wail. "You'll ruin it with your starch and your washboard."

Hettie covers her face with her hands. I made her feel bad. I feel bad, too.

"I'm sorry," I say, shuffling toward her, my ankles tied together with the slacks.

Hettie starts to laugh. She's in a much better mood now. So am I.

She talks while she folds the clothes that are strewn all over my bed. Whoever made all that mess was very inconsiderate.

"Listen carefully, Mary. Look at me! Zach is coming. I've still got lots to do. So sit here quietly and write. It's all set up for you."

"I don't know what to write."

"What are you thinking right now? Write about that."

I think that visitors are coming because Hettie is extra
upset and she's been cleaning. I try to help but I do it
wrong and she gets cross with me. I'm in her way. Seems
like I always am. She's mean to me. She pulls my hair
out when she combs it. I like purple.

sage

The bell rings. I rush to the door, barking furiously in case it's the *YooPeeEss* truck. Instead, a big upright enters. Before any of us have time to check him out, Gran rushes to him for a hug.

"Keith," she squeals.

Mom's mouth flops open. The newcomer's mouth does the same. Even Jesse's jaw drops. Mom recovers first, using her fake cheery voice, "*Let's-put-the-kettle-on-and-make-a nice-cup-of-tea.*"

In anticipation of a *Cookie*, which generally appears after this long word, I trot along to the kitchen. Gran follows, taking the big man's hand and leading him to the table.

Jesse grins and sings quietly, "Mary and Keith sitting in a tree. K-I-S-S-I-N-G."

Mom scowls at him.

He responds by giving orders. "Mary, *Come* and *Sit* here."

I do as I'm told but instead of giving me a *Cookie*, he says, "*Sage! Out!*" I'm confused — too many conflicting instructions. Again.

I sneak away to the other side of Gran, where Jesse can't see me, and I place my paw on her lap to get her attention. It works. She turns away from the newcomer and talks soft words to me. I'd prefer it if she shared her *Cookie* with me, but such is a dog's life.

The big man leans in close to Mom, briefly resting his hand on hers. "How are you holding up, Kayla?"

"Fine. I'm fine."

Jesse jumps right in. "Don't listen to her, Uncle Zach. Sometimes I think Mom is having a nervous breakdown."

The big man hesitates, glances toward Gran, who is immersed in her *Cookie*, then whispers to Mom. "I made an appointment for us to tour the home in town. Tomorrow."

Mom locks dagger-eyes with him, then forces a smile. "Let's not talk about this right now."

"Of course," the man says, squinting to make the one-eyed face that confounds me. "Did I tell you about my friend? Her name is ... um ... ur ... Susan! Susan's father had a stroke. He was always independent and never asked for help his whole life ... like someone else we know. But after the stroke, Susan quit her job to look after him. He'd always said he didn't want to be a burden on anyone, but that's exactly what happened."

He leans close to Mom and murmurs, "Look at it this way, Kayla. Would you want *your* kids to give up their lives and work themselves to death looking after you?"

Mom shakes her head vigorously.

"Hettie," Gran says, "please may I have a *Cookie*?"

"Who's Hettie?" the newcomer asks.

"I'll tell you later," Jesse says.

Their gaze shifts to Gran. Chocolate is smudged around her mouth. How did I miss that? I can't lick it right now because Mom is watching.

mary

The woman is whispering with my Keith. They seem to have a bond: a shared secret. They're sneaking around together! Something is going on! They're going out in the car! Keith is leaving me!"

Tears sting my eyes, and I can't stop them from falling. Not a deluge of uncontrolled weeping and wailing, but a silent trickle.

Toby nudges his nose under my hand. He's such a sweet boy. We wander around the house together, finding things Keith left behind: a single strand of hair on the bathroom counter, strangely softer than I remember; his scent —

A memory rushes in: I'm sitting in the closet, surrounded by Keith's clothes, burying my face in his favourite jersey and breathing in every last trace of him.

There's an open pack of Wrigley's gum on the dresser, along with his Ray-Ban Aviator shades. His blue pick-comb is still by the sink, a strand of dark Afro hair coiled in the prongs like a miniature Slinky. A sandwich bag in my jewellery box holds a wad of his hair … shaved from his head before the biopsy … the only part of him left. For years I sank my nose into the bag and breathed deeply. It used to smell of him, but then it didn't anymore.

I need to pee.

I can't find the bathroom.

I don't know where I am.

Oh, no.

sage

I hear *Minivan* prowl into the driveway and cough to a stop. I trot to the door to greet Mom, but she stays in the van, head down, shoulders heaving. I wait, peering through the smudgy glass, my breath clouding it until I can barely see out. Finally, when she comes in, she buries her damp face in my coat.

"Mom! Is that you?" Jesse shouts.

Mom leaps up like she was caught eating the garbage. Quickly blowing her nose, she makes the smiling face, but the weight of sorrow presses her down.

"Where's Uncle Zach?" Jesse asks.

"He got a taxi straight to the airport — we thought it would be better than coming back into the house and having to say goodbye to Gran all over again."

"That's heartless," Jesse says.

"Quite the opposite! We figured that if Gran thought Keith was leaving her again, she'd get really upset."

"What was the nursing home like?" Jesse asks quietly.

"Very nice! Clean. She'll have her own room, so she can have a few personal things, much like here. The staff are lovely, and there's a special wing just for dementia patients. It's locked, so they can't wander off and get lost. She'll be safe."

Despite Mom's best pretending moves, I can tell she's really sad.

"Sounds like a prison," Jesse says. "Did you put her name down?"

Mom sighs heavily. "It's not that simple, unfortunately. The system is designed to protect seniors from being shoved into old folks' homes by families who can't be bothered with them. I thought that because I have power of attorney, I could make the decision, but no! She has to be assessed by a governing body called the Local Health Integration Network, the LHIN. People call it Lin. They are the keepers of 'The List.' Do you remember when I was trying to get Gran into respite care and I used the *F*-word on the phone?"

Jesse laughs. "How could I ever forget?"

"It's the same people."

"Crap!" Jesse says. "They make the decision?"

"Yeah, they'll send someone to the house to assess her."

"Hope it's not the same person you swore at!"

"Me, too! The only other way is for Gran to sign herself in, and that's never gonna happen."

"How long will all this take?"

"I don't know. Even after we get the assessment done and her name is on the list, beds only open up when someone dies. There's a long list, so it could be years. And there's no guarantee the bed will be in the home that Uncle Zach and I just visited. Gran could end up in another town several hours away."

"But there are other homes in town," Jesse says. "There's one by the golf course."

"That's a retirement home. It's for people who are still independent."

"What about the place by the united church?"

"It's assisted living. The staff provide meals, I think, but Ma will need round-the-clock care from personal support workers and nurses." Mom sighs. "It seems like I should have dealt with this a long time ago. But it's a catch-22 situation because you can't get on the list until LHIN says you are ready and by that time, the list is years long! It's all crazy-making. The only good thing is that once she's on the list, if we get into a crisis situation, she'll be bumped to the top."

"How about I find us a movie to watch," Jesse says, putting his arm around Mom's shoulder. "A comedy? Something to cheer you up."

They head toward the couch, but as soon as Mom sinks her bare feet into the rug, she leaps backward, her voice deep and loud. "*Sage!* What have you done? *BadDog.*"

Uh-oh.

Dragging me to the wet spot on the rug, she pushes my nose into it. "*BadBadDog.*"

I tuck my tail, confused. The wet patch belongs to Gran, not me! She's been marking her territory recently, letting out a few drops of pee here and a few drops there. It's what I do in the broader spaces of my territory, spreading my scent as far as it can go — to tell the neighbourhood dogs I'm still here. But over the years, I've learned *not* to do this inside the den. Gran still needs to learn this lesson. Maybe Mom hasn't yelled at her enough.

"*Bed! RightNow,*" Mom orders, pointing her finger at me.

I slink off toward my bed, Mom's angry voice following me. Unfortunately, Cat is blocking the entrance, the steely look in his unblinking eyes saying he's in no mood to be challenged. I hover in the hall, stuck between Cat with his sharp claws and Mom with her anger and disappointment in me.

"It's bad enough having to look after Gran," Mom complains, "but now the dog is peeing in the house. I can't take it anymore. I just can't take it!"

"It's a good thing you signed Gran up for the nursing home," Jesse says.

"I can't wait for her to go!" Mom says.

I hear the sharp intake of her breath. "Ahhh, I didn't mean that. I mean, I wish … I wish …"

"What do you wish, Mom?"

"I wish I still had my Ma," she says, her voice quivering. "I wish I could watch a movie with her and talk about it. I wish I could tell her my worries and that she could tell me hers. I wish we could do mother-daughter things, go to the mall, enjoy a cup of coffee, eat lunch out."

"Why not do that?" Jesse says.

Mom scoffs. "You mean in public? It's okay for a child to eat with his hands, or spill things, or even have a tantrum, but seniors with dementia ... well, people stare! It's embarrassing. I feel that everyone is judging her ... and me — that I should be making her behave better."

"Mom!" Jesse exclaims. "You always told me not to care what people think."

She snorts. "Easier said than done! Oh, Jesse, I wish I could have the years back to live over. Relationships are what life is all about — I've always known that in my heart — but I didn't make it a priority, at least not with Ma. When we lived out west, I could have flown back to see her more often. I should have. Even when we moved here, I should have encouraged her to visit us more. But I was always too busy — with my job, with you kids, keeping a roof over our heads and food on the table. I put things off until next week, next month, next year ... to when I thought things would be less crazy. But they never were, and time raced by. If I could do it over, I'd spend more time with Ma ... because now it's too late."

Jesse wraps his arms around her. "Don't beat yourself up, Mom. You did the best you could."

"Did I?" she asks, pulling away. "So why do I feel like I'm a failure?"

Gran totters past me. I give her a good sniff. She's damp and cold and smelly, right down to her feet. I'm still in exile, but I creep after her on my belly, raising my eyes to watch for the slightest sign of an invitation from Mom. Yes — there it is! I heave myself to all fours, just in time for her to fling her arms around my neck and sob into my ruff.

"Oh, *Sage*, I'm so sorry I yelled at you. It was Ma who peed on the rug, not you!" She kisses the top of my head, and I wag my tail in contentment. All is well in my world.

kayla

"Hey, Kayla," Alicia says, through a crackling phone line. "How did the assessment go with LHIN?"

"Just let me shut myself in the bathroom. I hate to talk about Ma in front of her face. Okay this is better. The assessment? *Unfortunately*, Ma was in better form than usual. She chattered away almost like a normal person. And I was thinking, *Crap, the one time I want her to act demented and she's being little Miss Congeniality*. Although when she couldn't answer a question, she looked at me, expecting me to fill in the gaps, but I didn't, so she tried to change the subject or give an excuse."

"Yeah, she's good at pretending and deflecting."

"The assessor asked, 'Do you know what the date is today?' Ma said she didn't need to know the date because she didn't go to work anymore. But then she contradicted herself by saying she works at the library and that she's head librarian!"

"Aw."

"And the assessor asked Ma to show her where the bathroom was. Ma stood up, looked around, and didn't even know what direction to go in. And she doesn't even know what season it is. She stared out the window and watched the snowflakes falling ... those super big, lazy ones ... and she said it's spring. But the biggest thing was ... she couldn't remember any of our names, not one of us. She said I was Hettie."

"Who's Hettie?"

"The maid in her parents' house in Trinidad."

"Oh, Kayla, I'm so sorry."

"Hey, it makes sense. I'm Black and I do all the work!"

"I hope you don't *feel* like the maid."

"Nope," I say, laughing. "I don't get paid!"

"I haven't heard you laugh for such a long time. It sounds good! I'm guessing there's not much to laugh about these days."

"Actually, there's lots to laugh about — like when she has both legs in the same pant hole. But I stifle it because I don't want to hurt her feelings."

"We need to find a way of laughing *with* her, not at her. Laughter is so good for us. It floods our system with dopamine, the happy hormone. It reduces stress big time! Have you heard about laughing yoga? There's probably an online class."

"I don't need that, Leesh! *You* make me laugh."

"Okay, I'll make an effort to do it more often. So I'm guessing Ma didn't pass the assessment?"

"Oops, didn't I tell you that already? She passed! Or I guess she failed … whichever way you look at it. When I was showing the assessor out, I mentioned that Ma was usually so much worse. She said she sees enough people with Alzheimer's disease to recognize what's going on, and she has no reservations recommending her for long-term care."

"Excellent! What happens next?"

"We have a case file now! And she'll be put on the list for the home here in town. But I have to add five more homes as backups. That means I've got to research them, make appointments and go to visit them all. I don't know how they expect me to be the primary caregiver as well as do all that."

"I'll get Zach working on it. He can narrow the field down, maybe do virtual visits. Leave it to us."

sage

Uh-oh, the *Bath* word.

I race away, diving headfirst under Jesse's bed, tucking my tail to my butt so Mom can't grab it.

Gran hates the bath as much as I do, but she doesn't hide quickly enough. Mom catches her and uses her alpha voice. "Look here, Ma, you are getting in the *Bath* right now." But then her voice changes to the happy singsong one she uses for short ones. "We're babysitting Natalie this weekend. It will be such fun to have a child in the house again. Krista is dropping her off soon, so let's get you all cleaned up and looking nice."

I stay under the bed until the doorbell rings. It's Krista. She's not my favourite person, but I crawl out to greet her anyway. She ignores me.

"Hello, Mom. Traffic was so bad. I'm running late, so I can't stay long."

I push my snout between her legs.

"Mom!" she complains. "Can't you stop the dog from doing that? It's so rude."

My ears droop, and I'm about to slink away when I hear the happy shriek of a short one. I can tell by the scent that it's Natalie, but I'm confused — she's nothing like she was when I last saw her. At first, I wonder if my nose is mistaken, but then I realize that, like Jesse so long ago, she has transformed from a helpless four-legged puppy to a short upright, running around so confidently on her two legs that it's hard to believe she spent so long on four.

She races toward me, arms out, eyes bright with excitement, and unfamiliar words tumbling from her mouth. I buzz with anticipation, but before she can touch me, Krista yells, "Mom! Get this dog away from Natalie."

"For goodness' sake, Krista," Mom says, "*Sage* won't hurt her. You know that! She loves kids."

"Her breath stinks," Krista complains, wrinkling her nose while grabbing Natalie by the hand and pulling her away from me.

Natalie breaks free and flings her arms around my neck. It feels wonderful, reminding me of when Jesse was short and I was the most important thing in his life. But after a few moments, she sees Cat and races off to investigate. Krista follows closely. I want to tell them that Cat can be downright mean, but Krista is so out of sync with me that she'd never understand my warning. Compelled to protect the little one, I overcome my fear and rush to put myself between Natalie and Cat. He jabs at me instead.

"Looks like Sage is jealous," Jesse says, not understanding my altruistic gesture. He leads me down the hall to our room and leaves me there … alone. I flop onto the floor, pressing my nostrils into the crack at the bottom, sifting the many odours in the air, finding Natalie's salty aroma and revelling in it.

Before long, the door opens. Overjoyed, I wriggle my best greeting: It's Jesse! It's Jesse! It's Jesse! But then I see Natalie peeking out from around his legs, and I change the greeting: It's Natalie! It's Natalie! It's Natalie!

Krista is gone! Another reason to celebrate! So Natalie and I roll around on the floor, like puppies.

After a while, Mom interrupts us. "It's time for *Bed.*"

With halting steps, I head toward my bed, but Jesse laughs. "Not you, *Sage*! *Come* here. *You'reSuchaSillySage.*"

I wag my tail with the reprieve. "*Stay,*" Jesse commands. "*Down.*"

Tired from all the playing, I collapse at his feet and close my eyes.

When I awake, Natalie is climbing onto Gran's lap. "Read me a story," she says.

Gran gets argumentative. "Read it yourself."

"I can't read," Natalie says.

"Yes, you can. I taught you! You could read the newspaper when you were four."

Natalie holds up her pudgy fingers. "I'm f-ree. I just had my birfday."

Salt water wells in Gran's eyes and she folds herself around Natalie, rocking back and forth, crooning in a tender voice. "Your daddy loves you more than anything in the world. He'd stay if he could, but he was in too much pain and —"

Mom swoops down, like an owl catching a mouse. "Your daddy's just fine," she says, racing out the front door with Natalie straddling her hip. "He'll be back to pick you up tomorrow."

I canter after them, not wanting to miss an outing.

Jesse chases us. "Stop, Mom. You stay with Gran, I'll take Natalie to *ThePark*."

It's my lucky day! Soon, I'm heading down the street with Jesse and Natalie, without my leash. Instinctively, I know I must help care for this extra special short one, so I stay close to Jesse's leg, the way I'm supposed to.

When we reach *ThePark*, the leaves become our playmates, swishing and swooping and whispering in the breeze, begging us to chase them in their erratic journey to the ground — ooo-ooo-ooo, there's another one. And another! Natalie runs and tumbles and runs some more, and I bunny-hop at her side. Even the cheeky squirrels can't lure me away from her.

Weary from the chase, I roll in the leaves, squirming my spine to make them crackle and crunch. Natalie copies me. Then Jesse lifts her into the swinging chair and pushes her high into the sky. I watch from a safe distance, having learned long ago that dangling feet can give me a painful bump on the head.

As soon as we get home, Mom scoops Natalie up and twirls her around. I wait until she's back down on her two chubby little legs, then I greet her again, because she's been gone so long! Finally, I greet Mom with a face-lick. It's salty.

Later, when both Gran and Natalie have gone to bed, Mom talks to Jesse.

"When Ma held Natalie on her lap, I think it triggered a memory of when your Auntie Leesha was that age. Ma thought she was holding Alicia … telling her that Keith had died."

"What makes you think that?"

"I know the story about Alicia reading the newspaper at four. She was so precocious! Ma was saying that our daddy had loved us very, very much, and that he didn't want to go away and leave us."

"Like my dad did," Jesse mumbles.

I hear the pain in his voice, the lonely ache from deep inside. I lean into his leg, telling him I'm here if he needs me.

But then Jesse wraps his arms around Mom. Then, something even stranger. Mom sobs into Jesse's chest: big, heaving sobs that shake her whole body. This is confusing because it's the wrong way around, and it's never, ever, happened before.

sage

The pack is eating breakfast, and Gran is practising her new word.

"Do-I-have-to-go-to-that-place-today?"

Mom responds in her cheery voice. "It's nice to get out of the house and meet some new people ... make some new friends."

"But they are all so old!"

Jesse's laughter sputters into a cough. It works for me because a fine spray of food flies to the floor.

"You don't have to go yet," Mom says. "*Sit* down and finish your breakfast."

I sit, but Gran paces around, complaining, "I don't want to go. I don't want to go."

"Why not? You have fun there. You play bingo."

"No, we don't."

"A nice young man plays the piano."

"No, he doesn't."

"You sing songs, and you can dance if you want."

Gran frowns.

"It's mind-boggling!" Jesse murmurs. "She can't remember what goes on at the program, yet she remembers that she doesn't want to go and that all the people are old! And she remembers that Ian and Anna-Mae are supposed to come to dinner! She's still asking me if I've heard back from them."

"What do you tell her?"

Jesse grins. "That I spoke to them on the phone, but they're busy, or out of town, or that Ian pencilled us in for next month. I keep making up new excuses. Therapeutic lying ... that's what you call it, right?"

"You realize that you don't have to make up a new excuse each time? She won't remember what you already told her."

Jesse laughs. "I never thought of that! But just my luck, she would remember. It's like she forgets almost everything but gets obsessed with just a couple of things."

"*Do-I-have-to-go-to-that-place-today?*" Gran says.

Mom makes the one-eyed face at Jesse. "No, you don't have to go today, Mary, but I'm going to the store. Would you like to come with me?"

Gran stops whining and brightens up. She heads toward the front door.

"It's not time to go yet," says Jesse, getting up to follow her. So do I.

"Who's that?" Gran asks, looking at *Mirror*. Then, more agitated, "Who's that?"

I don't understand her problem. *Mirror* is a gentle dog, a little strange, but not dangerous.

Jesse speaks calmly. "It's just your reflection, Mary! You walk past it every day."

But Gran will not be calmed.

Suddenly, Jesse snatches up *Mirror* and carries her down the basement steps. I don't go. My hips are sore, and the steps are mean to me.

He comes back up the steps without *Mirror* and whispers to Mom, "What happens when you get to the program. Won't she notice she's been duped?"

"I'm gonna rip that Band-Aid right off!"

Jesse looks confused.

"Apparently, a certain person settles down as soon as I'm out of sight. She enjoys all the activities, especially the singing. She eats her lunch and enjoys the snacks. She's the perfect guest! So, from here on in, I'm going to peel her off me and get out of there as fast as my legs will carry me! I'm *not* gonna feel bad. And I'm gonna enjoy my day alone!"

sage

With a full moon shining through the window and the song of the Wild Ones rising up strong inside me, I tip back my head and howl along with Gran.

"Joy to the world, the Lord is come! Let earth receive her King."

Jesse pulls the pillow over his head. "Give me a break! It's the first day of the holidays! It's not even light yet."

I push my muzzle under his pillow and lick his ear. He pops his head out, irritated.

"How come she remembers the lyrics to Christmas songs, but she can't remember that I'm Jesse?"

He jumps out of bed and heads to the kitchen, where Gran is singing loudly, "On the first day of Christmas, my true love gave to me ... / a partridge in a pear tree. / On the second day of Christmas, my true love gave to me ... / da-da-da-da, and a da-da-da in a pear tree."

"This reminds me of when we were still in Calgary," Jesse says, "creeping into the living room with Kyle when it was still dark outside. The *Cookie* plate was empty!" He laughs, rubbing me enthusiastically behind my ears. "We thought Santa had eaten them, but it was you, *Sage*, wasn't it? You ate Santa's *Cookies*! You *Cookie*-eating monster, you!"

Although Jesse keeps saying the *Cookie* word, there are none in sight. I can't even smell them.

"That Christmas was the best ever," Jesse says, sadly. "It was the last one to hold any magic. After that, Dad left."

Feeling the loneliness in his voice, I nudge his leg — in part to comfort him, but mostly to get his mind back to the topic of *Cookies*. It doesn't work.

"How does she know it's Christmas?" he says.

"Maybe it's the smell of the Christmas tree," Mom replies. "They say that smells bring back memories."

Gran launches into a new song: "O Christmas tree, O Christmas tree, how lovely are thy branches."

Jesse raises his head and inhales deeply. "You're right! I remember cutting the tree that year in Calgary, getting sap on my hands. It was sticky, but it smelled so good. Dad looked like a real lumberjack in that red plaid jacket, remember? Then Krista got snow in her boots and wanted to go home. She always spoiled things."

"I have a surprise for you," Mom says, helping Gran into a sweater. "It's Rudolph the red-nosed reindeer."

Gran bursts into song.

Mom, Jesse, and I sing, too — a pack of Wild Ones!

"I bought reindeer antlers, as well," Mom says. "I even got a pair for you, *Sage*." She wrestles something onto the top of my head. "Aw, *Sweetiepie*, you look so cute!"

I wag my tail because, even though my head feels squished, any attention is better than none. But as soon as Mom turns away, I toboggan my face along the floor to dislodge the tight band from my head.

Later, Jesse and Gran hang shiny little balls on the tree. Gran claps her hands together, excitedly, but Jesse complains quietly to Mom, "She's putting all the decorations in the same place."

"She's happy!" Mom says. "Rearrange them later, if you must — when she's not looking."

Cat watches from behind a chair, his eyes fixed on the tree as if a bird is hiding in the branches. He's in hunting mode. Crazy cat!

mary

I love Christmas.

I sing along to a hymn playing on the radio. "Hark the herald angels sing … Glory to the newborn king. Peace on earth and mercy mild, God and sinners reconciled."

It takes me back to my childhood, to the old stone church in Southampton, to choral voices echoing around the vaulted ceiling, to the crescendo of the pipe organ … to Mummy standing and sitting and kneeling beside me, helping me find the page in the hymn book, using her finger to point to the words.

I pick an ornament out of the box to hang on the tree, a golden ball with red writing: *Baby's First Christmas*. Alicia has just learned to sit up. Her eyes are bright with wonder at the lights twinkling on the tree. She doesn't care that most of the decorations are cheap ones from Woolworths. I'm a stay-at-home mom now, so we need to economize. Despite this, Keith has bought this one special tree ornament.

While a chicken roasts in the oven, we go for a walk on Holmwood Common, Alicia sleeping in her cloth carrier, her little face smushed against Keith's chest. We are so much in love with her and with each other. Life is wonderful. And Christmas makes it even more wonderful.

After Keith died …

I'm not going there. I hate Christmas. Everyone is so full of peace and love … bubbling with the Christmas spirit … so damn happy.

Me, lonely and empty, bereft, yet pretending to be okay.

Living a lie is exhausting.

sage

In the middle of the night, a mighty crash wakes us all. I canter bravely toward the noise, barking non-stop, hackles up. Cat flies past me in the opposite direction. It's not until Mom arrives, making light shine, that I see the tree flat on the floor, shiny little balls rolling in all directions.

"Regis," Mom screams, chasing Cat around the house.

Under normal circumstances, I'd join her, but instead I chase the shiny balls. I can't stop myself. They're skittish and don't like to be caught — the best kind of chase.

Suddenly, there's a stabbing pain in my paw.

"Oh no!" Jesse says, his voice alarmed. "She's bleeding!"

Returning from her lap around the den, Mom, too, is alarmed. Their combined panic tells me that something dreadful is happening. Instinctively, I do my guard-dog routine, but with one paw out of commission, instead of growl, snarl, and lunge, I can only whimper, grimace, and hop.

"Blood's getting all over the floor," Mom says. "Let's get her to the laundry room."

"I thought those ornaments were plastic," Jesse says, lifting me into his arms.

Mom's voice quivers. "One ball was glass. It said *Baby's First Christmas*. I always pretended my daddy bought it for me, even though I wasn't born until after he died. Now it's broken."

"Oh, Mom, I'm so sorry," Jesse says, placing me on the laundry room counter. This is a first. Everything looks different from up here!

"*Sit*," he orders. "Give me your foot."

I look at him, perplexed.

"*GimmeFive.*"

I offer him my sore foot. He holds it while Mom peers into it.

"I can't see for tears," she says.

Jesse takes over. "Looks like a clean cut. I don't see any glass stuck in it. D'you think we should take her *ToTheVet*?"

I freeze at the word. Bad things always happen there. Doc usually sticks something very sharp into me, or he lifts my tail in the air and pokes something up my butt. I don't like it when he does that.

The first time Mom took me *ToTheVet*, I followed her into Doc's den without a care in the world, eager to introduce myself to the other dogs. But they smelled of sickness and fear, and they all had their tails clamped firmly between their legs, telling me this was no place for a dog. I cowered behind Mom and sat on my tail. She acted bright and cheery. I hadn't yet learned about her pretending ways, so I gobbled the yummy treats in her outstretched hand until they led to a crate. The door clanked shut and she left me there! Doc was pleasant, at least at first. Then he stung me like a bee, and I cried until I went to sleep.

When I woke up, I had a burning pain in my belly, and I felt yucky all over. Mom wasn't there. Neither was Jesse. I was just a young pup, and they'd abandoned me in Doc's lair! But Doc acted like he was pleased to see me, stroking me and speaking gentle words. And I trusted him. Stupid me!

"I know this cone will feel bad," he'd crooned, fastening a big thing around my neck, "but I don't want you chewing your stitches out. You'll get over the spaying in no time. And you'll have a long life looking after your humans instead of puppies."

When Mom reappeared, I was ecstatic, but this was my first experience with the dreaded neck-thing. I rushed toward her, and it got caught on everything in Doc's den, giving me a smack that sent another kind of pain shooting right through me. Mom attached my leash and escorted me carefully through the room where a new set of dogs sat with their tails between their legs and their heads down.

Back at home, the door, the table, the chairs, and the walls all sided with the neck-thing and knocked me around. If I stayed still and didn't go anywhere, I just had to deal with the fire in my belly, but when I moved, everything and everyone had it in for me. Jesse was still very short in those days, and all he could do was laugh.

Now, sitting on the laundry room countertop, my paw in Jesse's hand, I quiver in fear at the word *ToTheVet*.

"The bleeding has slowed down," Mom says. "Let's bandage it tight and see how it is tomorrow. If it needs a stitch or two, we'll take her in the morning."

When Mom's finished, Jesse lifts me down, and I hop on three legs to the door. It's closed.

"Sorry, *Sweetiepie*," Mom says, "but you have to sleep here tonight. I don't want you bleeding all over Jesse's bed." She kisses me on the top of my head. "*Stay*."

They escape, leaving me on the laundry room floor. Jesse reappears with my bed and blankie but then leaves again, and I'm alone. I whine in the darkness.

Gran comes in, creaking and groaning as she lies down beside me. She curls around me, one arm over me, protecting me. "It will be okay," she murmurs. "It will be okay."

mary

I curl around him, trying to embed the feel of him in my memory forever, letting him know I'm here ... that he's not alone. It's all I can do.

The doctor says that Keith is unaware of the tubes and hoses, whirring machinery and bedsores. He's wrong. Keith is trapped inside this broken shell of a body and he knows it. The anguish in his eyes tells me so. I can't stand knowing that he's feeling all this. Please, God, please let it be over.

The familiar dream comes to me.

> At first, it's idyllic,
> luring me in as always with its intimacy and warmth:
> Hand in hand we walk along the shore,
> our bare feet sinking into the damp sand at the water's edge ...
> I feel *safe*, *loved*, and so *happy*.
> At the far end of the bay, there's a dock with two chairs.
> It's where we are heading, where we are meant to be.
> Not yet.
> Not now.
> But in our old age ... to watch the sun go down on our lives. Together.
> Panic grabs my chest. I know where we're going next.
> I struggle to change the outcome, to take some other path.

But I can't.

It's out of my control.

The sky darkens and the wind springs up.

Keith lies on a gurney at the water's edge.

Paralyzed.

The tide has turned.

The wheels sink into the wet sand, water swirling around them, sucking them deeper.

I throw my weight against the bed, struggling to get it up the beach, to safety. But it won't budge. The wheels are stuck in the sand.

The water is rising.

I know what is going to happen, but I refuse to accept it.

Keith! I *will* get you to those chairs on the dock. We *will* watch the sun go down. Together.

But the sea rises relentlessly.

Around my ankles.

Around my thighs.

Soaking the mattress.

Lapping over Keith's beautiful brown skin,

Lapping at his face. His face ...

I wake up, my heart pounding.

I didn't save you.

I couldn't save you.

Toby nudges me until I reach out and stroke him. He's such a good dog.

sage

Once again, Doc has tied the dreaded neck-thing around my head. I can't lick my sore paw.

Gran clings to Mom's side as she moves around the kitchen. Lured by the aroma of turkey, I try to do the same, but I keep banging into things.

Mom points her finger. "*Out*, both of you! *Out* from under my feet. Mary, *Sit* on the couch. *Sage! Bed!*"

It's too many orders for both of us.

"*Sage! Bed!*"

That's clear. Careful not to provoke the walls or misjudge the doorway, I hobble toward my bed, flopping down and squirming to force the neck-thing to the shape of my head. In the end, my head is forced into the shape of the neck-thing.

The doorbell startles me. I scramble to my feet, ready to do my guard-dog routine, but I get hooked on the corner of Jesse's bed. Natalie rushes into the room on chubby little legs. She stops in her tracks, recoiling and running back to Krista.

By the time I free myself, a big male is clomping around on heavy feet. I've met him before — Dan. He's nice enough, but Gran doesn't like him one little bit. She pulls closer to Mom and whimpers, and when he moves in for a hug, she shrieks in fear.

I bark at Dan, telling him to leave Gran alone.

"Get the dog to back off," Krista shouts.

Jesse erupts. "Tell your husband to back off! Can't you see he's frightening Gran?"

Krista yells back, "She's not scared of Dan, you idiot — she's scared of the dog!"

Jesse's arms shoot upward. "Are you out of your mind?"

Mom tries to get the pack under control. "Calm down! It's Christmas Day. Time for peace and love."

But she's not using her alpha voice, so Jesse and Krista continue bickering like quarrelling dogs … until Natalie covers her ears with her hands and cries. They freeze, heads turned toward her.

Krista is the first to move, shaking her fist at me. "Look what you've done, you stupid dog — you've made Natalie cry."

The whole pack responds as one, quarrelling as before.

The doorbell rings again.

I bark louder, because that's my job.

Kyle comes in.

Gran screams harder.

Natalie cries louder.

I bark some more.

Mom bursts into tears.

Salt water streams down her face like the spring melt, and everyone stares at her. They don't know what to do. I do! I move in for a lick, but the neck-thing keeps me from reaching Mom's wet face. This is disastrous!

Jesse guides me to our room, protecting me from the walls along the way. "Merry Christmas," he snorts, shutting the door and leaving me alone — alone except for Cat, who peers out from under Jesse's bed, his evil eyes insisting that I leave the room immediately.

I can't! The door is closed.

Cat strolls to the middle of the room, stretching and yawning, showing me all his pointy little teeth. Then he sits down and washes his face slowly and deliberately. I want to get away from him, but there's no escape — no place outside the range of his jabbing claws. He controls the room.

I flatten myself against the door and wait, my tail so far between my legs that it tickles my belly.

Eventually, he springs onto Jesse's bed, kneading it with his sharp claws for what seems to be forever. I slink cautiously to my own bed. For a while, I try to reach the itch in my paw, flattening my snout against the neck-thing, nibbling, but it doesn't work. I give up and drift away to a place where there is no itch, no pain, and no neck-thing.

sage

Jesse comes to get me from the bedroom. "Listen, *Sage*," he says, gently holding the neck-thing and looking into my eyes. "Stick with me! Mom doesn't want you in the kitchen."

It's obviously an important command, but I don't recognize it.

He takes me to the far corner of the family room, where Kyle and Dan are drinking from dark bottles.

"Are you guys hiding?" Jesse asks.

"Yeah, from Gran," Kyle says. "We tried talking to her, but it's impossible. Anyways, she's scared of us. It makes no sense! We're family!"

"I know! It's not rational or logical, but I've learned a few things, if you want some suggestions."

"Sure!" they both say.

"First off, asking Gran questions doesn't work very well. I know it's the way we usually get into a conversation: 'What have you been doing lately? Seen any good movies? Do you want fries with that?' But the problem is … Gran doesn't know how to answer, certainly not at the speed most people ask, especially you, Kyle — you talk way too fast for her. Slow down. Use fewer words and shorter sentences. Try the six-second rule: give her six seconds before you ask her something else."

"That's hard," Kyle says. "I want to keep filling the silence."

Jesse nods. "And if you want to connect with her, you need to stand where she can see you … that's basically right in front of her, because her peripheral vision is gone." He makes circles with his fists and places them around his eyes. "Pretend you're looking down a pair of binoculars. That's what she sees."

All three of them, their eyes encircled by their hands, look around the family room.

"And unfortunately for you guys," Jesse continues, "she doesn't like men — you've already seen that ... especially big men who advance toward her or touch her. So the deck is stacked against you, Dan!"

"What's with that?" the big man asks.

"Mom thinks some guys must have hurt her, way back when, and that's the era she's living in now."

"God, that's awful! It's bad enough to go through something traumatic once in your life, but to be stuck in that time warp ..."

Kyle rests a hand on Jesse's shoulder. "I don't know how you do it, bro."

Jesse smiles. "I screw up all the time. Mom's always telling me to let Gran do the things that she can still do, but it's way easier and quicker to do it yourself. One thing I've learned for sure is that talking to someone with dementia is hard. Normal conversation goes back and forth like a tennis game, but talking with Gran is like serving ball after ball into the net."

Bored by their unfamiliar words and tempted by the smell of turkey, I hobble toward the kitchen, but the door frame snags the neck-thing with a jolt that drives my teeth into my tongue. Undeterred, I hop on, blood and drool splattering. Mom sees me with the eyes in the back of her head, but she gives me no sympathy. Instead, she waves kitchen utensils at me and yells, "*Out.*" I reverse toward the tile with the crooked crack. Going backward with the neck-thing is easier than going forward, but unfortunately, I land too hard on my sore foot, and the pain stops me in my tracks.

"*Out! Out! Out!*" Mom shrieks, not appreciating my problem.

Jesse comes to my rescue, lifting me in his arms. "We need to stay out of Mom's way today, old girl." He gently opens my mouth and peers inside, then wipes the neck-thing, so my visibility is better. "You'll live. Let's go back and hang out with the men."

Kyle pops the cap off one of the brown bottles and gives it to Jesse. Fizz comes out of Jesse's nose, along with laughter.

mary

There are pots and pans to wash. I like to help. I want to help. I don't like being useless. But the woman is impatient with me.

"Ma! You've already washed that pot! Wash another one! And turn off the tap! You're wasting hot water! Turn off the tap, for goodness' sake."

I get flustered. I don't understand what she wants from me.

"Did you hear me? Turn ... off ... the ... tap. You've used enough hot water to fill the bathtub."

There's too much noise. Too many strangers. I can't concentrate.

"Oh, for goodness' sake, let me do it. Get out of my way. *Out!*"

I do as I'm told. Keith might be waiting for me outside, at the corner. He won't come close to the house because my dad might see him.

It's almost dark. There he is ... behind the bougainvillea bushes. I nestle into his chest, and he wraps his arms around me. I feel protected. Safe. Loved.

My feet are cold, but my heart is warm. I don't know what's happened to the weather. It shouldn't be this cold in Trinidad.

"Go on back to the house now," Keith tells me.

But I don't know the way. And I'm sleepy.

sage

"Dinner's ready!" Mom shouts. "Everyone to the table, now!"

Steaming dishes of vegetables float over my head on their way to the big table in the dining room. I let them pass because I have my eye on the turkey, which is still in the kitchen. As soon as it flies past my nose, I'm compelled to follow — even though the dining room is another no-go place for me. Distracted by the turkey, I forget about the neck-thing and crash into the door frame. I flop down and drool onto my paws.

My humans put paper hats on their heads and talk loudly. One chair is empty. Something is wrong, but I can't quite put my paw on it.

"Where's Gran?" Jesse says.

Mom leaps up, the scent of her panic almost overpowering the turkey smell. She bellows orders, short and snappy, alpha style. "Krista, check her room … Jesse, the street … Kyle, the yard."

Everyone races away from the big table, leaving the food unattended. No one says *LeaveIt*. I cautiously sneak up on a teeny piece of turkey that's within stretching distance of my mouth, but before I can grab it, I smell a fresh spurt of fear from Mom.

I spin — just in time to see Jesse step into his boots and charge out the front door, carrying his coat.

With the neck-thing banging into everything, I crash out of the house and race down the street after him. Suddenly, I have to pee. I lower my hips and wait as the stream of urine melts the crusted snow beneath me. Jesse disappears into the darkness. Before I've finished, he's running toward me, reeking of fear and yelling. "Dogs are supposed to track people. Find her, *Sage*. Find Gran!"

I look at him blankly, raising my haunches. Find-Gran is not a command I know.

"*Sage*, you've gotta help me. Use your nose! Track her!"

I recognize the begging tone of voice and know he needs my help, but I don't know what I'm supposed to do. Over the years, I've learned that Jesse doesn't explain things well, so I swivel my ears, cock my head, and try my hardest to understand.

Jesse charges back inside the house and returns with one of Gran's shoes, stuffing it in my face. "Track her, *Sage*!"

The shoe smells of Gran. I take it in my mouth since he's offering it, but I'm not allowed to chew on shoes, so I don't know why he's trying to get me into trouble. He flashes me the *You'reStupid* face, then takes off running again — up the street this time. I make a valiant effort to run after him, shoe in mouth and tail tucked between my legs to stop the cold from scooting up my backside, but before I catch up with him, he races back toward me, skidding to a halt on the packed snow. I lean against his legs, trying to calm him, but it doesn't seem to help.

"*Sage!*" he whines, as pathetically as a newborn pup. "Where's she gone?"

I give the shoe back to him, nice and wet, then lick his hand, but that doesn't help, either.

It's quiet on the street. No dogs, no people, no cars. Enormous snowflakes the size of kibble float in front of my face. I try to eat them as they fall. It keeps me busy while Jesse frets and talks on *iPhone*.

Suddenly, I catch a whiff of Gran on the wind, and I understand what Jesse needs me to do.

Galloping on three legs, I follow my nose over the road and around the corner, cantering right past the place where I should plant my butt on the ground and wait for the words *Okay!YouCanCross*. I don't wait. My breath steams up the neck-thing, blocking my peripheral vision, but that's okay because I could find Gran even if I were blind. She's lying in a snowbank on the edge of the street. I squirm with delight, rubbing against her cold body until she nuzzles her head into me and sinks her icy-cold fingers into my ruff.

Jesse arrives, wrapping his coat around Gran. She's shivering. He's shivering. Even his voice is shivering. He lifts her into his arms and carries her along the road. I gambol merrily alongside, happy to be out without a leash.

As we near the den, a truck comes down the street, flashing, wailing, and screeching to a halt alongside us. Two burly uprights jump out. I hide behind Jesse where, emboldened by the safety of his legs, I woof quietly. But these uprights are not to be feared. They carry Gran inside and cover her in a sheet of shiny metal — just like the stuff that Cat is currently nosing off the turkey skeleton! I watch carefully as it slips off the bones … off the counter … and hits the floor. Mine! I pounce, lapping up the coating of turkey juice.

The burly uprights have stopped being nice and are now giving Mom a stern talking-to. She cries. If she had a tail, I know it would be tucked between her legs. I nuzzle her to tell her it's okay.

sage

My humans speak in urgent, yet hushed whispers.

"How could she disappear without any of us noticing? We were all right here!"

"I thought she was in the kitchen with you, Mom."

"I thought she was with you, Jesse."

"But whatever possessed her to go off like that? In her slippers?"

"She didn't even put a coat on! And it was minus two!"

"In her mind, that doesn't add up to frostbite or death!"

"Maybe she was looking for Toby ... *Sage*, I mean."

Mom's voice is close to tears: "No, that wasn't it. She went outside because I got cross with her. She was in my way in the kitchen, and I shouted at her."

The pack goes silent. I feel their sorrow, hear it in their sighs, smell it on their breath.

Krista speaks gently. "I'm sorry, Mom. I didn't realize that looking after Gran was so hard. It's like looking after a giant toddler. She can't be left alone, I see that now. I'm going to help you. I can come Thursday afternoons. I'll have to bring Natalie, but that might be nice for Gran, right? And at least you can have a bit of a break ... to pop out and do something for yourself. And I can swing by the grocery store on the way here and pick up what you need."

Salt water oozes from Mom's eyes as she hugs Krista. "Thank you. That would be wonderful. Now, I guess we should eat ... if Regis and *Sage* have left us anything."

She takes Gran's hand and leads her to the room with the big table. The others scurry around, taking up their places, and I settle down just outside, watching. Nobody takes any notice of me. Bored, I chew at the edge of the neck-thing, but even when I wriggle and squirm, and nibble and lick, it won't release me from its stranglehold.

Suddenly, I feel eyes turn toward me. I stop attacking the neck-thing and act innocent.

"It's a good thing *Sage* didn't help herself to all this food," Mom says. "Turkey is her favourite! *You'reSuchaGoodDog.* Right, *Sage*?"

I thump my tail on the floor.

"The dog's name is Toby," Gran says. "I don't know why you all keep forgetting that."

Laughter fizzes in everyone's noses, but they stifle it, except for Natalie, who giggles delightfully, tugging on Krista's sleeve and announcing, "That's not Toby! That's *Sage!*"

Gran gets ready to argue, but Jesse interrupts. "Toby was the one who found you, Mary!"

Gran frowns. "Found me?"

"Yes! I was going down the street in the wrong direction. If not for Toby ..."

He stops talking and looks at me. I feel the warmth of his praise, although I don't know what I did to deserve it.

Mom holds up her glass. The others copy her. "Cheers to Toby!" she says. "Our hero! *You'reTheBestDogInTheWorld!*" They all stare at me with smiles on their faces, repeating Mom's word. "*TheBestDogInTheWorld!*"

I know this means they love me but, quite honestly, I wish they'd stop looking at me because Natalie has dropped a chunk of turkey on the floor, and I'm waiting to sneak in and gobble it up. Eventually, they go back to eating, drinking, and talking, and I get my chance. Mmmm — turkey.

When chairs finally get pushed back and dishes get picked up, I lead the pack to the kitchen, just in time to see Cat slither off the counter. He's so stuffed he can barely move.

mary

The strangers leave. The woman puts me to bed, pulling the purple and yellow comforter up to my chin.

"I'm so sorry for messing up today," she whispers, her eyes brimming with tears.

I don't know what she means, but I tell her it's okay.

"I love you, Mary," she says, kissing my forehead.

I love her, too; I know I do — I feel that warm glow in my chest. But I don't remember exactly who she is. And I can't recall her name.

"I love you, too," I say, meaning every word.

kayla

My cell is ringing, but I really don't want to talk to anyone. I pick it up and see it's Zach and that he has already messaged three times. Reluctantly, I answer.

"Hi, Kayla," he says warmly. "I hear you had a traumatic Christmas Day."

"Yeah. I was too upset to even tell you guys. How did you hear?"

"Jesse called me. He said you're beating yourself up over it."

"Yeah. What if it had been minus twenty, not minus two? What if she'd been out there another ten minutes? She could have died, or lost her fingers or toes! And it would have been my fault."

"None of those things happened, so be grateful and move on. And no one blames you."

"I blame myself. *I'm* supposed to keep her safe, and I failed. She was in my way in the kitchen, and I lost my patience and told her to get out. I just meant out of the kitchen, not out of the house! I keep the front door locked all the time but in the confusion of everyone arriving, I must have forgotten to lock the dead bolt."

"Well it's good that there's a police report —"

"Yeah, with enough evidence to convict me for elder abuse!"

"No, I mean so the LHIN will understand the problem here and bump Ma up the list."

"That's true, I guess. But she'd be bumped up because of *my* failure to look after her rather than her deterioration."

"But that's part of the assessment — if no one can keep her safe, then she'll go to the top of the list."

"I wanted this Christmas to be good. It's probably the last one. Even if she lives for another ten years, she won't be here in this house with us, and she won't have her mind. So I wanted it to be memorable for all of us."

Zach chuckles. "It was memorable, for sure — the paramedics coming. You'll look back on this one day and laugh."

"Right now, nothing seems funny. And it's terrifying how quickly something can go wrong! What if she wakes in the night and wanders out of the house?"

"I think I have a solution for that. I found some kiddy-proof doorknob covers. It's the same principle as the kiddy-proof locks on the pill bottles: you have to squeeze and turn at the same time. People with dementia can't figure it out. You don't have to change your doorknobs—just slip these gizmos over the top. So if you want to make sure she stays in her bedroom overnight, put a cover on the *inside* doorknob. She'll turn the handle until the cows come home but won't be able to open the door! I've ordered you some. They're on their way."

"Gee, thanks, Zach."

"I got you a set of surveillance cameras, too, like nanny-cams. You can sync them with your iPhone and watch her from anywhere."

"You mean I can stay in bed and see what she's doing everywhere in the house?"

"Anywhere that's in sight of a camera. I've ordered three but we can add more if you need more."

"Zach, that sounds like a really good idea, but technology isn't my thing. Who's gonna set it all up? And even when it's installed, I probably won't be able to figure out how to use it."

"The install isn't difficult. It's all wireless. The cameras just stick to the walls … no screws required. Jesse will help you! He'll put the app on the phone and he'll sync everything. He's good at that … better than you! All you'll have to do is tap the icon on the home screen. Nothing to it!"

"Wow, thanks, Zach. I appreciate it. And I need to thank you for taking such an interest in Jesse, too. He's being much more helpful these days. Gosh, he's even pleasant at times! He's matured a lot over the last few months, and I think that might partly be because of you. So, thanks."

"You're welcome! I've gotta go. There's another call coming in. I hope the cameras make life easier. And next time something goes wrong, don't keep it to yourself. If we know what's happening, I can help — or try to, at least."

sage

I'm half asleep at Jesse's feet when he suddenly puts *Mac* aside and charges down the basement steps. I follow him warily, but the stairs hurt me all the same. It's worth it, though, because at the bottom, I find Jesse on all fours, crawling into the place with the low ceiling. I respond with the universal sign for *Let'sPlay,* pushing my butt in the air and resting my elbows on the floor, ready to spring into a mock attack as soon as Jesse lunges. Who am I kidding? I'm still wincing with pain from going down the steps. The stretch from the *Let'sPlay* pose feels good, though. Maybe I'll stay here for a while.

I inhale the scent around me. It smells of being outside all day and all night; of eating hot, fluffy treats cooked on sticks; of swimming in the lake. Memories of Dad waft across my vision like he's in the smoky haze of the fires he built. When I was young, Dad was the only one who took me on long walks. We both enjoyed being in the great outdoors, but we disagreed on one thing — squirrels. I wanted to chase them. Dad didn't. When he caught me, he growled angry words, yanking my neck so hard that I gagged. I'm not stupid. I learned the rule: No chasing squirrels. Getting my legs to obey, however, has been a lifelong struggle. After a while, my humans kept me on a leash. Squirrels cost me my freedom. But I'm still unable to silence the whine that rises in my throat at the sight of one of these magical mischief-makers.

Jesse rolls over into a sitting position, dropping his head into his hands. I mosey over to him, licking his hands until he takes them from his wet face and throws them around my neck instead. "How come we got the camping gear in the divorce?" he says. "Dad was the camper, not Mom. He could probably use it — now that he's got two more boys."

Jesse is hurting, not with the kind of pain that shot through me going down the stairs, more like the dull ache I get when he goes away and leaves me.

"Why does this still bother me?" he says, getting to his feet to struggle back up the steps, carrying a large, long object.

I follow cautiously.

"Look, Mary! It's a piano," he says enthusiastically.

"That's no piano," Gran says.

"Yes, it is! See, it's got all the keys, except for a few way at the top and a few way at the bottom, and you never use those, anyway. It's just missing the big old wooden cabinet."

Gran puts her fingers on the box and presses down. The only sound is a faint clunk. She turns away in disgust. "I told you, it's no piano."

Jesse ties its leash to the wall. "Try it now."

Her fingers press down again, and the box wails. A big smile lights up her face. An equally big smile lights up Jesse's.

In no time, Gran's fingers are moving back and forth.

Mom gets out of bed and joins us, grinning from ear to ear. "Thank you!" she says, hugging Jesse. "How did you get the idea to try that?"

"Google! Apparently, people who learned a musical instrument way back in their youth can sometimes still remember how to play it, even after they've forgotten most other things. Same goes for a second language."

Gran's hands stop moving and silence fills the air. Jesse and Mom clap enthusiastically. Everyone is smiling. Everyone is happy.

"I'd forgotten that you were such a good piano player, Mary!"

"I used to teach," Gran says.

Mom inhales sharply. "I can see other children sitting next to you at the piano!"

Gran looks around, perplexed.

"No! I mean, I see them in my head. I remember the other children ... your students! When was that? When did you teach piano?"

Gran shrugs.

"Did your piano have chipped ivory on one of the keys?" Mom asks.

"Yes! Middle C."

"Wow. And was the piano reddish brown?"

"Yes. Mahogany. Keith bought it for me right after we moved to Toronto. For my birthday. It was old and needed refinishing, but it was beautiful."

"What happened to it?"

"It's here somewhere," she says, getting up and wandering around.

I follow her up and down the hall, in and out of rooms, then I head back to Mom, who is in the kitchen. She holds my face with meat-scented fingers. "Kyle's coming for supper. He's bringing his new girlfriend to meet us, so we have to be on our best behaviour, okay."

The phone rings and within a few heartbeats, Mom deflates like a dying basketball.

"Kyle's not coming!" she announces, her crumpled face telling me that salt water will soon be running down her cheeks. "He's got the flu. We certainly don't want him here if he's sick."

"Does he think we're stupid?" Jesse mumbles, stomping off to our room with me hot on his heels. "It's New Year's Day! He's probably got a hangover."

Soon he's talking to *iPhone*, his voice high pitched and sharp. "Let me repeat that back to you, Kyle, so you can hear how selfish you sound: You're embarrassed to bring your girlfriend here because you don't want her to think our family is crazy."

Jesse stops breathing, as if he doesn't want to give his position away to a predator, then he explodes, angry words flying out of his mouth.

"But why lie to Mom? ... Well, you have hurt her feelings ... I'm so pissed at you!"

He tosses *iPhone* aside, then throws himself facedown on the bed, making it bounce. "Urrrgh! He's so self-centred. But I'm jealous, too. He has his own place. I can't wait to go to university and get away from here."

I push my head under his hand and feel his mood change.

He lifts his face out of the pillow and looks into my eyes. "To be honest, I don't blame Kyle for not bringing Sofi here. I haven't brought Ashley here for the same reason. If it was just Mom and me, I'd have invited her long ago."

sage

Mom has shut me in the laundry room and driven away in *Minivan*. It's extra upsetting because Natalie is just outside the door. I hear her voice, as well as her little feet running up and down the hall. I want out, but I don't have hands, so all I can do is press up against the crack at the bottom and listen.

"Gran," Krista says. "I mean, Mary! Can you help Natalie do this jigsaw puzzle? It's Bambi. Let's start with the corners. Who can find a corner piece? It has two straight edges.

"Well done, Natalie.

"Gra ... Mary, can you find a corner, too?

"Thank you, Natalie! Let's see if Gran can find one now.

"Thank you, Natalie, that's all four.

"Mary! Look at this piece. See, it's got grass at the bottom and Bambi's legs, so where do you think it goes? No, I think it goes at the bottom. Can you put it at the bottom? No, don't eat it! It's not a *Cookie*, it's a puzzle piece. Take it out of your mouth! Don't swallow it! *OhMyGod*. Spit it out!"

I hear a chair being pushed back and the cookie tin opening.

"Look at what I have, Mary. A *Cookie*! Spit out the puzzle and you can have the *Cookie* ... phew, thank you."

They are eating cookies and I'm getting none.

Krista speaks again. "Okay, we can do some colouring or we can play with Play-Doh. Which do you want?"

"Play-Doh!" Natalie says. "I want Play-Doh."

"Good choice. This will be fun. Look, Mary, you squeeze it with your hands like this and make shapes ... No! You can't eat it.

Huh, the label says it's non-toxic ... says it's edible. How does it taste, Mary? Yucky? ... Good idea, spit it out ... Oh, for goodness' sakes, Natalie. We don't eat Play-Doh ... you know that!"

"Gran is eating it," Natalie says.

"I know she is, but she shouldn't be. Let's try colouring."

I didn't plan on napping. It just happened. The next thing I know, Jesse is saying *Walkies*! I come to my senses and scamper around looking for Natalie, but she's gone.

Jesse clips on my leash and I drag him to the snowbank at the edge of the street, to the tree that he brought into the house a while ago and then hauled back outside. Neighbourhood dogs are using it as a marking post, so despite its prickliness, I'm compelled to squat and leave my scent as close as I can.

"Hurry up, *Sage*," he says. "It's too cold for standing around."

The clouds sit on top of my head, throwing icy pellets at me. I snap at them as we walk while telling Jesse to toss a snowball for me, but he doesn't. He rarely does these days. In fact, he rarely plays at anything the way he did when he was short. Back then, he rolled alongside me in the snow or splashed in puddles, kicking the water so I could catch the splatters in my mouth. Or with me racing alongside, my ears flapping in the wind, he'd hold out his arms and we would fly down the hills like birds. Now, he trudges the snow-covered sidewalk, hood up and head down, disappearing into himself. I don't like it when short uprights get tall.

Ashley comes looming out of the blisteringly cold air and it's like the sun pops out from behind the clouds, lighting up Jesse's face, putting a sparkle in his eyes and a quiver to his legs. While he struggles to get them under control, I lick the icy crystals from inside my nose. It requires a certain talent.

And then we are off, racing toward my all-time favourite place and skidding to a stop outside. I never get to go in. I always wait outside, the delicious smells driving me into a slobbering frenzy as I await the moment Jesse reappears with my special treat: *Pickle!* Just the thought makes my mouth pucker.

"We can't leave *Sage* outside in this weather," Jesse says.

Ashley peers through the window. "Nobody else is in there, and anyway, I know the guy at the counter. He had a crush on me in Grade Eight."

We enter. I'm so excited I can barely contain myself. Delicious meaty aromas float out from behind the counter, tempting me, but I must be a *GoodGirlSage*. I don't want to do anything that will get me tossed back out to the street and tied to the lamppost.

Jesse and Ashley sit facing each other, a small table between them. Sadly, they don't get the delicious red meat or the tangy *Pickle* ... just the drinks that make the fizzy sound. I don't like fizzy drinks because the bubbles go up my nose. Not that it matters what I like or don't like because neither Jesse nor Ashley think to offer me any.

They are quiet for a while, sipping their drinks and looking uncomfortable.

"Are your parents divorced?" Ashley asks.

"Yup. Since I was six. Dad hooked up with his secretary when we lived in Calgary. They have twins now. Boys."

"Ouch!"

"Yeah."

"Do you know that your brother and my sister used to date?"

"Seriously, you're Tara's sister?"

"Yeah. She's in university now. *OhMyGod*, I love having the house to myself."

"You're so lucky," Jesse says. "Soon after Kyle moved out, my Gran moved in. She's pretty high maintenance."

"Why?"

"She's got Alzheimer's. She gets confused. Really confused."

"My great-uncle is the same way. Dad just says that poor old Bill is losing his marbles, but they're pretty sure it's Alzheimer's. *OhMyGod*, the last time we went to see him, he kept telling me

this story about his school friend from thousands of years ago …
same story … same wording. He must have told me ten times … no
exaggeration! I wanted to scream, but I wanted to cry, too, because
it was really sad. I'm sorry about your Gran."

"Yeah, me, too. When she first moved in, she drove me crazy,
but these days, I try to imagine myself in her shoes. Sometimes it
helps. But hey, listen to this! We just discovered she can play the
piano, really well … except she plays the same piece over and over,
so it gets on your nerves a bit. Beethoven is great, but some variety
would be nice."

Ashley's hand creeps across the table, touching Jesse's. He grasps
it, his scent instantly changing. I pay attention, still hoping a *Pickle*
might materialize, but nothing. They have eyes only for each other,
not for me, so I let my front paws slide along the shiny floor until I
am flopped under the table, the perfect place for licking up spills.

Suddenly, they push back their chairs and we leave.

What? No *Pickle*!

kayla

Hi Zach and Alicia,

I'd totally forgotten it was Valentine's Day until long-stemmed roses arrived. Thanks so much, Zach! And for the note saying you hoped they'd lift our spirits. It was a lovely thought. But who knew that Ma doesn't like red rosebuds!!! I hope you're not upset. The good news is that they sparked quite a conversation with Ma and she revealed a few big moments in her life … in all our lives, actually. I grabbed my iPhone and recorded it. There's a long silence just after two minutes. You might think the conversation is over. I did! I felt emotionally exhausted and imagined she felt the same way. But then she started speaking again, cradling her belly as if she were still pregnant. Pregnant with me!! It makes me wonder if I crossed paths with Keith, like ships in the night — me coming and him going. I like to think that's what happened. It makes me feel whole — even though I never really knew that part of me was missing.

Sending the audio file.

[Audio file]

"Why don't you like red rosebuds, Mary?"

"I bought four on the way to the crematorium to put on the coffin … one from me, one from Alicia, one from Zach, and one from the baby. Nobody would have known I was five months' pregnant — I hadn't eaten enough to gain an ounce all the time Keith was in the hospital, and I hadn't slept much, either. Alicia carried her own rose and she didn't want to put it on the coffin. She wanted to keep it for herself! After a few seconds, she reluctantly laid it on the coffin — away from the others and at the wrong angle. I wanted to move it, to make it look symmetrical. But I knew that would be wrong, so I left it. There were no other flowers … just the four red rosebuds. It was simple, and perfect. The coffin was draped in a royal-blue altar cloth with knife-edge folds on the corners. Somebody did a good ironing job. Hettie, was it you?"

"Ummm. Yes, I expect so."

"Not many people came to the funeral. We'd only just moved to Canada. We hadn't had time to make friends. Mummy came. In fact, she was already here. She'd come from England to help take care of Zach and Alicia while I was at the hospital. Keith's parents came, too. They all said I shouldn't take the children to the funeral — that they were too young to understand. I compromised … Alicia came, but not Zach. He wasn't even two. He could never have sat still — he'd have been climbing over the pews. My father didn't come."

"I'm so sorry."

"Alicia was only three, but she was a grown-up from that point on. She sat next to me in the front row, holding my hand, comforting *me* rather than the other way around. She paid attention to the service and asked questions: Why did the man call Daddy 'Brother Keith'? And where is Daddy's head? It took a couple of days for me to figure that one out. People use the word 'body' to describe the deceased, so Alicia thought that Keith's *head* had gone to live with God and his *body* had been left behind. She literally thought that Keith's decapitated body was in the coffin! But the hardest question was: Why can't we keep him? Why do we have to put him in a box and burn him?"

"Good Lord, Mary! What did you tell her?"

"That dead people go rotten like bad meat!"

"Oh, God!"

"Yeah, I felt bad saying that! But it was okay because when she climbed on Keith's bed right after he died, she learned that death was different from life. And when the coffin started the journey through the curtain to the cremator, she turned to me and said, 'Don't worry ... Daddy can't feel anything anymore!'"

[Silence]

"This baby is the best gift Keith could have left me with ... like a Christmas present labelled *Do Not Open Until December Twenty-Fifth* or, in this case, February. It's something to look forward to."

mary

"What's all that noise?" I ask the woman.

"The neighbours are building an extension," she tells me. "This rain isn't helping them much. It's a quagmire out there."

I look out the window at the mud, remembering our brand-new home in Toronto. The inside was perfect when we moved in, but the subdivision was still a construction site. It was April and the snow was melting fast. Alicia and Zach didn't care that the mud came without trees and grass, birds, and critters. Watching heavy machinery was way more exciting.

"It's a good thing that Alicia and Zach still have their red rubber boots from England," I tell the woman.

She looks at me askance. "Yes, that *is* a good thing, but we aren't going out in this rain, anyway. It's a good day to stay inside and write some more of your book."

She's always telling me what to do:

Sit here, sit there.

Put this on. Take this off.

Get in the bath.

Play the piano.

Get out of my way.

Write your story.

She opens my laptop. I stare at the words on the screen, sounding them out, but before I get to the end of a sentence, I forget what the beginning said.

She asks me how my story is coming along. I tell her that it makes no sense, that there are so many mistakes it's impossible to read. I tell her that if it was written better, I'd be able to follow it more easily. After all, a misplaced comma changes everything.

The woman chuckles and says we can have a tea break as soon as I've written one sentence ... just one sentence.

I stare at the letters on the screen. They taunt me with their meaningless message. I feel sad. I am a writer. A woman of words. Words were always my friends. But now we are strangers.

In the silence, Keith comes to me, saying he's watching over me just like I watched over him when he was in the hospital, when I didn't want him to be alone.

The woman calls out, asking if I have written a sentence yet.

I don't want to write. It takes forever. It's hard. I hit the keys like I'm playing the piano.

duklyhweetiAmskdn9645637891;..jgjdfgd.
yoopplreokw4-5i346kgrgfhghj90rwu50923oijergo
idjsgsdjoetetjhwoitjdfjgijnmuivhbfkbdsfksdbfsdfus
ihiueriwehuskdfbskdfhsfhihwiehefsdkfskfsfhsfhsfhs-
ffgiorgrt76956809u434jggeerhgfj45o8y489yw3498
3489q348hq988998t98tue-r0tue0r9gjs0er9utw03
4u3utw04tuw0u304wutw304ut3w40ut34w0tu340
tu30tu930w9utergogjdfogjdpu34m09iges0h-8tu3-
4905u23q27685684567959ghjfgfgqy8q2wg-=47p-jk
TEH ENNNNND.

The woman brings me a cup of tea. I ask her to please bring a cup for Keith, too. Her smile is sad.

"Write about him," she says.

I look around, hoping Keith will help me, but he's gone; I think he left because the woman didn't bring him tea. He knew he wasn't welcome. I'm angry at her.

"Don't tell me what to do," I screech. "I'm not a child."

The woman hangs her head and apologizes, then she hugs me. It feels familiar and comforting.

She leans over me and reads from the screen. The words sound familiar, too. Very familiar. Suddenly, I know they are *my* words! I wrote them!

"How did that get on the interweb?" I ask. "Did someone steal it and put it there?"

She touches my arm soothingly. "No, Ma, no one stole it. This is *your* writing. It's *your* story — right here on your laptop. You write really well, Ma. You are so clever!"

I'm cleverer than her, that's for sure. She doesn't even remember my name is Mary. She calls me Ma! What kind of name is that?

"What do you know about Keith's family?" she asks.

I start to tell her, but she orders me to type it. I slap the keys in a burst of frustration.

"Don't do that!" the woman shouts. "You'll break it. How about if you talk, and I'll type, okay?"

"Talk about what?"

"Keith's family? Start with his parents. You knew them, right? What did they look like?"

"They were both brown skinned, like him. Mixed. African and something. Portuguese, I think. A young man sailed from Madeira in eighteen-something ... settled in Arouca, a reserve in Trinidad for Amerindians. I think he may have gone there as a missionary. Anyway, he married an Arawak girl and stayed ... became the village teacher. They had about twelve children. One was Keith's great-grandfather."

The woman's mouth drops open. "Wow! I've got Amerindian genes, as well as genes from Portugal and Africa!"

"What a coincidence," I say, surprised, "same as Keith. No wonder you are both so good-looking!"

The woman smiles broadly. "But Bowen is a Welsh name, I'm told. Did Keith have any Welsh ancestors?"

"There are lots of brown-skinned Bowens in Barbados."

"*Barbados?* I thought Keith was Trini."

"He was," I tell her, "but his father was Bajan."

The woman types silently, leaving me in peace.

Toby nudges me, his soft brown eyes saying he'd rather be at my side than any other place in the whole world. I smile at him, feeling loved, feeling sleepy.

The woman wakes me with an excited voice. "I found something online: *Genealogies of Barbados Families.* Guess who was one of the original settlers?"

I look at her, perplexed.

"Anthony Bowen!"

"I don't know him."

"He was before your time, Ma!" she says, giggling as if I've made a joke. I wish she wouldn't do that. It makes me feel stupid. "He was granted land in Barbados by the British Crown in 1629. Do you know what year we're in now?"

"1970," I say.

She smiles at me, her eyes sparkling with reassuring familiarity.

"Listen to this!" she says. "Sixteen thousand acres were divided among several settlers. Anthony Bowen was one of them. He was from Glamorgan, Wales."

"Who was?"

"Anthony Bowen."

"I don't know him. But Bowen is a Welsh name."

"I've found census records, Ma! Perhaps we can track Keith's ancestors like they do on that show, *Finding Your Roots!*" Her mouth flops open. "Oh my God ...! This is from a will in 1703: I, Ann Bowen, bequeath my slaves to my four sons, and the cows to my daughter!"

"Sounds about right," I tell her. "Slaves were like livestock, bred and worked for profit."

The woman's voice quivers. "Oh my Lord, generation after generation of slaves passing from one generation of owners to the next. This is how my people lived."

She blows her nose, wipes her eyes, and continues to stare at the screen. Suddenly, she brightens up. "In 1809, Benjamin Bowen freed a woman and a child in his will. Good for him! He must have decided slavery was wrong."

I snort. "He probably had a liking for that particular woman and her child."

"You don't mean …"

"Where do you think brown-skinned Bowens came from?"

Tears trickle down the woman's cheeks.

I don't know why she's so upset. Toby leaves my side and comforts her.

sage

TeeVee is talking non-stop. Mom looks at it with deep lines etched on her face. She doesn't say much — just the occasional *OhGod* whispered under her breath. She's trying to keep her worry inside, but I feel it. Gran does, too.

I know we'd all feel better if we went into the yard and played fetch — or, even better, if we went to *ThePark*. I tug at the end of my leash until it falls off its peg, then drag it to Mom, whining. It doesn't take long before she notices me and understands.

"*Let'sGoToThePond*," she says. "We'd better get out while we still can. Looks like we're heading into a lockdown."

Any word starting with *Let'sGo* is a good word, unless it's followed by *ToTheVet*, so I wag my tail and wait patiently as Mom stuffs Gran into her clothes. It takes a while, but finally we are heading out the door, Mom holding my leash with one hand and Gran with the other. When we arrive at the pond, Gran eases herself onto a bench. Squirrels in the overhead branches goad me to chase them. I whine, straining against the leash, now tied to the bench, telling Mom how much I want to be free.

"I'm sorry, *Sage*," she says, "I don't trust you off the leash. You've chased squirrels too many times. I need to look after Gran now, so I can't be running around after you."

Understanding that this is the long way of saying *Down*, I ease myself to the ground beside her, rest my chin on my paws and watch the swimming birds paddle past the remaining patches of ice.

Mom hands Gran food. The swimming birds paddle faster and I perk up, drool instantly gathering in my mouth. Mom is always trying to starve me, so whenever I can, I scrounge additional snacks, such as catching the food that Gran drops. She misses her mouth a lot. Even her clothes are often delicious enough to lick, although the fibres that stick to my tongue sometimes make me gag. Right now, the food in Gran's hand is up for grabs, but experience tells me that during this ritual called *FeedTheDucks*, the greedy birds get all the food, and I get none. All the same, I watch Gran closely, willing her to share with me, but she throws the food into the water. Disappointing.

More swimming birds arrive, quacking and squawking and fighting. I strain at the leash until I throw up. I don't even take the time to gobble it back down — I get right back at it, this time running in circles until the leash is wrapped around Mom's legs.

"*Sage! Sit!*" she yells.

Trembling with excitement, I do as I'm told, until a chunk of food flies through the air, not far from my nose. I stretch and snap … and miss. It lands in the wet grass, out of my reach.

The swimming birds lumber onto land, slapping their large, webbed feet in the mud, squabbling. I woof in discontent. Gran understands. She stops throwing food at the birds and offers me a handful.

Then she eats some herself.

Mom groans. "*No!No!No!*"

I must be doing something wrong, but I can't tell what. Regardless, I shrink down and press my belly against the damp earth in submission.

Gran leans down and offers me another handful — crunchy and frozen.

"For goodness' sake," Mom moans. "Don't give it to *Sage* — it gives her gas."

I lick up every trace, seasoned with the warm saltiness of Gran's hand. I like Gran.

Mom sighs. "Don't blame me this evening when Sage is farting up a storm."

Two uprights approach, a tall one and a short one. The short one strains to reach me, but the tall one holds her back.

"*Sage* is good with kids," Mom says. "You can stroke her, if you like."

The short one gazes into my eyes, her warm little fingers stroking the top of my head.

Gran gets in on the action, patting the short one's head. "Kayla! You are looking so pretty today."

Mom gasps. "Ma! That's not Kayla."

"Of course it is," Gran scolds.

"No, Ma! *I'm* Kayla."

The tall upright struggles to pull something over her face, covering her mouth and nose, hiding everything except for her panicked eyes. She's afraid of me! She drags the short one away as if I've rolled in dead skunk.

I stare longingly as they disappear into the distance.

Gran tries to follow. "Kayla! Where are you going? Come back here! Right now!"

Mom holds Gran back. "Mary! That little girl is not Kayla! She looks like her — like me! A mop of dark curls and big hazel eyes. But she's *not* Kayla."

Gran's shoulders slump. "I miss Kayla. She doesn't visit me anymore."

"Who do you think I am?" Mom says.

Gran's face creases into a deep frown. "I don't know."

"I'm Kayla."

Gran smiles. "My daughter's name is Kayla. It's such a nice name."

"I think so, too," Mom says, swiping her arm across her damp face. "Let's go home."

We walk. Slowly. Quietly. Sadly.

kayla

Hey guys, here's the weekly update I promised you.

Ma's ability to read, write, and organize her thoughts is fading fast. I doubt she will be able to write much more of her story, so *I've* started writing. It's called *The Caregiver's Tale*, and eventually, I plan to weave it into Ma's story. I've been thinking about the title for her memoir. How about *Tangled Tales*? It's a cool play on words because plaques and tangles characterize Alzheimer disease! Tangles develop when the microtubules (which carry nutrients to the brain cells) twist, collapse and get tangled. I just found out that a protein called Tau keeps the microtubules from twisting. Tau reminds me of hair conditioner! When I don't use it, my hair is so frizzy and tangled that I can't get a comb through it!

No rush to decide on a title. A published book is a long way off. But for now, I figure my notes will help you guys follow along with what's happening. So here goes.

***

The Caregiver's Tale — Part 1

Becoming a full-time caregiver has been harder than I anticipated. There are so many ups and downs and so much to learn. I feel like I'm always one step behind! By the time I learn how to deal with one behaviour, Ma has moved on to a new one or, more accurately, back to an earlier one.

Thank God for the Alzheimer Day Centre. It made a huge difference in my life. Sure, we had a rocky start. Ma fought hard about going, and when I picked her up at the end of the first day, she was angry at me for making her go to the centre. It upset me so much that I was ready to quit — it didn't seem worth the effort and aggravation. But then after two weeks, there was a sudden shift in Ma's attitude. She was *keen* to leave the house in the mornings, saying the people were so nice.

So, with two days of freedom each week, I rejoined the world. I actually went to the church office instead of working from home ... planned the Easter services and spoke to other people! At the grocery store, I read the labels, picked the best fruits and veggies, and shopped for the deals. As a result, I became a better caregiver — more patient and more loving. I even had moments of joy and satisfaction.

But then, as you know, Covid-19 changed the world, wreaking an extra burden of havoc on dementia patients and their caregivers. Social distancing, masks, virtual funerals, banned gatherings, cancelled classes, and, devastatingly, no Day Centre.

Once again, I'm struggling.

Some days, I do a reasonable job. But on nights when Ma has a nightmare, or is rattling the kiddy lock on the door all night, my nerves get frayed and it's easy to snap. I know I shouldn't be irritated, but I am. Then I feel bad. And I'm so tired. Weary to the bone.

Without the mental stimulation of the Day Centre, it seems to me that Ma is slipping away faster. She is getting increasingly emotional. (Me, too!) Sometimes she cries. (Me, too!) And sometimes, she's angry and acts out, like Jesse when he was little and didn't have the words to express his frustration, so he screamed and had a temper tantrum. I hate to admit it, but sometimes I'm on the brink of doing that, too, especially when Ma calls me "Hettie." I feel like shaking her and yelling, "I'm Kayla! I'm not the frickin' maid. I'm not just the woman who looks after you — I'm your daughter. Can't you see me?"

I haven't actually said that, but I've been close and have locked myself in the bathroom. In my defence, I have surveillance cameras in the house now, so I can watch what she's up to on my cellphone. (Thanks, Zach!) It makes me feel like I'm spying on her secret life, which of course I am, but at least I can relax a little, knowing that she's safe. And after a break from her, I can start afresh.

The Alzheimer Society transitioned to virtual programming, and I've done a few webinars with Teepa Snow, the guru for dementia caregivers. Role-playing with her has given me a real feel for how soul-destroying it must be to do your best, yet have someone respond with impatience and irritation.

I understand with my heart that the most important thing I can do for my mother is make her feel safe and loved. All the other things I had placed value on are immaterial. It's far better to set aside the chores and sing "If you're you happy and you know it, clap your hands," or read *Love You Forever*, or throw the beach ball back and forth in the hall, or sort playing cards into suits, or just sit side by side, her head resting against my chest. When Ma smiles and laughs, I do, too. When she feels loved, I feel good, too. Yet, despite knowing all this ... at times I still snap. And then I feel bad.

So there you go. It's a real Jekyll-and-Hyde lifestyle ... altruistic aspirations on the one hand, reality on the other.

I'm attaching a video clip. Ma is singing along with Steve, a gentleman from the Alzheimer Society. It's a YouTube recording, but Ma interacts with Steve as if he's in the same room, responding to his questions. It's cute. Steve always starts with the national anthem. Ma gets to her feet, stands up straight as a ramrod and belts out: "God keep our land glorious and free! O Canada, we stand on guard for thee." It's so heartfelt and patriotic and inspiring.

sage

Days and nights merge. Gran wakes in the middle of the night, acting like it's the middle of the day. Mom gets up, too, stripping the bed and taking the sheets to the laundry room. I follow her because there's an interesting smell. Jesse sleeps through it all. He stuffs plugs into his ears. Sometimes he leaves them on the table at the side of his bed. They make a tasty snack, but I have to sneak them when no one is looking because Mom gets really mad, yelling, "They'll clog up your tummy and kill you."

mary

The woman makes me wear pull-ups like the ones toddlers wear. But they are confusing. Sometimes I don't know how to pull them down. Sometimes I don't know how to pull them up. It should be simple, but it's not.

Why is there pee on the floor? Who did that?

Why are my socks wet?

The woman gives me dry socks and helps me get them on right.

sage

Mom sits at the big table — the turkey table. Sighing heavily, she pushes papers around, piling some up but crumpling others and tossing them onto the floor. Taking this as an invitation for a game of catch, I surge into the room, mouth at the ready. With a noise resembling a growl, she drops her head into her hands. Uh-oh, she doesn't want to play, and she doesn't want me in the turkey room. I reverse out as fast as my legs can carry me.

"What's going on?" Jesse asks, coming into the dining room.

"Taxes," Mom groans. "I left it way too late. The problem is, I have to do Gran's as well as my own, and she hasn't filed for four years! Her memory must have been failing long before I realized it. And since she moved in, I've been too busy looking after her to even think about taxes."

"Hang on," Jesse says, "I'll call Uncle Zach ... he'll know what to do."

"He says he'll find a tax accountant in town. He'll call them and set it up — you'll just have to drop everything over to their office. Take yours as well as Gran's ... don't worry about how much it costs because he'll take care of it."

"Phew! That's a relief. Thanks for doing that, Jesse. I would never have asked him. I don't know why I find it so difficult to admit I need help, especially from Zach. I always think I should be able to do everything on my own."

Jesse smiles. "You know, Mom, I think sometimes people *like* to help. It feels good."

I don't know what is happening to Jesse these days, but he's different. I like it.

Mom pushes her chair back from the table. "Spring is here. It's a glorious day. *Sage! Let'sGo. Let'sGoToThePark. Come* along, Mary, you need to get some sun. You're looking far too pale."

With a wagging tail, I fetch one of Gran's shoes, hoping to hurry her out of the house, but Mom doesn't appreciate my effort.

"*Sage! DropIt. You'reSuchaSweetiepie*, but these are Gran's house shoes. She needs walking shoes."

Finally, we're out the door. Scent after glorious scent blows on the soft breeze, telling me it's the kind of day when squirrels have love on their minds, the kind of day when they are preoccupied with each other and may allow me to get close.

After a slow amble, we make it as far as *ThePark*, just missing *MitzyTheSharpei*, who trots off in the other direction, her tail curled high over her back. But something is wrong. The entrance is fenced off. We can't get in.

"Crap," Mom says, "it's closed. Bloody Covid."

I sniff through a patch of fluff in the grass. It gets stuck to my damp nose, making me sneeze, shooting the fluff into the sky. Gran watches it float on the breeze, her bottom lip trembling.

"Dandelions!" she complains. "Right after the funeral, Alicia picked some that had gone to seed like these. She wanted to give them to her daddy, like she'd given him the red rosebud. But there was no coffin for her to lay the dandelions on. I puffed at a few, to blow them to heaven! I thought I was helping, you see, but they drifted back down and landed on the grass. Alicia pouted a bit — the way she does, you know — and then she tipped her little face up to mine and said, 'If I think really hard, can I think them to Daddy?'"

Gran's face creases into a smile, but I sense the heaviness in her heart. Mom's, too.

A squirrel moves close with short, jerky movements, flicking his tail over his back in a graceful curve. I refuse his invitation to play — Mom and Gran both need me.

When we get home Mom heads inside, saying the long word for Cookie: *"Let's-put-the-kettle-on-and-make-a-nice cup-of-tea."*

I try to follow her, but she takes me back to the yard, ordering me to *Sit* and to *Stay*. I sprawl out in the sunshine at Gran's feet. Life is good.

A noisy blue jay catches my attention, squawking as it flies overhead toward the cedar hedge at the bottom of the garden. I cock my head to watch it settle on the soft fronds. Gran watches it, too, her face peaceful.

Suddenly, Gran's face puckers. Salt water trickles down her cheeks. But before I can get in there to clean it up, another upright wipes her eyes. That's strange! I didn't see him arrive. Usually I bark to warn the pack of intruders, but this stranger carries no threat. He's unusually bright, shining like the sun, but fuzzy around the edges. After a while, he backs away and vanishes, so I approach Gran to lick her face. It's already dry.

mary

The woman ushers me outside, telling me it's a lovely spring day.

"We're going to plant some flowers," she says. "Look! Pink and purple impatiens. Aren't they beautiful? I thought we'd put them in the border under the front window. They like shade and they'll be a nice splash of colour right through to the fall."

"They should go under the silver birch tree," I say.

"Uh, we don't have a silver birch tree, Mary."

"Yes, we do! Keith planted it to remind me of Holmwood."

I look around but the silver birch isn't there. I keep searching, confused and lost. The tray of flowers in the woman's arms makes me sadder still. I remember that awful summer when the impatiens bloomed under the silver birch tree. By the time Keith died in October, the flowers were dead, too.

The woman hugs me, then tells me to sit on the porch in the new two-seater rocking chair and watch her plant the flowers.

A familiar car drives slowly down the road. My heart leaps in my chest. It's Keith in his new company car, a bronze Caprice Classic with all the bells and whistles. I jump to my feet, waving, but the driver doesn't stop. He goes past, glancing at me with a quizzical expression.

A memory comes to me, so powerful that it hurts my heart: The children and I watch from the porch as Keith reverses his shiny, new car out of the garage. It's our routine. No matter if he's going to the office in Toronto or flying to the other side of Canada, we wave him off each morning from the front porch. But on this memorable day, instead of driving away as usual, he stops on the street, separated from us by only the small expanse of newly laid sod.

I see the bigger picture: the leaves of the silver birch trembling in the early morning air; dust motes dancing in the shafts of sunlight; pink and purple impatiens flowers freshened with the dew of dawn.

Zach is balanced on my hip, wearing just a T-shirt and a diaper, his fingers twirling my sleep-scruffy braid. Alicia is at my side. She's wearing a short pink jumpsuit — velour with white ties on the shoulders — and has bare arms, bare legs, bare feet. I don't remember what we talked about that morning, whether we ate breakfast, whether we kissed goodbye. Yet I can still see Keith vividly as he rolls down the window of the car, rests his arm on the frame, and turns to me with his beautiful smile.

And I flash back a decade. Keith in the Sunbeam Alpine on the first day of university, his arm draped loosely over the window frame. The same warm smile. *That* moment was the beginning of our life together. With a gut-wrenching jolt, I know that *this* moment is the end. Never again will I see him heading off to work, waving, smiling.

Time slows down. I fix him in my memory.

"Don't go," I whisper.

But he drives away, turning out of Goldberry Square and merging into traffic, heading to the airport for a short business trip to Calgary.

If not for Zach on my hip and Alicia at my side, and all three of us barefoot, I'd have run after him. Instead, I stand on the porch, dazed, with my heart in my mouth.

Years earlier, I'd had a premonition that I was going to lose the love of my life. It hadn't come true. Sure, he'd been beaten up by skinheads, but he'd recovered. He was invincible. I tell myself that my imagination is working overtime. All the same, as the morning passes, I flick back and forth between *Sesame Street*, *Mister Rogers*, and the news, expecting to hear about a plane crash. There is no plane crash. Keith calls to say he landed safely. And I forget about my second premonition.

"How do you like the new rocker?" the woman says. "Is it relaxing?"

I ignore her because Keith is telling me why he missed his flight home from Calgary. "I was lying in bed in the hotel room," he says, "wanting more than anything in the world to be home with you and the children. I knew I had to get to the airport, yet I couldn't get out of bed and call a cab — my body wouldn't co-operate. And time made no sense to me. When I arrived at the check-in, I'd missed the flight by several hours! I couldn't understand how that had happened!"

"You were exhausted from the new job," I tell him, "and the stress of moving us to Canada and starting a new job ... and travelling all over the country."

"Who are you talking to?" the woman says.

"No one! Go away and leave us alone."

"Are you talking to Keith?" she asks, her voice incredulous, her brow furrowed.

"No!" I say, on the brink of tears.

Her face softens. "It's okay, Mary. I won't tell your daddy. I'll stand guard for you! I'll be right here ... planting flowers ... keeping my eyes peeled so no one sees you. Sit on the porch with Keith and have a nice chat together."

kayla

Hi Siblings!

You're gonna think I'm crazy, but I just recorded Ma talking to Keith!!! I couldn't see him or hear him, but *she* certainly could! She wasn't dreaming, I swear. Her eyes were wide open. And, before you ask ... I hadn't taken any of her CBD oil! And I hadn't been drinking, either.

She was sitting on the new two-seater rocker on the porch, rocking gently. Her body was skewed a little to the side, and her head tilted ... as if someone were sitting next to her ... except no one was there. Well, at least no one I could see. I wish I could have.

I didn't record the first part of their conversation. I was planting flowers ten feet away and I didn't realize her mumbles were so important. She was talking about someone missing a flight home. As soon as I clued in that it was Keith who had missed the flight, I hit record. I'm attaching the audio file. There are dead spaces where Keith must be talking back to her. I wish I knew what he said.

Listen to the file and let me know what you think. It certainly puts a different slant on his death. We always suspected he was murdered, right? Or that he died in a racist attack ... something that was so traumatizing for Ma she couldn't talk about it. Seems that's not the way it happened. I can't fit the pieces of the puzzle together.

[Audio file]

"I made excuses for you when you missed the first flight home, but not when you missed the second one. I was mad ... really mad. You weren't pulling your weight. I was only two months' pregnant, but I could barely function. The exhaustion was overwhelming. I needed you home to help with the kids. There was so much to do ... we hadn't even unpacked the boxes or hung the pictures. You joked that you were having a sympathetic pregnancy. I wasn't amused."

[Silence]

"I'm sorry, too, Keith. When you finally got home — two days late — you tripped through the doorway and almost fell ... said your leg had gone to sleep. I should have called an ambulance right there and then, but you said you just needed to go to bed, that you'd be fine in the morning. I believed you, or maybe I was just too darned tired to do anything about it. But in the morning, you were worse! You couldn't dress yourself and your speech was slurred. At the clinic, the doctor couldn't find a reflex in your feet. I knew that was bad. By the end of the day, you were in the neurology ward at Toronto General. You couldn't stand, or even sit in a wheelchair without slumping over. You had to be strapped in. It was heartbreaking. If I'd acted faster ... got you to the doctor sooner ..."

[Silence]

"No, Keith! All the signs were there. You were deteriorating in front of my eyes, minute by minute. I could see that, yet at the same time I was blind to it!"

[Silence]

"I get it! You wanted life to stay normal for as long as possible."

[Silence]

"You knew, didn't you? Before that trip, you insisted we make our wills, and you checked that your life insurance policy was adequate. You showed me where all the important documents were and how to pay the bills. When I asked why, you said that with the extra travelling and the family growing, you needed to make sure that the children and I would be okay if, for example, the plane went down. Day after day for weeks, you were trying to tell me! But I didn't want to hear. It wasn't until after the biopsy that I started to accept reality."

[Silence]

"I knew you didn't want the biopsy. The evening before, you tried to get out of bed to go home. You collapsed in my arms. You said the doctors weren't going to make you better. But for me, it was the only hope of finding out what was causing the problem and giving you a chance of survival. I promised to take you home right after. If only I'd listened to what you were trying to tell me, instead of making decisions for you as if you were a child. Those were the last words you ever spoke to me — at least the last words I understood. It's obvious now that you were saying you wanted to die at home with me and the kids. I denied you your dying wish. I'm so sorry."

mary

My ankle hurts. The woman says I fell. I don't remember falling. She says we need to go to the emergency room for an X-ray. She says we have to wait.

Sitting in the corridor next to the nurses' station, I wait for the surgeon to give me the results of the biopsy. It's late afternoon when he finally appears. Even then, he's busy — talking with staff, reading charts, making notes, disinclined to notice me. Finally, I interrupt him. With staff and visitors milling around, he tells me the shocking truth: there is nothing to be done. Keith will become demented to the point of death within the month.

How?

A virus. The JC polyomavirus. In my years working in virology, I'd never heard of it. I had, however, seen interferon kill viruses in my own cell cultures in the lab — as groundbreaking, I thought, as the penicillin fungus that stopped the growth of bacteria in Alexander Fleming's Petri dishes. The first clinical trials of interferon had started in humans.

I phone the head of the department and beg. Nothing is available. I make more phone calls to doctors and researchers around the world. Nobody has a solution for us.

There is now no avoiding the prognosis. Death has to be faced. I make up my mind to tell you as soon as you wake up from the surgery. But when you finally regain consciousness, you can't speak. Your words are jumbled, your sounds incoherent. For two days, you try to talk, but I can't understand a single word. You obviously know what you want to say, but the messages are short-circuited. After two days, you stop trying.

You can still clutch a pen, and with a shaking hand, you write me notes, but they are illegible. I can't read a word. I print out the letters of the alphabet and try to get you to point to them, but you have no control over your hands — not even to squeeze *yes* or *no*. The muscles of your eyes are partially paralyzed, too, so you can't blink an answer to my questions, either. It's all too dreadful to bear.

I feel so helpless. I'm letting you down. Over the years, you'd occasionally shared your thoughts on life and death, but I wasn't interested. Now, it's all I think about.

I remember the little maroon book crammed with your handwritten notes: scribbled shopping lists and household expenses, but also poems and prose ... your gems of wisdom. It's in the top drawer of your desk, and I eat up your words like I am starving. On a page titled "Creation," your words jump off the page and hit me in the face. "Life on earth is a time to understand your purpose, to develop and prepare for your return to the Creator."

You lie in a hospital bed, mute, your own handwritten words in a little maroon book speaking for you. You are ready for your return to the Creator, and I am nearly ready for it, too. But your suffering is now the problem, a challenge for my budding faith: infection after infection; seizure after seizure; raging fevers; bedsores. The agony written on your face and in your eyes tells me it's torture — body and soul. Yet you keep on living — two months past the prognosis given by the neurologist. You are young and your heart is strong. It refuses to stop beating. This extended time gives me pause to hope again. Has God heard my prayers? Are we going to get a miracle? I feel like I am riding on a seesaw, flying into the sky with hope, then plummeting to earth again in despair.

The thing that bugs me the most is that you are a man of God, yet God gives you no mercy.

The woman interrupts me. "No bones broken," she says. "Let's go home."

mary

The woman says that Alicia's birthday is coming up and we need to write in a card. She gives me a pen and a card, but I can't catch my thoughts … can't hold onto them … don't know what to write.

"Practise on this first," the woman says, putting a pad of paper down in front of me. "Say 'happy birthday.'"

"Happy birthday."

She smiles. "My bad! I mean *write* 'happy birthday.' To Alicia. It's her birthday soon."

I try, but it's hard to create the letters.

hapy day aleesha

The writing pad reminds me of Keith's final message. And my stupidity for not being able to read it. He wrote the same message over and over, scrawled it across the page diagonally. Each time it had the same shape and the same pattern, but it got bigger and bigger, bolder and bolder, like he was screaming at me to understand. Yet, I still couldn't read it. I felt so helpless, so stupid.

I feel a wrenching pain in my chest as if my heart is being split apart. This is what it's like to be broken-hearted.

The only thing I could do for Keith was snuggle into his chest, weaving my body around the tubes and letting him know I was there … that he was not alone.

Now it's my turn.

Now *my* brain is dying … my abilities leaving me.

I'm scared.

Stay with me, Toby. Don't leave me.

sage

Gran gets out of bed early and goes to the kitchen. I follow, hoping for a snack, but there's nothing.

"This hotel isn't very good," she says, sitting at the table. "No breakfast. Not even coffee."

Jesse joins us, briefly, but he throws his hands over his eyes, calling for Mom, and almost trampling me in his rush to get out of the room. I don't understand what's wrong.

"What's going on?" Mom yells back.

"Gran is topless!" Jesse replies. "I've been seriously damaged! Permanently scarred! Old people should *never* take their clothes off."

"Don't worry," Mom says, chuckling. "I'll get her dressed."

"It's not funny, Mom. I can't get the image of Gran's boobs out of my mind!"

Mom tries to stifle her laughter, but it shoots out of her in a whoosh of warm breath.

Jesse leaps into the rain room, letting the water fall on his head for much longer than usual. When he gets out, I can tell he's going somewhere, but I don't know if he plans to take me along, so I pay close attention, watching for clues. I can tell from his heartbeat and aroma that he's excited and a little bit anxious. He puts on *Walkies* clothes, so I wag my tail in anticipation, but then he rips them off, tosses them to the floor and puts on others that have a fresh new smell — not *Walkies* clothes. My tail droops. But then he puts on shoes — *Walkies* shoes — and clips my leash to my collar. Yay!

"Aren't you going to eat something?" Mom calls out.

Jesse shivers. "Seeing Gran like that has turned me off food for life. I'll never eat again!"

Mom laughs again. She's obviously having a good day, but there's no time for me to share her joy; Jesse is leaving, and I'm going with him.

Mom gets serious as we reach the door. "Don't forget social distancing! Don't let your guard down. I know they say that young people don't often get Covid … at least not badly, but you could bring it home to me and Gran. She's vulnerable, so please be vigilant. Do you have your mask?"

"Do I ever go anywhere without it?" he says. "Don't worry, Mom. I'll be careful."

As soon as the door closes behind us, Jesse seems happier. There's a bounce to his step. Or maybe it's just a bouncy kind of day. Birds twitter, chasing each other through the sky, and squirrels chatter, chasing each other through the branches. Even the trees whisper to each other, as warm gusts of wind rustle their newly unfurled leaves. And I'm with Jesse! What could be better?

Then Ashley appears. She offers me her hand, but I pull away. It smells of the harsh goop that seems to cover all humans these days, goop that deadens the delightful smells of food and sweat and dirt; goop that stings my nostril when I sniff it and tastes yucky when I lick it.

She leans into Jesse. He doesn't mind the goopy smell. He drapes his arm over her shoulder and pulls her close. They walk slowly. I shorten my stride to match theirs.

"It feels weird, doesn't it?" she says. "To be outside, I mean. I thought that not going to school would be great, but it sucks, right? I miss seeing my friends."

MitzyTheSharpei is coming toward us, taking her human for *Walkies*. *Mitzy* and I usually stop for a quick sniff, but Jesse is in no mood to slow down. He herds Ashley off the sidewalk and onto the street, tugging me along with him. It's troubling because I'm not allowed to walk on the street as a rule. There's a scent of fear in the air, too. It hangs over all the humans like a cloud. For some reason that I can't put a paw on, they are all scared of each other.

"I miss *Basketball!*" Jesse says, leading me back onto the sidewalk. "And I've missed you, Ashley. FaceTime is great but it's not the same as this, right?"

TerrorTheTerrier drags his human toward us. *Terror* is small but surprisingly strong. He's fast, too. Fast enough to catch a squirrel and shake it to death. If I ever caught a squirrel, I'd let it go so we could play catch all over again. As they get closer to us, Terror's human flattens himself against the hedge while we, once again, hop down the curb onto the street.

Eventually, we reach a place I've never been to before.

Jesse stands on a dark circle on the ground and talks to *iPhone.* "Jesse here … yeah, we're booked for 11:15 … okay … will do."

"What did they say?"

He taps *iPhone* and talks. "We have to read the rules and answer the questions. Do you have a fever? Cough? Blah blah blah? Have you been out of the country? In contact with anyone with Covid-19? Name and number for contact tracing? I'll put mine. Must maintain physical distancing. No group bigger than five. One hour maximum. Masks to be worn at all times …"

Suddenly, Ashley is alarmed. "Are dogs allowed in?"

"Sure … they just have to be on a leash."

She pats me and speaks soft words. I'm beginning to see why my boy likes her so much.

Soon, they are hitting little balls with long sticks, making them disappear down holes. It's my kind of game — the balls are the perfect size to fit in my mouth, but Jesse won't let me try. I wouldn't have chewed them, anyway; they smell like the yucky hand-goop. I *Sit* and *Stay*, watching Jesse stand behind Ashley, his nose in her hair and his arms around her. Together, they hold the stick and swing it. She giggles. He smiles. They're having fun and ignoring me. I feel left out.

"We still have fifteen minutes," Jesse says. "I think there's a concession stand over by the gate. *Sage! Let'sGo.* You want *IceCream?*"

I bounce alongside them, wagging my tail and whining, *Yes, yes, yes.*

They sit on a bench, but there's no *IceCream.*

Jesse is disappointed, too. "Closed until further notice. Damn Covid!"

Ashley smiles. "Never mind. I had fun. I even let you win!"

"Ha ha," Jesse says.

She reaches out to touch his hair. "I love your curls."

"Are you kidding me? I'm way overdue for a trim. But everyone is, right?"

She nestles into his chest and he pulls her close — absorbed, I think, by the scent of her hair. He doesn't notice the group of uprights who strut toward us like alpha males, sticking their chests out, big and menacing.

The hairs on the ridge of my back bristle and my heart races, priming me to protect Jesse, but at the same time, I want to hide behind his legs and pee. I hold my ground, leaning against him, telling him to get his face out of Ashley's hair and pay attention. But he ignores me!

The uprights home in on us, the aroma of aggression hanging like a thick cloud.

"A fuckin' nigger!" one says.

"And a fuckin' nigger lover!"

In an instant, Jesse's aroma changes from love to hate. Rage and fear burst from them both in a thick soup of scent that drives me into a frenzy. A low growl rumbles from so deep inside me that I startle myself. Hackles up and lips pulled back in a snarl that shows my long canines, I yank the leash right through Jesse's hands, lunging first at one upright, then another, pivoting between them so fast that it makes my head spin. Feral and free, I borrow moves from the Wild Ones and even from the Big Cats on *TeeVee*, nipping at their ankles, snatching socks and skin in my jaws, and shaking my head the way *TerrorTheTerrier* showed me.

The uprights high-step away from my snapping teeth, screaming like hurt bunnies. Then, tucking their non-existent tails between their legs, they run. I give chase, barking ferociously. At my age, running is hard. Barking as well as running wipes me out in no time, but I've done enough. They won't return to mess with my precious humans. I give one deep, sonorous woof; then, with my hackles settling back down, I trot back to Jesse with as much spring in my step as I can muster.

He exhales. "Wow! That's a first. I've lived in this town for years and nobody has ever said that before!"

"It's because you're with me," Ashley says. "They don't like that. I guess that's what my dad meant. He isn't a racist, believe me, but he's worried about us dating."

She reaches down, stroking the top of my head, her hand trembling like a leaf in the breeze. "Thank goodness you were here, *Sage*."

"*Goooodgiiiiirl*," Jesse murmurs, rubbing the spot between my front legs.

Usually, I'd squirm with pleasure, but not today. Jesse is carrying a weight of sorrow. I can feel it through his fingers.

That night, Jesse tosses and turns in bed. Every few moments, I have to find a new position and settle in again.

"I can't stop thinking about what happened today," he tells me. "It's like a video on replay. It keeps looping around. And I keep thinking of all the things I could have said and done, or should have said and done — like taking out my phone for one, and hitting video. How could I forget that? We both had phones in our pockets and neither of us thought to take them out! Guess we weren't thinking straight."

I nudge my nose under his hands until he strokes me. "If you hadn't been there, we wouldn't have stood a chance! There were five of them! If I'd said anything to provoke them, they'd have beaten me up, for sure. Ashley, too. Was that what happened to Gran and Keith?

"*You'reSuchaGoooodGiiiirl*," he whispers. "It's strange, because you're so gentle, and yet today, you were more like a police dog than a golden retriever. You knew how to protect Ashley and me. Thank you. *GoooodGiiiirl*."

I bask in the warmth of his love. Soon his breathing takes on a gentle, even rhythm, so I go to be with the Wild Ones.

In the morning, he sits up and scratches his head. "*Sage*, I had this crazy dream! I was ringing Ashley's doorbell. Her father opened the door. I told him I'm Jesse — that I'm picking up Ashley. He said, 'I don't think so! Not with nappy hair like that! Anyway, she has a boyfriend. His name is Ian.'"

I lick his hand, and he strokes me.

"It was just a dream, right? Let's get something to eat."

mary

The woman makes me have a bath.

I forget her name.

I don't know why I need a bath. I'm not dirty.

She says I smell and that it's been a week.

It's not true. She lies to me all the time.

I hate baths.

Naked.

Wet.

Besides, I don't have a shilling to put in the meter. The hot water will run out. I'll get cold.

And I don't know how to get dressed — it's embarrassing.

I want to get away from these feelings. I try to tell the woman but the thoughts in my head won't come out as words. She doesn't understand me.

I try to escape with Toby, but the yard boy blocks me. I'm a prisoner! They're keeping me here against my will. It was the woman's idea. I think her name is Hettie. The yard boy is in on it, too. They're as thick as thieves.

I want to go home, but I don't know how to get there.

sage

Jesse is out late. Mom goes to bed at her usual time, but I flop onto the mat by the front door, waiting.

When he comes home, I sense his sadness, even though he seems pleased to see me. Soon we are snuggled in bed and he talks — so many words, but I don't understand any of them.

"Tonight was a disaster! It was supposed to be special because I don't know when I'll see Ashley again. Camp starts tomorrow ... at least that's the plan, but the Covid rules keep changing and everything is so messed up. Right now, camp is running at reduced capacity, but that could change any day and it could close right down at a moment's notice. I don't know if I'll be up north for two days or two months! Neither option is great. I don't want to be stuck here with Gran for the rest of the summer. But at camp, the internet sucks ... no Zoom or FaceTime. And even if Ashley wants to visit, they won't let her. Plus, I won't be allowed to leave camp even on my days off! Covid sucks! Will we have to live like this forever, stuck in our own bubbles?

"That's why tonight was so important. But it didn't go well. The movie theatre was closed, of course ... so I'd made a reservation for the outside patio of the Italian restaurant. Walking down Main Street, Ashley reached for my hand. I pulled away, saying we have to social distance, but that wasn't the reason. I was scanning the body language of everyone in sight ... with one hand in my pocket, ready to whip out my phone and hit video should things go bad. A cop car came toward us. No big deal, but after it passed, it did a U-turn and followed us! My heart almost leaped out of my chest. For years Mom has prepped me for this, so I looked down and got ready to do the 'Yes-sir-no-sir' routine. I always thought she was being overdramatic, and a bit of a wimp, but things have changed. The George Floyd video shook me up, big time. I haven't been able to *un*-see it — him face down on the pavement, arms wrenched behind his back and a cop's knee on his neck. And now cops are tailing me! Stalking me, waiting to pounce. There are two strikes against me. I'm Black and I've crossed the line ... I'm with a white girl.

"Wow, *Sage*, I think that's the first time I ever said that I'm Black. I didn't see myself that way before ... not until George Floyd.

"Anyway, that cop car scared the crap out of me. I was angry, too, but I couldn't let that show. I had to be submissive. God, that was hard. Rage was right at the surface, ready to explode.

"Honestly, *Sage*, I don't know how much longer I could have held it together. Fortunately, I didn't have to. The cops pulled ahead and turned into the parking lot of the donut shop. I'd over-reacted ... this time. But my gut tells me there'll be another time, one that won't end so well. You're lucky you're a dog. This is really heavy stuff to deal with."

Jesse sighs and strokes me for a while, but he's not focused on me. His mind is a long way off. Nevertheless, I pay attention to his words, waiting to hear a familiar one.

"By the time we got to our table, I was hoping for better things. Ashley ordered the risotto, but she didn't realize it came with sea-food. She doesn't like seafood. So she spent the whole time picking bits out. I ordered the pizza but it turns out that arugula, ibérico, and olives are not the greatest toppings. We should have gotten takeout from the pizza place. I spent fifty bucks on a crappy meal! And you won't believe what she said when I told her I was gonna miss her — 'Aw, thank you, Jesse! That's so nice.'"

He turns off the lights, thumps the pillow a few times and turns away from me, mumbling to himself. Then he laughs out loud and speaks in a strange voice that sounds a lot like Gran. "Fifty fuckin' bucks! That's a fortune! A fuckin' fortune! Fifty fuckin' bucks!"

Finally, he settles, and I know it's safe for me to take up my favourite spot with my nose close to his butt. He's not peaceful for long, though. He tosses and turns, winding himself up in the sheets. Whenever I start to drift away to be with the Wild Ones, he thrashes some more.

In the morning, he leaps out of bed, waking me with a start — racing around the house and putting things into *GymBag*. This is not unusual, but today the air feels charged, like just before a storm — when everything rumbles and the den shakes, when the sky cracks with flashes of light, and when I generally run for cover under Jesse's bed. I'm not hiding under the bed yet, but I'm ready.

I wait with my nose against the rain door as he bathes, even though I hate the falling water. And I sit at his side as he eats breakfast although Gran is dropping more food than usual. Finally, he puts on shoes, so I know he's going out. I ask to go, too, but his mind is elsewhere and he doesn't hear my silent plea.

Mom hugs him, long and hard, and then he picks up *GymBag* and opens the door. I try to rush outside with him, but Mom holds me back. The door closes and Jesse is gone.

I drop onto the mat by the door and wait, as I always do whenever Jesse leaves the den, standing up occasionally and stretching my neck to see what's happening in the street, hoping to catch a glimpse of him returning.

I hold *FloppyBunny* in my mouth, waiting for the comfort that his softness usually brings, but Jesse is gone. What if he never returns? Mom offers me Kong. He's filled with dry, meaty treats, but I can't be bothered to wrestle them from his mouth.

A sleepy fly crawls across the glass, right in front of my nose. With nothing better to do, I sniff at it. Cat opens his eyes and catches sight of the fly. He likes flies. He's quick enough to snatch them right out of the air. Stifling his yawn, he crouches in hunting mode, eyes focused intently. I don't much like the taste of fly, although sometimes I gobble one up just to deprive Cat of the treat, but Jesse is gone and I feel indifferent to everything, so I let Cat catch it. He swallows, then, without acknowledging my generosity in any way, nonchalantly grooms his elegant ears with spit-wettened paws. Ingrate.

I heave myself onto Jesse's bed, pushing my nose into the pillow where his scent is strongest. The night goes by, with Mom making a midnight trip to the laundry room, carrying Gran's wet sheets.

Another boring day. Another lonely night. I suck the remnants of Jesse's aroma from his bed. Eventually, all I can smell is myself and Cat. I rummage through the laundry basket until I find Jesse's socks. I lick them until I've absorbed every trace of his comforting scent.

In the old days, I would send Mom messages by staring up at my leash on the peg by the door until she understood that I wanted to go *Walkies*. These days I don't care if I ever go *Walkies* again. Mom doesn't seem to care, either.

But then Ashley comes by. Her face is covered so all I can see is her eyes, but I recognize her scent. "Hi, *Sage*. Would you like to go for a walk with me?"

I have no idea what her words mean, but I wag my tail hard.

Gran is excited to see Ashley, too, rushing toward her. "Anna-Mae! It's wonderful to see you!"

Mom holds Gran back. "No hugging! We have to put on our mask, like I showed you. Here! Let me help ... the elastic goes around your ears. Perfect! You look like a surgeon!"

Mom, Gran, and Ashley are now all reduced to eyes. Their words are muffled, which is a problem since I don't understand most of their words at the best of times. Thank goodness for my nose. They still smell the same!

"Anna-Mae, you dyed your hair!" Gran squeals. "I love it blond! How's Ian? We have so much to catch up on."

Ashley smells uncomfortable.

"Good timing, Anna-Mae," Mom says, with the one-eyed expression. "I've just made muffins. They're still warm."

Suddenly, I have an appetite again!

My knower tells me that Ashley wants to join our pack, but Mom is keeping her on the fringe, the way a good alpha does when checking out a newcomer. If Ashley were a dog, she'd roll onto her back and expose her soft belly, saying she's happy to submit to Mom's leadership, even if it means getting a bite where it really hurts. I demonstrate this submissive gesture to Ashley, but she just leans over and gives me a belly rub.

Then she clips on my leash, and we go *Walkies!* It's a good day.

kayla

Hey Siblings. Here's the latest instalment of my caregiver notes.

The Caregiver's Tale — Part 2

It's quiet in the house these days. Ma doesn't talk to me much, although sometimes I get the impression she's talking to someone I can't see ... maybe someone in her head. I mentioned it to the doctor. He says she's probably hallucinating, seeing and hearing someone who isn't there, and that it's common in dementia. I hope he's wrong and that Keith drops by sometimes to keep her company ... waiting for her to join him. It makes me feel good to think that. I wish I could see and hear him, too! I never knew him, but all the same, I miss him. How can you miss someone who was never here? The doctor would probably say I'm losing touch with reality, too.

Ma still wanders around looking for things that she never finds, but she doesn't get as agitated or argumentative as she used to. Maybe the CBD oil helps. There are fewer repeated questions, too, and fewer retold stories. Strangely, I almost miss it! And I never thought I'd say this, but now that Jesse is away at camp, I miss him, too! The last three months of virtual schooling had their ups and downs. We aggravated each other so much, but we laughed, too, and even talked. And miraculously, he spent quality time with his gran. They watched YouTube videos of Motown artists, singing along and even dancing ... copying the moves. They had *fun!* It was a joy to watch.

Jesse played "basketball" with her, too, using a light, bouncy ball from the Alzheimer Society. They bounced it back and forth in the hallway, then moved to the laundry room to shoot "baskets" in the sink! I had to remind Jesse to dial the energy back because Ma isn't as steady on her feet as she used to be, and I worried about her falling. A broken ankle or hip would be the end in terms of me being able to care for her at home.

With Jesse at camp, there's no one to stay with Ma while I go to the store. I tried taking her with me. You'd think I'd have learned my lesson, right? I mean, why would things have gotten any easier, especially now we have to line up outside and keep a six-foot distance, and go around the store in the right direction. Ma has no idea why she should keep her mask on, or why she should stay away from people. Thank God, the stores are offering curbside pickup now, so I won't have to take her inside the store ever again. But I wish Jesse was here to help me figure out the app. The first time I tried, I got ten eggplants instead of one!

Keeping Ma entertained is harder than it used to be. TV isn't much help. She can't follow movies or TV series, or the news. *Judge Judy* is still helpful. I recorded six episodes and she watches them over and over. It's new each time! Fortunately, the Alzheimer Society has pivoted to virtual programming ... exercises, singalongs, webinars, and support groups. Ma can't follow along like she used to, but for me, it's a focus for the day, and provides a social aspect to my own life, which is sadly lacking right now. Covid is taking its toll on everyone, so I feel like I shouldn't complain, but I will! Being a dementia caregiver in the time of Covid is hard. On a positive note, we both enjoy Steve playing his guitar online. Ma sometimes claps or taps a foot — way behind the beat, but that doesn't seem to bother her. And the MP3 player the Society gave us, with all her old favourites, is a huge help. I cannot imagine enduring dementia without music.

On a more cheerful note, I'm attaching a video. It's funny as heck but sad, too. The background story is that I had bought a carton of pull-ups for Ma. When I opened the box and got one out, she thought it was a hat! She put it on her head with her face through the leg hole. I kid you not. She was wearing it like a balaclava! She was quite pleased with herself. You'll see the smile in the video.

sage

Judging by the hollow pit in my stomach, Mom should be in the kitchen, making *dindins*. But she's still in bed, moaning. Something is wrong. I need to check her out, but I'm unsure if she will welcome me. I creep cautiously over the no-go line. She sees me and leaps from the bed in one enormous bound. Quick as I can, I reverse out of the room, but she's not coming my way. Instead, she races to her big water bowl, throwing herself onto all fours like a dog. She wants to play with me! *Yippee!*

I gambol to her side, just in time to see her vomit into the water. I get right in there, nostrils twitching, but Mom groans and pushes me away. Soon everything edible disappears in an angry swirl, except for the traces around her mouth and nose, which I clean up, much to Mom's displeasure.

Gran totters up behind us, saying, *"I'll-put-the-kettle-on-and-make-a-nice-cup-of-tea."* This long word often means *Cookie*, so I follow Gran optimistically into the kitchen. But she just wanders around, the way she often does. "Where's the thing to boil the water?" she shouts.

Mom's voice is weak as she replies. "The kettle is on the counter by the sink. You have to put water in it."

"Shall I feed Toby?"

"Yes, please."

Gran wanders around some more, then ambles back to Mom's bed, with me on her heels.

"Shall I feed Toby, dear?"

"Yes, please."

"Where's the ..."

"Kibble? In the pantry, in the big white can."

We mosey back to the kitchen, and Gran opens the kibble can, the aroma making me feel even hungrier, but instead of filling my dish, she puts the lid back on again and totters back to Mom's bed. I follow.

"Did you feed the dog?" Mom asks.

"Yes."

"Why is she here, then? Why isn't she eating?"

"Maybe I forgot."

Ravenous, I follow Gran back to the kitchen, but after one lap, she returns to the bedroom, mug in hand, me licking the spills along the way.

Mom takes a sip. "Mmm ... did you turn the kettle on?"

Gran's face collapses.

"This is good," Mom says in her encouraging voice. "I like cold tea. Did you make one for yourself?"

"I don't remember," Gran says, returning to the kitchen. She nibbles a piece of my kibble from the can, then spits it out. "Blah! These *Cookies* are bad! And this tea is dreadful! Who made it?"

Mom's laughter trickles down the hall, but I have my head in the depths of the kibble can. Even with my nose coated in crumbs, I pick up the delicious scent of fresh meat.

"Sausages!" Gran says excitedly.

I'm excited, too. I love all meaty things. Dry kibble is okay in a pinch, but it goes down much better with meat.

"The woman who cooks isn't feeling well," Gran tells me, "so I'll make supper."

Then she wanders off, probably looking for her bone again. I nosedive back into the kibble can, eating until my belly is stuffed. Even then, I eat more. When I'm down to the last crumb, I notice that the meaty scent smells alarming. My hackles go up and I bark, but Gran has gone to her bed and isn't interested in what I have to say. I rush to Mom's room, flying over the no-go line and barking right in her face.

"For heaven's sake, *Sage!*" she whines. "Are you still waiting for Gran to feed you? Give me a break, for goodness' sake. I feel dreadful. You'll have to wait."

Then her nostrils twitch and she races to the kitchen, where crackling flames flicker up the side of the pan, growing taller and fiercer.

"*Fire!*" Mom shouts, rushing to Gran's room. "Ma! Get *Out!* Get *Out*, both of you."

I don't obey. Instead I bark at the shooting flames that lick the walls, and I growl at the ominous coils of smoke that rise to the ceiling, drifting in a band to where the dead bird sits on top of the cupboard. The flames and smoke defy me, searing my throat and choking me. Plus, there's another problem now: an ear-splitting screech coming from above our heads.

Coughing and spluttering, Mom herds Gran and me out the back door and down onto the grass, screeching, "Fire! Someone call 911!"

I bark the alarm and *KingDoberman* echoes it.

Gran is screaming, too. "The cat! The cat! The cat!"

Suddenly, Mom is running back into the smoke, ordering me to stay. I don't stay for long. She needs me! But she's already on her way back out, eyes streaming, Cat dangling from her clenched fist by the scruff of his neck. She deposits him in Gran's waiting arms and flops onto the grass, coughing and reeking of smoke. Overjoyed to see her, I lick her stained face. It tastes nasty, but I push past the bad flavour and do what I have to do.

Within a few wags of my tail, a big truck is racing down the street, sirens blaring, screeching to a halt outside our den. It terrifies Gran. She flattens Cat against her chest. He yowls in a strangled kind of way, his bulging eyes wild and frantic.

"You're frightening Regis," Mom shrieks. "Let him go before he scratches you." But Gran's eyes are glazed and she doesn't hear or understand.

It's all up to me. Keeping a cautious eye on Cat's teeth, I nudge Gran firmly with my snout until she looks at me and relaxes her grip on Cat. He leaps from her arms, bounds two strides to the big tree and scales it, glaring at me from a high branch with no appreciation for the part I played in his rescue. But Gran's hands are now free to stroke me, and after I nuzzle and whine to get her started, she does a good job. It's only then I realize that uprights from the noisy truck are inside the den! I shrink down in shame ... I should not have let that happen.

KingDoberman's human appears. "I'll just stay here with you, *Sage*," he says, clipping a *King*-smelling leash to my collar. "I don't want you getting out on to the road. You were a brave dog, *Sage*. Such a brave dog." His words sound like *You'reSuchaGoodDogSage*.

Before long, a huge upright clomps out the back door, looms over us from the deck, then lumbers down the stairs. My heart pounds. I've never seen an upright like this one. He walks on two legs but has no human scent and nothing that resembles human skin. Where eyes should be, he has a giant raccoon mask. Terror clutches my gut. Gran's, too, I think, because she hides behind Mom.

"The guys are just finishing up," he says, popping off his raccoon mask to reveal a smiling human face framed by short sweaty hair. He lumbers toward Mom, his bulky legs swishing. "The medics are here now so they'll check you out."

Strangely, Mom's not scared of him, her gushing breath speaking of relief and gratitude.

"No thanks are needed, ma'am! We're just glad that no one was hurt and not much damage was done. You'll have to replace the blinds and the kitchen cabinets and repaint everything. But there's no structural damage. You were lucky — really lucky. You called us right away, and we got here fast."

Mom strokes me. "*Sage* raised the alarm before the smoke detector went off."

"What a good dog," the man says. "It looks like a pan was left on the stove, eh?"

"It was my mother," Mom says quietly. "She has Alzheimer's."

The upright shakes his head sadly. "That's hard. You'll need to sleep somewhere else for a few days, so you don't breathe the fumes. If you tell me what you need, I'll go back in and get you a few essentials: medicines, car keys, cellphone, a change of clothes ... just enough to get you through the night. Do you want me to call anyone for you?"

"Yes, my brother, please."

"What's his number?"

Mom's face puckers and she starts to sob. "I don't know! It's in my cellphone and that's in the house ... beside my bed."

Despite my efforts to hide from the big man, he sees me. "There's the hero!" he says, trying to pat me.

I don't like his smoky smell, so I don't encourage him.

He turns back to Mom. "Let's get both of you over to the ambulance so the medics can check you out."

Gran backs up to me, whimpering, her heart racing and her skin damp and clammy. I know I should protect her, but I get distracted by other uprights entering the backyard, carrying the aromas of my doggy friends. They stroke me with dog-licked hands and speak reassuring words. More uprights arrive, offering food and drinks, and blankets. I can tell which ones are not looked after by dogs because they don't carry doggy smells, plus they ignore me or tentatively pat me on the head, making my knower wobble.

I catch my favourite doggy scent — *MitzyTheSharpei*. But it's just her upright, coated with her aroma. He greets me warmly and replaces *KingDoberman*'s leash with a *MitzytheSharpei*-smelling one. Thinking he is taking me to meet my wrinkled friend, I follow him willingly. He lifts me into a car that also smells of *MitzytheSharpei*. Cat is there, too, meowing pitifully in a crate. I happily sniff around ... until the car springs to life with a low growl and starts to move, and then I quiver with fear. No Jesse! No Mom! No Gran! As we motor down the street, I see a masked boy, running and bouncing a basketball. I woof, "Jesse! I'm here! I'm here!" But it isn't him. The boy keeps running and the car keeps moving.

"It's okay," *MitzytheSharpei*'s human says. "Don't worry, it will only be for a few days."

His tone is comforting, but it does little to calm me since we're heading in the direction of *ToTheVet.* We motor past it and I breathe a sigh of relief. Then I panic ... am I going to a new den?

The car stops and *MitzytheSharpei*'s human tugs gently on the leash. With mixed feelings, I follow him into the new den, expecting to see *MitzytheSharpei*, but she's not here. Instead, the space is filled with so many canine aromas that my nostrils are overwhelmed. Under normal circumstances, I'd be nose-to-the-ground, inhaling the latest news on all the dogs for miles around. But not today. Today, I want Jesse. I want Mom. I want Gran. I *don't* want to eat, I *don't* want to drink, and I *don't* want to talk to anyone — two-legged or four.

I curl up in a corner and tuck my head under my tail, pretending I'm not here and saying loud and clear, "Leave me alone."

But I hate being alone!

An upright sits on the ground beside me, talking in a soothing voice and offering me treats. In no time, she wins me over, and I'm scampering around with the other dogs and eating and eating, and eating some more! These uprights aren't trying to starve me like Mom. The treats keep coming ... and coming. I like it here.

kayla

The firefighter brings me my phone. I stare at it blankly in my hand, unable even to find Contacts, let alone Zach's number. My brain has seized up. Crap! I'm getting Alzheimer's!

The phone startles me by ringing.

"Hi Kayla. I'm up to speed," Zach says. "Jesse called me."

"How did he know? He's up north."

"One of his basketball friends called him. Listen! I'm just throwing a few things into a bag and will be on my way to the airport in ten minutes."

"Where are you going?"

"Toronto, of course!"

"Here? I thought you meant you were flying off on business."

"I am! This is my business! I'm booking you and Ma into the hotel in town. All you have to do is get there. Once you've settled in, send me a list of all the things you need and I'll get them the moment I arrive. And the animals are taken care of, so all the important things are done."

"Thank you." I want to say more, but I know I will cry. I have to stay strong. I have Ma to think about.

"I'll contact the insurance agent. Who are you with?"

Once again, my mind is blank. "It used to be State Farm, but they were bought out by someone. The information is in the house."

"Does the same company handle your car insurance?"

"Yes."

"So the pink slip will be in the glove box. Take a photo and text it to me. When I arrive tomorrow, we'll figure out the extent of the damage and I'll organize a building contractor. And Leesha will speak to LHIN ... so don't worry about a thing. Have a nice meal at the hotel and get a good night's sleep. I'll see you in the morning."

He hangs up and the tears come.

mary

I don't know where I am.
   Where's the bathroom?
   I can't find it.
   Where's Toby?
   He's not here!
   Neither is the cat.
   It's just the woman and me. Sharing a big bed.
   Where's the bathroom?
   I can't find it.

The food is good.
   They call me *madam*.
   There's a ceiling fan. It reminds me of a place I lived once.

Where's the bathroom?
   I can't find it.

sage

When Mom appears, I try to act indifferent, telling her I'm mad she left me … but I can't control my feet, my body, my tail, or my voice for long. Soon I am dancing and squirming and wagging and whining in pure joy. I repeat this exuberant greeting with Gran, miraculously not wetting myself in the process.

Back at the den, I sniff at everything long and hard, eager to discover what I missed while I was away. There are lots of new smells that I don't like and, sadly, none of Jesse. He's not here. As for Mom and Gran, neither of them is doing well. Gran paces around and around, upset because she can't find her bone. I work on her first, following and nudging. Eventually, she gets tired and flops onto her bed, freeing me up to check on Mom. She's a mess — fraying like a rope pulled between two big dogs. It's unravelling and weakening. Any moment now, it will snap in two.

That first night back at home, I step boldly over the no-go line at the entrance to her room and stand close to her bedside, half expecting to be reprimanded. She ignores me, so I jump onto the bed and gently snuggle down alongside her. She's silent. I sense that there's much she needs to say, but she's keeping it inside. I nuzzle close, encouraging her to stroke me. She does, and eventually she whispers. It's a sound like aspens trembling in the breeze. But then her chin quivers and words rush out.

"I don't know how to keep going, *Sage*. Looking after Ma is too difficult, too dangerous. Look what happens when I take my eyes off her! And a week in that hotel was a nightmare. Good Lord, she couldn't even find the bathroom, and it was right there! I mean, how far away can the bathroom be in a cheap hotel room? She would have peed in the closet if I wasn't there, watching her constantly."

She rubs behind my ears, her fingers angry and harsh against my skin, but I don't pull away because it's helping Mom feel calmer.

When she speaks again, I concentrate hard, knowing her words are important.

"And you don't understand a word I'm saying, right?"

I lick her wet face.

A faint smile lifts her lips. "*Sage, You'reSuchaGoodGirl.* You smelled the smoke and gave me a heads-up. Without you, there would have been much more damage. I dread to think what might have happened." Planting a kiss on the crown of my head, she rolls over. "Goodnight, *Sweetiepie.*"

My job is done. But before I can slip away into the land of the Wild Ones, Gran starts wandering around, distressed. Mom doesn't hear her light footsteps or her soft whimpers. Jumping off the bed, I investigate, drawn by Gran's aroma. She smells of urine. By the time Mom joins us, Gran is sobbing like a short one.

"What's the matter, Mary?" Mom asks.

"I couldn't find the bathroom," she wails.

Mom hugs her. "It's okay, Ma. It's okay. That's why we wear pull-ups. Let's get you cleaned up and into a nice dry one."

kayla

Hey Siblings. Here's another installment of my caregiver notes.

The Caregiver's Tale — Part 3

You hear about people with Alzheimer's putting a pan on the stove, forgetting it, and burning the house down. But I never thought it would happen to us. We worried about it when Ma lived alone in Montreal. In fact, it was one of the reasons I brought her here to my house ... to keep her safe. I didn't think it was a risk here because I'm with her all the time and I do all the cooking! But I got sick and had the day in bed. That's the thing ... a full-time caregiver can't have a sick *minute*, let alone a sick *day*! You can't take a break for an hour, never mind a week.

And there are hazards you never even think about. Yesterday, when we were driving back from the hotel, I stopped at a traffic light. Ma got out of the van and walked right into the intersection! For heaven's sake, she needs help getting in and out of the van all the damn time, yet suddenly she's as nimble as a frickin' mountain goat, leaping out the door and cavorting into oncoming traffic!

Thank goodness we live in a small town — everyone stopped while I got out and caught her, but it was embarrassing because, well, I shouted at her: "Are you crazy? You're gonna get yourself killed." I lost it, right there in the middle of town. She didn't deserve that. But it's so hard to stay calm and be patient and kind. She could have gotten herself killed or caused a major accident. I didn't even see her take her seat belt off! Did I forget to belt her in? There are so many distractions, so many interruptions, it's easy to miss things.

And everything keeps changing. You adjust to the new normal, but then you have to figure out how to cope with the next thing. It's hard to keep up. My track record says I'm *not* keeping up. She nearly froze to death in a snowbank, I lost her in the grocery store, and she almost burned the house down: the three major hazards associated with Alzheimer's, and I score three out of three. That's probably a record!

I always thought I was a relatively smart and capable woman, but this caregiving job has confounded me ... yet society expects us to fit it into our normal schedule and do it for free.

After my F-bomb fiasco with LHIN, Alicia took over as advocate. She told them about the fire, and everyone agreed that Ma should be designated "crisis." They ranked her as four out of five, which means she gets bumped almost to the top of the wait-list, surpassed only by people currently taking up a hospital bed. Alicia also worked her magic to ensure that Ma will get into the care home right here in town, and not in the next town over. Problem is we don't know when. It could be six months or maybe only six days. It all depends on when other residents die! I need to be ready *whenever* the call comes — emotionally ready, I mean, because if you change your mind at the last minute, you go back to the bottom of the list and could be waiting for years. The idea of that makes my stomach sink. On the other hand, if the call came today, I still wouldn't be ready! I feel like I need to do more. For longer. But I can't even be sick for a day.

I reason that, basically, Ma is already gone. I can't even play a hand of cards with her or have a glass of wine. Alzheimer's has stolen all that from us. Alzheimer's has stolen my Ma. She's gone. I miss her so much it hurts.

sage

I pick up *TennisBall* and drop it in Gran's lap, asking her to roll it along the floor. We played this game all the time when Gran first joined our pack, but now, the ball stays on her lap. She doesn't roll it, or throw it, or even hand it back to me. I pick it up and drop it in her lap again and again, but she doesn't accept my invitation to play.

Eventually, I give up and lie on my back with *TennisBall* in my mouth, lifting it from my teeth with my paws, holding it in the air, then letting it fall back into my mouth. It's a trick I learned long ago after Jesse stopped playing with me. Sometimes *TennisBall* skids out of my stubby paws and misses my mouth. Hands and fingers would make the job so much easier, but I do the best I can with what I've got.

I get weary and settle down at Gran's feet for another dull day. But then I sense something is happening. Mom is singing! Dancing, too! And tantalizing smells waft from the kitchen.

"He's coming home, *Sweetiepie*!" she says excitedly. "Camp is over!"

I wag my tail, knowing that the *Sweetiepie* word means she loves me lots.

I push *TennisBall* into her hands and she rolls it along the floor, not just once but over and over. Life is good!

Then suddenly, Jesse is at the door!

I squirm with excitement — *Jesse is home!*

I vibrate — *Jesse is home!*

I stand on my hind legs, or rather, I try to. He catches my front paws and holds me steady while I lick his face, then he lowers me gently to all fours. Bending over, he scratches my back, making me squirm all over again.

I break away and romp off to get him a gift: *Mouse*. He doesn't squeak anymore, and he doesn't have a tail, but he's still very special to me. I grab him by a foot and race back to the door.

But the mood has changed. Gran is holding Jesse in a hug. "Keith! You're home! I missed you so much."

Jesse pulls away.

Mom intervenes, steering Gran to the kitchen. "Oh my goodness, Mary. *Let's-put-the-kettle-on-and-make-a-nice-cup-of-tea.*"

Jesse bolts to the bedroom like a startled deer.

I want to follow him, but my belly is pulling me toward the kitchen and the hope of a *Cookie* that goes along with the long word. My paws, however, have minds of their own. They trot after Jesse, incapable of letting him out of sniffing distance.

He throws himself onto his bed. I stand alongside, nudging him until he reaches out and strokes me. His agitation flows into me.

Before long, Mom comes in, flopping next to Jesse on the bed.

"How can she think I'm Keith?" he wails.

Mom chuckles. "Weren't you the one who explained all this to Uncle Zach? You look a lot like Keith when he was sixteen. And with that tan, goodness, you're as dark as I am! And your hair's gotten so long! You look like Lenny Kravitz when he was young."

"Who?"

"A singer from my day. Anyway, Gran's already forgotten about it. Out of sight, out of mind."

"But if every time she sees me, she thinks I'm Keith, what are we going to do? What if she hits on me?"

"It's just a phase she's going through. She'll move on. Or back. She always does. And she's on the crisis list now, so it won't be too long. What with school starting in a few weeks, and *Basketball*, you won't be home much."

"Mom! What universe are you living in? They're talking about online learning at home again! And no sports *ever*!"

She kisses the top of Jesse's head. "This won't last forever. I'd better go check on Gran. I'll bring you a cup of tea."

"Bring my *Mac* and my phone, too. Bring the whole *GymBag*. It's all by the front door. A television would be nice, as well."

"Don't push your luck," Mom says, walking away.

kayla

Hey Siblings. Here's another installment of my caregiver notes.

The Caregiver's Tale — Part 4

When Jesse came home from camp, Ma thought he was Keith. It was troubling for a while, but she seems to have gotten over it, now. Jesse is back to virtual learning and rarely gets out of his room, let alone the house. No sports, either. I feel bad for him. Will this pandemic ever be over? Will life ever get back to normal?

I know that regardless of what the virus does, my role as caregiver will not last forever. Sooner or later, it will come to an end. Some days, I see this as a light at the end of a tunnel, but other days it's an even darker darkness. The doctor says I'm depressed and I have a lot to deal with. He suggested trying antidepressants for a while to help get me through this patch. They aggravated my tachycardia, so I quit. Better to be depressed than to have a rocketing heart rate. Knowing that my time as a caregiver is limited should make it easier, right? But Ma requires more work now for *everything*, so the job keeps getting harder ... feeding, bathing, dressing, toileting (I never knew the word *toilet* could be used as a verb until Ma started down the path of incontinence). She wears pull-up diapers all the time now, but I have to pay close attention or she will throw it in the toilet and flush. I anticipate worse things to come — fingerpainting with poop being the one I dread most. I have rubber gloves and a jar of VapoRub on hand for that scenario. Apparently, a sliver under your nose helps with the smell. I think that loss of bowel control will be the end of the road for me. But, hey, I've already adjusted to bladder incontinence. A few months back, I thought *that* would be the end of the road! So the goalposts are moving. On the other hand, I don't know how much longer I can keep going. Looking at couples where one partner is caregiver for the other ... the caregiver, in the case of Alzheimer's, is more likely to die before the partner. It's the stress that kills us. Caregiver stress is higher for Alzheimer's than for any other illness.

Through it all, I find myself looking out for the "lasts." Will this be the last time Ma spoons food into her own mouth? Or is able to brush her teeth? Or can push her arms into the sleeve of her sweater when I offer it up? It's like watching for the "firsts" when you have a baby — the first step, the first word, the first pee in the potty — except it's all in reverse and instead of celebrating the achievements, you mourn the losses. And the problem is that you never know it's a last until it's gone; like the last time Ma called me by my name. It's been so long! And it's so very sad.

sage

The urge to pee sneaks up on me ... suddenly ... urgently. As soon as Mom opens the back door, I trot across the deck as fast as I can, desperate to get down the three steps to the grass. Suddenly, I find myself slipping and sliding, pain shooting through me as I land spread-eagled on the grass.

"Oh, *Sage*! My poor, sweet baby," Mom says, rushing to my side. "What happened? Can you get up?"

She circles her arms under my belly and tries to lift me to my feet, but I don't help her — it hurts too much. I just want to rest on the ground that is turning warm with my pee.

Jesse comes. I feel comforted.

"What happened?" he says.

Mom's eyes brim with salt water. "There was dew on the steps. It must have made them slippery. We'll have to take her *ToTheVet*."

I don't want to go, but I'm too weak to fight. Together, Mom and Jesse lift me into *Minivan*.

"You'll be okay, old girl," he says, kissing the top of my head. "Doc will fix you up. Don't worry."

I wish he was coming with me, but Mom goes boss-dog and orders him to *Stay*.

Minivan growls to life, and soon the twists and turns of the route confirm my worst fears. When we stop, I don't need to see out the window to know where we are. Doc carries me into his lair. Usually, I struggle to get away from him, but today I let him lay me on the cold, slippery table. All I can do is clamp my tail between my legs and hope he doesn't go there. He strokes my head, talking in a soft, gentle voice, pretending to like me — the way he always does. But I've fallen for this trick before. Just when I begin to trust him, that's when bad things happen. I won't fall for it again.

kayla

Kayla: I'm at the vet's, waiting for X-rays.

Zach: What happened?

Kayla: Sage slipped down the back steps.

Alicia: Oh, no. Is she okay?

Zach: You must be so upset.

Kayla: Quite honestly, I feel like throwing up. Not only am I dealing with putting Ma in a home, but now this might be the end of the road for Sage.

Alicia: She's been such a good dog.

Zach: A great dog!

Kayla: But it's not fair for her to live in pain, just because I still need her around.

Zach: She's fifteen, right?

Alicia: That's old for a golden retriever.

Zach: We have options for animals that we don't have for humans.

Kayla: Yeah, when there is no real quality of
life, we can euthanize them. But it's gonna be
so hard.

Zach: Wait and see what the X-rays say.

Kayla: I need to prepare myself. If she's
broken anything, then I'll euthanize her. I have
to!

Zach: It's the right thing to do. The kind thing.

Alicia: You'll make the right decision, I know
you will.

sage

Doc and Mom peer intently at shadows on the wall. "No broken bones," he says, "but there's a lot of arthritis in her hips and the ball-joint right here has worn away significantly. Golden retrievers are such wonderful family dogs — therapy dogs, too. The problem is breeders have selected for that calm, intuitive disposition, but the hip dysplasia and mobility issues have come along with it. They must be on the same gene, so when you select for one, you get both." Doc strokes my head and speaks quietly. "She's had a good, long life."

Mom breathes in sharply. "You don't mean ..."

"One step at a time," he says. "We can try anti-inflammatories and pain meds. Perhaps some glucosamine and chondroitin. They should make her more comfortable. And exercise will help ... gentle walks. You can add fish oil to her diet, too. That might help with her joints. If none of that works, then we'll talk about the next step. But we need to do some blood work first. We'll start with a physical."

He strokes behind my ears. His voice is soothing, and I start to relax. Then, when my tail is no longer clamped securely to my backside, he pokes something up my butt. Asshole!

After that indignity, we go home and Mom drizzles fish over my dry kibble! It's almost as delicious as bacon, and it reminds me of the way that *MitzytheSharpei* smells.

Things start to look up. I get fish oil every day, plus cheese treats, although Mom goes to a lot of effort stuffing bitter pills into them. I figure that the more times I spit out the pills, the more cheese I get, so I continue to play Mom's game. Eventually, she says, "What-are-we-gonna-do-with-you-Sage?" I think it means she loves me. And bonus, Jesse takes me for *Walkies* every day.

"D'you want to go to *ThePond*?" he asks.

I yip, *yes, yes, yes,* because I love going there with my boy. Ashley joins us, and once the greeting ritual is over, they ignore me. It's okay, because the swimming birds entertain me, racing toward us as they always do, churning up the water and squawking. Some even fly in, their bodies lurching from side to side and their feet dancing on the water before disappearing under the murky surface. With a quick shake of their feathers, they join the frenzy, rudely demanding treats, but there's nothing for them to eat! This never happens when Mom takes me to *ThePond*. Mom always has food.

The swimming birds hop out of the water and waddle closer, making absolutely sure there is no food. Jesse and Ashley ignore them. She's nuzzling against him, but I sense Jesse's anxiety — he keeps looking around. I tell him not to worry, because he is safe. The humans close by do not smell of aggression.

Disgruntled, the birds ruffle their plumage, plop back into the water, and paddle away. I try to chase after them, but my leash is tied to the bench. All I succeed in doing is throttling myself until I throw up. I wolf it right back down, enjoying the fish oil for a second time.

I rest my chin on my paws and wait. Another dog approaches. He doesn't have an upright with him. Wagging my tail in a friendly greeting, I move toward him until my leash is taut, but he pulls back his lips and snarls, flashing his immaculate fangs. The air suddenly fills with the sharp scent of fear — mine! I can't escape because I'm tied up, so I flatten my ears and look away, saying I want no trouble. He takes no notice of my submissive gesture; in fact, he ups the threat, a low, ferocious growl rumbling in his throat. I press against Jesse's leg with a nervous whimper.

He gets it! Jumping up, he waves his arms and yells, "Get outta here!"

The dog tucks his butt and spins away, tossing his head back for a parting glance. I bravely bark at his retreating rump.

Jesse laughs. "Thatta girl," he says, "see him off."

I bark some more, since Jesse seems to like it. He strokes my head and I nuzzle in close.

"We're even now," he says.

Soon he is stroking Ashley's head instead of mine, so once more, I rest my chin on my paws and close my eyes.

Eventually, I feel their attention shift to me. I cock my head and prick my ears, concentrating.

"I don't remember life without her," Jesse says. "Mom says that at the beginning, we were like a couple of puppies crawling around on all fours. But I never noticed she was getting old. She doesn't run like she used to — never a flat-out gallop, just a stiff little canter. And if she spots a squirrel racing along the ground, she doesn't chase it for more than a few paces. She mostly just stands and barks at it."

"Why not let her off the leash, then?"

Jesse leans down and unclips my leash. I wander from his side, totally at the whim of my nose. Bliss. A squirrel catches my attention.

"*GetHimGirl*," Jesse says.

What? I must have misheard! Looking at Jesse, I wait for further clarification.

"It's okay, girl, *GoGetHim*."

I don't believe my luck. Gloriously free, I give it my best shot, but the squirrel bounds to a tree trunk, grasping it in a full-frontal hug, and circling it in a jerking dance of now-you-see-me, now-you-don't. I race around the base, getting dizzy. After a while, the squirrel dashes for the treetops and I amble back to Jesse, leaning my weight into him until he rubs that place I can't scratch myself — right between my front legs.

"Poor old *Sage*," he says. "You must be over ninety in human years."

I hear the sorrow in his voice, but it doesn't last long. Soon he and Ashley are nuzzling each other again, their hearts beating faster and their scent changing. I flop to the ground and wait.

kayla

I don't get many calls on the home phone these days, so when it rings, my heart skips a beat.

"Hello, Kayla. It's Vivian from the long-term care home. Good news ... Mary can move in on Wednesday."

"Wednesday! It's Monday already."

I thought I was prepared. But I'm not. I'd weighed up the pros and cons and had reached a verdict. But now I'm a mess — an indecisive mess, and an inner voice is screaming at me. *We're in the middle of the worst pandemic in a hundred years. Seniors in long-term care homes are dying like flies. How can you condemn your mother to death?*

"So can you confirm that you want the bed?" Vivian asks.

I don't say anything. I can't.

"If you've changed your mind, Kayla, that's okay. You're allowed to do that. I know it's a very difficult decision. Everyone struggles with it. Especially right now. But if you say no, your mother will lose the crisis status. She'll go back to the bottom of the list."

My stomach knots. *It will kill you! You've got atrial tachycardia. You need to reduce your stress.*

I pull the scattered parts of me together and try to act normally. "With Covid-19, am I sending my mother to her death?"

"We have a stellar track record. Not a single case! All our staff is full time — they don't do shifts at different homes, which helps. Unfortunately, we've had to cancel our volunteer programs, so our activities are limited, and we restrict visiting. Right now, you can visit outdoors in the garden, but I don't know what will happen in the winter …

"… Are you still there, Kayla?"

"Yes, I'm sorry. This took me a bit by surprise. It's shocking."

"I can give you half an hour to decide. I need the papers signed by end of day, or we will offer the bed to the next person on the list."

"Okay, I'll call you back."

I hang up and continue the dialogue with myself. *You've been through all this before — weighing up the pros and cons, agonizing over the options, deciding that long-term care is the only way. Why do you feel so guilty about it?*

A voice sounds in my head, a lyrical voice. "Kayla! You've done as much as you can for as long as you can. Now you need to let go. Without guilt. Without remorse. It's time to pick up the reins of your own life."

I'm stunned. I never knew Keith. I never saw him or heard him. Yet, somehow, I recognize the sound of his voice.

I look around, hoping to see him, but he's not here. I close my eyes, hoping he will appear in my head. He doesn't. But warmth radiates from my chest in a surge of comfort — a father's love. It's a feeling I've missed my entire life. I want to hold on to it forever.

Suddenly, my mind is clear about how to proceed. I'll accept the bed. I won't tell Ma anything. Instead, I'll keep things as normal as possible. On Wednesday morning, I'll say I'm taking her to the Day Centre. I'll drive her things over afterward, in a separate trip. Just two more days. It's the right thing to do.

sage

Mom comes out of her room, greeting Gran with the singsong voice she uses right before bad things happen.

"Are you okay, Mom?" Jesse asks.

"Yes, I'm okay," she says several times over, patting Jesse's arm reassuringly. "It's happening! Wednesday!" Then her face crumples.

Jesse hugs her, and she holds him tight like she never wants to let him go.

"Can you hold down the fort for half an hour?" she asks, her voice quivering. "I have to pop over to the home to sign some paperwork."

"Sure," Jesse says, pulling away from Mom. "Let's make some tea, Mary — with milk and sugar, just the way you like it. And I know where Mom hid a pack of chocolate chip *Cookies* — your favourite. She said they were for a special occasion. I figure this is it."

He's acting like something good is happening, even though my knower tells me something bad is lurking in the shadows. I glance around furtively in case Cat is waiting to pounce. There's no sign of him.

"I'm glad you came to live with us, Mary," Jesse says. "I'm glad ..." His voice trails away, as if he doesn't know what to say.

Something is going on inside him that I don't quite get. Something is going on inside *me* that I don't quite get, either. It's not the rumbling growl of my gut telling me I'm hungry or I need to poop; it's more my knower quietly trying to tell me something, but I don't know what.

Gran finishes her *Cookie* without dropping a crumb. Jesse wipes her hands with a warm cloth, so there's nothing for me to lick. Disappointing.

"I have a photograph to show you," he says. "Do you know who this is?"

She looks at it for a very long time. Then she holds it to her chest, a trickle of salt water slipping silently down her cheek.

I lick it away.

A new day dawns. And then another.

The weight of foreboding grows heavier in my heart. Jesse leaves the house early, before Gran is up.

Mom puts on her coat and shoes. Under normal circumstances, I'd be keenly aware of the potential for *Walkies*, but the accumulating dread over the past couple of days makes me think that the next word out of Mom's mouth will be *Let'sGoToTheVet*.

Instead of shadowing her, I hide under Jesse's bed. She makes no attempt to pull me out and wrestle me into *Minivan*. Instead, she leaves with Gran, and they drive away. I flatten myself against the far wall where the dust bunnies live.

Alone.

Afraid.

mary

The woman leans over to undo my seat belt. "Okay, Mary, we're at the Day Centre."

"Do I have to go?" I ask quietly.

She nods and helps me out of the car, enthusiastically telling me how much I love it. Something doesn't feel right.

A masked stranger greets us at the door.

"Have fun!" the woman says in her cheery voice. "I'll be back for you soon."

The stranger takes my hand. She feels safe and comforting, but something is wrong. I turn back to the woman, pleading with her not to leave me.

There's a smile on her face, but tears in her eyes. "I'll be right back!" she says, blowing me a kiss.

I see other people. Older people. Way older than me. Some of them act really strangely. I think they've lost their minds.

I look around for the woman. She's already out the door.

"Don't go!" I yell. "Don't leave me here!"

But she does.

sage

Gran is gone. I pull her track pants from the laundry basket and lie down on them.

YeeHaw is gone, too, lifted into the gaping mouth of an enormous truck. Good riddance! Miserable creature.

Cat is still here, but he doesn't harass me like he did before. Seems like he doesn't have the energy. I think he's sad.

I'm sad, too. I miss Gran — not enough to stop eating entirely, but enough so that Mom notices and gives me scraps of human food. She's in a funk, as well, spending far too much time in bed, facing the wall and occasionally talking to herself. "Kayla, you've got to get out of bed," and many other words, none of which I understand. My knower tells me that her aches and pains are the lonely kind that she feels in her heart.

When Mom finally re-enters the world, she does so with a vengeance, brandishing the sharp gizmo that she uses for my nails. "Don't be such a baby! I've *got* to cut your nails. They're clicking on the floor! You can't go to the nursing home with talons like this! You'll scratch Gran's skin."

The harder she holds my paw, the more I struggle to get free, until she goes totally boss-dog on me.

"If you won't let me do it, then it's time to go *ToTheVet*. He'll do it!"

I brace, allowing Mom to have her way.

"You don't smell too good, either," she says when she's de-fingered me. "*TimeForaBath*."

I make a run for it, wriggling under Jesse's bed, but Mom catches me before I reach the safety of the wall. Holding my collar, she drags me toward the bath. I resist, but my de-fingered paws have no grip and I slide along behind her. Once there, I submit — except for the tail, which stays clamped firmly to my butt. Mom has to work really hard to wash under there.

Afterward, she rubs me briskly with a towel, which almost makes the whole experience worthwhile, and then brushes my coat until my skin tingles.

Finally, she leads me to the back of *Minivan*, enthusiastically saying *Hup*. I don't respond. "Okay, old girl," she says kindly, "I'll help you."

"Old girl" is a relatively new word that gets used a lot these days. I don't know what it means yet, but I think it's another word for *Sage*.

Mom cradles my chest and lifts me, then she sits alongside me, stroking me tenderly and talking.

"You've got a few more white hairs on your muzzle, and your eyes aren't as bright as they used to be."

There's no joy in her touch, only sorrow. I lick her face, and she smiles.

"You're always so good at making me feel better."

Then she slams the back door of *Minivan* and we drive away. I clamp my tail to my butt, but as soon as we pass *ToTheVet*, I relax.

When we stop, Mom helps me out. I see other dogs. One rushes toward me and soon we are spinning in circles, each searching for a good under-tail sniff. The leashes get tangled and Mom intervenes. I nuzzle her hand, saying I'm glad for the help because the other dog was way too pushy.

A big, masked man rushes toward Mom in much the same way as the pushy dog just rushed up to me. Mom retreats in fear, acknowledging that the big man is the alpha. She obeys his commands, leading me into the belly of the big den. Then, one by one, we dogs have to obey, too.

Sit. Stay. Come. Down. I obey perfectly.

But after that, the big alpha gets rough with me, patting me way too hard for comfort and grabbing my fur. Jesse did this when he was young, and Gran did it sometimes, too, but I always knew they were both doing their best. This upright knows better! He's not being honest. It's worrisome. Mom's anxiety spikes, too. She holds her breath until he moves on to the next dog, who growls at him.

Then a chair rolls toward me on big wheels! I want to pull away, scared that it will run right over my toes, but Mom is at my side, talking softly, so I hide behind her. The chair rolls past, and Mom reaches down to rub the sweet spot between my front legs.

After that, the big upright talks, and I doze off.

Mom's excitement wakes me. "You passed! You're officially a Therapy Dog! Who says you can't teach an old dog new tricks?"

She shows me a metal tag, clipping it to my collar so that it jangles against the one Doc gave me right after he stung me like a bee. "There's a scarf for you, too," Mom says, tying bright fabric around my neck. Standing back, she smiles at me. "You look so pretty. *Let'sGo*, let's visit Gran."

We get back in *Minivan* and go to a new place. Mom leads me to a door, but we don't go through it. We wait. When it slides open, a strong smell wafts out, reminding me of Doc and his lair. I'm apprehensive.

A voice says, "New rules from the Ministry of Health. No indoor visits until further notice. Go around to the back. You can visit in the garden."

Mom turns me around and leads me down a path edged with flowers and through a gate into a garden. Floating among the smells is the distinct aroma of Gran. I home in on it, wagging my tail enthusiastically and dragging Mom behind me.

Gran is slumped in a moving chair, except it's not moving. Her head is flopped onto her chest, her eyes downcast. I rush toward her, whining with pleasure, pushing my nose under her hands. Gran's head pops up, and her eyes brighten. I vibrate with excitement.

"There's my boy," she whispers, stroking the top of my head. "*GoodBoyToby.* How's my boy?"

Mom talks to Gran but Gran doesn't talk back, and soon Mom runs out of words, too. For a deliciously long time, they both stroke me in silence. Other old ones call out to me and Mom lets me run to the extent of my leash to greet them. Some stroke me or pat me, thinking they know me, calling me by many different names. I feel loved.

When we get back to where we started, Mom leans over, slips her mask aside, and kisses Gran.

"Do I know you?" Gran asks.

Mom smiles, even though I can tell she's sad. "Yes, I'm Kayla."

"That's my daughter's name. It's a nice name. My Kayla is so smart and so pretty, and she sings like a bird! All over the world. I wish she'd visit. I haven't seen her for a while."

Mom sighs, her eyes glistening.

"Do I know you?" Gran asks again.

"Yes, you know me," Mom replies, dabbing at her eyes. "I'm Kayla. And I love you. I always have, and I always will."

Mom stands up and pulls her keys from her purse. I know it means we're going back to *Minivan*.

Gran knows it, too. "Don't leave me," she says, grabbing Mom's arm and clinging tight. "Please don't leave me. All the people here are old. I want to go home … I'll be good. I won't be any bother."

Mom sits down again, patting Gran's hand. "I'm not going anywhere, Mary."

After a while, Mom puts on her bright, cheery face. "Toby needs his supper! I'll go feed him and be right back, okay?"

She gently tugs on my leash. "*Come*, Toby, let's go get *dindins*." It's usually a word that makes me dance, but today I feel she's not being honest. Anyway, Gran still needs me.

"Don't leave me," she whines. "Please don't leave me."

Mom sits down again. "Don't worry, Mary. I'm staying right here with you. But it's getting chilly, so let's go back inside where it's nice and warm. Maybe we can make a cup of tea." Mom pushes Gran back to the doors and we wait. Soon, they slide open with a scary buzz. Gran goes through, but Mom and I don't.

Back at *Minivan*, Mom pulls off her mask in a rush of warm breath. And I sniff at the trunks of trees where other dogs have left their scent. It feels good to get doggie smells back into my nose. Mom doesn't say, "*Sage! HurryUp*," the way she usually does when I take too long doing my business. She's content to wait while I sniff out the perfect spot.

When we get home, Cat is sitting on the mat right inside the front door, as if to greet us. Mom picks him up and cuddles him. "Aw, poor Regis. You miss your mommy, don't you? I know! I miss her, too."

"How was it?" Jesse asks.

"*Sage* did an amazing job! She calmed Gran with just a nudge of her nose. And when *Sage* visited the other residents, we had to stay six feet away, but it was priceless to see their faces light up. Some of them thought she was their own dog from years ago. One gentleman called her Spot, and a woman called her Goldie. Sage didn't care what they called her. She didn't tell them they were wrong. She didn't humiliate them by reminding them they couldn't remember ... she accepted whatever identity they gave her and just loved them regardless. She's the definition of unconditional love! *GoodGirlSage, You'reSuchaGoooodGiiiirl.*"

mary

I walk up and down the corridors, in and out of rooms, looking for the bed with the yellow and purple comforter. Some of the old people get mad when I choose the wrong bed. Others don't care. I don't think they know where they are, either.

Masked strangers try to help me, but I don't know if I should trust them. I can't see their faces. Are they smiling? Are they angry? Toby would know the difference. When he wags his tail at a stranger, I know all is well, but if his tail goes between his legs, then I should be wary.

I look for Toby to help me out with these strangers. I can't find him. Maybe he's outside, chasing chickens. I'll go check. I walk up and down the corridor, in and out of rooms, but none of them lead outside.

"This isn't your room, Mary. Come with me, and I'll take you there. Here it is, see. Your name is on the door: *MARY*. And there's your photograph!"

I see the bed with the yellow and purple comforter. I snuggle under it and pull my knees to my chest.

Suddenly, a masked stranger is throwing the covers off me, trying to undress me! I fight. I scratch. I scream. "Get off me! Help!"

It works. She backs away. But another stranger enters, older. They plot quietly, talking about someone else.

"Shall I give her a sedative?" the younger one asks.

"No!" the older one replies. "You just need to talk her through it, and give her time."

The younger woman's voice quivers as if she's close to tears. "I don't have time. I've got two more patients to bathe before lunch, and I'm already behind."

"She needs to trust you and that takes time," the older woman says. "Imagine if a stranger charged into *your* bedroom and started ripping *your* clothes off. What would *you* think was happening? People with dementia live in the past. She might be remembering someone else taking her clothes off, someone she didn't like. Who knows what she's been through in her life. She's not being unco-operative just to annoy you! Remember what you learned in the training video?"

"I didn't watch a training video," the young woman sobs. "They were short staffed. I was put straight on the job."

The older woman seems angry. "That's not acceptable. I'll sort it out. I suggest you take a break. When you come back, Mary likely won't remember what just happened, so you can start afresh."

I don't know what they are talking about, but they go away and leave me in peace.

kayla

I'm clearing out Ma's room, planning to redecorate and make a nice guest room, for when Covid is over. Alicia or Zach might want to stay here when they visit Ma. Or Natalie might want to sleep over occasionally, now she's getting older."

"You think Covid will ever be over?" Jesse says.

"Sure it will. How's the virtual learning going?"

"It's not! The school's computer system crashed, so I have nothing to do. Do you want some help?"

"Yes, please! Moral support would be nice! I know that Ma is never coming back, but discarding her things makes me feel like I'm throwing part of her away. Regis isn't helping. He's been sitting on everything I lay on the bed to take to the charity shop."

"What needs doing?"

"Take the drawers out of the chest and tip them upside down, please. Tap out the dead ladybugs. We'll vacuum after."

Jesse wrestles with one drawer, then another, and another. Suddenly, he puts the drawer down, picks something up off the floor and hands it to me — an old Manila envelope. "This was under the lining paper."

Peering inside, I almost stop breathing. "Oh my Lord. It's a wedding photo of Ma and Keith. Look! They're laughing with each other, like they're sharing a private joke. It's lovely!"

"You never saw this before?"

"No! Never! It's priceless!"

"It's brown!" Jesse says. "I didn't know they had colour filters back then."

"It's sepia, Jesse. The real deal. Black and white photos turn sepia with age."

"There's something else," he says, pulling a large sheet of paper out of the envelope.

I snatch it from him.

"Watch yourself," he says. "That paper clip is rusty."

"Oh my Lord, it's Keith's death certificate! Date of death … that's no surprise. It's about the only thing Ma ever told us about him. Cause of death … progressive multifocal leukoencephalopathy. That makes no sense. Why would Ma treat it like a deep, dark secret if it was just some disease?"

I turn the page, the paper clip disintegrating into shards and leaving rust marks on the paper, which is high quality, with the name and address of a doctor in embossed letterhead, and a note, handwritten in black ink.

To Whom it May Concern,

Progressive multifocal leukoencephalopathy (PML) is caused by a polyomavirus that acts like multiple sclerosis, stripping myelin from the nerve fibres and short-circuiting them — like house wiring that is stripped of its insulation. The virus can lie dormant for years, then progress quickly.

The disease is rare, but the virus is surprisingly common. It becomes lethal only when embedded in the brain, and even then is harmless, sometimes lying dormant for decades, until the patient's immune system is compromised. For this patient, there was a perfect storm of circumstance. The virus gained access when he sustained a severely fractured skull with brain edema. He was prescribed prednisone for those and other injuries, which included broken ribs and a ruptured spleen. Prednisone undoubtedly helped the patient survive his injuries and return to a normal life. At the time, it was regarded as a wonder drug, but too many physicians were, and still are, ignorant of the devastating long-term effects on the immune system.

My legs feel weak. I slide down the wall, wrap my arms around my knees, and rock.

sage

Mom is curled into a ball. Despite my nudging, she won't let me in. She reminds me of a little critter named *Hedgehog* that Krista kept in a cage, long, long ago. When I sniffed him, he pulled himself into a ball of prickles. I couldn't see his head, his belly, or his feet. I learned that if I watched him quietly, with my chin on my paws, he would eventually poke his nose out and uncurl. I try the same technique with Mom, quietly watching and waiting, but she doesn't uncurl.

Jesse, in the meantime, pounces on something that flutters to the ground, like a moth caught in a draft. He opens its wings.

"Mom! This was in the envelope, too … an old newspaper clipping. Should I read it?"

She nods weakly.

> This week marks the one-year anniversary of a vicious skinhead attack that happened right here on Clapham Common. Not in Birmingham, where the poisonous climate of Enoch Powell's repatriation scheme still lingers, and not under the cover of darkness, but on a sunny Saturday afternoon in South London. Mixed-race newlyweds Keith and Mary Bowen had walked from their flat to the Common. The gang initially targeted Mary (white), calling her offensive names and making lewd gestures. Things escalated quickly. Keith, who has no

memory of the event, fought to protect his wife, until he was beaten and kicked to unconsciousness, sustaining critical injuries from which he was fortunate to recover. Mary was not physically harmed but was traumatized by the event. Since then, has there been an investigation? Have the police arrested anyone? Has justice been served? On all counts, the answer is a resounding no. This stands out as yet another example of the injustice we live with.

Jesse slides down the wall next to Mom, his arms wrapped around his knees, too. A pair of hedgehogs.

"Nothing has changed, Mom," he says. "This could have been written yesterday."

Mom uncurls and turns to him, a wave of grief washing over her. It reminds me of the first time I felt an ocean wave. I'd been happily smelling the salty air and had cantered into the cold water, as I'd done many times before in lakes and streams. Then, out of nowhere, the wave hit, knocking me off my feet, swirling and churning over me until I choked for air. Dad hung on to me, fighting the water as it tried to tug me away, or maybe I was fighting the water as it tried to tug *him* away. Whichever way around it was, we had more strength together.

Mom and Jesse have more strength together, too. He holds on to her as she gasps for air, keeping her safe until the wave retreats.

kayla

Sage barks non-stop. It's a delivery truck, so I shut her in the laundry room. When I let her back out, she charges around the house, checking that no one has breached the barricades. She's so funny.

"What is it?" Jesse asks as I rip into the package.

"Hopefully, a life-size baby doll," I reply. "Oh my goodness. It's perfect — just like a real baby!"

"What the heck?" Jesse says. "Aren't you a bit old for dolls?"

"It's for Gran! Quite a few of the ladies at the home have baby dolls. They've lost so much, yet they still know how to hold a baby in their arms and rock it. I had to order this one online — the toy store in town only had white ones." I grab Sage's leash. "Let's see what Ma thinks of this. *Let'sGoSeeGran.*"

Sage jumps up and down, wagging her tail.

I tie the scarf around her neck, and we head out.

As soon as I give Ma the doll, she is enthralled, cuddling it, smiling tenderly.

"What's your baby's name?" I ask.

"Kayla," Gran whispers.

It's been more than a year since Ma called me by name. All this time, I thought she couldn't remember me because I wasn't a good enough daughter. I thought I wasn't lovable enough. I wasn't memorable enough. I should have made a permanent mark on her brain — like with a Sharpie — that even Alzheimer's couldn't wash away. But now, I know without a shadow of a doubt that my mother did love me, and that she still loves me even if she doesn't know who

I am, even if she calls me by the wrong name, even if she calls me nothing. Love transcends all that.

On the drive home, I turn on the radio, hoping for a distraction. "Dance with My Father" comes on, and feelings of self-pity and grief and anger bubble to the surface, but mostly regret. Regret that I never got to dance in my father's arms. He lifted Alicia and Zach up, spun them around and carried them up the stairs to bed, just as in the Luther Vandross song. My brother and sister felt his love. I long to feel it, too, and I'm mad with Alicia and Zach because they don't remember it. If I'd danced with my father, even once, I'd have remembered it for sure.

I weep so hard I can barely see the road through my tears, so I pull over onto the shoulder, hanging on every poignant word of the song, making it my own, aching for a chance to dance with my father and for a song that will never, ever end.

Eventually, I wipe my eyes and drive home, but when Jesse asks if Ma liked the doll, I choke up again, telling him that it was like watching myself as a baby, snuggled in my mother's arms.

mary

A song wafts in the air — a familiar, raspy voice. I can't put my finger on the name of the singer, but I can see him in my mind's eye. He's old and very dark-skinned and sometimes he plays a … damn it … I can't remember what he plays. No matter, he's not tooting it now. He's singing about blue skies and white clouds and a world that's wonderful. It reminds me of the Caribbean. It's a Wednesday afternoon. Keith and I are at Maracas Bay, lying in the sun on damp beach towels, warming up after body-surfing the waves. Salt drying on our skin. Sand stuck to our feet. A raspy voice wafts from Keith's transistor radio, the offshore breeze whipping the sound away.

We're in love and it *is* a wonderful world.

Soon, my skin is burning. I go back into the ocean until I shiver.

Exercises? No thanks. I'm tired. I ache all over.

Bingo? Okay.

Number four — knock on the door. Number five — man alive.

I'm peeing. Ouch, that burns.

kayla

Kayla: I need your help! Right now!

Zach: What's up?

Kayla: Ma has a UTI. She's running a fever of 102.

Alicia: A bladder infection? Can't they just give her an antibiotic?

Kayla: That's the issue. We have to decide if it's what we want.

Alicia: You mean we have the option of *not* treating it … to let it rage out of control and possibly kill her?

Kayla: Yes. She might get over it without treatment, or she might not.

Zach: If we treat her, she might live another four or five years, deteriorating day by day.

Alicia: Yes, but to withhold treatment … isn't that against the Hippocratic oath?

Kayla: Not in this situation. We have the power of attorney for her health. We get to choose.

Alicia: Oh good Lord, no! This is awful!

Zach: When I was setting up the power of attorney, I talked with Ma about this exact situation, except it was pneumonia, not a bladder infection. She said she'd rather die from pneumonia than linger for years with end-stage Alzheimer's. She made it clear that she didn't want to be alive after her brain was mostly gone. And she didn't want us sitting around, watching her die, for literally years!

                 Kayla: But that was months ago. I can't believe that she'd be okay with dying *today*!

Zach: I disagree! This could be her way out! I think she'd want us to let her go.

                 Kayla: But her quality of life isn't that bad! She's settled into the home well. She's healthy in all other regards. I don't think she's ready to die!

Zach: I think you're saying *you* are not ready for her to die? And that's not what's important, here. We have to make the best decision for *her*. What do you think *she* would want if she still had a sound mind?

                 Kayla: If she still had a sound mind, this wouldn't be an issue.

Zach: That's true! But I know what her mindset was eighteen months ago. She told me ... loud and clear.

Alicia: If she was in dreadful pain with no hope of improving, then I'd agree with you, but life is so precious. We want to hold onto it for as long as possible. What we thought of as being unacceptable somehow becomes acceptable.

Zach: The bottom line is … do we think *she* would rather die now, or go on living with someone having to bathe her, change her, feed her … take care of her every need?

Kayla: How can we be expected to make this decision! It's not fair.

Alicia: When does the doctor want an answer?

Kayla: Now! If we're gonna start antibiotics, the sooner the better.

Zach: Let's put it to the vote.

Kayla: Vote? On whether we kill our mother!

Zach: Do you have a better idea?

Kayla: I guess not. I can't get my head around it.

Zach: Okay. Let's hold off with the decision until tomorrow?

Kayla: That's effectively saying no to treatment. She's already got a fever. I think we need to act now or never.

Zach: I say no antibiotics. Honour her wishes.

Go the palliative care route. If she gets over
it … wonderful. If not, then we keep her
comfortable …

                    Kayla: God, Zach. You are so cold-hearted.

Zach: I know it sounds harsh, but this is what
she would want.

                    Kayla: I disagree. I say treat her.

Zach: Alicia, it's up to you.

Alicia: I can't believe this is happening! My
heart says it's too early. She's not ready to die
yet. Let's treat her.

sage

The light is fading.

A fog descends, swirling around me in a misty haze, clouding my mind as well as my eyes. Everything is blurry — like when I used to duck my head underwater to reach the stones that Dad would throw in the lake. Back then, the blurriness disappeared as soon as I came up and had a good shake, the water flying from my fur in all directions. Now it doesn't.

I can see Jesse in the kitchen, but he's fuzzy. I walk toward him, down the narrowing hallway, the walls bouncing into me, first one, then the other. Jesse rushes to steady me. There's panic in his voice.

He scoops me up and carries me to our room. I feel like a puppy in his embrace. I try to lick his face, but my tongue won't do what I tell it. He puts me on his bed. I can tell he's scared. I gaze at him with love, trying to tell him that I'm happy to just be held in his arms. But he doesn't understand. He's always been so slow.

"Crap! I need to find Mom," he says, running away from me, talking on *iPhone*. His words are filled with fear, and again I try to tell him to please come back and hold me. If I had the magical gift of words, he would understand me. Instead, I have to rely on gestures, even more limited now that I can barely lift the weight of my own head off the bed.

Finally, he gets it. He climbs onto the bed and curls his body around me. He holds my paw and talks.

"GoooodGiiiirlSage, GoooodGiiiirl. You'reTheBestDogInTheWorld!"

Salt water wells in his eyes. I'd like to lick it, but I can't reach.

"I love you so much, *Sage. You'reSuchaGoodGirl, SuchaGooood-Girl.*"

A Wild One stands at the end of the bed, an alpha female.

"Not yet," I tell her.

Suddenly, Mom is with me, her head against my chest, her arms around my neck, her sobs muffled in my fur.

"Oh, *Sweetiepie*! You've been *TheBestDogInTheWorld.* Thank you, *Sweetiepie. My Sweetiepie!*"

The Wild One is shimmering now. She is energy. Wisdom. Compassion. Peace. Love. "Your job is done, *Sage*," she says. "*Come.*"

I leap effortlessly from the bed and follow her.

sage

Holy shit … I'm dead!

Why didn't I realize this before? It's so obvious now! I watched as Jesse placed *FloppyBunny* between my paws, tenderly wrapped us in my blankie, and carefully lowered us into the hole he'd dug under the big tree where I used to doze in the heat of summer. Mom and Jesse were crying, yet strangely, I'd felt peaceful, like the earth was snuggling me back into her arms, claiming me as her very own *GoodGirlSage*. And anyway, I figured they'd come back and dig me up later, like a favourite bone.

They didn't dig me back up. Shit! Shit! Shit! Shit! Shit! I *am* dead. To heck with the earth claiming me back … I don't want to be dead. I want Jesse and Mom to know I'm here. Gran, too. As far as I can tell, that's the biggest difference between being alive and being dead — my humans can't see me.

Mom looks at my leash, which still hangs on the peg by the door, but she can't see me right there, beside it. She's blind and not using her knower.

Mom's not the only blind one. Jesse can't see me, either. Of course, there's nothing unusual about this. For big chunks of my life, Jesse ignored me. I've often been invisible to him.

The Shimmering One has sent me back on a mission. I'm here, but I don't remember what my mission is. Crap! Instead of being a dog without a job, I'm a dead dog without a job. I'm a mess.

Jesse is a mess, too. He was shocked when I left his bed to follow the Wild Ones. He wasn't ready for it, and he still isn't. He swallows his tears, but there's a hole inside him shaped a lot like me. His memories reel me in, like a fish on a line. Slowly at first, then whoosh ... flop ... I'm floundering at his feet. We can be at *TheBurgerJoint*, where he picks out the *Pickle* and lays it wistfully aside. Or in the kitchen, staring into *TheFridge* for a snack. We can be in his bed where, half asleep, he tosses a comforting arm over my non-existent ribcage. Or on the couch, watching dogs scamper across *TeeVee*. I don't understand how I get to any of these places since I'm leg-less. It just happens! But sadly, when I arrive at Jesse's side, he can't see me. He doesn't know I'm here.

Gran sees me! Her other senses have faded, but her knower is keener than ever. "*Toby*! There's my boy," she says when I whoosh in and lay my head on her lap. A man with a radiant smile is always there, too, standing at her side, watching her, loving her. The nurse reaches right through his golden glow to check Gran out. "You don't have a fever," she says, making her mark on the chart that hangs at the end of Gran's bed, "and your blood pressure is fine. You're having hallucinations, but at least you're happy, right, Mary?"

At the end of my visit with Gran, I don't have to wait for someone to buzz me out. I just zoom back through the heavy doors, marvelling that they no longer hold me captive.

I whoosh through the front door of my old den, over the cracked tile and right into the kitchen. Mom is sitting at the table, her hands hugging a mug of tea, her eyes sad. Cat sits next to her on Gran's old chair, spreading his toes wide and nibbling at the fur between them. He looks up, giving me a stare that says, *Not you again.*

Mom follows his gaze. "What are you looking at, Regis? Sometimes I swear you see things that aren't there."

He flicks his tail — a clear sign that he's not happy. But let's be real, is he ever happy?

I advance boldly toward him. He looks away. That's a first!

I rest my knower on Mom's lap, sending her my love with all the strength I have. She smiles and whispers my name! In a flash of

light, I remember my mission: I need to show Jesse and Mom how
to see with their hearts, as well as their eyes.

Jesse barges through the door, dropping *GymBag* and trapping
Basketball in the corner. I greet him as best I can, considering I
don't have a body or an all-important tail — sending him *all* my
love with my knower.

"Wow, Mom," he says, a smile lighting up his face. "I just had
such a strong memory of Sage ... it was like she was right here,
wriggling and whining a greeting."

"I know what you mean," Mom says, hugging him. "I can feel
it, too. I think she came by for a visit."

"*GoodGirlSage*," the Shimmering One says. "*Come. FollowMe.*"

I take one last look at my human family, then, with a wag of my
non-existent tail, I follow the Shimmering One.

mary

Someone stole my purse. I'm looking for it everywhere, but I can't find it. One of these old people stole it.

A masked one finds me. "Mary, what are you doing in Ada's room?"

"She stole my purse."

"I'll help you find it later, okay, but right now, it's music time! Your daughter is coming to sing for us again. Won't that be lovely! I hear she's doing a tribute to some of the greats. I hope she does Whitney Houston … she's my favourite. Let's go to the big room."

She holds my hand and takes me to the room with a ceiling fan and lots of chairs. I sit under the moving blades and listen to the quiet *whomp-whomp-whomp*, feeling strands of hair tickle my face.

The boy with the big smile will be coming soon. I must find my binder and fill my pen with ink. Where's the ink?

Suddenly, music is playing and the boy is holding me in his arms. I snuggle my head against his chest. Nestling against him. Two pieces of a jigsaw fitted together.

Home!

No building.

No location.

Just me and the boy.

Feeling safe.

Feeling loved.

The music stops, but the notes hang in the air long after they are played. Then a single kick of the drum and another perfectly

timed pause. Finally, the key shift and a magnificent voice. "I ...
will always love you ..."

My heart feels full ... growing warm in my chest.

Love!

"I will always love you, too."

author's note

Gone but Still Here is a work of fiction, but it's also my memoir. The character of Mary, or at least the self that Mary recalls, is me in the 1960s and '70s ... a naive yet rebellious teenager who fell helplessly in love across the colour line, challenging parental and societal norms to embark on a tumultuous interracial marriage that spanned Trinidad, England, and Canada, and which ended in tragedy far too soon. I was thirty years old when Keith died from complications caused by an earlier skinhead attack in England. Our daughter was three and our son a month shy of two (and they really did speak the poignant words recorded verbatim in the book). Like Mary in the story, I was five months pregnant and we had just migrated from England to Canada, looking for a safer place to raise our children, a place they could reach their full potential and not be held back by skin colour. Keith's death was hard to accept, despite my earlier dreams and premonitions. Like Mary, I buried the painful memories deep, soldiering on to raise three biracial children alone.

My ability to tell my love story through the perspective of Alzheimer's comes from being caregiver for my second partner. As an executive editor for the action adventure division of Harlequin, Feroze had edited drafts of my earlier novels, helping me to be a better writer. By the time I was ready to share this manuscript, he could no longer read. If I read to him aloud, he was unable to retain the storyline. He had always been a walking dictionary, yet when I asked him for an alternative word, he would get frustrated, saying,

"I was a man of words and now I have none." Despite this, he was a major contributor to the story, his words, actions, and fears coming to life in Mary.

The emotion I have felt about my unexpected caregiving role is woven into the tapestry of the book, oscillating between compassion and impatience, between love and frustration, between my desire to do the right thing and my resentment at having to. I confess that I've acted like Jesse at his worst, but also Kayla at her best. Some days I'm emotionally in control, others I'm overwhelmed. Often, I'm exhausted. I've screamed inside my head and out loud, and I've laughed. Along the way, I've learned that these conflicting emotions are part of the caregiver journey.

The first draft of this novel, completed in 2016, was very different from the story you have just read. Reaction to my previously published books had led me to believe that my forte was writing for young adults through the eyes of animals, so I planned to write about Alzheimer's exclusively through the voice of Sage, the wise and empathic golden retriever who shared my heart and home for fourteen years. Long before Alzheimer's made a personal appearance in my life, Sage, wearing her St. John's Ambulance Therapy Dog scarf, would visit the local nursing home with my then-teenage daughter. Sage's ability to bring comfort to those in need was the initial inspiration for this book.

In the story, I wanted Sage to behave and think like a real dog, not a human on four legs. Her limited understanding of human words ultimately made this approach too challenging, so I created Jesse to help narrate the story of a teenage boy and his dog, both of their lives disrupted when Gran and her cat move in. Several students who read the first draft said that Jesse behaved like their brothers, but teachers thought that he was too selfish and therefore not a good role model for young readers. Reluctant to tame down my belligerent teen, I decided to take a stab at turning the material into an adult novel.

Alzheimer's patients often live in the distant past, vividly remembering people and places from decades earlier while unable to remember what happened five minutes ago. I knew I could use this symptom as a means of accessing Mary's long-suppressed secrets about the love of her life ... which increasingly became the suppressed secrets of *my* life. But although I had the outline in my head, my writing was put on hold for several years because caregiving left me with little free time. I was holding on to my own health by the skin of my teeth. Things came to a head in March 2020, when Covid-19 forced the day program to close down, leaving me with no respite. Over the next few months my mental and physical health became so fragile that Feroze was moved into long-term care (as much for my benefit as his). At that point in time, seniors were dying from Covid-19 in care homes all around the world. Guilt and relief pulled me apart like a tug-of-war, but we were fortunate that he settled in well and has remained physically healthy. This allowed me to concentrate on my own failing health, discovering that my "funny spells" had been caused by multiple TIAs, which have resulted in mild cognitive impairment. Although there is a genetic component behind these symptoms, the stress of caring for Feroze no doubt exacerbated the condition.

Suddenly, the urgency to finish this book became very real. Ironically, I had planned for this story to raise awareness about dementia, but I found myself wanting to hide the diagnosis. I felt ashamed of my confusion and lack of competence, and worried that if I told people — especially my publisher and my readers — that I would be dismissed as being useless and no longer taken seriously. Yet, at the same time, I was able to really get into Mary's head in the early stages of her disease. As published authors in our seventies, Mary and I struggled to finish our shared memoir, reliving the trauma of the past, confronting our memories, both good and bad, and facing our fears for the future. In the process, we gave Keith back the voice that I had silenced.

Finally, with encouragement from editor Robyn So, I added Zach and Alicia to the cast of characters and turned the story into a family affair.

I hope that by sharing this very personal story of dementia, I will raise awareness and help others on the same path. I also hope to shed light on racism, past and present, and show the value of pets in caring for the cognitively impaired.

Jennifer Mary Dance

Keith, 1966   Keith and Jennifer Mary, 1971

acknowledgements

First, I thank Keith, my husband for nine years, half a century ago. Through our shared life, which is dramatized in the pages of this novel, Keith inspired me to take a stand for justice and equality. He changed me. Also, I thank Feroze. Although Alzheimer's disease prevented him from understanding the storyline of *Gone but Still Here*, his contribution to the story was immense. Without him, it would not have been written.

I thank the Canada Council for the Arts for their confidence in me as a writer and for the Creative Writing grant that enabled me to pay for help around the house, thus freeing up blocks of time for writing.

I thank the Alzheimer Society of York Region, for its programs and staff, especially Rebecca Wardlaw, Jaime Cruz, and Lisa Day; the staff and volunteers at the Stouffville Day Centre; the staff at Bloomington Cove Care Community; and Teepa Snow for her Positive Approach to Care (teepasnow.com).

I sincerely thank those who, like me, are walking the Alzheimer's path as caregivers, especially Sandi Jones, Lawrence Gelberg, Sharon Pearson, Nancy Zalman, and Anne Vatistas. Our shared experience fuelled this book and enabled me to laugh in the face of heartache. But of all the people I have met during this journey, I owe the deepest debt of gratitude to Carolyn Watt. As both an Alzheimer's caregiver and owner of an old golden retriever coincidentally named Jesse, Carolyn supported me when

I was ready to give up, encouraging me to rise above rejection and criticism. She made me believe in myself and in the story.

I thank the following readers for their honest feedback and suggestions: Linda Hutchison, Brenda Reid, Jenn McGuggin Greenham, Jane Warren, Alex Jones, Josie Norton, Christine Payne, Jo-Anna Cromie, and Marie Bertuzzi and her students at Bayview Glen Independent School, especially JiaJia Jiang and Naomi Kongham.

My deepest thanks go to Robyn So for her editorial insight, which led to a better story, to Paula Eykelhof, and to the team at Dundurn Press.

And finally, I thank my family — Joanna, James, Kate, Tarik, Matthew, Erin, and Kim — for your confidence in me, not just as a writer but more importantly these days as a caregiver. Love you all.

about the author

JENNIFER DANCE is an award-winning author, playwright, and composer with a passion for justice and equality. She has published three novels for teens, *Red Wolf*, *Paint*, and *Hawk*, two of which were nominees for the Ontario Library Association's Forest of Reading program. In 2016, in recognition of her significant contribution in raising awareness about residential schools, Jennifer received an Achievement Award from the Government of Ontario. She was also nominated as a Woman of Excellence in the J.S. Woodsworth Awards and is the grateful recipient of a prestigious grant for creative writing from the Canada Council of the Arts. Jennifer is a caregiver for her second life partner, who is journeying through the decline of Alzheimer's disease. She lives on a small farm in Stouffville, Ontario, where she enjoys horseback riding and walking.